More Critical Praise for *Bedrock Faith*

• Named a Notable African American Title by *Publishers Weekly*

"Eric Charles May might be the surprise hit from this list. This Chicago native writes a novel set in a small Black town. Really it's a block community where an ex-convict returns home and turns everything upside down with the religious conversion he underwent in prison. He wasn't the best juvenile, and turns this small world around via accusations, losing friends, gaining enemies, and more. *Bedrock Faith* isn't a short read, but it's a rich one, and the characters are engaging." —*Ebony*

"In this vivid, suspenseful, funny, and compassionate novel of epiphanies, tragedies, and transformations, May drills down to our bedrock assumptions about ourselves, our values, and our communities. As sturdy as a Chicago bungalow and bursting with life, May's debut is perfect for book clubs." —*Booklist* (starred review)

"May's expansive first novel reveals the complicated emotional economy that holds together a neighborhood in crisis . . . May's vivid descriptions of the rhythms of life in the suburb . . . reveal vibrant lives in ordinary houses." —*Publishers Weekly*

"A compelling look at a tight-knit community battling a threat from within." —*CS Modern Luxury*

"The depth and the magnetism and the humor of Eric Charles May's truly unforgettable characters makes this a neighborhood well worth visiting." —*New York Journal of Books*

"*Bedrock Faith* is an entertaining and heartfelt novel, and it provides an important look at a side of Chicago that is under-represented in today's literary fiction." —*Chicago Center for Literature and Photography*

"In *Bedrock Faith*, Eric Charles May has created a world inhabited by unforgettable, believable characters—the fervid Stew Pot Reeves, the patient Mrs. Motley—who will linger in your heart long after you've finished their story. A bittersweet, timeless book." —Valerie Wilson Wesley, author of *Dying in the Dark*

"An impressive debut with truly memorable characters and an epic story line by an author who has appeared on the literary landscape fully formed." —Colin Channer, author of *The Girl with the Golden Shoes*

BEDROCK FAITH

BY **ERIC CHARLES MAY**

Published by Akashic Books
©2014 Eric Charles May

ISBN-13: 978-1-61775-196-7
Library of Congress Control Number: 2013938810

Akashic Books
Brooklyn, New York
Twitter: @AkashicBooks
Facebook: AkashicBooks
E-mail: info@akashicbooks.com
Website: www.akashicbooks.com

Acknowledgments

In the ten years' time it took me to finish this novel, excerpts were read at numerous public readings in Chicago and at the Stonecoast Writers' Conference in Maine. The positive reception my readings received over the years from audiences—the reinforcement that I was on the right track—were invaluable when I hit those periods of doubt caused by frustrations over plot and character and wordage, the inevitable result of the writing process. So to all who laughed at the right passages or gave a supportive comment or a kind word with regard to my story, please know that it was greatly appreciated. That goes especially for my Fiction Writing colleagues at Columbia College Chicago, my second family. (And that includes the students.) Excerpts of the novel were printed in F and *Criminal Class Review* magazines. Thanks to John Schultz, Betty Shiflett, and Kevin Whiteley for that support. In addition to my mom (my dad died some years ago), the support of my siblings Marc, Craig, Mitchell, and Alison has been a blessing. Thanks to Linda Naslund for copyediting a draft of the novel, and to those people who took time to read the entire manuscript before its acceptance for publication, and who gave me helpful feedback: my mom again, Stacey Basham, Catherine Hovis, Alexis J. Pride, Karen Ryan, Susan Smith-Grier, and my good and longtime friend Adrienne Clasky. Thanks also to Elinor Lipman for her support. A special thanks goes to attorney William P. Murphy for answering my many questions about defense lawyer procedures and the old Chicago Police central lockup. Last but not least, thanks a million to the crew at Akashic Books who have been a joy to work with.

The Old Neighborhood

If you're driving to Parkland from Downtown, your best bet is to take the Dan Ryan Expressway (I-57), which cleaves like a wide river, with a bend here and a bend there, through Chicago's vast South Side. Parkland is on one of the farthest edges of the city, what Blacks from other parts of town call "out south." Pull off at Exit 351 (which is just a ways beyond the 125th Street overpass) and hang a right at the top of the ramp. You'll now be headed west and after a couple of blocks you'll pass through a viaduct. On the other side is Parkland's main drag, a quarter-mile or so of small businesses—two saloons, a barbershop, a dry cleaners, a drugstore, and such as that; nearly all the buildings storefront affairs with display windows and hand-crank awnings, and every one situated along the south side of the street (to your left going west) because on the north side is a forest preserve that offers up, during warm weather months, a high green wall of thick foliage. Turning off the main drag is the only way into the neighborhood because Parkland is kind of hemmed in: a cemetery directly east (where mostly White folks are buried), a railroad yard directly west, and the Cal Sag Channel, a man-made waterway, directly south. (If viewed on a map, Parkland is an irregular rectangle of Chicago proper wedged between two larger suburban towns.) If you turn off the drag and onto a Parkland side street, you'll see tall trees in the parkways lining either side of the road. The modest homes are mostly brick stand-alones, none higher than two stories, with tidy yards and front doors painted eye-catching colors like canary yellow, or sky blue, or fire-engine red. There's also the occasional two-flat or wooden four-square, as well as several houses of worship, all of the churches Christian and none of them the foot-stomping, shout-it-out variety. On late Sunday mornings, if the weather's good, there'll be gatherings out front of those places as people, dressed in their finery, enjoy some after-service commiserating. Weekdays during the school year there's relatively few people about, and on summer evenings, plenty of kids bike riding and double-dutching and what-have-you, while the adults, home after a hard day's work, water lawns with garden hoses or converse on front steps, their polished midrange cars sitting curbside. And as you take all this in, with that never-ending expressway traffic providing an ambient noise, the thought may occur to you that Parkland looks like any number of Chicago-area neighborhoods you could name, and you'd be right. However, don't tell residents out there that their bailiwick isn't special, 'cause if you do you'll get an earful about how Parkland has been all-Black since the 1870s when the first Colored settlers arrived from Dixie, squinting from under the shade of bonnets and straw hats at the surrounding prairie and onion-scented marsh. The territory's original residents were, of course, long gone by then, and the local White folks, the first beneficiaries of the Native's forced departure, were living in a small town set on a ridgeline a few miles west. Though hardly happy at the sight of strange Negroes, these Whites had no interest in lynching anybody, which for the Colored settlers was a big improvement over the Whites they'd left behind. And so, the new arrivals dropped their bags and declared themselves home. Within a few years there was a small community with a whitewashed church and a scatter of cottages painted bright colors, which was the neighborhood's first use of the sky blue, and the canary yellow, and the fire-engine red.

A hundred-some years later, which by the way is when the following story takes place, only a handful of Parkland's ten thousand–plus residents could trace their ancestry directly to those first settlers. A fact that did not stop the ten thousand–plus from taking great pride in the intrepid-Colored-settlers-come-north story, just as they were proud of their neat houses and the Parkland High School graduation rate; a vainglory that did not sit well with some. Blacks from South Side neighborhoods like Morgan Park and Pill Hill, who took a backseat to no one in the proud-of-themselves department, claimed Parkland people acted as if they were the only Black folks in Chicago who knew how to keep their property up. Blacks from less prosperous enclaves, on the South Side and beyond, who were no less proud, swore that there were more Uncle Toms per square foot in Parkland than anywhere else in town. (As for Chicago-area residents of other races and creeds, whenever they thought of Parkland, which was seldom, most saw it as just another piece of the city's Black Other World.)

Parklanders, as they liked to call themselves, viewed the criticism from other Blacks as sour grapes and the disinterest of those from outside the tribe as just more of the same old, same old. Which is not to say Parkland inhabitants were naïve or unrealistic. They readily admitted (when talking among themselves) that Parkland had in recent years, like numerous other communities across the nation, experienced some of the effects of drug abuse and other crimes, committed by this or that homegrown miscreant; however, in their opinion those effects had not been too severe, for there were no street gangs, graffiti, drive-by shootings, or open-air drug dealing in the neighborhood. And as they gazed from yards and porches at their tidy little world, residents told themselves they could still state with confidence that regardless of what others might spitefully say or misconstrue, they knew what their predecessors had struggled so hard to establish and what their efforts had, so far, managed to sustain. And they saw that it was good.

BOOK I

Blues for Mrs. Motley

CHAPTER ONE

1993: A Homegrown Miscreant Returns

By seven that evening, every resident on the 1800 block of 129th Street knew that Stew Pot Reeves was out of prison and back home; home being his mom's redbrick two-flat located at the very east end of the block where the road came to a halt before the high stone wall of a railroad embankment.

As a chilly wind waggled naked tree branches beneath an overcast sky and sent bits of debris pinwheeling across bare, damp ground, word of his return traveled from house to house. Some called neighbors on the phone, while others threw a wrap over their shoulders (it was early March) to trot next door or across the street with the bad news, each messenger beginning their bulletin with: "Did you hear? Stew Pot's back!"

Those receiving the news widened their eyes in surprise or winced in anguish. "Stew Pot's *back*? The judge gave him thirty years. It hasn't been half that long. Who was it said they saw him? Was it Mrs. Motley?"

Yes, it was Mrs. Motley. Tallish with a body that kinder neighborhood souls called slender and harder hearts labeled as bony, she had a skin tone the color of butterscotch and a head of silvery white hair combed back in a tight bun. A former school librarian, by then five years retired, she lived next door to the two-flat in a large wooden four-square with a teal paint job and black stationary shutters. That afternoon around four she'd been sitting on her blue living room couch sipping tea from a china cup, the saucer held chest high, when a yellow taxi stopped in front of the two-flat. (Although she had not left the house that day and expected no visitors, as usual she was dressed as if important company was coming or she had somewhere important to go: beige silk blouse, black ankle-length pencil skirt, stockings, and black low-heel shoes.) There was a row of lace-curtained windows across the front of the room with the couch backed against the sills. Mrs. Motley set the cup and saucer on the nearby in-laid coffee table, lifted a white lace panel aside, and looked past the railing of her roofed porch. Her round wire-rim glasses were set low on her long nose and she had to tilt her head to see over her bifocals.

The house's high first floor gave Mrs. Motley a commanding view of the street, and she was able to make out the forms of two people within the shadows of the cab's backseat. Folks in Parkland seldom took taxis, so she was surprised when the cab's rear door opened and her next-door neighbor, Mrs. Reeves, stepped out.

Normally a Nervous Nelly sort of person, that afternoon the petite Mrs. Reeves looked unusually at ease in a green headscarf and a worn gray coat. A tall man, much darker than she, followed her out. He had a shaved head and a goatee, and wore an open peacoat and denim overalls. A bit of white T-shirt was visible above the bib and the pants hung loose on him, the front hems bunched over the insteps of black brogans.

There was a turning circle at the base of the embankment wall and after the tall guy closed the cab door, the driver made a slow turn-around and headed back west. Leaning closer to the window, Mrs. Motley saw that the tall guy was also broad across the shoulders, his thick goatee a furry frame around his wide mouth, and his shaved head was shiny, even under the overcast sky; the noggin reminding her of the smooth side of a greased coconut.

Standing alongside him at the curb, Mrs. Reeves's brownie face barely reached his chest. The man said something to her which Mrs. Motley could not make out, and for the first time in ages Mrs. Motley saw Mrs. Reeves smile: a spread of tiny teeth in her small, almost chinless face. It caused Mrs. Motley to wonder if the two were lovers, and if so, how much cash Mrs. Reeves was forking over to him; money being the only reason Mrs. Motley could think of for why such a strapping fellow, who appeared to be in his early thirties, would be with a woman old as Mrs. Reeves, who was sixty if she was a day.

The idea that her east-door neighbor was keeping a honey pie in walking-around money bothered Mrs. Motley more than a little bit. The two-flat's parkway and front yard were neighborhood anomalies: weedy and trash ridden. The windows were hung with dingy sheets, the white paint on the window frames and doorways were flaked and faded, and the downstairs apartment had been vacant for years. Like other immediate neighbors, Mrs. Motley felt the two-flat's condition brought the whole block down; a situation made all the more maddening for the neighbors by the fact that money was not the issue, for Mrs. Reeves had a perfectly good job Downtown clerking in the Department of Motor Vehicles.

The couple strolled up the walkway to the two-flat's front door, where they paused so Mrs. Reeves could insert her key. While turning the lock she said something over her shoulder. It was then that the young man smiled, revealing a white wall of large teeth within the frame of the goatee. And when Mrs. Motley saw *that*, a chill swept over her.

After the young man merrily followed Mrs. Reeves inside, Mrs. Motley dropped her hand and the lace curtain fell back into place. Sliding to the front of the couch and with her arms crossed, she leaned forward and slowly massaged her goose-bumped biceps.

When Stew Pot Reeves had gone to prison fourteen years before at age eighteen, he'd been a tall, skinny boy without enough hair on his face to weave a sweater for a fly. That's why she hadn't recognized him at first. But there was no mistaking that big-tooth smile; she'd seen it too many times to ever forget it. Mrs. Motley had always assumed he would remain in prison till the end of his sentence, by which time she figured she would be in either Heaven or the old folks' home. But here it was, 1993, and he was back. The maker of so many Parkland mayhems—arson and pet murder, just to name two—was back. Her first impulse was that she could not take the stress of living next door to him again, that she would have to move. But could she do that? Could she actually leave this house that her grandfather had built, and where she'd been raised, and where she'd raised her own child, and where her parents and husband had taken their last breaths?

To her left, glistening like a hearse, was an upright piano where she and her mother had once played side by side. To her right was the redbrick fireplace, its innards charcoaled from years of use where as a youngster she had done her first reading, lying on her stomach as the flames cast wavering light across the pages, an image that was repeated years later when she sat on the floor with her toddler son, reading aloud to him from storybooks. She now gazed beyond the sky-blue living room, with its white moldings and ceiling, through the wide passageway to the apple-green dining room where the furniture—an aircraft carrier of a table, a dreadnaught of a sideboard—were like most of the house's furniture, heavy, dark, ornate wooden pieces she polished to a high sheen. (The same went for the hardwood floors which were like honey glaze in color and gleam; the varicolored rugs spread across them presents her now grown son had purchased overseas.) The house and everything in it had come to her, she the only child of sibling-less parents. She saw it as her legacy, and though she'd been raised to believe vanity a terrible thing, she couldn't deny the immense pride her legacy gave her, even though she knew it set her apart from many of her neighbors, the majority of whom lived in homes far less elaborate. (A few of these folks, and she knew this for a fact, considered her pride nothing more than snob arrogance.) She loved her house, despite it being drafty in winter and hard to cool in summer, despite having to haul laundry up and down the basement steps, despite all the rooms that were becoming more and more of a problem for her to keep clean. *But*, could she stand living next to Stew Pot? Just the thought of it brought a sour expression to her face.

For twenty minutes or so, Mrs. Motley sat there on the couch fretting over her dilemma. Coming to no conclusion she rose slowly, for her knees gave her a bit of trouble, and exited the room carrying the china saucer and cup of now cooled tea. With perfect posture, she walked to the back of the house through a wainscoted hallway, moving past a grandfather clock and the thick posts of a stairway balustrade.

At the end of the hallway was a big yellow kitchen—yellow walls, yellow fridge, yellow stove—where the air was thick with the fumes of lemon-scented cleaner. As Mrs. Motley poured the tea down the drain of the stand-alone sink, she heard the two-flat's screen door bang shut. Setting the cup down, she went to her own back door and peered through the window's parted yellow polka-dot curtains. Next door Stew Pot was headed toward the alley with an armload of phonograph albums. He wasn't wearing the peacoat, and his white T-shirt showed off his robust arms. When he reached the chain-link gate, he kicked it open and dropped the records into the black garbage can.

Afraid he might catch her watching, Mrs. Motley yanked down her door's window shade before Stew Pot could turn around; but after only a few seconds her desire to see became overpowering and she pulled gently at the edge of the shade to take a peek. She saw Stew Pot heading back toward the two-flat and let the shade go as if it were hot. His black brogans thumped loudly on his porch steps and when the screen door bang wasn't followed by the slam of the inside door, she knew he wasn't finished.

Scared to look but too curious not to, she waited behind the safety of the shade. Before long the screen door banged again and Mrs. Motley peeked once more. Stew Pot had another tall armload of albums that he also dumped in the garbage can. When he turned around that time, she saw that his jaw was fixed in a grimace and his eyes in a furious squint; however, he didn't so much as glance over the chain-link fence separating the yards. Feeling safe from discovery, she kept on peeking.

Stew Pot took one more trip carrying albums, two trips carrying stacks of magazines, one trip carrying a stereo and speakers, and one carrying a clock radio and a portable TV. The magazines he dropped atop the records, the electronic equipment he stacked behind the fence. He then made two trips with women's clothes—dresses, blouses, skirts—that he piled on the records. When the screen door bang after the second clothes trip was followed by the inside door slamming, Mrs. Motley knew he was finally done.

She sat at her broad kitchen table which was covered with a yellow oil cloth. *Have Stew Pot and Mrs. Reeves gotten into an argument already?* she wondered. *Should I call the police?* Though she held Mrs. Reeves primarily responsible for the way Stew Pot had turned out, at the same time Mrs. Motley had never wished the woman ill.

She decided not to call the police, since it wasn't likely that 911 would send a car simply because she'd seen Stew Pot throwing stuff away. Using her yellow wall phone, she instead called first one, then another nearby neighbor, who were also retirees. (She spoke in her usual unhurried way, her mellow pronunciation as precise as her handwriting or posture.) Later on these folks contacted other neighbors on the block, which got the word-of-mouth rolling, and by seven thirty, as they sat down to their suppers, neighbors on the block knew not only that Stew Pot had returned, but that he was already acting the fool.

CHAPTER TWO

Neighbors on the Block Weigh In

Maybe prison finally taught him a lesson."

"Who do you know ever got better from being in jail?"

"Never can tell, sometimes folks change for the better."

"Change for the better? You heard what Mrs. Motley said about Stew Pot throwing his momma's clothes away. If you ask me, looks like he's going to put his momma out."

"How can he do that? She owns the two-flat, not him."

"An ex-con big as Ali says, 'Hit the road,' you going to argue with him?"

After the suppers were done, a number of these immediate neighbors telephoned neighborhood friends and relatives to inform them of Stew Pot's return. No one they spoke with took the news lightly. Although he wasn't the first Parkland boy to go to prison, to everybody in those parts, Stew Pot was a legend. Stew Pot could destroy your home using fire *or* water. Stew Pot could sneak up to your window and eavesdrop on your most intimate acts and conversations and laughingly tattle it all to the neighborhood. Stew Pot would slaughter your pet just for laughs. He'd done these and other infamies to people in Parkland and had never suffered once for them because he did his deeds with great stealth and left behind no incriminating evidence. True, he had eventually been caught burglarizing a White woman's apartment way up on the North Side, but after the details of the case became public during his trial, Parklanders saw his capture as more a case of cop dumb luck than any lack of skill on his part.

On Stew Pot's first night home, in the noisy confines of Parkland saloons and the quieter quarters of Parkland homes, folks thought long and hard about him. This included Mrs. Motley, of course.

By eleven she was in the second-story bedroom at the front of her house where the walls were painted dove gray. Fresh from a bubble bath, with her silvery hair down to her shoulders and wearing a white flannel nightgown, she gingerly lowered herself beside her four-poster bed, a practice she felt honor-bound to do, achy knees or no achy knees. As always she asked God to watch over her son and granddaughter. (The son, a career soldier, was a master sergeant stationed at Fort Sill, Oklahoma, while the thirteen-year-old granddaughter lived with the son's ex-wife in Germany.) Mrs. Motley also asked for guidance in regard to the Stew Pot situation, for she was still undecided as to what to do. After saying her amen, she stood with a soft groan and climbed aboard the bed's high mattress, which was no easy feat for her either.

Unable to sleep, Mrs. Motley lay in the darkened room contemplating what lay ahead. She imagined Stew Pot would get himself another pit bull like the ferocious one he had owned before his incarceration; a dog that had snarled and barked anytime it had caught sight of her. And she bet that instead of walking the beast twice a day like somebody with some sense, Stew Pot would let the animal do its business in the Reeves's backyard, just as he had done with the first dog. Which meant that before long the ground over there would be covered in dog mess, the carpet of droppings drawing flies from spring through autumn and fouling the air so bad that on some warm days she'd have no choice but to keep her back windows shut. And at no point during such times would she be able to relax in her elaborate backyard gardens, because who wanted to sit on the deck with a yard's worth of dog dung next door? Who'd invite guests to such a place? A pig farmer, she supposed. But she was no pig farmer. She was a lady whose parents had sent her to Mrs. Walker's Day School for Colored Girls, which is where she'd learned her perfect posture, along with tea etiquette and some French.

And Mrs. Motley also knew that if she were to knock on the two-flat's door (when Stew Pot wasn't home) and ask Mrs. Reeves if something *please* couldn't be done about the backyard, that her neighbor would stand in the doorway looking sheepish. Then in a squeaky voice that to Mrs. Motley's ears sounded irritatingly like Butterfly McQueen (Oh, how Mrs. Motley loathed *Gone with the Wind*), Mrs. Reeves would say: "I don't know what to do, Mrs. Motley. I tell the boy he ought to clean up after Hitler"—for Hitler had been the first pit bull's name— "but he never seems to have time."

That's what had happened years earlier when Mrs. Motley had complained about the dog mess. Not three weeks later she'd awoken one hot night to find her garage on fire. The firefighters who knocked the blaze down (trampling her gardens in the process) said she was lucky her house hadn't caught fire too. And although a subsequent investigation by police and fire officials resulted in no arrests, there was no doubt in the mind of Mrs. Motley or any other neighbor that Stew Pot had done it. From then until he went to jail the following year, hardly a fortnight passed without Mrs. Motley experiencing a nightmare wherein she awoke in the dream to find her bedroom burning.

This evening some neighbors had telephoned her with questions she had no answer to: "What is Stew Pot doing now?" "Is Mrs. Reeves okay?" Gazing now at the darkened ceiling she wondered, *What will he do next?* As it turned out, that question was answered early the next morning; and once again, it was she who was the first to know.

CHAPTER THREE

Mrs. Motley Makes a Momentous Decision

In the middle of the night Mrs. Motley had a fire dream. Lying faceup to the blaze, she saw the flames undulating hideously while a weight-force kept her helplessly pinned to the mattress. Just as the encroaching flames began to sting lightly at her nose, she awoke into the safety of the darkened bedroom with her forehead damp and her breath short. Though it was nearly an hour before she got back to sleep, she arose later at her usual six a.m. time, for she prided herself on being the sort of person who did not lollygag in bed.

The sky was as forlornly cloudy as the day before. By seven, dressed in a maroon blouse and charcoal-gray skirt, she was at the kitchen table with eggs, bacon, toast, coffee, and the obituary page of the *Chicago Tribune*. Every morning, without fail, she looked for familiar names in the death notices; sightings which had, over the previous ten years, become more and more of an occurrence.

She was on to her second coffee when the front bell chimed.

Mrs. Motley's foyer was at the end of that aforementioned first-floor hallway, separated from the hall by translucent double doors. You can easily imagine her surprise and trepidation when she swung the doors open and saw Stew Pot's face peering through the square window of her main door.

She worriedly glanced at the deadbolt lock and security chain to make sure both were still engaged. Stepping carefully forward she asked Stew Pot what he wanted. He smiled and wished her a good morning. The storm door was locked too, and the two glass panes muffled his deep voice as his breath clouded the area in front of his mouth.

She returned his greeting, but with none of the pleasantness she usually employed when making such responses. If Stew Pot noticed her cool demeanor, he didn't show it. Still smiling he said in his booming voice: "Sorry to come by so early, but it's kind of an emergency. See, I was wondering. Could I borrow your Bible?"

Mrs. Motley would not have been more surprised if Stew Pot had asked for her hand in marriage. Her befuddled expression greatly amused him and he said cheerfully: "Bet that's the last question you ever expected to hear coming out of *my* mouth."

"Why do you want a Bible?" she finally managed to say.

His eyes widened in excitement. "Oh, I read the Bible every day now. The Lord came to me in prison. He found me, saved me, and made me a new man."

"Oh really," she said. "So where's that Bible now?"

Mrs. Motley looked for some evidence—his eyes darting away perhaps—that would show that she had thrown him off balance through a quick and clever discovery of the hole in his story. Without hesitating, however, Stew Pot told her that some years back, another inmate, upon leaving prison, had given him a Bible. Through daily study, prayer, and contemplation, he had managed to "get into The Light." The day before, when he had left prison himself, he'd given the book to another inmate.

"I figure it this way," Stew Pot added, "that Bible helped me, now hopefully it'll help someone else."

Mrs. Motley felt her apprehension dissipate and her hopes lift. Her dilemma—move to safer surroundings, stay and live in terror—might in fact be no dilemma after all. The idea that the Lord sometimes works in mysterious and unexpected ways was, for her, not just a saying. And what could be more mysterious and unexpected than what she saw before her now—a God-fearing Stew Pot!

She told him to wait and that she would be right back.

Her favorite Bible was a thick volume with a soft red-leather cover and large print. No way was she going to give him that one. Fortunately, she had several others in the house, one of which was in the living room book cabinet. She took the black hardback copy from the top shelf and hesitated before pushing the glass door closed. Her sense of apprehension was still on duty and it told her that Stew Pot's story might be nothing more than a trick to get her to open the door so he could force his way in.

Mrs. Motley closed the cabinet, rationalizing her actions with the thought that her initial response to Stew Pot's revelation had been positive. One of her mother's guiding philosophies had been, *Always follow your first mind*, advice that had seldom steered Mrs. Motley wrong;

besides, after telling Stew Pot to wait she couldn't very well *not* give him a Bible. How would she explain such a sudden change of heart? She was a Christian, was she not? How then in good conscience could she refuse him?

Approaching the door again, her apprehension beseeched her to please take some sort of precaution, just in case her initial feeling had been wrong. Thinking quickly, she devised a strategy.

Stew Pot smiled at her through the glass, looking like a child who has just caught sight of the longed-for present. Holding the book with both hands, Mrs. Motley told him that she would let him borrow the Bible on one condition. "Step back from the door and down the steps so I can leave it on the porch railing."

His smile vanished, then just as quickly it returned. He nodded his head.

"It's all right, it's all right. After all the bad I've done, I understand folks wanting to be careful around me."

Stew Pot walked down the high steps. He stopped at the bottom and turned around, looking up at her expectantly.

Mrs. Motley waved a hand for him to back up further. He obeyed her gesture, stepping away until he was at the end of her walkway, his black boot heels on the sidewalk.

Keeping an eye on him, she unlocked and unlatched the inside door, and then did the same with the storm door. She stepped onto the porch and into the cold air, set the Bible atop the railing, and went back inside.

It wasn't until she had relocked and relatched both doors that Stew Pot came forward, bounding up the steps. He picked up the Bible and held the book over his head.

"Thank you *so much*, Mrs. Motley."

He turned and walked down the steps while Mrs. Motley, on instinct, inspected doorways and picture windows across the street for signs of someone watching. She saw no one, and feeling relieved, she shut her inner door again. As she did so, the thought hit her that what she *should* have done was tell Stew Pot to *keep* the Bible, for she did not doubt that he'd return the book; which meant he'd eventually be back at her door. Though happy at the surprising news of his religious conversion, old fears die hard, and she could not repress a new apprehension at the prospect of future face-to-face talks with him on her property. In her life she had seen the sort of joy Stew Pot had just displayed; the joy and relief of having finally found the Lord. It had been her experience that people in the throes of such elation had a tendency to latch onto some like-minded person as a kind of mentor for praying and long talks about the Scriptures. And though she felt guilty for feeling so, she did not want to be that person for Stew Pot. He'd have to find that elsewhere.

In the hopes of preventing any future intimate conversations, Mrs. Motley went to her living room telephone. It was on the end table nearest the foyer, alongside an answering machine and a thin spiral notebook. Sitting at that end of the blue couch, she thumbed through the notebook for the Reeves's number, which she'd gotten decades before. The original blue ink of her precise cursive writing had, over the intervening years, faded to gray. After tapping the code with a clear-nailed forefinger, she nestled the receiver to her ear and waited for the ring.

CHAPTER FOUR

Mrs. Motley Receives Two More Visits
and Does Some Reminiscing

Mrs. Motley heard no ring. Instead she got a chime followed by a recorded voice saying the number she'd called was disconnected and there was no further information about it.

She hung up and returned to the kitchen table where she poured herself a fresh cup of coffee. She was stirring the cream and sugar when the front bell sounded again.

Mrs. Motley sighed exasperatedly. *Now who?*

This time it was the round, pug-nosed face of Mrs. Hicks, her thickset neighbor from directly across the street, peering through the window. Mrs. Motley assumed Mrs. Hicks had been out walking her dog, and sure enough, as soon as she began the unlocking process, she heard the yelping barks of Pinky, Mrs. Hicks's small white-haired poodle.

Only a few years younger than Mrs. Motley, Mrs. Hicks still worked as an office clerk at the neighborhood grade school where Mrs. Motley had been the librarian. Mrs. Hicks's face had a squad of tiny moles ringing her left eye and plump cheeks bracketing the pug nose. That morning she was in her usual attire: army-surplus field jacket, cuffed chinos, and white athletic shoes. Under a blue wool cap her head sported a set of shiny, coppery curls that were obviously artificial. The wig was one of several Mrs. Hicks wore to cover her extensive hair loss; this coppery number wasn't Mrs. Motley's favorite because she didn't think it went well with her neighbor's gingerbread color.

As soon as she and the dog were inside the foyer, Mrs. Hicks stated why she had come: "I was wondering if anything new had happened this morning with You-Know-Who."

Although very different in style and demeanor, Mrs. Hicks and Mrs. Motley had become, over the previous thirty years, very good

friends; too good for Mrs. Motley to feel comfortable about withhold-
ing information of an important nature. So while Pinky paced about
the women's feet, Mrs. Motley crossed her arms and gave a full account of her encounter with Stew Pot that morning. When she got
to the part about giving him a Bible, Mrs. Hicks gave her a perturbed
look and said: "What'cha do that for?" This reaction didn't surprise
Mrs. Motley since she knew Mrs. Hicks never read the Bible and only
set foot inside a church to attend wakes or funerals; and only then if
the dead person was someone Mrs. Hicks had especially liked.

"The man asked for a Bible," Mrs. Motley said. "What was I supposed to tell him?"

"How about, *Git*?"

"That wouldn't have been a very Christian thing to do."

"Yeah, but it would have been sensible."

"Look, if Stew Pot has come to God, I for one am not going to
throw a roadblock between him and the Bible. If reading the Scriptures keeps him on the straight-and-narrow, he can read a Bible of
mine any day."

Because Mrs. Motley was a person that Mrs. Hicks especially
liked, she didn't make any more of it. They were still speaking a minute later when they heard the door to the two-flat open and close.
They stopped talking as Mrs. Reeves headed down her walkway and
turned left past Mrs. Motley's house. Usually, Mrs. Reeves trudged to
and from the commuter train station with her head down, and if she
encountered anyone along the way and received some sort of perfunctory greeting, she gave the person a quick nod of recognition before
lowering her eyes back to the ground and continuing on. This morning, however, she had her head up with an almost grin on her face, her
arms swinging easily at her sides in time to an energetic walk.

Mrs. Motley and Mrs. Hicks watched Mrs. Reeves until she was a
few doors away.

"Well, at least now we know Stew Pot didn't kill her," said Mrs.
Hicks. They spoke for a few minutes more and then Mrs. Hicks said
she and her husband had to leave for work. As she and Pinky moved
onto the porch she said over her shoulder: "Be careful with that Stew
Pot. Born again or no, you watch your step with him. Hear me?"

Mrs. Motley promised to be careful. After closing the doors she
went back to the kitchen, and shortly after returned to the living room

and the couch with a reheated cup of coffee and the day's crossword puzzle.

Moments later her attention was broken by the sight of Mrs. and Mr. Hicks heading down the walkway from their house (a brick Cape Cod with a pink front door), the two engaged in lively and smiling conversation which Mrs. Motley assumed was about Stew Pot.

Mr. Hicks wore no hat, exposing his cropped white hair and big ears to the cold. The same hue as his wife and just as thickset, he was a couple inches shorter, with a belly bulging his brown waist jacket and bowed legs that gave his walk a rocking gait.

The two left for work together every weekday morning, and Mrs. Motley knew, the way you know the habits of people you've lived across the street from for thirty years, that they would walk west on 129th for two blocks until Mrs. Hicks turned south for the grade school and Mr. Hicks headed north to his shoe shop on the main drag. And as sometimes happened when Mrs. Motley took notice of a couple enjoying the simple pleasure of each others' company, she felt a twinge of envy and thought of her husband and the times when they had enjoyed such delights. Their daily just-the-two-of-us times were marked by silent companionship—he closeted behind the wall of a morning paper as they breakfasted in the yellow kitchen, or she reading on the blue couch while he sat in a club chair by the living room fireplace, puffing on a pipe and reading one of his Civil War histories full of mustached generals. She had never complained about their lack of conversation because in the mornings she felt her husband needed peace and quiet before setting out for a day's work at the city insurance company where her father had been a founding officer. And at night she felt it was more than understandable that he wanted to rest in the comfort of his books after his long day. No, she had never complained about that, just as she had never complained about the white dress shirts that he wanted starched and ironed just so, or the soft-boiled breakfast eggs he wanted cooked just so, or the myriad other just-so things he had required. A neat and trim man, a precise man her husband had been, with immaculate fingernails and hair thinning across the top of his head, along with a narrow mustache and a gap between his top front teeth. In her formative years it had been the depictions of gentlemanly men in books and movies—William Powell, Heathcliff of *Wuthering Heights*, Zorro—that had stirred her blood, and continued to thrill her as she matured. Brawny types had never done anything for her; although as a youngster she'd desperately desired a wide-hipped and big-legged body for herself. She had imagined that the touch of burly boys would be inarticulate. She had loved her husband's touches. His intimate plucking had brought her such physical ecstasy that before her marriage, she would never have believed such intensity possible; a fact she'd admitted to no friend save Mrs. Hicks. And though she still occasionally had fond memories of the physical ecstasy—a fact she told no one—she considered such pleasures to now be a closed book of her life. Yes, she had loved her husband; had felt herself lucky to have him, for despite her well-to-do father and education, she had not considered herself much of a catch with her skinny, nearsighted self; an assessment that had been cultivated by her somewhat fulsome mother. Once, when Mrs. Motley was a teen trying on outfits in a dress shop dressing room, her mother had shaken her head slightly at her daughter's lack of curvature and said, out of a sincere desire to be of help: "Well, dear, we'll just have to work with what you have." Looking in the full-length mirror that day, Mrs. Motley, who was Miss Brownlee back then, had seen herself in yet another dress that to her fifteen-year-old mind hung on her as droopy as if from a hanger. (She also had no enthusiasm for her eyeglasses, which she thought made her look boringly bookish.) Upon hearing her momma's comment, the girl had felt a mean pinch of pain in her forehead, which her mother never knew of because by that age, Miss Brownlee had learned when caught in such humiliating situations to freeze her face in expressionless unrevelation.

Now, on her blue couch with her coffee and crossword puzzle, Mrs. Motley felt the pinch again, though not as intensely as that day in the dressing room. She did not hold against her momma what her husband had called "your mother's frequent and unintended lacerations of the soul," for she, Mrs. Motley, had made her peace with all that long ago.

By the time she came out of this reverie, Mrs. and Mr. Hicks were out of sight. Mrs. Motley went back to her puzzle, but after only a few minutes her concentration was broken yet again, this time by the sight of an avocado-colored four-door sedan that cruised to a slow stop in front of her house. The car belonged to Mr. Davenport, who lived with his wife and daughter midway down the block on Mrs. Hicks's side of the street. A teacher at Parkland High, he was the block club president who in the last citywide election had, many said foolishly, challenged the long-time alderman who represented Parkland on the City Council. In the years leading up to Stew Pot's imprisonment, Mr. Davenport had been a fierce opponent of the boy, and the night before he'd been one of the people who had called Mrs. Motley for Stew Pot updates.

Mr. Davenport had his head lowered over his steering wheel, gazing through the car's windshield at the two-flat like he had caught sight of something out of the ordinary. Curious, Mrs. Motley left the couch and moved to the edge of her porch. Upon seeing her, Mr. Davenport stepped out of the car. Leaving the driver's door open and the engine puffing exhaust, he trotted to her walkway and up the high steps.

Mr. Davenport's color was what some might call olive. He was stocky with a plump face and a trimmed mustache. He wore no coat over his dark blue suit and no hat on his head of relaxed hair, which was parted at the side and so strongly scented with cologne that Mrs. Motley's nose gave a twitch at the first sniff.

He stopped on the step below Mrs. Motley. With her arms wrapped around herself for warmth, she bid him good morning and asked if something was wrong. "I was headed to work," he said, "and decided to take a look at the two-flat to see if anything was amiss."

Before Mrs. Motley could even think about whether she should tell him about giving Stew Pot a Bible, Mr. Davenport was saying that he had decided to call an emergency block club meeting for that evening.

"We need to form a contingency plan," he said. "After that business with his mom's belongings, there's no telling what he might do next. Does eight o'clock work for you?"

She said yes, and before she could say anything else Mr. Davenport told her he was running late. He wished her a good day and headed back down the steps.

When she returned to the couch Mrs. Motley's thoughts became occupied with an issue she hadn't taken into consideration in those first heady moments when she'd pulled the Bible from the cabinet— namely, how immediate neighbors would react when they learned she had befriended Stew Pot. Because she was on generally good terms with people, she imagined most would be no harsher than Mrs. Hicks; however, a few were certain to be cross. She put the guesstimate at two. Three if she included Mr. Davenport. She didn't think he'd censure her for her actions, but when he found out what she'd done, he was likely to feel hurt she hadn't made a point of telling him just now. And she didn't doubt it would eventually all come out, because in Parkland stuff always came out. Neighbors reacting negatively would demand an explanation, and with a block club meeting set for that evening, demands and explaining might be coming sooner rather than later.

Mrs. Motley's worry over this issue flittered in and out of her thoughts as she completed the puzzle. (Only one clue gave her any real trouble—ACROSS 15: *Rousseau novel*.) By a quarter past eleven, after doing a load of laundry, she finally worked out what she would say in her defense. Basically, it was an elaboration on what she'd told Mrs. Hicks: out of Christian charity she'd come to Stew Pot's aid, et cetera et cetera.

Later on, while folding clothes in the yellow kitchen, she told herself giving someone a Bible wasn't *that* big of a deal. Not like she'd loaned Stew Pot money, or welcomed him home with open arms, or done him some other sort of intimate kindness. When he came to return the Bible, she'd tell him he could keep it and send him on his way. If he asked her for mentoring, she'd kindly but firmly suggest one of the Parkland deacons or ministers, or even its lone priest, telling Stew Pot it'd be better for him to take instruction from a man. Relieved as well as a bit proud at her problem-solving skills, Mrs. Motley now looked toward her next encounter with Stew Pot and the block club meeting with a calm, if not serene, confidence.

CHAPTER FIVE

*Hear My Plea: Wherein Mrs. Motley's Confidence
Is Proven to Have Been Unduly Optimistic*

After her noontime lunch (slices of cheddar cheese with olives, a piece of reheated chicken, and buttered whole wheat bread), Mrs. Motley was at her kitchen table making a list for her supermarket trip the next day when she heard the slam of the two-flat's back door and then the screen door. Wondering what Stew Pot might be up to this time, she left her pen and pad on the table and stepped to her back door window. There she was startled to see Stew Pot, with his peacoat unbuttoned, grabbing the top bar of the chain-link fence with his right hand and vaulting into her yard. His booted feet landed square on a stepping stone of her still wintered garden—brown stalks, dead leaves—before he bounded over to the steps of her deck, which had a fallow wood stain and extended the width of the house.

When he took the first step up, he saw her and his face got all toothy smile and wide eyes. As he neared she did not see the Bible and she wondered what on earth he wanted this time, but then when he reached the door, his head all big in her window again and clouding the glass with his breath, she saw him reach into the bib of his denim overalls and pull out the black book.

"See," he said, raising the book to the side of his dark face, "I'm returning your Bible."

Not wanting to appear rude by speaking through the window and storm door, Mrs. Motley was obliged to open her inner door and part the outer one, the cold air wafting her face and chest as she spoke through the foot-wide space.

"I got to thinking of that man giving you a Bible in prison—"

"Yes," he said, "and?"

"And it occurred to me I could do the same for you."

Stew Pot now got a look on his face as if he could not believe the wonderful news he was hearing. He thanked her softly, then bowed his head and closed his eyes. "Dear Lord, thank You for Mrs. Motley. A lot of people would've turned away a man who'd destroyed their property, but she's offered a helping hand in my efforts to stay in The Light."

With a vehemence that surprised them both, she said: "You admit to burning my garage?"

With eyes open again, but head still lowered, he said, sounding all sad and contrite: "Yes, it was me."

He then raised his head, and he looked as if he was suddenly in physical pain, his bottom lip trembling and his eyes tearing. Then just like that, Stew Pot dropped to his knees. Her right hand still held open the door a bit, and she watched as Stew Pot thrust his left arm into the open space and pushed the storm door wide open. She stepped back, her apprehension articulating in that split second that this is what Stew Pop had been waiting for all along, a chance to get into her house and at her. Terrified, she stepped backward, ramming against the end of the table. She was about to move sideways to make her escape down the hallway when Stew Pot, still on his knees, moved toward her.

"I have no right to ask," he said, "but can you find it in your heart to hear my apology?"

Mrs. Motley was not a woman given to public displays of high emotion, and whenever other people did so in her presence—men especially—she found the experience uncomfortable. This reaction only intensified as Stew Pot continued closing the space between them until he was kneeling directly in front of her. He clutched the low hem of her gray skirt, which made her flinch. For Mrs. Motley, having someone beg her in such a manner made her feel as if she were arrogantly assuming the role of a Divine. However, at the same time, she was not unmoved by the entreaty.

"All right," she said, "I'll hear your apology, but not like this, not on your knees."

She told him to stand and he did so. He was a head taller and her eyes were now inches from his hairy chin and her nose was full of the industrial-soap scent coming off his body.

"Do you want to sit down?"

He said yes and moved to the other side of the table and the chair nearest the wall. She thought of making a run but nixed the idea. If he truly meant to harm her, he'd catch her within a few steps.

At a loss for what to do, she said as calmly as she could manage: "Would you like some tea?"

CHAPTER SIX

Tea for Two

So what do you plan to do with yourself, now that you're home?" said Mrs. Motley. She was sitting at the kitchen table opposite Stew Pot who had draped his peacoat over the back of his chair. Along with a silver tea kettle, the china cups, saucers, and sugar bowl were arranged on the table between them. His apology, which he had just finished, had been long and rambling, and they had now moved to discussing his life situation.

"I'm going to get a job," he replied. "And I mean honest work. Mom says there's a *Help Wanted* sign at the car wash over on the drag. Probably just part-time, but it could be a start. No more crime for me. This change is for real."

"Well you certainly look different," Mrs. Motley said.

"There's not much to do in the joint constructive. I read the Bible and lifted weights. At first the lifting was just to pass time, but I eventually saw it was good discipline."

"And is that discipline what brought you to the Bible?"

"Oh no, my spiritual awakening came as a result of counsel from Brother Crown."

"Who?"

Stew Pot grinned and set his cup on its saucer.

"Brother Crown is someone I met when I was inside. He's a man of God, a great man of God walking day and night in The Light. He's turned a lot of fellows in prison around. The way I see it, sinning Stew Pot is dead. God gave me the strength to kill him."

"So, are you going to get another dog?"

"I was planning to," he said. "I like pit bulls, and I think I know what your concern is." He broke into a smile again. "I won't let this one do its business in the yard."

She thanked him, then asked what else he'd done in prison besides read and lift weights.

"I listened to gospel music, and I'm not talking about gospel that sounds like honky-tonk. I mean no-frills gospel. Anything else is Devil racket. I talked to Mom about that. Now don't get me wrong, Mom is a good woman. But even good folks make mistakes. I told her a person is either walking in The Light or they're not. And you can't be walking in The Light if you're listening to songs straight from the Devil's piano. If music doesn't praise God, I don't want it. Don't care if it's jazz, country, or opera."

"Opera?" said Mrs. Motley.

"*Especially* opera," said Stew Pot, pointing at the yellow oil table-cloth with a forefinger. "Most operas you hear aren't even sung in English. Right off, that ought to make you suspicious. You ever read translations of opera lyrics? Sin, pure and simple. Opera is the same as rock and roll, just more melodic. It wraps sin in a prettier package."

Stew Pot nodded his head in agreement with himself.

"That's how the Devil gets to folks," he continued. "He wraps sin in a pretty package. In the case of music, a package that gets people bobbing their heads and tapping their feet to the point that the bobbing and tapping feel so good, people don't *listen* to what the lyrics are *saying*. That rock and roll, and that opera, and that country music, and that nasty blues like my dad used to listen to, are all about the same thing—drunkenness and salaciousness.

"So like I said, I had a talk with Mom yesterday. I took those records of hers by Ray Charles—ha, now there's the blind leading the blind—and Johnny Mathis, and so on, and I tossed them in the trash. I threw out all her soap opera magazines too. Soap operas are as bad as regular opera—a lot of wanton behavior masquerading as *entertainment*. But then what can you expect? TV is the Devil's twenty-four-hour playground. Radio is just as bad. And *movies*? Don't even get me started, same for novels and poetry. I threw out her TV, radio, and record player because they were tainted from all the sinful programming that had run through the circuits. Her phone service got shut off awhile back, which is just as well because those receivers were probably tainted too. When we get the service back on we'll get new, clean telephones. I dumped her revealing clothes because no decent woman should be in blouses with the tops collarbone low or skirts and dresses with the hems knee-high.

"Yesterday I struck a blow in my fight against sin. I'm dedicating my life to walking in The Light and I'll take on Satan wherever I see him. I'm going to spread the Word. And if anybody tries to stop me they better watch out, 'cause I got the Lord for backup."

He took a long sip and Mrs. Motley did likewise. She'd heard such uncompromising arguments before, most notably from her mom's mom. According to Grandma Lucy, Jews hunted Christian kids for sport, nuns and priests had sex orgies every night, and Muslims sacrificed Protestant virgins to Muhammad. Grandma Lucy could never be argued off such beliefs and Mrs. Motley made no attempt to argue Stew Pot off any of his. (She could just imagine what he'd say about her record collection in the living room which included operas and Broadway musicals, as well as more than a few albums by Mr. Charles and Mr. Mathis.)

"I've given it a lot of thinking," said Stew Pot, "and the first thing I feel I should do is apologize to anyone on the block that I may have hurt or offended in the past."

Using a measured tone, Mrs. Motley said she didn't know if that was such a good idea. "Perhaps you should wait, give folks a chance to get used to your being back."

"I understand what you're saying, Mrs. Motley, but you can't delay repentance." He grinned again, drained his cup, and glanced at her wall clock over the sink. "I should be going, but before I do, would you pray with me?"

She nodded yes, but only because she didn't see any way she could get out of it. From her experience with her grandmother, she knew how uncompromising people could get angry when refused. And she did not want to run the risk of irritating Stew Pot even a little bit because it was now sunshine clear that Stew Pot was more than a little off.

"Would you place your hands on the table?" he said.

Mrs. Motley did so. He placed his large hands palms-down over the backs of hers and her arms got goose-bumped. His short fingernails were clean and the pink undersides of the hands surprisingly smooth. He closed his eyes and bowed his head. She followed suit.

"*Our Father,*" he began softly, "*Who art in Heaven . . .*"

Minutes later they were both standing at the table as he pulled on his peacoat, he smiling and she anxious for him to step through the kitchen doorway. However, as he was buttoning up he said: "Okay if I leave by the front?"

There was no way Mrs. Motley would ever order another Black person to leave by the back door, the way so many had been forced to do for so many years by so many Whites.

Stew Pot headed down the wainscoted hallway with the Bible in hand. She followed close behind, his broad torso making it impossible for her to see past him. Mrs. Motley sent up a silent prayer that she would make it through this second Stew Pot visit the way she had the first, without her neighbors seeing any of it.

This prayer was answered, sort of.

As Stew Pot moved through the doorway, directly across the street a lanky mailman named Mr. Bird was pushing his cart down the Hicks's walkway after making a delivery to their letterbox. Although he didn't reside in Parkland, he'd been delivering mail there for so many years that his face was as familiar as any in the neighborhood.

Mr. Bird stopped cold when he caught sight of Stew Pot rocking down Mrs. Motley's steps. She watched helplessly from the foyer as Stew Pot crossed the street. She imagined Mr. Bird was recalling the days when Stew Pot and Hitler had made mail deliveries to the block a scary thing, because Mr. Bird had a look on his face like people get when they're caught in the open by someone they owe a lot of money to. When Stew Pot reached him and began chatting away, all Mr. Bird could manage at first was a weak smile.

Mrs. Motley knew Mr. Bird to be a fine man. Save for vacations, he hadn't missed a day in years. However, he did have one professional failing—he greatly enjoyed trading in gossip. He could often be seen exchanging the latest Guess-what? with this or that resident on the sidewalk or at a front doorway. (He never did this with Mrs. Motley because early on she had politely told him she was not interested in such talk.)

Mrs. Motley saw Stew Pot gesture with the Bible toward her house. Mr. Bird's eyebrows arched. Then he asked Stew Pot something. Stew Pot responded with affirmative nods, which caused Mr. Bird to snatch a glance across the street. He said something else to Stew Pot, who got even more animated, which caused Mr. Bird to slowly nod yes to show he understood everything he was being told.

CHAPTER SEVEN
Say What?

After Stew Pot bid him a happy goodbye and strolled off westward, Mr. Bird renewed his stop-and-go pace in the same direction. From the blue couch Mrs. Motley watched the mailman until he was out of sight. (He had already delivered the mail to her side of the street.) She had no idea how many neighborhood folks Mr. Bird would speak to that afternoon about his conversation with Stew Pot, but she knew it would be at least a few, and a few would be more than enough. There was no doubt in her mind that by suppertime, on the block and beyond, her conversation with Stew Pot that afternoon would be the hot topic of conversation. She was right about that.

The most common reaction from immediate neighbors was bewilderment.

"Motley let him in her <u>house</u>? What in the world for?"

"Mr. Bird said Stew Pot told him that Stew Pot and Mrs. Motley had tea in her kitchen, and then they prayed, and that he—Stew Pot, that is—found God while in prison and that Mrs. Motley gave him a Bible as a welcome-home present and now Stew Pot's going to be an evangelist. Oh yeah, he also said he's going to apologize to everyone on the block."

As for Parkland-at-large, the judgments were generally less harsh, the admonishments diminishing in intensity the further away you got from Stew Pot's home. A few such Parklanders, upon hearing of Stew Pot's religious conversion, were even willing to move him from the neighborhood's "weird and dangerous" category, to "weird but harmless," reserved for Parkland residents whose behavior was considered by the majority to be merely oddball, arousing little fear or face-to-face mockery. On Mrs. Motley's block, a goodly number of neighbors said she had some serious explaining to do at the block club meeting, with a few wondering out loud if she would even show.

At supper Mrs. Motley gave the no-show option serious consideration. Although her argument for why she'd given Stew Pot a Bible was clear in her own head, an explanation for why she'd seated him at the kitchen table was not. In her mind the kitchen encounter was like a weird dream—Stew Pot on his knees sobbing, his strange fears and judgments, his vague evangelical plans.

As usual she took her evening meal in the apple-green dining room where the sheen of the rectangular expanse of table produced a near flawless reflection of the crystal chandelier and its minor constellation of lights. Her place setting was formal as well: china plates, sterling silver flatware, and a crystal water glass which, depending on one's point of view, was either something very classy or something kind of sad.

She idly moved her pork chop and peas around with her heavy fork. If she didn't attend the meeting, folks were sure to see it in the worst light. However, she also had no desire to stand and deliver, as it were, before nearly every neighbor on the block, some of whom would not be happy. One neighbor who she knew would be especially angry was Mrs. Butler, who lived with her teenage grandson in the corner house at the west end of the block on the other side of the street. She and Mrs. Motley had a history going back to the early 1970s when Mrs. Butler, who sported a big afro at the time, had led a Parkland group that sought to have certain books—*Huckleberry Finn* and *Moby-Dick* among them—taken off the library shelves of the grade school where Mrs. Motley was librarian. Mrs. Butler's crew contended that the books on their hit list were racist and a threat to the healthy emotional development of Black children. Mrs. Motley had vigorously opposed those efforts, which produced a lot of angry finger-pointing and name-calling from Mrs. Butler and her crowd—"Boot-licking Uncle Toms" being one of the less profane descriptions they'd used for Mrs. Motley and those who supported her. The whole thing fizzled after only a few months, the victim of community indifference as much as anything, but not before hard feelings had developed on both sides. Eventually Mrs. Motley got over hers, as victors often do. As for Mrs. Butler, in the tradition of many a failed revolutionary, she'd never forgotten or forgiven. (According to Mrs. Hicks, Mrs. Butler's resentment was also due to envy: "Your husband left you in good financial shape, while hers just up and left.")

At her dining room table Mrs. Motley put her fork down. To her left, on either side of the wide window that overlooked her west yard, were a couple dozen framed photographs of various sizes; black-and-white images depicting previous generations of her family. There wasn't a smiling face in the bunch. Usually she found the stern looks comforting, proof of the determination they'd used to free themselves from poverty. Now the faces seemed to admonish her. *What are a few cranky neighbors*, the faces seemed to say, *compared to Klan nightriders?* Embarrassed, she looked to her right at the hulky sideboard. There sat photos of her husband, son, and granddaughter; all with high foreheads, chestnut hues, and gaps between the top front teeth.

If her husband were alive, Mrs. Motley knew he'd have seen Stew Pot's return as a perfect reason to sell the house, since he had never much liked living in it. (He'd had an equally negative attitude about working at her dad's insurance firm, though not so negative that he ever quit.) And if Mrs. Motley were to call her son at Fort Sill with news about Stew Pot, Master Sergeant Motley would surely say, as he'd done many times before: "Ma, that house costs a fortune to heat in winter and another to keep cool in summer. Why hang onto it?" As for the granddaughter, Mrs. Motley didn't know what the child might say. She hadn't seen her grandbaby in eight years. The girl's mother had full custody and refused to let Alison-Jean visit the US. One of Mrs. Motley's cherished hopes was to one day sit alongside her granddaughter on the blue couch as they turned heavy black pages of leather-bound albums filled with family photos and memorabilia.

Giving up on supper, she cleared the table and went to the living room couch. Along with its red leather cover and large print, her Bible had lots of illustrations. On more than one occasion her son had laughingly pointed out that the illustrations were inaccurate because in every picture the people, with their pale skins and straight hair, looked as if they'd arrived in the Holy Land directly from Oslo. Such comments never failed to irritate Mrs. Motley, who always replied that the people's color was not the point.

That evening she sought solace, as she often did, in the Book of Psalms, beginning with the well-known Chapter 23: *The Lord is my shepherd, I shall not want* . . . When she got to Chapter 27 she paused, then read a line aloud: *"The Lord is my salvation; whom shall I fear?"*

CHAPTER EIGHT

Showdown at the Davenport Corral

The Davenports' yellow-brick Dutch Colonial had a screened front porch (uncommon for such houses) and a front door painted orange. The first-floor furniture was Swedish Modern, and although no one ever said so to the Davenports, most neighbors on the block found the style off-putting, which was also their opinion of the "modern art"—paintings with splotches and irregular lines—that hung on the peach-colored walls.

There were two dozen metal folding chairs set among the sleek furniture to help accommodate the thirty-seven guests crowded into the living room and adjacent dining room. Mrs. Motley, Mrs. Hicks, and Mr. Hicks sat three-in-a-row on a burnt-orange couch set against the wall that was perpendicular to the picture window. Mr. Davenport, dapper in a paisley ascot, white shirt, blue blazer, and gray slacks, stood at a wooden podium by the carpeted stairs and opened the meeting with an apology.

"Unfortunately, my wife had an engagement planned for this evening that she couldn't break." Folks nodded politely at this, although some nods camouflaged mean spirits snidely wondering if Mrs. Davenport's "engagement" included gin and a lemon twist, since her affinity for martinis and dislike of block club meetings was well known.

"And, of course," Mr. Davenport continued, "Delphina will take the minutes." He gestured to his right where he and his wife's fifteen-year-old daughter sat near the front door with a pen and pad. In both shape and face she was the image of her mother, rangy and brown with large eyelids that gave her a sleepy look. Her dad had appointed her the block club note taker (nobody else wanted to do it), and if the flat smile she displayed at meetings was any indication, Delphina wasn't happy for the job. She did it well, though. Her handwriting was so good she never typed the minutes; instead she photocopied the longhand version and distributed it to people's mailboxes.

"All right," said Mr. Davenport, "let's get to it. Like a bad penny, a certain someone has returned. Stew Pot now claims he had a religious awakening while in jail."

A few people chuckled, and from various angles heads swiveled to look at Mrs. Motley. Despite feeling self-conscious, she kept her eyes on the stairway bannister that rose at an angle above and behind Mr. Davenport.

"If Stew Pot has had a religious turn," Mr. Davenport went on, "then all I can say is, *hallelujah*. However, it would be foolish, given his past, to not be ready with a plan in case he starts cutting up again. Stew Pot says he wants to apologize to folks. Of course, according to Mr. Bird, Stew Pot also claims that he threw out his momma's TV because the circuits were tainted."

This got a big laugh and Mr. Davenport smilingly waited for the mirth to subside.

"Now, you'll have to excuse me if I'm a little skeptical about *anything* Stew Pot says. We're civil people who believe in giving others the benefit of the doubt. However, we should also prepare for the worst."

Mrs. Motley raised a hand. Again heads swiveled her way.

"Yes?" said Mr. Davenport, looking a little surprised.

Mrs. Motley lowered her hand and others leaned forward in anticipation. Many had come expecting sparks to fly and now it looked as if the first one was about to be struck.

"Mr. Davenport, there's something I want to say."

"Well, as you know, Mrs. Motley, we have a time scheduled for comments from the—"

"I'm aware of that. But this is an emergency meeting about a specific issue of which I have become involved. As a longtime friend and neighbor, I beg your indulgence."

"Um, well, of course, Mrs. Motley. Would you like to step to the podium?"

"No," she said, "I'll speak from here."

She slowly rose to her feet. The people sitting in the folding chairs turned sideways to look at her. Drawing upon her experience lecturing to students, she reminded herself to shift her gaze as she spoke and make eye contact at different points around her audience.

"As I'm sure you all know by now, Stew Pot came to my house this morning and asked to borrow a Bible. I gave him one. He returned it this afternoon and I told him he could keep it. I know some people are not happy about that; but if someone comes to my door and asks for help in keeping their faith, I'm not going to turn them away. Now don't get me wrong. I'm no fool about Stew Pot. He set fire to my garage and—"

"But he didn't drive your aunt to an early grave." The interruption came from a woman seated in the passageway between the living and dining rooms. Her name was Erma Smedley and she lived on the block's west corner on Mrs. Motley's side of the street. Erma's late aunt, who'd been that house's previous owner, had left the place to her. Just past forty with black hair styled in a bob and a scatter of freckles across her nose, Erma's color was so light that all her life she'd evoked worship from some Blacks and scorn from others, as well as being the object of numerous hot desires.

Mrs. Motley turned to Erma, who had her arms crossed over the front of a lavender blouse. "I'm not trying to equate my loss with yours."

Erma's scowl softened, but only a little. Mrs. Motley went back to moving her eyes among the group.

"Yes, Stew Pot was in my kitchen this afternoon. Yes, we had tea, and yes, we prayed. I believe that as long as a person draws breath, there is a chance for salvation, and only by forgiving those who have harmed me can I hope to enter Heaven. I know not everybody believes as I do, and I know I've disappointed some of you, perhaps many of you. All I can say is that when it comes to matters of faith, I have to do what I feel God wants me to do, even if those things are difficult."

Mrs. Motley sat down. For a few seconds nobody said anything. Many there considered themselves God-fearing and her words had a persuasive effect on more than a few, who acknowledged their feelings with approving nods.

Mr. Davenport thanked Mrs. Motley and was about to say something else when Erma spoke again: "Well here's what I know: Stew Pot killed my aunt's cat, gouged out its eyes, and then left the head on her doorstep. My aunt went from being a woman active in the community to being too scared to leave her house."

Erma was, of course, repeating facts that everyone already knew. Those who were in strong agreement voiced their feelings by clapping. When the racket subsided, Mr. Davenport, in an attempt to regain control of the meeting, said: "What should we do?"

Several suggestions were called out almost at once and people started talking over each other. Mr. Davenport reached inside the podium stand, grabbed a wooden gavel, and rapped the podium top until there was silence.

"We need to form a committee to watch Stew Pot," he said. "The best way to get him back in jail is to catch him violating his parole and report it to the authorities."

An older woman sitting in the first row of chairs near the podium stood up. This was Mrs. Butler. One look at the falcon-like features of her chocolate face and you saw why generations of neighborhood kids had called her Hawkeye behind her back. As usual, she was dressed all in black. She had a black cape draped over the back of her folding chair and the rest of her noir ensemble consisted of a sweater, stretch pants, and ballet slipper shoes. Her long salt-and-pepper dreadlocks (she hadn't had an afro for a long while now) were swept back from her forehead, and as she surveyed the room over the tops of half-moon glasses, another sense of anticipation, far stronger than the first, swept through many attendees. (Her aforementioned teenager grandson, Reggie, tall and gangly, sat beside her, his eyes fixed on the floor.)

"I personally think all this talk about Stew Pot finding religion is nonsense," Mrs. Butler said in her clipped, precise diction. "I think he's using it to get people to lower their guard. He's counting on finding gullible people with whom to ingratiate himself, people who'll in turn try to convince the rest of us that he's *changed*. You know, *some* people get so caught up in how *they* feel that they forget what they owe their other neighbors. They should quit all the worrying they're doing about Stew Pot and consider the memories of those he has harmed."

A few voices called out in agreement and heads swiveled to Mrs. Motley's direction once more, but all they got was the sight of her sitting quiet and looking calm. The faces then shifted back to Mr. Davenport who was saying that Mrs. Butler had a good point; although it was not clear to anyone exactly what point he was referring to.

"So it's agreed," he said. "We'll form a watch committee. Who wants to be on it?"

Erma piped in that those living closest to the two-flat should be on the committee. "I nominate Mrs. Motley."

From all over, Mrs. Motley got expectant stares, with two notable exceptions. Delphina leaned back in her chair and gazed upon the room with an expression of condescending bemusement. Meanwhile, Mrs. Butler's grandson Reggie glanced sideways at Delphina with a longing look, before returning his eyes to the floor. She saw his look and knew exactly what it meant, which only increased her bemusement.

Peering at Mr. Davenport, Mrs. Motley said calmly: "If I see Stew Pot doing something wrong, I'll of course report it. But are you sure we need—"

Mrs. Butler was still standing and she let loose an exaggerated sigh. "You live next door to him, Mrs. Motley. You have the best vantage point to observe his actions."

Still calm, Mrs. Motley began: "As I said before—"

Mrs. Butler cut her off again. "We *heard* what you said. I wonder if you'd feel so blasé if Stew Pot had gotten *your* children hooked on drugs?"

Her grandson's shoulders flinched in reaction to this reference to his mother. Fortunately for him, folks were so focused on his grandma they didn't notice this clear indication of his shame, the young man keeping his acorn-brown face, with its full-bodied nose and lips, aimed at the floor.

"What does Stew Pot have to do to convince you he's evil?" Mrs. Butler continued. "Burn your house down too? Some of us can't afford to lose our homes. Some of us didn't have the luxury of wealthy fathers and husbands who left us inheritances from the blood money they accrued by exploiting the poor with usurious insurance policies."

"Mrs. Butler—" Mr. Davenport said.

"Some of us are not so foolhardy as to believe the leopard has changed its spots."

"Mrs. Butler—"

"Some of us are not obsessed with making grandstanding shows of piety—"

"Mrs. Butler, please . . ."

At this point Mrs. Hicks stood, leaving her husband looking up at her.

"Keeping an eye on Stew Pot is everyone's responsibility," Mrs. Hicks said with a sweep of the arm, "not just a few. Everyone must be watchful. If we are, then no one has to turn their life inside out keeping tabs on him."

This was loudly seconded from numerous quarters. Mrs. Butler sat down shaking her head to let everyone know how angry she felt. Erma didn't look too pleased either.

The rest of the meeting was spent discussing how people should report on Stew Pot's movements. Mr. Davenport said he would take reports from neighbors and act as a clearinghouse for information. While this talk was going on, Mrs. Motley leaned over to Mrs. Hicks and whispered: "Thank you."

The meeting broke up twenty minutes later, and as people filed out, Mrs. Butler could still be heard complaining to Erma about Mrs. Motley. Reggie, following behind, gave a last glance over his shoulder at Delphina, who responded with a *pu-leaze* expression, which caused him to embarrassingly snap his head forward, a move that a few people caught and were amused by, although no one commented on it until Reggie and his grandma were out of earshot. Mrs. Motley said she felt sorry for the poor boy, while the others in the small group around her had fun chuckling at his situation—just as later, a number of the other immediate neighbors had fun phoning around the news of all that had happened that day between Mrs. Motley and Stew Pot, along with details of the block club meeting. The Parkland Gossip Line, as Mrs. Motley snidely referred to it, consumed and regurgitated these reports well into the night in homes and nightspots. Not being a gossiper, she called no one, though later that night, after giving prayerful thanks for Mrs. Hicks's intervention, Mrs. Motley did lie in her dark bedroom and conduct her own review of the meeting.

In addition to having gotten over her animosity toward Mrs. Butler, Mrs. Motley had given up hope Mrs. Butler would ever get over hers, which included her socialist resentments. (The mean words about her father and husband had infuriated her.) Of course, Mrs. Motley reminded herself, there were other issues fueling Mrs. Butler's rage that evening, which the woman had mentioned. Mrs. Butler's son had been a teenage running buddy of Stew Pot's, despite her many attempts to end the friendship. According to Mrs. Butler, Stew Pot had introduced drugs to her son and then her daughter, with both kids then taking paths to addictive despair. The son eventually got clean, only to disappoint Mrs. Butler by marrying a White woman he met at a Drug-Anon meeting and moving to Maine. As for the daughter, no one knew where she was, including Mrs. Butler. (Or so Mrs. Butler said.) The daughter left a baby behind (no one knew who or where the father was), and Mrs. Butler had raised Reggie on her own, the boy now a junior at Parkland High where he played on the football and basketball teams *and* got good grades. Reggie had never wanted for anything, Mrs. Butler working all sorts of jobs—laundromat attendant, motel clerk, to name a couple; and though she was a year older than Mrs. Motley, Mrs. Butler was still working, these days as manager of a food pantry in nearby Blue Island that provided free groceries and meals to the poor. And Mrs. Motley knew the woman would work until Reggie finished college. Mrs. Motley readily acknowledged that she had more than a grudging respect for Mrs. Butler's efforts; an opinion she'd never shared with anyone because she knew it would not have been appreciated by Mrs. Butler if she had ever gotten wind of it.

At this point Mrs. Motley again thought of the Parkland Gossip Line, which she imagined was running full blast, and she blew an audible breath of exasperation, for she was sure that the next day, when she ran her neighborhood errands, she herself was going to get an earful.

CHAPTER NINE

Parkland, Sweet Parkland

Mrs. Motley's garage was a copy of her house with the teal paint job, black shutters, and white lace in the windows. The car she parked there was a boxy, four-year-old, Swedish sedan that still had its new-car smell. She'd nicknamed it Ingrid. She'd nicknamed all her cars, for good luck: Julia Belle, Betty Lou, Elvira, to list a few. Her husband thought the habit silly and so did her son, but in all her driving years she'd never had a serious crash, so what did they know?

The day after the block club meeting, wearing a tan trench coat, tan beret, and tan gloves, she pulled from her garage in the midmorning under yet another gray sky. Anxious over her upcoming gossip ordeal, she drove down the concrete alley to the west end of the block and turned left onto Honore Street (pronounced Hoh-nur by the locals), rolling to the next intersection where she turned right on 129th Place and continued west.

Normally Mrs. Motley loved being out in the neighborhood where every block was like her own—the colorful front doors, the tall trees lining the road—and where nearly every street had a spot that had been the site of some happy event from her sweet long-ago. For example, on the block she was driving through now, over on her left, sat a red four-square, similar in size to her house. At age eleven, it was there that she had attended her first formal tea wearing a sky-blue dress and elbow gloves outfit sewn by her mother. She and the other girls from Mrs. Walker's School had nibbled on finger sandwiches and sipped Earl Grey flavored with honey while a June breeze carried the scent of lilacs through the window screens. A couple blocks later, on her right, there was a brown brick bungalow where at age sixteen, in the backyard beneath a weeping willow on a perfect August evening, she had experienced her first real kiss from a boy; the fellow an out-of-town cousin of her best girlfriend (who'd acted as matchmaker). A sophomore at Howard with a thin mustache, the cousin's color had reminded the demure Miss Brownlee of a roan horse, and although he was later killed in the war by the Germans at the Battle of the Bulge, and though the friend had died the previous year after a long and ravaging illness, the memory of that first kiss and the events around it were still a pleasantry for Mrs. Motley. And as she drove on, she tried lightening her spirits further by softly singing, "*Parkland, sweet Parkland*," the opening line to the high school's fight song. (P-High was a few blocks north, a maroon-brick edifice where she'd enjoyed many a triumph: four years on the honor roll, yearbook editor, senior class vice president.) These thoughts lifted her mood, but only a bit.

With every relative of consequence either residing far away or gone to their rewards, Parkland was really all Mrs. Motley had; a fact she'd been aware of for some time. Two days before, during all her fretting on the couch, she had not wanted to remind herself of that, but she did so now. Parkland was all she had—although she knew that one day her son (assuming he wasn't killed or rendered disabled in some combat action) might well have to deposit her in an institutional warehouse where she'd waste away among strangers. (A fate that had befallen a number of people she knew.) However, as long as she was able to operate on her own recognizance, there was only one place she wanted to be. And thinking of that brought to her mind another issue she'd managed to avoid. Namely, that moving from her house (the epicenter of her Parkland joy) was not really an option. Residents in Parkland tended to stay put. If she sold her house, it wasn't likely she'd find another in the neighborhood large enough for all her things. In other words, she wasn't going anywhere. She had to stay right where she was. No matter what Stew Pot might do, she had no choice but to stay.

CHAPTER TEN

The Wit and Whimsy of the Parkland Gossip Line

It was earlier stated that nearly every establishment on the main drag was a storefront business. One of the two exceptions was a supermarket located at the neighborhood's northwest corner. It was through the intervention, some said machinations, of the city's 51st Ward alderman that Diamond Foods, a Chicago-area chain, had built the supermarket in Parkland and not Blue Island, which was just the other side of the nearby rail yard. The suburban town was so old that in style and demeanor it looked no different from the city neighborhoods it bordered. It was now home to many Blacks and Hispanics, though Mrs. Motley well remembered the days when non-Whites had not been welcome there. (The suburb the other side of Parkland, Calumet Park, had had an even meaner attitude toward Negroes back in the day, though you'd never know that now with the town's mostly Black population.) When the Diamond store had opened twenty-some years before, it had been so grand with a staff so integrated that Whites from Blue Island ventured into Parkland, making grocery shopping the first joint activity for residents of the two communities; racial harmony through retail, if you will.

With her thoughts back onto her concerns, Mrs. Motley pulled into the lot. The supermarket was one of her favorite neighborhood stops. She enjoyed rolling a cart among the shelves of colorfully packaged items and seeing employees in their purple knit shirts. That morning she meandered among the aisles for nearly an hour, luxuriating in the scent of floor wax before finally pushing her cart to a checkout line.

There the cashier was a young, honey-colored woman with dyed blond hair done in a ponytail. Years before, she had been a student of Mrs. Motley's at the grade school. (The name tag on the purple shirt read, KEISHA.) The cashier gave Mrs. Motley a happy good day which Mrs. Motley returned in kind. However, her mood quickly changed when Keisha said, between smacks of gum, that she'd heard Stew Pot had come home from prison two days before and, after beating up Mrs. Reeves, had run off with all of her money.

This was just the sort of thing Mrs. Motley had feared. Folks gabbing inaccurate nonsense really got on her nerves. Speaking politely despite these feelings, she gave Keisha a quick and correct account of Stew Pot's nonviolent homecoming.

"Are you *sure* about that?" Keisha said as she handed back change. "The person I spoke with said they had it on *very* good authority that Stew Pot beat his momma."

Mrs. Motley, recalling now that this Keisha had been a girl more interested in flirting and passing notes than in getting her lesson, assured her that no beating or stealing had occurred. Keisha thanked her, although it was clear from her flat expression that she was not pleased with Mrs. Motley's tamer version of the story.

At the Parkland Co-op Credit Union, midway down the main drag, it was more of the same. At the teller's window, a fellow with lips that reminded Mrs. Motley of raw liver asked if it was true that Stew Pot was now seven feet tall. Again hiding her irritation, she politely set the teller straight. And so it went at the drugstore, and the dry cleaners, and hardware store, and the flower shop; folks coming at her with either mangled versions of Stew Pot's return—he had set fire to a pile of his mother's clothes in the two-flat's backyard—or with questions based on things that had never occurred: Why had she invited Stew Pot over for a welcome-home supper? Why had she decided to start a Bible study group with Stew Pot?

The exception to all this was the 51st Ward alderman, whose office was located in a storefront between a diner and a beauty parlor. His name was Vernon Paiger and at the time of Stew Pot's return he'd represented the ward for twenty-six years and was a recognized big deal on the City Council. Not tall but not short either, he was mostly bald with a color similar to that of peanut shells, with bushy eyebrows set above hazel eyes that gave him an owlish look. Several businesses on the main drag bore his name: Paiger Insurance, Paiger Realty, Paiger Construction, Paiger Flower Shop; all operated by a relative. (Another business, Paiger & Paiger Mortuary, was located on a Parkland side street across from Eden Rest Cemetery, which sat on a high bank above the Cal Sag.) He was a year younger than Mrs. Motley and had been a widower longer than she'd been a widow. After her husband's death (two years after, to be exact), they'd dated briefly—four dates. Mrs. Motley had ended the relationship, and though disappointed by her decision, he'd remained on good terms with her.

After leaving the supermarket lot Mrs. Motley had parked in front his office before heading to the credit union. (The forest preserve across the busy street presenting a high background of brown bare branches.) He was standing a ways back inside the office behind the large display windows, dressed that day in a dark gray three-piece suit with red tie, white shirt, and black wingtips. She hadn't seen him but he'd seen her, and knowing her routine, he made sure he was near the glass door when she returned some time later. By then she was carrying two white plastic bags and a bundle of cut yellow flowers in one hand, and two dresses on hangers (from the dry cleaners) in the other.

He waited until she had her back to him, and as she tried to figure out how to manage getting her keys from her closed purse without setting down her items (the purse hanging by a strap from her forearm), he slipped behind her.

His softly spoken baritone of a hello startled her and she nearly dropped the flowers. In a voice just as soft but with even less inflection, he said: "Let me help you with that," and reached for the long stems.

The initial look of surprise she cast over her shoulder disappeared when she recognized him, replaced by an expression of pleased agreeability.

"Oh—hello," she said, and turned halfway around so she was facing him. Without any further instruction she raised her arms, and one by one he took the items from her. She retrieved her keys and opened the rear door of the sedan, whereupon the one-by-one procedure was reversed with Mrs. Motley setting her stuff inside the car.

When that was done and the door closed, she turned to him and asked how he was doing. He said fine and that he was wondering the same thing about her, what with Stew Pot back home asking for Bibles and dropping to his knees and hauling perfectly respectable clothes to the garbage can. "Not to mention Mrs. Butler, who is apparently up to her old tricks." He spoke this with a touch of sarcasm to let Mrs. Motley know that he was on her side, and she, appreciating the gesture, responded with a grin. And in response to that, he shifted tone again, this time gently asking: "So you're okay?" And with a smile she said yes, all things considered, and thanked him for his concern.

He then asked about her son. After telling him her boy was fine she asked about his children—two sons, two daughters; none of whom were in politics or living in the Midwest. They were all fine, he said, as were his grandchildren. He didn't ask about her granddaughter, knowing that situation was a sore point with her. And that pretty much exhausted their ammunition of small talk, and since neither wanted to venture into anything of a serious nature, Mrs. Motley said she'd better be going and again thanked him for his assistance. He said it had been no trouble at all, and if any problem arose as a result of Stew Pot, she should feel free to call him. She thanked him for that too and told him she would, and they said their goodbyes without so much as a light hug or her mentioning that she thought Stew Pot was, at best, a bit unbalanced.

She got in her car and he walked back inside his office. As she drove away, she glanced in her rearview mirror and saw the empty sidewalk area in front of ward office door, her mood greatly brightened now with the sort of breezy feeling of supremacy that comes when you run into someone that you know was once enamored of you (and perhaps enamored of you still), who was a good enough sport to not hold it against you or act unpleasant because you hadn't (and still didn't) feel the same way about him.

Unfortunately for Mrs. Motley, these high spirits did not last. Folks simply would not stop pestering her about Stew Pot. That evening she received three phone calls from neighbors, none of them Mrs. Butler or Erma, thank goodness, who all wanted to know if she had anything new to report. She didn't, because she'd had no sightings of Stew Pot, nor did she the next day, or the day after that, which did not stop folks from calling, or others in Parkland from inquiring during her other ventures into the neighborhood—a dental checkup, a hairdresser appointment.

By Saturday evening she'd about had enough, and over the phone she told Mrs. Hicks that if folks around Parkland were so interested in what Stew Pot was doing, they could darn well sit in front of the two-flat and watch for themselves.

CHAPTER ELEVEN

The Little Church on the Corner

Mrs. Motley attended Wesley-Allen A.M.E. Chapel, named for the founders of the Methodist and African Methodist Episcopal churches respectively. Located on a residential corner a few blocks to the south and west of her house, Wesley-Allen was not to be confused with Allen A.M.E. Chapel, located a half-mile north at 128th and Honore.

The two churches were related beyond the Allen name and A.M.E. affiliation. Way back in 1912 the hot issue in Parkland had been whether it should remain an independent town or become part of Chicago. Nowhere in the neighborhood was the debate more heated than within the walls of Allen Chapel. When the neighborhood referendum to join the city passed by a handful of votes (sparking a brawl on the church's steps), the members opposed to the idea—twenty-three families in all—left to form a new church.

Mrs. Motley's paternal grandparents had been among those disgruntled people. A few years after the schism, the group built a square, two-story, brown-brick building just yards from a winding creek that at the time formed Parkland's southern boundary. (During the 1920s, after much digging by the Metropolitan Sewage District, the creek became the Cal Sag Channel.) Wesley-Allen had no basement or high steps leading to the front door. Its roof was flat and the first-floor windows were a translucent sea green; not very fancy when compared to other neighborhood houses of worship like Seven Sorrows Catholic Church, or Parkland Presbyterian, or Allen A.M.E., with their large stain-glass windows and high steeples.

Mrs. Motley had spent nearly every Sunday of her life at Wesley-Allen. Her Grandpa Brownlee had been one of the original deacons and her Grandma Brownlee the first pianist. Mrs. Motley was very proud of these facts, as she was of the motto her mother had coined to describe the house: *Wesley-Allen, plain and small.* After four days of being pestered with Stew Pot queries and comments, she very much looked forward to attending church, which had always been a haven for her.

On that gray, damp Sunday morning she parked Ingrid directly across from Wesley-Allen's main door on Tubman Street, which at that point T-boned into 132nd Place, a narrow lane that ran in east-west parallel with the Cal Sag. The channel was around fifty yards wide, its olive-drab surface visible just beyond the bare bush branches of its rocky bank.

After pulling open the church's heavy wooden door, Mrs. Motley stepped inside the maize anteroom, the door closing behind her with a thud. The air there had the sort of heavy, wet smell you often find in old wooden places, and despite her penchant for stuff like lemon-scented cleaners, Mrs. Motley did not find this clammy smell unpleasant.

The walls of the main room were painted sage and the center aisle had a pine-green runner. That aisle divided the sitting area into north-south sections of a dozen rows each, the dark brown benches long enough to seat maybe ten adults comfortably.

Mrs. Motley's usual seat was in the north section (to the right as you entered), fourth row and on the aisle. After draping her trench coat over the pew back she stood in the aisle and engaged in pre-service chat, one of the things she enjoyed most about church.

The people she spoke with were, for the most part, other Wesley-Allen Old Guards, a baker's dozen of men and women she had known since childhood. There were folks like Mrs. Roberts, who was white-haired like herself, but much wider in the body and wearing another of her flowery hats, today's cover a sky-blue number with a wide side brim; and Mr. Govan, dressed as usual in a brown suit with his salt-and-pepper hair arranged in the slicked-back "sportin' waves" style of their youth; and Mr. and Mrs. Lewis, who'd been a couple since grade school and who now used canes to get around, the thick lenses of their glasses making them look almost like twins.

None of the Old Guards asked Mrs. Motley about Stew Pot, for which she was most grateful, and as she stood in the aisle conversing comfortably with these familiar faces, it was as if the past six decades, with all the accumulated regrets and losses, had not happened and they were still young, with years of future ahead of them.

The congregation in attendance numbered about sixty people. When services started, they all stood and sang the hymn "At the Cross"—

Alas and did my Savior bleed,
and did my Sovereign die,
Would He devote that sacred head
to such a worm as I . . .

When that was done, the congregation sat and the choir, in maroon robes Mrs. Motley thought a bit garish, remained standing on the raised area at the front of the room. The choir was all younger folks who Mrs. Motley felt were nothing like the choirs of her day. However, one of the songs they did that morning was "When We Get to Heaven," a favorite of hers, so she sat there in her aisle seat and sang along in her full, slightly off-key voice:

When we get to Heaven,
what a day of rejoicing that will be.
When we all see Jesus,
we'll sing and shout the victory . . .

By sermon time, Mrs. Motley felt as good as she had in a week.

Wesley-Allen's pastor, one Reverend Wilkins, wearing what he referred to as "my simple black robe," took the lectern in front of the now seated choir. He was what some tribal members still liked to call "a pretty Black man." (A few Wesley-Allen middle-aged women said he favored Sam Cooke, which Mrs. Motley thought was going a bit far.)

Brown and slender, the reverend was a congenial fellow (sometimes to a fault) who had been at Wesley-Allen only two years. During that time he'd managed to enlarge the congregation significantly, with most of the newcomers joining from outside Parkland.

As with every sermon, he glanced over at his wife with a beaming smile. A honey-colored woman with hair a brassy shade of bottle blond, that morning she was encased in a white woolen sweater dress and sitting in her usual first-row aisle seat, where she returned her husband's smile with a toothy one of her own.

Although Mrs. Motley liked Reverend Wilkins well enough, at the same time she found his sermons underwhelming (an opinion she had never shared with anyone). It wasn't his delivery, for he had a strong voice and he made frequent use of animated hand gestures; it was just that his sermons leaned toward the boilerplate. That morning, for example, he launched into a sermon about the prodigal son. After a minute it was clear to her that he wasn't going to say anything she hadn't heard plenty of times before, and her attention drifted, her thoughts occasionally fondling some memory evoked by her surroundings.

She remembered how on her wedding day the June heat had been so intense that the long candles had gone limp in the holders. And years before that, as a teenager, which is when she'd inherited the pianist duties from her grandma, on Saturday afternoons, after practicing the next day's hymns and with the church to herself, she'd played Broadway show tunes, which she was forbidden to do at home. And in winter the heat went full blast and the radiators hissed and clanged. And back in the day, when the Cal Sag had been an open sewer as much as a commercial waterway, during the summer foul smells sometimes wafted through the open windows . . .

Eventually Reverend Wilkins finished, and after leading them in prayer and initiating the passing of the collection plate, he surprised everyone by saying he wanted to offer "a special word for Sister Motley." From all over folks turned to look at her like at the block club meeting. "As you all know," Wilkins continued, "she extended a Christian kindness to a soul in need this past week who returned to our neighborhood. Though some have reportedly found fault with this, I want to acknowledge her. Well done, Sister Motley. Well done."

The reverend then proceeded to clap and others quickly picked this up. Mrs. Motley, after recovering from her initial surprise, acknowledged the applause with a wan smile and nods of the head in this and that direction.

Newer members who had no previous experience with Stew Pot were the most enthusiastic, while the Old Guards of the church exchanged discrete glances that revealed their unspoken skepticism. But then, after the applause died away, the reverend did himself one better by happily saying: "And Mrs. Motley, you tell Mr. Reeves—and his mother too—that they are welcome to worship with us any Sunday. Will you promise me you'll tell them that?"

Given the circumstances, Mrs. Motley felt she had no choice but one, and she responded with a positive shake of her head and something that was almost a smile.

CHAPTER TWELVE
Offers Extended, Offers Rejected

Around nine that night, Mrs. Motley was on the couch with her red-leather Bible when her kitchen bell chimed. When she got back there, Stew Pot was standing in the glare of the motion light set above the outside of the doorway.

She opened the main door but kept the storm door latched. She had yet to contact Stew Pot about the reverend's offer, having spent a good part of that afternoon and evening trying to figure a way to avoid carrying out her naïve pastor's request without lying to him later when he asked her (as he surely would) what Stew Pot's answer had been in response to the offer to worship at Wesley-Allen.

Stew Pot got right to the point of why he had come. After apologizing for calling on her so late, he said he'd been thinking of how thankful he was for all she'd done, and what he might do in return. "That's when it came to me, and I had to tell you right away. Remember the other day when I spoke of Brother Crown? How he got me walking in The Light? Well I'm sure he could do for you what he did for me. You could become a follower of Brother Crown. He's a powerful man of God. He's a great man, a true man."

Hearing this, Mrs. Motley suddenly realized—more a flash of impulse than a coherent thought—that here might be her way out, and without further consideration, she said: "Actually, I was going to ask you the same thing. Reverend Wilkins, my pastor, asked me this morning at service to extend an offer to you and your mother to come worship at Wesley-Allen. But with your being so loyal to Brother Crown you probably don't . . . Is there something wrong?"

Stew Pot's smile had evaporated and in its place was a hardened look similar to what she had observed when she'd seen him dumping his mother's items: narrowed eyes and a frowning mouth.

He was silent for a few scary seconds and she asked again if something was wrong. He was silent a couple of seconds more before finally speaking in a low, curt voice.

"Just because you befriended me, Mrs. Motley, doesn't give you the right to insult me."

Stammering just a bit, she said she had meant no offense, and he responded, "I explain to you how important Brother Crown is to me, how he helped me find my way into The Light, and you come at me with the suggestion that I abandon him?"

"Not at all," Mrs. Motley replied. "In fact, my point was just the opposite. I understand that in light of your relationship with, uh, Brother Crown—"

"And my mother's relationship as well. New though it is, don't forget her."

"*And* your mother's relationship—I felt you would not be able to accept Reverend Wilkins's offer. I was simply, out of politeness to him, passing his offer along."

"Well if you understood my position, Mrs. Motley, why didn't you just tell Wilkins that in the first place and spare me the indignity of having to hear his insulting offer?"

"I'm sorry. I didn't realize you'd react so strongly about it."

Stew Pot's expression softened some. "Apology accepted," he said. "Now back to *my* offer. What do you have to say to that?"

Mrs. Motley paused for a few seconds as her thoughts frantically sought wordage that would not anger him.

"I've attended Wesley-Allen all my life. My grandparents were founding members. And just as you feel strongly about your Brother Crown, I feel—"

"Yes," Stew Pot interjected, "but with all due respect, Mrs. Motley, Wesley-Allen is not walking in The Light."

"Now it is you who have insulted me," she said.

"No, I don't think so. To ask someone to *step out of* The Light, as Reverend Wilkins did, is an insult. To give someone the opportunity to *step into* The Light, by way of proper study and instruction, is coming to another's rescue. Brother Crown rescued me and I in turn am attempting to rescue you."

"Well, be that as it may," said Mrs. Motley, "I could never leave Wesley-Allen."

The look on Stew Pot's face again went hard, his voice low and curt. "Well now that's two insults you've given me. Good night, Mrs.

Motley." And with that he spun around and stomped down the steps of the deck and over the stones of the flower bed. Then he vaulted the chain-link fence the way he had the first time he'd come to her back door.

CHAPTER THIRTEEN

The Fire Next Time

Later that night, after a bubble bath and washing and drying her hair, Mrs. Motley slipped on a pink flannel nightgown and sat down at her bedroom vanity. It had originally belonged to her Grandma Brownlee and was so old that the silver backing on the round mirror had bubbled in several spots.

As she leisurely stroked her hair with an ivory back brush that had also belonged to her grandma, Mrs. Motley could see, behind her and on the other side of the room, the arched headboard and tall spires of her four-poster bed. Its frame had, over the years, held the mattresses where she had been conceived, and where her parents had died, and where her son had been conceived, and where she had awakened one January morning to discover that her husband's soul—at the ripe age of fifty—had taken flight during the night, leaving behind a tepid shell with half-closed eyes.

Over the previous four nights, following the fire dream the first night that Stew Pot was home, her current mattress had been a place of nocturnal peace, which she took as a sign that her largesse toward Stew Pot had been the correct course. Now, however, after the latest episode at the kitchen door, she was not sure. That sudden and volatile turn she'd witnessed when he'd dumped his mother's clothes was, as she had suspected sitting across from him at the kitchen table, not an isolated incident.

When the brushing was done, Mrs. Motley went to her bedside. During prayers she didn't ask why she'd been beset with her troubles of the past week, because she thought such inquiries presumptuous. Once under the top sheet and quilt, and with the lights out, she lay with an arm draped over her eyes, her agitated thoughts going round and round about Stew Pot. How long would his newfound anger toward her last? How would it manifest itself next? How long would he and she be joined at the hip as topics of neighborhood gossip? It wasn't until nearly midnight, which was way past her usual sleep time, that her weariness finally overcame her worry and took her down.

Mrs. Motley slept till nearly three a.m. when she had another fire dream. After her mind finally managed to tear itself back into safe wakefulness, she raised herself to a sitting position. When her sobbing had subsided a minute later, she wiped her face with the back of a hand. As she breathed hard to catch her breath, she wondered how long she could go on suffering like this. And then all the reasons for why she could not move came upon her again, and the frustration of it all, not to mention her fatigue, caused her to cry some more. When that round of tears was done, she fell back to the bed with her arm flung once again over her eyes and she sent up a plea for some sort of relief.

As it so happened, her desperate request would eventually be answered—in a manner of speaking; for in less than a week's time, Stew Pot's intense attentions would be redirected toward another resident of the block, producing an engagement so riveting that it would keep Parkland's imagination burning and its tongues wagging for months, causing folks to forget, for a good long while, all about the goings-on between he and Mrs. Motley.

BOOK II

Stew Pot vs. Erma Smedley

CHAPTER ONE
Laying the Groundwork for a Future Offense

The day after Stew Pot made his offer to Mrs. Motley, he made good on his vow to apologize to everyone else on the block. With the exception of Mrs. Motley's house, his own home, and the house directly across from the two-flat (where the homeowner was still on winter vacation), Stew Pot went to every house, twenty-six in all, to make his amends.

In his peacoat, denim overalls, and brogans, clutching "Mrs. Motley's Bible," as folks had come to call it, he stood on stoops and porches giving folks an abbreviated version of the spiel he'd presented in the yellow kitchen.

Despite all the tough talk voiced by many at the block club meeting, Mrs. Butler was the only person who refused to listen to him. The rest eyed him warily through the relative safety of storm doors; some out of macabre fascination, others because they wanted to give him a piece of their mind. Stew Pot took whatever tongue lashings he received without complaint. He told folks harsh admonishments were what he had coming. This response tended to anger the tongue lashers rather than placate them.

Not surprisingly, Erma Smedley took particular offense at Stew Pot's mea culpa. That Monday evening when he came to her place, a two-story amber-brick four-square that's commonly referred to as a Georgian, she angrily repeated the points she'd made at the block club meeting about her aunt feeling like a prisoner in her own home and so on. When she was done she slammed her maroon door before Stew Pot could say another word, the force rattling the panes of her living room bay window.

Meanwhile, directly across the street, Mrs. Butler, in her dark brick Tudor-style house with a maize front door, stood watching through her picture window, the receiver of her black phone in one hand and the other poised to punch 911.

After Erma's door slammed, Stew Pot remained standing on the stoop. Mrs. Butler saw him bow his head, which she thought very suspicious. She was about to press the 9 on her phone when Stew Pot turned around and headed down Erma's walkway to the sidewalk. He was smiling all big, which also struck Mrs. Butler as a bad sign. She kept watching as Stew Pot took a left around the nearby corner and walked south down Honore, past the west side of Erma's house and out of her sight.

Mrs. Butler phoned Erma immediately and for the next few minutes the two took turns running Stew Pot down, Mrs. Butler calling him detestable and Erma quoting her late aunt's favorite Stew Pot description: "A progeny of an inebriate and an ignoramus."

Their words might have been even harsher if either had known what Stew Pot had done after Erma slammed her door. With his blurred reflection showing back at him in the glass of the storm door, he had raised his right hand to his lips, whereupon he smooched the fingertips, blew a kiss toward the door, and closed his eyes while whispering a brief prayer of heartfelt hope.

CHAPTER TWO
Snow Job

The Friday night after Stew Pot's apology to Erma, the Chicago area was hit with one of those not-unheard-of March snowstorms. About ten inches fell, not nearly enough to shut down the snow-savvy city, but enough to be an inconvenience, especially if your house was on a corner lot and you had, in addition to your front sidewalk, a property-length stretch of sidewalk running alongside your home that had to be cleared.

On the morning after the snowfall, at around ten thirty, Erma sat in her living room by the bay window contemplating just that problem. Although in good health, she smoked a pack of cigarettes a day and at her age she had no intention of shoveling snow.

Wearing a gray sweatshirt and black stretch pants, and with her first cup of coffee and second cigarette of the day, she was on the lookout for one of those men who roamed the neighborhood after snowfalls, offering to shovel sidewalks for a few dollars. She was halfway through her cup when she heard a noise from outside. It came from the side of her house, metal scraping concrete, followed by silence, then more scraping, then silence, then more scraping, etc.

In addition to a front and rear entrance, Erma's home also had a west door that opened onto Honore. After opening the inside portal, which was maroon like the front one, Erma gazed through the leafy designs of the wrought-iron burglar door. Stew Pot was about twenty feet away, shoveling the sidewalk in her direction. He was wearing the peacoat, along with a red wool hat that sat to one side of his head. His methodic movements reminded Erma of a machine, his broad shoulders shifting as the coal shovel he used scooped up piles of snow that he then flung with apparent ease onto the parkway.

Unlocking the burglar door and taking care not to get any snow on her fluffy pink house slippers, Erma leaned her head out the doorway, the cold chilling her face.

"What in the world are you doing?" she said.

Stew Pot looked up as he was about to fling another shovelful. He held the load in midair for a few moments, suddenly mesmerized.

"I *said*, what are you doing?"

He came out of his reverie and tossed the load, then set the shovel scoop down in the snow of the parkway like a person might stand a pitchfork. He took a step forward, but before he could take a second one, she said: "Close enough."

"I'm shoveling your walk, Miss Erma."

"Why? I didn't ask you to do that."

"I know. I figure it's the least I can do after all the trouble I caused your aunt."

"As I said the other evening, you caused her a lot more than just trouble."

"I know, Miss Erma. That's why I'm trying to make amends."

"By shoveling a sidewalk? My aunt is the one you hurt. There's no point trying to make up by doing favors for me."

She watched Stew Pot bow his head, the peak of the red wool cap drooping like a limp antler. When he looked up there were tears brimming at the edges of his eyes. He glanced off in the distance for a moment, sniffled, then turned back to her with an expression on his face like he'd just figured out something very important.

"Oh my goodness, Miss Erma," he said softly, "you're right. You're absolutely right. All this time I call myself doing good and all I've really been doing is ducking responsibility for what I've done. Thank you, Miss Erma, for opening my eyes. Now I'm going to finish your walk."

"I'm not paying you."

"I'm not asking for pay."

"In that case, do the front walks too and the porch. I'll leave a couple bags of rock salt here by the door. When you're done shoveling you can spread the salt around."

A big smile came across his face. "Be glad to, Miss Erma."

"And quit calling me Miss Erma, you make me sound like some-body's grandma."

"Okay, Miss Smedley," he said cheerfully.

"Just plain Erma will be fine."

About an hour later Stew Pot was finished. The sidewalks at the side and front of the house were clear, as was her front walkway, her stoop, *and* the backyard walkway between the rear door and the alley. He rang her front bell when he was done salting. When she answered she made a show, with squinted eyes and a frown, of looking past Stew Pot to inspect his work. She nodded her head slowly as if to say that while the quality of the shoveling left something to be desired, it would have to do.

With a smile on his face displaying his wall of teeth, Stew Pot clutched his red cap in front of his chest and thanked Erma for the opportunity to serve penance.

With her frown still in place, Erma gave him a dry "You're welcome," and then, with a flick of the hand, she closed the door in his face.

Erma stepped to the bay window and watched him walk past the front of her house and around the corner. She had greatly enjoyed seeing Stew Pot toil for her benefit, and she felt an aesthetic pleasure at the clear lanes of wet, grayish sidewalk between the white bluffs of fresh snow. The squint, frown, dry tone, and closing the door in his face had been her way of keeping Stew Pot in his place, lest he get the wild idea that shoveling her sidewalks was the start of some sort of friendship between them, for she he had recognized the look he'd given her when she interrupted him at the side of the house. It was a look she knew well. Boys and men had been reacting that way toward her since she had transformed, at age thirteen, from a runty tomboy into a curvaceous wonder. Now that she was past forty, such reactions didn't happen nearly as often as in the past, but they happened enough for her to know that on occasion, for some fellows, she still had the old power.

S tew Pot's shoveling of Erma's walkways did not go unnoticed by others. When Mrs. Butler, from her living room window, spied Stew Pot throwing snow across the way, she telephoned Erma and asked if she was aware of what Stew Pot was doing. When Erma explained what was up, Mrs. Butler questioned the wisdom of such a move. Erma just laughed and said that if Stew Pot had decided to be good, she of all people deserved to benefit. "Besides," she said sarcastically, "it's about time he did some honest work."

A retiree named Mrs. Powell lived, along with her husband, in a redbrick Georgian directly east of Erma. After noticing Stew Pot shoveling Erma's front walk from her living room bay window, she phoned Erma too. When Erma offered to order Stew Pot to do the Powells' sidewalks as well, Mrs. Powell was momentarily tempted to accept. Her husband, who worked nights and was asleep upstairs, was sixty-seven, and despite his age he still insisted on shoveling snow against his doctor's warnings; however, Mrs. Powell knew he would not like the idea of waking up to find they had received a favor from Stew Pot, so she regretfully declined Erma's consideration.

After Mrs. Powell hung up she watched from her purple living room couch as Stew Pot moved methodically up the walkway toward Erma's door. A dark woman with flecks of gray in her curled, shoulder-length hair, she was slender, although not nearly as slender as Mrs. Motley. At the block club meeting, Mrs. Powell had been one of the people who'd supported Mrs. Motley's comments, which surprised no one since the two women, who'd attended high school together, were sisters under the skin when it came to their demure deportments. (Mrs. Powell had, in fact, been the first person Mrs. Motley called about Stew Pot's return.)

Despite the anger Erma had displayed at the block club meeting, her chortling over getting Stew Pot to do her bidding didn't surprise

Mrs. Powell. To her mind that was just Erma being Erma. Mrs. Powell well remembered the days when, as a little girl, Erma had visited her aunt next door and played with other girls on the block like Mrs. Powell's daughter and Mrs. Hicks's oldest girl. Erma had been bossy even then, dominating conversations with her loud voice and opinions; so much so that Mr. Powell had, behind the child's back, jokingly dubbed her Erma the Imperious.

When Erma was in high school she had continued making frequent visits to her aunt, and on many a warm evening Mrs. Powell had heard, through the front-door screen, Erma chatting and laughing with a flock of boys on the stoop next door.

That allure, in Mrs. Powell's opinion, was still very much at Erma's command. Since Erma had taken over her aunt's house some seventeen years before, Mrs. Powell had noticed, along with just about every other woman on the block, how the men perked up at block club meetings when Erma arrived; and conversely, the looks of subtle but unmistakable disappointment when she didn't attend. Mrs. Powell counted her husband as a member of this group, though she held no grudges against Erma for that.

Long ago Mrs. Powell had decided that some women were just like that: men very much liked them and they, the women, very much liked the being liked. If you weren't the sort of woman that men very much liked—Mrs. Powell placed herself in that category—there wasn't much you could do about it.

Mrs. Powell knew that some women on the block, like Mrs. Davenport for instance, were not as philosophical as she was about Erma. She supposed her own lack of angst was due to her never having felt a moment of insecurity as to her standing with Mr. Powell, his membership in the Erma Fan Club notwithstanding. Once, she had admitted to Mrs. Motley and Mrs. Hicks: "My husband worships the ground I walk on. Do you think that's bad of me to brag like that?" To which Mrs. Hicks had laughingly replied: "Honey, if it's true, then it ain't bragging."

Watching Stew Pot shovel with his coat open and his dark face and neck glistening with perspiration, Mrs. Powell smiled at the thought of Mrs. Hicks's comment. And she told herself that the Erma Smedleys of the world could keep their allure and flash. In the end, what did it get them? No guarantee of happiness, that was for sure.

Poor Erma's marriage had crashed and burned two years before she'd moved into her aunt's house and there she was now, living alone with no man. One wild rumor claimed she had a North Side boyfriend—a jazz musician—who she never brought around because he was White. This was a plausible scenario to Mrs. Powell since such a relationship would have raised the ire of at least a few neighbors, most especially Erma's close friend, the interracial-romance-hating Mrs. Butler.

While Mrs. Powell considered Stew Pot's shoveling nothing more than another example of Erma's addiction to being bossy, other folks on the block had their own ideas, which they wasted little time in expressing to one another. This following conversation at Miss B's House of Beauty (located on the eastern end of the drag) was typical.

"All of that talk at the block club meeting and she turns around and has Stew Pot hopping and jumping. How could she let him do that after what he did to her aunt's cat?"

"Her aunt's dead, and as you may or may not have noticed, Erma doesn't own a cat."

"Meaning what?"

"Meaning, she's a divorced woman with no man, and he's a single man. A big hunk of a single man, I might add."

"But Erma can't stand Stew Pot. She never could."

"Like the song says: 'There's a thin line between love and hate.'"

"Oh stop."

"Stop nothing. These days, some sisters feel they have to take what they can get."

"No woman's that desperate. Leastways not one with any sense. Besides, what would Stew Pot want with a woman old as Erma?"

"Forty-one isn't old. You act like you haven't seen Erma in a dress lately. Ain't nothing wrong with those hips. And she's got that light skin and green eyes, and you know a Black man is always going get his blood up over a redbone."

Being the weekend, with most folks at home, word of all this made it very quickly through the neighborhood, the possible romance/sex angle easily knocking talk of Mrs. Motley's actions aside.

"Erma and Stew Pot?" folks across the neighborhood said. *"Lord, Lord, Lord."*

CHAPTER FOUR

Weather Report

Two days after the snow fell, a warm front moved through the Chicago area (another not-unheard-of occurrence) which melted most of the snow. This was then followed by another cold front that brought more low temperatures and cloudy skies.

During this time Stew Pot did not, as far as anyone could tell, find a job; however, he did get a dog. Mrs. Reeves, who was still all smiles whenever folks saw her on the street, was apparently so overjoyed with Stew Pot that she gave him money to buy another white pit bull. Where he managed to get ahold of a full-grown dog he did not say and no one asked. This one he named John the Baptist; and oh, how folks wailed when they heard *that*, "blasphemous" and "sacrilegious" being the most frequent descriptions used.

As soon as he got the dog, Stew Pot altered his walking route. He left with the dog through the two-flat's front door and used the alley only for return trips.

Within days, neighbors found that a Stew Pot–owned pit bull by any other name was just as ferocious. This new dog growled at almost everybody it encountered. Stew Pot had to yank hard on the leash to make the beast shut up, after which he always offered apologies, which did nothing to ease people's apprehensions.

Such encounters happened a lot more than they ever had with Hitler because Stew Pot kept his promise to Mrs. Motley and walked this new dog twice a day, causing some to say that on this count at least, Mrs. Motley's gain was everybody else's loss.

Stew Pot had the dog a little over a week before the police stopped him. He and the pooch were walking south on Honore, alongside Mrs. Butler's house, when two plainclothes cops in a dark sedan pulled to the curb and called him over. While the dog sat quietly on the parkway, the cops, both Black, warned Stew Pot they had better not hear of him scaring folks like he had with Hitler.

Bending at the waist to bring himself face-level with the cop on the passenger's side, Stew Pot told them how God had rescued him in prison and he was a new man, etc., etc. The cops, who'd heard such tales before, listened dispassionately and told him they and the other cops in the district would be watching him.

Mrs. Butler watched this encounter from her dining room. Afterward she reported what she'd seen to Mr. Davenport and others, which told neighbors two things. Firstly, the police were watching Stew Pot, which was good. Secondly—and this was not so good—it seemed Stew Pot's dog was perfectly capable of being quiet when he needed it to be quiet. This meant that all the growling the dog did was not the actions of an unmanageable dog, which cast a whole new light on why it growled at people like Mr. Davenport, and Mrs. Butler, and Mrs. Hicks, and not at folks like Mrs. Motley and Erma.

April arrived and the only notable observation of Stew Pot came from Mrs. Powell. On Tax Day she told Mr. Davenport she saw Stew Pot in the alley. When Mr. Davenport asked what Stew Pot had been doing, Mrs. Powell said he hadn't been doing anything. "That's what was so strange," she said. "He just stood there staring at Erma's house."

CHAPTER FIVE

A Very Important Date

The Friday after Tax Day, Erma celebrated the end of her busy season by taking a cab from the Downtown office where she worked to a North Side restaurant. The occasion was a dinner date, the latest episode in a weeks-old romance that had begun in her office with exchanged glances over tax forms and credit card receipts, and had now advanced to the smooching/patty fingers stage. The meal was tasty—sushi, maki, and sake—and the conversation enjoyable, so much so that Erma felt the prospects were good that joys of a more nakedly intimate nature were in the offing for later that night.

This particular eatery was a two-story place on Wells Street, at an intersection about halfway between equally busy Division Street and North Avenue. The gentrification of the surrounding area, which Chicagoans called Old Town, was by then almost complete. Although the sidewalks and streets were as busy that Friday as during Old Town's counterculture heyday, the mostly White crowd sported clothes similar in price and conservative style to Erma's black dress and knee-high black boots.

When dinner was done and the bill paid, she stepped from the restaurant ahead of her date and into the chill night air, whereupon she pulled the top of her dark wool coat closed. The date got caught behind a large party of gregarious patrons leaving the restaurant, the group barging into the gap formed by the date pausing to let Erma pass through first. Erma waited on the corner as this drunken group—nearly two dozen in all—proceeded to then make a slow, single-file exit through the narrow doorway. She turned around to face the street and saw Stew Pot, of all people, standing just a step away. Bareheaded, he was wearing his peacoat and overalls, and had his hands on his hips.

In angry surprise she said: "What're you doing here?"

"What am I doing? I'm trying to stop you from making a big mistake."

"What in the world are you talking about?"

"I'm talking about whatever man you're sneaking around with up here on the North Side. I can't let you do this."

"Do what?"

"Sin, that's what. This is how it always works, right? First, there's a fancy meal, and then—sex; gluttony, followed by debauchery."

"Have you completely lost your mind?"

"No, I haven't. What I've been doing is keeping an eye on you. I've been taking the train Downtown every other evening or so and waiting across the street from where you work so I can see what you've been up to. Until today all you did was take the train home. When I saw you get a cab this evening, I got one too and followed you. I guess you met your boyfriend inside. I looked in the window but I didn't see you. You two have supper in the upstairs level?"

Being as tall and Black as he was, Stew Pot drew the attention of the mostly White passersby, who gave him and Erma a wide berth.

"Leave me alone!" she said. Her voice was still angry but her eyes looked frightened.

"Don't sell yourself cheap, Erma," Stew Pot pleaded. "You wouldn't just hand over your house to a man, why give him the most precious gift God gave you?"

"Go away!"

The gregarious party, now almost completely through the doorway, crowded the corner, laughing and talking loud. Catching Erma completely by surprise, Stew Pot took a step forward and gently enveloped her in his arms. Not wanting to cause a scene in front of all these strangers, she refrained from pushing away from him. Gazing up at his face, she said in a low but angry voice: "Let me go."

"Erma, I know it must hurt a woman's confidence to have a marriage go bad, but—"

"What's all this?" These words were spoken by a woman who'd come onto the street at the tail end of the gregarious party. Unbeknownst to Erma and Stew Pot, she had paused in the restaurant doorway, brought short by the sight of Stew Pot and Erma in what appeared to be a loving embrace.

Stew Pot let Erma go and took a step back. The woman moved to Erma's left. She was a bit shorter and looked to be about the same age. If a passerby were to guess, he or she would probably have said she was Hispanic, what with her tan skin and long dark hair, although she could just as easily have been Black or Mediterranean. She was wearing a pine-green trench coat and was carrying an expensive-looking leather briefcase.

Turning to Erma, the woman said: "Who is he?"

"My name's Gerald," said Stew Pot. He extended his hand. The woman peered at the large paw as if it were a rotten vegetable, then turned back to Erma.

"He a friend of yours?"

"No," said Erma, and she turned to face Stew Pot. "He's just an idiot from my neighborhood butting his nose in where it doesn't belong."

"Is *that* what you think of me after all I've done?" asked Stew Pot in a voice of genuine-sounding hurt.

Upon hearing this, the other woman arched her eyebrows at Erma in the classic *Oh, is that so?* expression. Then she said brusquely, "I'm outta here," and with a snappy left turn headed away from the corner and up the street in the direction of North Avenue.

Erma brushed past a stunned Stew Pot, for whom the dawn was only just now arriving, and caught up with the other woman after only a few steps. Erma slid in front of her to block her progress, but the other woman deftly stepped to the right and kept going. Erma wheeled around and caught up to her again, this time walking alongside her, gesturing vigorously with her hands as she spoke. The other woman kept on looking straight ahead.

"I can explain this," Erma said.

Speaking softly but firmly, the other woman said: "I told you how I feel about that switch-hitting crap. You said you felt the same way. Now it turns out you lied."

"That fool is not my boyfriend, for Christ's sake."

"Oh sure," replied the other woman sarcastically, "he just comes all the way to the North Side to keep tabs on you."

They kept moving down the street, past other restaurants, a comedy club, a parking lot, a cigar emporium, the sidewalk becoming more crowded the closer they got to North Avenue. Erma's gestures drew a few glances from people walking nearby, who also noticed the furious expression on the other woman's face.

"Erma!" called Stew Pot from somewhere behind them.

The other woman gave a backward nod. "Your *man* is calling you."

"Can we please go someplace and talk?" Erma said.

"There's nothing to talk about," responded the other woman. "I've been down this road too many times before with too many trifling women."

Erma reached out tentatively and touched the other woman's shoulder. The other woman knocked the hand aside with a sweep of her arm, a swift and violent move so startling to Erma that she stopped in her tracks.

The woman took a step and then wheeled around and came back, her angry expression causing a little shudder to tremble through Erma.

"Please do not call me on the phone or come to my house," the woman said.

This was heard by a couple of passersby, a White man and White woman walking hand-in-hand. Erma thought for sure she saw the White woman smirk. Erma's date, meanwhile, made another snappy turn and continued in the direction of North Avenue, which was now just steps away.

Erma wanted to follow, to explain, but was terrified that she might receive a rebuke even more heated that would draw even more smirking attentions.

"Was that what I think it was?" she heard Stew Pot say from behind. He sounded like a grandmother scolding a child. "Because if it was, then things are a lot worse than I thought."

Erma watched her date walk with the rest of the foot traffic across North Avenue. Looking bewildered, Erma turned around and saw Stew Pot close by, his shiny head cocked to one side with an angry expression clutched on his face.

Stepping between parked cars, Erma looked again in the direction of North Avenue, this time for a southbound cab.

Stew Pot called out: "Where do you think *you're* going?"

Erma said nothing. Because of his size, Stew Pot wasn't able to get through the narrow space between parked cars and had to stop at the curb.

"You're not going after her, are you?"

Erma ignored him.

Shifting his voice to a soft and entreating tone, Stew Pot said: "I came up here to save you, Erma. You're an angel, a beautiful angel. That's what I saw when you opened your door on the day I asked you to hear my apology. It doesn't matter to me that you're divorced and not pure, because I learned in prison that if you're willing to step into The Light, then you can be cleansed like new. And I don't care that you aren't young, because I know you have wisdom, and wisdom is an invaluable thing for a man to have in a wife."

Erma continued to act as if she didn't hear him. She frantically waved her right hand in the air for a cab as Stew Pot's voice shifted back to an angry tone.

"The Devil has gotten into you, Erma Smedley. He dressed himself up in a pretty package with long hair and smooth tan skin. There's still a chance to escape his clutches. But you'll have to step into The Light to do it. You're going to have to face your sin, see it for what it is, and admit that sin out loud to the Lord and everybody."

A cab pulled to a stop alongside Erma. Still ignoring Stew Pot, she got in. The cab moved slowly away in the thick traffic and Stew Pot's face became full of malice. Extending his right arm, he pointed at the cab.

"Lesbianite!" he shouted. "Fornicator! Violator of nature! If you won't come to The Light, I'll bring The Light to you! You hear me, Erma? I'm bringing The Light!"

That got the attention of just about everybody around him. Heads turned and necks craned. Even folks across the street looked at him. All those White faces staring; some curious, some frightened, some irritated, a few bemused. And a few Black faces too, these people fixing Stew Pot with looks that were a combination of embarrassment and anger. And you didn't have to be a genius to imagine what all these people were thinking: that he was probably some crazy from the nearby projects over on Sedgwick Street or Cabrini-Green; that he was scary looking, big as he was, big enough to play linebacker for the Bears, with his bald head and furry goatee and booming voice.

Those nearest darted their eyes from his gaze when he turned their way, surprised by the deer-in-the-headlights look that was now in his eyes. These folks quickly moved on. Those further away felt safer and watched awhile longer. They saw him jam his hands into his coat pockets, turn around, and walk south on Wells toward Division Street, headed for who knows where.

CHAPTER SIX

Getting the Word Out

Mr. Powell loved to barbeque. Weather permitting, he had his grill going at least three days a week. And he didn't wait around until Memorial Day either. The first day it was warm enough outside so that you couldn't see your breath, he was at it. The Sunday after Erma's incident on Wells Street, the weather was sunny with the temperature in the mid-fifties. Mr. Powell fired up the grill right after he and his wife returned from morning church services, and by midafternoon he had already done three slabs of ribs and was working on some chicken. His grandchildren were with him in the backyard. The girls, aged eleven and ten, ran around kicking a soccer ball, the older in a red tracksuit and the younger in a blue one. Although it struck Mr. Powell as odd that girls would be doing such things (whatever happened to girls playing jacks? he wondered), he was glad to have them there. Both were long-legged, round-nosed, and so beautifully brown, reminding him of his daughter when she was young, reminding him of his wife too.

And just like that, as he was standing there moving pieces of chicken around the grill with a large prong, he saw in his mind's eye a vision of his wife when she was in her teens, sitting in Sunday service at Parkland Presbyterian. In the memory, she is between her parents and he is a few rows behind, watching slyly at the graceful sweep of her long brown neck as he sends up his weekly prayer for God to give him the courage to ask her if she'd like to go with him to the drugstore sometime for an ice cream. Not that he thinks she will actually say yes. He is sure she will not be the least bit interested in him. (With his long brown face and droopy, sad-looking eyes, his nickname around Parkland at that time had been Hound Dog.) If he asks her out, he thinks, he's sure she'll look at him with one of her eyebrows arched the way she does when she thinks someone has said something particularly odd. Until finally one Sunday, in the vaulted room, looking at that neck, he will finally decide to ask her, even though he knows what her answer will be. *But at least I will have tried*, he thinks. *I can live with that.*

As he stood in the backyard with his granddaughters and the barbecue, Mrs. Powell walked out onto the back porch. Standing above and behind him, she asked if he wanted her to bring him a can of pop. He glanced up from the patio and saw her there in the sunlight, that oval face of hers, that long neck. (Her childhood neighborhood nickname had been Goose.) The still-bare tree branches cast a web of shadows across her and the porch, and he threw his head back and laughed like someone who just found out he won the lottery. His wife looked at him puzzled and said: "What are you laughing at now, Powell?" She had always called him Powell, never by his first name.

Mr. Powell looked sheepish and just shrugged. Then he saw her face go sullen, her eyes fixed on something in the distance. He turned toward the direction of her gaze, toward the alley. His granddaughters were standing still in the middle of the yard, the soccer ball immobile on the ground between them. Their heads were also turned to the alley, where Stew Pot had just entered with his dog. The animal barked. Stew Pot shook the leash and said: "Shhhhh."

The dog shut up.

Stew Pot stopped by the back gate of the Powells' waist-high chain-link fence.

"Hey, Mr. Powell, Mrs. Powell. Isn't this a wonderful day God has given us?"

Mr. Powell's first impulse was to call the girls into the house. However, he didn't want to be too obvious, lest Stew Pot suddenly do something wild. The gate did not have a lock and it would be a simple matter for him to unlatch it and send that dog snarling after all of them. Yet at the same time, he felt he had to do something. Carrying the prong, he strolled down the walkway to the alley.

As he neared the gate the dog began barking and straining again and Stew Pot had to jerk the leash a couple of times to silence it.

"Those two your granddaughters?" said Stew Pot, smiling.

Mr. Powell answered with a slow nod of the head.

Stew Pot called over to them: "How are you today, ladies?" As they tended to do with all strange adults, the granddaughters responded with barely audible hellos.

"Such lovely, lovely girls," Stew Pot said.

"Something I can do for you?" asked Mr. Powell.

"Actually, there's a thing I wanted to speak to you about."

Mr. Powell glanced at the pacing dog and slid the prong in a back pocket.

Stew Pot leaned over the fence and spoke in a low voice. "There's something you ought to know, especially since your granddaughters visit."

"Pardon me?" said Mr. Powell.

"It's about your neighbor," and here Stew Pot nodded toward Erma's house.

From the back porch Mrs. Powell could not tell exactly what was going on, but from the gestures and the glances it obviously had something to do with Erma. Stew Pot did most of the talking, pointing with his free hand at Erma's place, causing Mr. Powell to occasionally glance back over his shoulder. She told herself she didn't know why in the world Powell was wasting his time talking to that fool. To be on the safe side, she called the girls in. They came reluctantly, taking looks back over their shoulders. Although shy, they also had that young person's radar for sensing a potentially dramatic scenario.

Mrs. Powell followed them inside. She got another prong, went back to the grill, and began turning the chicken, glancing every few seconds at the fence while the girls watched through the storm door, their brown heads peeking around the doorway.

Stew Pot was now gesturing and talking in an animated fashion that frightened Mrs. Powell. Her husband waved a scoffing hand and Stew Pot responded by placing his own free hand palms-down over the bib of his overalls in the universal expression of sincerity.

Behind and to her right, Mrs. Powell heard Erma's kitchen door open. She turned and saw Erma walk out onto the screened porch, and was taken aback by the woman's appearance. There were dark blotches below her eyes and her hair was unkempt and bunched to one side of her head as if she had just gotten out the bed. She was wearing a blue terry cloth housecoat and her pink fluffy slippers.

Taking no notice of Mrs. Powell, Erma shouted: "Stay out of my business, Stew Pot!"

The two men looked in her direction, Mr. Powell having turned halfway around.

"Well, what do we have here?" said Stew Pot. The dog barked and he silenced it with another yank of the leash.

Erma marched down her walkway. "I said, stay out my business!"

With a sneering smile, Stew Pot replied: "Yes, your business. I was just telling Mr. Powell about *your business*. That business you do on the North Side when you think no one's looking, where you think no one can see."

The dog snarled; Erma paid it no mind. Pointing a forefinger at Stew Pot she said: "Shut your filthy mouth."

"Hmph," Stew Pot snorted. "That's fine talk coming from you, considering where *your* mouth has been lately."

Erma's face flushed and she began frantically searching the ground for something, anything, to use as a weapon. Scooping up a handful of gravel, she fired a spray of black nuggets at Stew Pot, who ducked his head behind a raised left arm.

Mr. Powell took a step back in surprise. The dog went nuts. It leaped at the fence, barking like it intended to chew through the chain link to get at Erma.

"Powell!" called his wife from the grill, but he didn't hear her. He didn't know what to make of this. Stew Pot's story, albeit fascinating, had been too fantastic to be believed. But now here was Erma, looking like two miles of bad road, yelling at Stew Pot. Maybe that talk about her and Stew Pot romancing was true. She certainly looked like an angry girlfriend, her flushed face reminding him of a boiled lobster, her green eyes a rage as she shouted: "WHY ARE YOU DOING THIS? WHY ARE YOU DESTROYING MY LIFE?"

"Like I told you Friday night, Erma: I'm trying to save your life. I'm trying to save it before you flush it down the toilet."

"SHUT UP!"

"Shut don't go up," snapped Stew Pot, "but one day you will. You'll be up for judgment before the Lord and then there'll be a merciless accounting. That cute little gal you're so crazy about won't be able to help you then. Running down the street pleading with her to take you to bed won't fix things then."

Erma grabbed her face with her hands and let out an agonizing scream that echoed off the surrounding houses.

Then there was a shout from the barbecue grill: "POWELL!"

This time he heard his wife, and he turned to see her at the other end of the yard looking distressed. He knew she wanted him to get away from the fence where the dog was still leaping and barking and Stew Pot was going on and on about Hell, and Judgment Day, and some woman. He looked over at Erma; her face was wet with tears now.

She pointed a shaking finger at Stew Pot and in a voice made hoarse from her scream, she shouted above the barking dog: "*You're* the Devil! *You're* the one! Something out of Hell is what you are!"

She turned around and stalked back toward her house. Halfway there her foot hit a raised section of walkway. She stumbled slightly, caught her balance, and kept on.

The whole while Stew Pot yelled at her and struggled with the leash. "Harlot! Lesbianite! You can run but you can't hide from the Lord, Erma! You better get in The Light! You better get yourself in The Light while you still can!"

Without looking back she went into the screened porch and then her house. After the kitchen door slammed shut behind her, Stew Pot looked over at Mr. Powell.

"See," he said triumphantly, "you heard it yourself. She used invectives, and she made accusations, but she did not deny what I said. You're my witness, Mr. Powell. She didn't deny a thing I told you. Not a word. If I were you, I'd keep an eye on those granddaughters; no telling what Erma might try and pull if she gets the chance. Now, I know you probably think my saying such a thing is the Stew Pot calling the kettle black, but I'm telling you, I saw examples of the male version of Erma's perversion while I was in prison. The female type is just as insidious, just as ravenous." He looked at Erma's house, spit on the ground, and muttered: "Lesbianite!"

He gave the leash a jerk to the right and the dog, which had calmed down, stepped away from the fence.

"C'mon, John, let's go."

With the dog straining at the leash, Stew Pot started down the alley in the direction of the two-flat.

"You're my witness, Mr. Powell," he called back over his shoulder. "She didn't deny any of it. Not one bit. She didn't deny a word I said."

CHAPTER SEVEN
Wildfire

It took a little over twenty-four hours for news of the alley incident to get around Parkland. After Mr. Powell returned to the grill, he told his wife he would explain it all to her later. The granddaughters were disappointed when he refused their requests to tell them what the commotion had been about. On the way home that evening, from the backseat of the car, they told their mother (who had sad-looking eyes like their grandpa and a long neck like their grandma) all that they had seen that afternoon. When they got home their mom called her mom: "What's all this about Stew Pot and Erma?"

Mrs. Powell, who usually kept her daughter up-to-date on the latest goings-on concerning the block, and who felt guilty for not having done so earlier, said: "You're father doesn't think it's a good idea to talk about it."

There followed a half-minute of hard badgering in which Mrs. Powell's daughter, who now went by the name of Mrs. Sims, swore on a stack of Bibles she would not tell a soul. Finally Mrs. Powell caved, and after checking to make sure she could still hear the TV going in the basement (where Mr. Powell was watching a basketball game), she spilled every bean. When she was finished her daughter had all kinds of questions, the last one being: "And Erma didn't deny any of it?"

Later on Mrs. Sims told her husband what her mother had said. Mrs. Sims did not consider this a violation of her promise not to tell a soul since telling your husband stuff was, to her mind, part of the marital bargain. She did swear him to secrecy and he agreed; however, some things are just too good to keep to oneself.

The next night, Monday, Mr. Sims was having a beer at Sonny's Tavern (which was next door to Diamond Foods), following the bimonthly Knights of Peter Claver meeting at Seven Sorrows Catholic Church. (Mrs. Sims had converted to that faith as part of her acceptance of his marriage proposal.) Midway through his second beer he repeated what his wife had told him to one of the other Clavermen. As it so happened, the fellow he spoke with had gone to Parkland High with Erma. When he heard what Mr. Sims had to say, he immediately called over another Claverman who back in the day had also pined long and hard for Erma. Before you knew it, there was a small gathering of men at the back end of the bar, listening to Mr. Sims repeat the various and juicy details. (Mr. Davenport, who was also a Seven Sorrows Claverman, was not among them, having chosen to go directly home after the meeting.)

A tall fellow with a large forehead and receding hairline, Mr. Sims, unlike many of the other Knights of Peter Claver, had never gone away to college, or served in the military, or traveled to anyplace interesting. He had a mundane office job with the federal government and never had any ribald stories with which to enthrall other men. Leaning at the bar curve at the back end of the room, his faint smile suggested that he was very much enjoying himself. His listeners, four to either side, hung on his every word. He told how Erma had come rushing out the back of her house with her robe half-undone and so drunk she wasn't even aware that her breasts were showing, which got him hoots and howls all around.

At one point during his telling, the bartender came over to hear what was going on. He was a dark moon-faced guy who wore a long white apron on the job. This bartender didn't know Erma personally, nor had he ever pined after her, but he knew of her. He also knew a good story when he heard it. After the Clavermen left, the bartender told the Erma story to at least a dozen other people. This included a pizza-delivery guy who came in to drop off some food for one of the customers, and a couple of Black plainclothes cops who routinely spent their lunch break in Sonny's sipping colas, playing video games, and making free calls on the phone behind the bar.

The following day, Tuesday, the Erma/Stew Pot story was *the* hot item on the Parkland Gossip Line. Of course, Parkland being Parkland, the story acquired certain embellishments along the various paths it took around the neighborhood. Mrs. Hicks heard from one of the other office clerks at the grade school that Stew Pot had caught Erma with another woman in a cheap motel up on the North Side just as the other woman was throwing Erma out of the room. In the Parkland High School teacher's lounge, Mr. Davenport heard that Erma had been in a

North Side lesbian bar and that Stew Pot had caught her walking out and begging a White woman to be her live-in lover.

As soon as Mr. Davenport got home he told his wife, who taught elementary school in nearby Morgan Park, ending his tale with: "What I don't understand is why a woman like Erma would want to be *like that*? It's not as if she's ugly."

While this and other chatter concerning her was happening, Erma remained unaware. She spent that Tuesday as she had spent most of the previous three days—holed up in her house and more or less incommunicado. Some people tried calling her, but only got an earful of continuous ringing for their trouble because Erma had unplugged all her phones. That Tuesday evening Mrs. Powell, and later Mrs. Butler, came by to see how she was doing, yet all they got was Erma's voice through the closed front door saying she was fine save for a touch of the flu.

Meanwhile, all over Parkland opine and speculation continued. During a conversation over the phone, Mrs. Davenport said to Mrs. Powell: "The whole thing is kind of funny if you ask me. For years the men around here have been getting themselves all worked up over Erma and now it turns out she wasn't even thinking about any of them. Guess they can forget all of those nasty fantasies they've been having about her."

Of course, as any man could have told Mrs. D, for those neighborhood fellows entertaining salacious thoughts about Erma, the idea of her being with another woman did not stop their "nasty fantasies." In fact, it had just the opposite effect. The fantasies continued unabated. All the new information did was change the cast members of the fantasies, taking these fellows' imaginative turns to newer, and for them, even more exciting flights of fancy. That Tuesday night, in the neighborhood drinking establishments—the bowling alley and the pool hall and the two saloons—many a man gave laughing voice to these thoughts, taking some of the sting out of the sense of rejection many had originally felt when they'd first heard the news. They asked each other rhetorical questions about Erma and the woman Stew Pot had caught her with, such as which woman was "the man" and which one "the girl." Most said they'd put their money on Erma being the man. Bossy as she was, they could see her taking command in a lesbo situation. Yeah, they could definitely see her doing that.

CHAPTER EIGHT

Erma's Side of the Matter

The woman Erma had gone on the date with was named Gina. After taking the cab from the Wells Street Disaster, Erma was almost to Union Station when she gathered her resolve and redirected the driver back to Gina's house in Wicker Park, which was a few miles west of Old Town.

As it turned out, Gina did not refuse to speak to her, though she did refuse to let her inside. With Erma pressed against the outside of the locked storm door, Gina spoke around the corner of the parted inner door. Erma listened to Gina recount the rogue's gallery of lovers who had hurt her with their turncoat bisexual ways. Through the parted door Gina explained, as she had on their first date, her theory of love, which was that everyone had a well of trust and every time you fell in love you had to pull some of that trust from the well. If you were reckless and kept falling for this person and that person, one after another, one day you would throw your bucket down and it would come up empty because you had used up all your trust. And when that happened you were in a world of trouble because that meant you would never get any love. Because to get love, you had to trust—both the other person and yourself; otherwise, you wound up a bitter old crone sitting at a bar, sipping martinis, and scoffing at the mere mention of anyone else's happiness: *Falling in love? Oh yeah, I heard that story once. Take it from me, honey, the ending ain't very pretty.* Your routine made all the more pathetic because the pose of hardboiled cynicism hid nothing and fooled no one.

Through the parted door Gina told Erma she did not want to end up like that; after so many disappointments her well had only so much trust left, and she had to protect it.

Erma spent the next day, Saturday, behind the draped and shaded windows of her house, weeping and drinking vodka with soda. She didn't bother to bathe or brush her teeth, and wallowed in the odor of her body funk, bad breath, and self-pity. After years of wandering in what she had come to see as her personal wilderness, she had finally met someone she desired eagerly, and who seemed to desire her just as eagerly, *and* who also didn't get on her nerves, a combination which hadn't happened for her in a long, long time. Then, at the last tantalizing minute, it had all been destroyed by Stew Pot.

The day after that, midafternoon Sunday, Erma had been in her bathroom taking a pee (she'd already consumed a couple of drinks by then) when she heard a dog barking in the alley. After she returned to the house following the confrontation, her memory of the incident was hazy. She did recall that Stew Pot had ducked, so she knew she must have thrown something at him. As for what he had said to her and her to him, she could not have told you beyond the fact that the angry language had been loud, for her throat felt strained.

Sitting sideways on her bed later that evening, Erma told herself Stew Pot would surely continue to bother her. In the past she'd been hounded on telephones or followed about, by this or that lovesick fellow who, for whatever reason, could not take "it's over" for an answer. Stew Pot lived right down the street, which would give him plenty of opportunities to be a nuisance.

And it was then that the distressing thought came to her that she might have to move. As with Mrs. Motley, Erma had a powerful attachment to the house she lived in and to Parkland as a whole. Her parents had divorced when she was little, and Erma and her mom had lived in a series of rented basement apartments around the neighborhood.

Whenever she came over to visit her aunt and got to spend the night in the spare bedroom on the second floor, Erma felt, for that night at least, as if she were just like everybody else, sleeping in a regular upstairs bedroom instead of a basement. And although years later Erma came to see many of her neighbors as narrow-minded and unsophisticated, she could not deny that she also savored the lilt of their Black-folks speech and the roll of their laughter. She found solace in their no-nonsense view of the world, that was, for all its tough-mindedness, surprisingly full of hope for the future; not only for themselves but for their children; and in some cases grandchildren. On their first date she had tried to explain her love of the neighborhood to Gina, who'd asked why she lived in an area that was "so provincial."

Erma flopped faceup on the mattress in what had been her aunt's bedroom, staring at the motionless ceiling fan and asking herself why she was making such a fuss over Gina. She hadn't even made love with the woman, only kissed her a couple of times. That lame rationale lasted in her mind only a moment, Erma coming clean with herself that those intimacies, although brief, had produced gooseflesh and tight breath and a pleasant dizzy feeling. The combination of Gina's scent and touch had created something that was exquisitely definite and at the same time wonderfully impossible to place. And there on the mattress, the pressing pain of realization that such salvation was now gone got her tears going again, and she lurched to her feet and headed to the kitchen for more vodka and soda.

The next day, Erma was too distressed to go to work. She plugged in her bedside phone, called in sick, and then unplugged it again. She did the same thing Tuesday morning. (That evening when she sent Mrs. Butler and later Mrs. Powell away with her fib about the flu, she had felt too embarrassed about her smelly and haggard condition to face anyone.)

On Wednesday morning she showered, brushed her teeth, and applied extra makeup to mask the splotchy skin below her eyes.

So preoccupied had Erma been with her grief over Gina and rage at Stew Pot, she hadn't thought about the Wells Street Disaster making the rounds of the neighborhood talk circuit. Sitting at her sun-washed kitchen table that morning in a sleeveless black sweater and a black wool skirt, it suddenly occurred to her.

She didn't doubt for a second that wild versions of what had happened were running rampant. Neighbors would call the whole thing freaky, acting as if they had never heard of a gay person before, even though there were several such people in the neighborhood who had lived more or less openly for years. In the next block west lived two old and slender gentlemen—Mr. Williams and Mr. Collins. They had lived in their brick ranch house together with a pea-green front door since Erma had been a teenager. They attended Parkland First Baptist, and were frequently seen strolling with a pair of dachshunds waddling in front of them. And there was her old first grade teacher Miss Figgins who lived with her "friend" Mrs. Dawson, a widow, a few blocks away in a bright yellow four-square. And there were others like them in Parkland, some old, some not so old, and no one ever said anything negative to or about these people.

"But of course you know why that is," said Erma out loud at the kitchen table. The reason people like Mr. Williams and Mr. Collins and Miss Figgins and Mrs. Dawson and the others were not ostracized was because they never acknowledged that they were "that way," as Parklanders liked to put it. As long as a person never actually said they were what they were, most people in the neighborhood were willing to carry on as if nothing was out of the ordinary.

Erma could easily imagine the disapproval an open acknowledgment would evoke from Mrs. Butler and Mr. Davenport, not to mention others who would make her the subject of neighborhood ridicule.

Erma didn't want to move, of that she was certain, which meant that if she were to salvage the situation she'd have to call upon every bit of her skillful aplomb. Her defense, she decided, would be simple. She'd just say Stew Pot was nuts; his word against hers.

Through the kitchen window Erma saw the long shadows of the trees stretch like bars across the backyard lawn. Her explanation for her seclusion of the last few days would be the same as she'd given at her door the previous evening: she'd had the flu. As for the alley confrontation, that had been an angry but perfectly understandable reaction to having a crazy man going around telling lies on you. Erma knew some people would never buy it, but she knew others would if her performance was right.

A short while later, coated and gloved and determined to handle her business, she stepped from the confines of her shaded living room and into the sky-bright morning.

CHAPTER NINE
The Weight

When Erma reached the commuter train stop at 129th Place, the platform was crowded. There were plenty of people there Erma knew, and as she moved to her usual waiting spot midway down, she nodded and said hello to those she made eye contact with, making a point to appear neither overly friendly nor overly reticent. She managed this despite the fact that some people looked at her oddly, as if she had grown a second nose, while others had grins playing at the corners of their mouths.

She had bought a newspaper from a box before entering the small station house. When she reached her place at the edge of the platform, she opened the paper and began reading so that she would not have to converse with anyone. She was just about to compliment herself on a good initial effort, when from behind she heard: "So there you are!"

Erma did not know if Stew Pot had followed her or had arrived there by coincidence. What she did know was that how she conducted herself in the next few minutes would be crucial. Everyone on the platform was waiting to see how she'd react. She told herself she must not glance down the tracks to see how close the train might be, for onlookers would read that as a sign she was anxious to get away.

As Erma turned toward the direction of Stew Pot's voice, she reassured herself with the thought that this was actually a stroke of luck for her. This time, Stew Pot had outsmarted himself by giving her a chance to knock down his story before witnesses.

He was standing with his hands in the pockets of his peacoat and he wore no hat. He was smirking with his head tilted forward, the sunlight catching his dark, shiny crown.

From experience Erma knew that the best defense was a good offense, so before he could say anything else she moved to strike the first blow. In a voice of condescending irritation she said: "Will you quit following me around? Every time I look up, there you are. For the last time, I have no interest in being, how did you put it? Oh yes, your *angel*. I don't want to be your angel."

So well did Erma deliver her lines—just the right amount of mirth, just the right amount of scorn—that a wave of grins and laughs rippled through the people in her and Stew Pot's immediate vicinity. Stew Pot frowned and it was clear to everyone she had won the opening round. However, for reasons she could not explain, Erma felt a tightness clutch her chest as if she were out of breath. And then suddenly it was if she were hearing things from outside herself. Everything had a slightly tinny sound, like television broadcast audio that's on secondary power.

Speaking through his frown, Stew Pot said: "From what I understand, you're not interested in being *any* man's angel." So unenthusiastic was his voice, you could tell he realized she had gained the tactical advantage. If she kept coming at him with her irritated-beauty-brushes-off-lovesick-boy routine, he would be hard pressed to counter, since at bottom, lovesick was precisely what he was.

Erma knew what she should say next; she could hear the sentences clearly in her mind. After a sharp, laughing scoff she should say: *Oh yeah, right. I don't want to be bothered with you, so the only answer must be that I'm a lesbian. It couldn't be the fact that you're an uneducated convict with no job. It couldn't be that, could it?* But when she reached for the sentences, she could not find them. It was as if her inner self could not muster the necessary strength to respond. And as the seconds ticked by and she got further and further from the moment where the sentences would have had maximum rhetorical effect, she began to feel lightheaded. And in the silence she felt a shift in the mood of the men and women around her. The ripple of smiles and laughter came back, directed at her this time because she was just standing there looking at Stew Pot and saying nothing, denying nothing. And the seconds continued to tick, mounting one on top of the other, and a look of recognition came over Stew Pot's face, as if he could not believe his good fortune, like the boxer who is on the ropes and about to go down and then suddenly sees the opponent foolishly drop an arm, leaving the ribs and midsection wide open.

So many seconds had ticked away—at least twenty—that Stew Pot had to know that whatever Erma said now, no matter how witty and sharp, it would be too late. So he let a few more moments pass before letting her have it.

Speaking casually, he said: "What's the matter, Erma? Pussycat got your tongue?"

From somewhere nearby, someone guffawed. All around there were giggling murmurs and Erma knew that even at this late moment, she ought to mount some sort of counter, no matter how weak; but again she could not quite reach the sentences.

Smirking again, Stew Pot said: "*Put to death therefore what is earthly in you: immorality, impurity, passion, evil desire, and covetousness, which is idolatry. On account of these, the wrath of God is coming.* That's from Colossians, chapter three, verses five and six. You'd best heed it."

Erma looked around at the surrounding faces, some which belonged to people she'd known her whole life, and some so embarrassed for her they darted their eyes away. Erma dropped her newspaper and stepped quickly to the platform's swinging doors.

When she was safely back home and had called in sick, she told herself the reason she hadn't been able to reach the necessary sentences was that she was still weary from her ordeal of the previous four days. It would be months before she realized that she was only half right in that assessment. She'd been weary, all right, but not just from the ordeals she'd experienced that fateful weekend. The weariness that blocked her on the station platform was from a weight she had first started carrying decades before when an inner voice had made its first faint call. For years she refused to listen to the call, despite mounting evidence of the mind and body, until finally she allowed herself to fall into the voice's waiting arms. Although this had been a relief, acknowledging the voice in her heart while denying it in her public life had produced a second and far heavier weight.

It was the weariness from hauling that weight around for so long that had sapped her strength on the platform. That's what Erma would realize six months later when she returned to the neighborhood to attend a funeral. In her kitchen following her flight from the station, the only other thing she was sure of, as she sipped a vodka and soda, was that despite her previous hopes, she was going to have to leave Parkland.

CHAPTER TEN

Let's Make a Deal

As was mentioned earlier, Paiger Realty was located on the main drag. This business was operated by Vernon Paiger's niece. At age forty-one, she was twenty-eight years younger than her uncle and easy to spot at a distance because she always wore loud dresses and pantsuits—orange, hot pink, lemon yellow. Her talk was as sassy as her outfits. For instance, she liked to tell folks she was from Vernon's "dark-meat side of the family."

When the alderman's niece worked South Side neighborhoods like Morgan Park, Pill Hill, and Chatham, she conducted business in standard realtor fashion with classified ads, mailings, and publicized open houses. In Parkland she had to operate differently. People in the neighborhood frowned on things like FOR SALE signs on the grounds that such things were tacky, and they didn't like the idea of newspaper ads because then everybody and his brother would know how much money you wanted for your property.

These touchy attitudes were why no major realty company had ever managed to get a foothold in Parkland. The niece handled the situation by never advertising a Parkland property in any way. Prospective buyers had to come to her office, a storefront with Venetian blinds across the display windows, and inspect the listings in her photo book which featured snapshots of available Parkland homes. Because folks in Parkland seldom moved, a lot of the time the photo book was empty. If the buyers wanted, she would put their name on a first-come/first-serve waiting list. Because most buyers were eager to get their hands on a new home, few took her up on that option. However, there were always a few names listed, because there were always at least a few Black folks (cruel comments from outside the neighborhood notwithstanding) who felt they just *had* to live in Parkland.

The morning Erma made her decision to move, she called the alderman's niece. The niece didn't ask any nosey questions about why

Erma wanted to sell (though she certainly had her suspicions), nor did she gossip to anyone else about it.

The evening after the Station Platform Disaster, the prospective buyer at the top of the list, a single man who operated a neighborhood auto repair shop, came to look at the house. It was a bit of a cloak-and-dagger deal. Sensing Erma's needs, the alderman's niece donned a long dark coat to hide her red pantsuit and had the man drive them over, instead of bringing them in her pink Cadillac that was known throughout Parkland. When they got to Erma's, she had the man park on Honore and they entered the house via the side door.

After looking the place over, the guy immediately made an offer. Erma immediately accepted, and the house was sold before anyone in Parkland even knew it was for sale.

The man told Erma he could move in as soon as she could make arrangements to leave. The next day she secured a large two-bedroom apartment for a May 1 move. The flat was on the North Side in Rogers Park, which was as far north as you could get and still be in the city.

Erma told no one she was moving. She felt guilty about not telling people who had always been nice to her, like Mrs. Powell, but she felt she had no choice. If she told folks she was going, they'd just hassle her with a lot of questions she didn't feel like answering. She did not want to try and explain stuff like the Voice, or the Weight, or Gina producing a feeling perfectly clear and impossible to place, or the humiliation she herself had experienced when those people had turned their faces away on the train platform.

During the fortnight between the final closing and her move, Erma kept her contact with neighbors to a minimum. She rented a car and drove to work before dawn and didn't arrive home until way after dark. She did this every day, including Saturdays and Sundays. She refueled the rental, got her hair done, and did all her shopping outside the neighborhood. When she was home, she kept her windows draped and shaded, and only took her trash and garbage out after midnight. If people telephoned, she let the message engage and didn't call them back.

During this time she had direct contact with only three neighbors. Mrs. Butler came over and knocked on Erma's door, and this time Erma let her in, Mrs. Butler full of hot talk over how angry she was at Stew Pot.

"He's been slandering your name with these tales of perversion. I've told everyone I've talked to that his stories are nothing but lies."

Erma sat on the couch and said nothing. Eventually Mrs. Butler stopped talking. After an uncomfortable silence Mrs. Butler looked at her over the top of her half-moon glasses and said: "Erma, what does this mean?"

Erma shrugged and said: "This is what it is." It took a few moments for Mrs. Butler to realize what Erma meant, and the expression on the older woman's face shifted from one of puzzlement to one of disgust, as if she had smelled a terrible odor. Then, in a harsh whisper she said: "Never have I felt so betrayed."

The night after that, Mrs. Powell came over, and when she asked Erma through the storm door if she was still sick, Erma smirked sardonically and said, "No, not anymore."

Mrs. Powell didn't know what to say after that, so she bid Erma a polite good evening and left.

Two nights after that, much to Erma's surprise, Mrs. Motley came by. When Erma opened the front door, Mrs. Motley, in her tan trench coat and matching beret, asked softly: "Are you okay? I mean, I know you're okay. But are you *okay*?"

Erma felt she could have asked Mrs. Motley the same question, for the older woman's face looked tired. And then Erma remembered the way she had spoken to her at the block club meeting, and she felt bad for the way she'd acted, for Mrs. Motley had been a teacher who had always encouraged her.

Erma told Mrs. Motley she was all right and Mrs. Motley told her that if she needed anything, all she had to do was ask.

"You still have friends, Erma. Don't forget that."

Erma thanked her, and as Mrs. Motley turned to leave, she said: "I'm sorry for what I said at the meeting."

Mrs. Motley offered a tired smile. "You were just sad over memories of your aunt. I knew that."

Erma gave her own tired smile in appreciation, causing Mrs. Motley to say, "It'll be all right. You'll see." And something about seeing the skinny old lady walking away to an empty house seemed to Erma so profoundly sad. *Perhaps because,* she wondered, *it's a glimpse of my own future?*

CHAPTER ELEVEN

So Long, It's Been Good to Know You

By the day of Erma's move, the weather had warmed and there were buds and young leaves on the trees and bushes. It was also raining hard.

A white moving truck pulled alongside her house around noon. The moving men, four brown muscle-bound fellows, didn't seem the least bothered by the downpour that left their faces and bare arms gleaming wet. They used thick drop cloths to cover the furniture as they made their way out the side door and into the truck parked on Honore. They were done in under an hour. Shortly after the quartet squeezed into the cab and headed off, Erma stepped onto the front stoop wearing a black windbreaker and orange scarf.

Mrs. Powell saw her from her living room couch. Mrs. Butler had telephoned her earlier, blurting a report about the moving truck. Mrs. Powell had not seen Erma since that evening when she had come to ask if she was still sick. Watching Erma lock the door for what she now knew would be the last time, Mrs. Powell got up and opened her own door. Erma was walking toward the street holding a royal-blue umbrella over her head.

"Erma!" called Mrs. Powell. "You take care, you hear?"

Erma stopped and turned around. Even from there, Mrs. Powell could see the dark blotches under the younger woman's eyes. She looked like she'd aged ten years.

"Thanks, Mrs. Powell. Tell Mr. Powell I said goodbye."

Mrs. Powell said she would. She stood behind the screen door and watched Erma walk quickly to the dark rental sedan. Though the rain splattered through the screen and dampened her white blouse, Mrs. Powell did not move. She saw Erma get the car door open and, after collapsing the umbrella, toss it on the backseat. She got behind the wheel, and for a few moments Mrs. Powell lost Erma in the blur of rainwater on the windshield. Then the engine started and the wipers did that metronome-like movement across the glass, and she got a clear view of Erma's brightly covered head in the car's darkened interior.

Her sad feelings notwithstanding, Mrs. Powell had to admit to a tinge of relief at Erma's departure. Ever since Stew Pot had told folks what he had seen up on the North Side, Mrs. Powell had been haunted by memories of all the times Erma had played, unsupervised, with her daughter.

At one point during the previous few weeks, unable to contain her curiosity, she had taken her daughter aside and asked if Erma had ever attempted anything of a sexual nature. Mrs. Sims had looked at her incredulously and said, "No!" Mrs. Powell felt ashamed of herself, but not so ashamed that she was sorry she had asked.

Mrs. Powell watched Erma back the car slowly toward the intersection and then around the corner so it was facing north on Honore. The car paused, and then rolled across the intersection and out of sight.

Not until then did Mrs. Powell close her door. She suddenly felt tired. Her husband would be up soon and she'd have to fix his breakfast. (He always wanted breakfast food when he awoke in the midafternoon.)

Wanting to get out of the dampened blouse and not wake him, she went to the laundry room in the basement where she had folded clothes that morning. The washer and dryer were still busy with other loads, so she didn't hear Mr. Powell's footsteps until he reached the first floor. She listened to him move toward the living room.

In the light cast by the laundry room's naked bulb, she exchanged the damp blouse for another white one. When she reached the kitchen she peered down the hall to where her husband was standing in his cotton plaid pajamas, looking out the bay window.

As she moved into the living room, she became aware of a shouting voice outside. It was Stew Pot.

She stood alongside Mr. Powell at the window. Stew Pot was pacing slowly in front of Erma's house. His head was bare and he was wearing a yellow poncho that glistened like his rain-slicked head. The dog was walking at his side, leashed and quiet. Stew Pot had his free right arm high above his head with the fingers spread. The bare lower part of his arm extended out of the yellow poncho sleeve and his face was tilted back, taking the rain full force. His pace carried him from Erma's walkway to the corner where he circled back, smiling as he shouted to the skies.

"The lesbianite has been cast out! Thank you, Lord, for delivering us from the corrupter! Let the water carry her sin down into the sewers below where all sin belongs! The lesbianite has been cast out! This house is *clean!*"

BOOK III

For the Love of Mrs. Motley

CHAPTER ONE

Mr. McTeer

Although Mrs. Motley was well past what some would call her heyday, as was shown earlier with Vernon Paiger, she was not without her admirers. At the time of Stew Pot's return she'd been twenty years a widow and during that period a number of men had joined Vernon in making romantic approaches. Her Parkland neighbors had duly noted (and discussed) those occasions when Mrs. Motley was seen leaving her block in a car driven by Mr. So-and-So or Mr. That-a-One. In addition to Vernon, these hopefuls had included a retired dentist, a retired doctor, an undertaker, a used-car salesman, the janitor at the grade school where Mrs. Motley taught, and an older man from Wesley-Allen (since deceased).

Only a few suitors had gotten to a second date, and as with Vernon, none had ever advanced to the hand-holding and smooching stage. Mrs. Motley was closed-mouthed as to why none of these potentialities reached fruition. She confided in Mrs. Hicks, but Mrs. Hicks wasn't talking. A few of these fellows (the alderman was not among this smaller group) let it be known that the problem lay with Mrs. Motley. According to them, she was simply too picky.

Mrs. Motley received the majority of these romantic overtures in the first seven years of her widowhood. After that the offers had dwindled, and in the years immediately preceding Stew Pot's return, she'd had no man in her life, unless you counted Mr. McTeer.

Now, some in Parkland counted Mr. McTeer and some didn't. Those who did based their classification on the fact that Mrs. Motley and he were often seen together; those who didn't took the two at their word when they said they were just friends.

The retired and widowed Mr. McTeer lived in a maroon-brick Tudor-style house next door to Mrs. Hicks and directly across the street from the two-flat. The reason no mention has been made of him before now is that during the first seven weeks of all the Stew Pot sound and fury, Mr. McTeer had been in North Miami Beach, where he had wintered every year since his wife's death in the early 1980s. He stayed with his youngest daughter, the only one of his three children he was still on friendly terms with.

Originally from West Virginia (after all his years up north his voice still carried a distinct Southern seasoning), Mr. McTeer was seventy-two years old and wore black horn-rim glasses with thick lenses that greatly magnified his eyes when you looked directly at him. He had a bad right leg, the result of an injury he'd received during World War II, and he walked with a wooden, glossy-black varnished cane, swinging the stiff right leg as he moved briskly forward. He wasn't tall, five-five at best, and maybe only twenty pounds heavier than his old army weight, with a hue similar to Mrs. Motley's and a jutting jaw that had earned him the nickname Bull Dog. He'd carried the tag in high school, the army, and the Chicago Transit Authority, where he had aggravated the war injury by driving a bus for nearly thirty years.

While away that winter he had received a call from Mr. Powell about Stew Pot; however, the call had come only a couple of days after Stew Pot's return and had been brief. (Children of the Depression, both men thought extended long-distance phone conversations to be a wasteful extravagance.) As a result, when Mr. McTeer arrived at O'Hare Field the Tuesday after Erma's departure from the neighborhood, he had only a few details concerning Stew Pot.

That evening he wore a dark suit, black shoes, white socks, and, atop his bald head, a baseball cap emblazoned with the panther–head logo of the armored unit he'd served in.

Mr. Powell met him at the airport. Mondays and Tuesdays were his nights off, and every year since Mr. McTeer had been going to Florida, Mr. Powell had driven him to O'Hare in January and picked him up in May.

The clear sky was in the last pale of twilight when they pulled onto the Kennedy Expressway in Mr. Powell's roomy brown sedan. During the hour-plus ride home, Mr. Powell told Mr. McTeer all there was to tell concerning Stew Pot. Mr. McTeer's dislike of Stew Pot was somewhat stronger than Mr. Davenport's but not as volcanic as Mrs. Butler's, and his reactions to what he heard varied, from a profane response to Stew Pot throwing out his mother's things, to a look of dismay over Mrs. Motley giving him a Bible, to befuddled amazement when learning about Erma. "*Erma?*" he said. "But she's *beautiful*. Why would she want to be . . . that way?"

When they finally pulled up the ramp and into Parkland, Mr. McTeer went quiet at the nighttime sight of familiar surroundings. He'd left on January 2 and the bare branches he'd seen then now wafted shaggily in the breeze.

He lowered his window. It had rained heavily that afternoon and there was still damp in the air. Mr. McTeer drew a long sniff, which brought to his mind images of pine trees and wet stone. Happily, he said: "*May, with all thy flowers and thy green!*"

And though Mr. Powell didn't know what poem Mr. McTeer was quoting from this time (he knew so *many*), he was happy to see his friend happy and he cheerfully replied: "Welcome home, old son!"

CHAPTER TWO

Be It Ever So Humble

The east side of Mr. McTeer's maroon-brick house was, like the two-flat, just feet away from the railroad embankment. (Passing Amtrak trains vibrated the windows on that side.) There was a driveway along the house's west side running up a slight incline from the street and to a garage at the back of the property. The garage was also maroon brick and equipped with red folding doors across its front. The outer walls of both house and garage were matted with ivy vine, and as the brown sedan pulled in the driveway, the leaves, not yet at full growth, undulated in the cool breeze.

Mr. Powell carried Mr. McTeer's black suitcase, as he'd done at O'Hare. Normally Mr. McTeer didn't like such help (at the airport in Florida he'd angered his daughter by insisting on struggling with the case), but it was different with Mr. Powell. He was a veteran too, of the navy, and his favors didn't trigger Mr. McTeer's often intense pride.

After moving slowly up the three steps of the concrete stoop while grasping the wrought-iron handrail, Mr. McTeer opened the red door that was rounded at the top. Mr. Powell followed him into the dark living room, setting the suitcase just inside the door.

The two embraced and Mr. McTeer expressed his thanks. Mr. Powell said it was no trouble and they promised to get together for a game of chess that coming Saturday.

After Mr. Powell had driven away, Mr. McTeer, with his coat and hat still on and the lights still out, looked through the circular window of his front door at Mrs. Motley's house across the street. There, the living room and the front bedroom windows were dark.

His hopeful anticipation of seeing her on his first night home, which had been growing in intensity for the past week, dissolved and he turned from the door in disappointment.

After putting away his hat and coat, he dropped his red suspenders, clicked on the overhead light in the living room, and began pulling white sheets from the furniture, which he had draped back in January. Though tired from his day of travel, Mr. McTeer, as he had frequently lectured to his children, had no intention of "putting off to tomorrow what needed doing right now." (While they were growing up he'd used a collection of time-worn sayings to motivate them. One of his favorites being: *If a job is first begun, never finish until it's done. Whether the job is large or small, do it well or not at all.* His kids hadn't much appreciated such instruction when they were in his house and now that they were grown and gone, they appreciated it a whole lot less.)

Moving carefully in the living room, Mr. McTeer unveiled a long gray couch, a coffee table, a club chair, two end tables with lamps, an upright piano, and a TV console.

That done, he pulled a sheet from the Queen Anne–style table in the dining room, sat down, and wiped a hand across his damp brow and the top of his bald head. As he got his breath back, he silently scolded himself for getting pooped after so little effort, then just as quickly thought: *Who are you kidding, McTeer? You're old.*

Because his bad leg made it difficult for him to negotiate stairs, Mr. McTeer confined his living quarters to the first floor of the house. This had required a few adjustments and one redesign project. The first-floor powder room, which was located off the kitchen, had been expanded by workmen and plumbers to include a shower stall and door. Inside the stall, Mr. McTeer had placed a white plastic lawn chair that allowed him to sit while taking a shower. His small den, on the east side near the embankment wall and at the back corner of the house, had become his bedroom. There was only enough room in there for a twin bed, which was fine with him. After his wife had died, he'd had no desire to sleep in the queen-size bed they had shared for so many years and where she'd spent so many agonizing days and nights before her last trip to the hospital.

The rest of the first floor was pretty much as it had been when the place was full of his family. The flower-print wallpaper first hung in the early 1960s was still there, the pink of the rose petals now so faded that where the lamp light was weak, it was difficult to discern the petals from the paper's gray background. The carpeting, originally light gray, was older than the wallpaper and bore bald spots and stains from its many years of service. The kitchen was crowded, for not only had it lost space with the expansion of the powder room, he had also put a stacked washer and dryer in there. You had to squeeze sideways past the white machines to get to the back door, which led to a screened porch where he liked to sit and read when the weather was good. There was no exhaust fan over the old white stove. Along with the musty smell of dust, the house often reeked of whatever Mr. McTeer had recently cooked, which was as often as not something from a can since he'd never been any great shakes when it came to meal making.

At the dining room table he told himself he'd better get going before he got too sleepy. He pulled himself up and went to first the kitchen and then his bedroom, removing more sheets. When he had pulled off the last one and had folded it along with others and put it in a basket, he stood with his back to the front door observing his handiwork and enjoyed the satisfaction that he always felt when he could cross a chore off his to-do list.

The doorbell rang, startling him, and he almost lost his balance. He had not put on his outdoor light, and all he could make out through the door window was the shadowy head of someone. He glanced at his wristwatch—it was nearly a quarter to ten—and stepped toward the door with his thoughts full of hope once more.

CHAPTER THREE
Welcome Back

After hurriedly pulling his suspenders up, Mr. McTeer opened the door to the happy face of Mrs. Motley, who had a gray cardigan draped over her shoulders and a foil-covered plate in her hands. Smiling way wider than he had upon first seeing Mr. Powell at the airport, Mr. McTeer stepped aside and with a sweep of the arm, gestured for her to enter.

Across the threshold Mrs. Motley came. This momentarily put her back to Mr. McTeer, and as he closed the door he sneaked a peek at her from the waist down. She was ensconced in yet another long pencil skirt, this one dark green.

He stepped around to face her again. She shifted the plate to one hand and gave him a hug, having to bend over a bit as she did so because she was a couple of inches taller. Where her arm and cheek touched him, his skin became lively, as if brushed with a feather. His nostrils were full of her lilac perfume, which she wore the way he felt a lady always should: lightly, so that the scent was discernable only when you were very close.

She stepped back from him, still smiling. "So, how are you then?"

Mr. McTeer said he felt fine and that it was good to see her too. As he did so, he took note of her smile. Over their decades as neighbors he'd come to realize that Mrs. Motley had several smiles in her arsenal. The one she displayed now was her toothy smile, which produced prominent dimples in her jaws.

"I didn't know if you'd eaten or not, so I brought you a little something," she said, nodding at the plate. By the lumpy contours of the foil, he knew it was packed high with food and he could smell a medley of spices.

He said that he could use a bite and without further ado she headed for the kitchen. He followed slowly, and when he reached the dining room she was already at the kitchen counter, peeling away the foil with one hand and opening the silverware drawer with the other. He told her she didn't need to bother with setting a place for him, while at the same time feeling thrilled that she was doing so. She told him not to be silly. He'd had a long trip, it was the least she could do.

He eased onto the chair where he'd been sitting before, at the end of the dining room table nearest the passageway to the living room, and listened to the clinking sounds of silverware and glassware being retrieved and gathered.

Mrs. Motley placed a china plate with a flowered border gently before him. On the plate, fitted like puzzle pieces, were two plump pork chops. The rest of the offering consisted of a heaping pile of collard greens (cooked in smoked turkey as a bow to health), a thick spread of black-eyed peas, and two yellow squares of cornbread. It was the sort of meal he'd been raised on back in West Virginia, and the sort of food his wife had often dismissed as "common."

Mrs. Motley retrieved a folded cloth napkin from the sideboard drawer and handed it to him along with the silverware. She went back to the kitchen and ran water from the sink and returned with a tall glassful, which she set beside the plate.

She then sat down in the chair to his immediate left, watching him eat, her left elbow resting on the table and her chin in her hand. As he chewed, Mr. McTeer noticed she had shifted to her bemused smile, where she pursed her lips and these cute little indentions bracketed her lips. After swallowing a mouthful, he asked how she was doing.

Sounding rueful, she said she'd been better: "I assume Mr. Powell filled you in on Stew Pot?"

Mr. McTeer nodded.

"And I bet you're wondering why I gave Stew Pot a Bible."

He paused, searched for words, and came up with: "What makes you say that?"

This produced yet another Mrs. Motley smile, a lopsided one that veered to the left of her face, accompanied by a knowing look sent to him over the top of her glasses.

"What makes me say that?" she teased. "I didn't just meet you five minutes ago."

Is there anything sweeter than being playfully scolded by the one you love? To this latest assault on his senses Mr. McTeer could only say: "I *was* kind of wondering . . ."

"I bet you were," she replied, again using her big smile with the deep dimples.

He looked at his plate and pushed greens around with the fork. "I didn't mean to imply that you owed me an explanation."

And she said, "I know that's not what you meant," and gave his left wrist a single pat, sending the rubbed-by-a-feather feeling spiking across the skin of his wrist bone.

Mrs. Motley, who seemed unaware of the effect she was having on him, folded her arms close across her stomach. This had the unintended affect of pulling her white blouse tight to her body, causing the design of her bra to become suddenly discernable through the thin cotton fabric, like a paper watermark.

And as she went about explaining the whys and the reasons of her actions in regard to Stew Pot, Mr. McTeer returned to his food. While he ate, he heard what she was saying but only caught about half of it, so concentrated was he on the moments when her eyes moved from him and he could snatch a glimpse at the watermark's leafy design.

When she was done explaining her Stew Pot actions, she unfolded her arms and the watermark vanished. By then Mr. McTeer was full. He had managed to finish only one of the chops, a cornbread square, and about half of the greens and peas. (He knew Mrs. Motley had purposely overloaded the plate so he'd have some for his next day's supper.)

Mrs. Motley took the plate to the kitchen for refoiling and placement in the avocado-green refrigerator. She then washed the silverware and water glass, talking over her shoulder through the doorway. At some point during this, Mr. McTeer fell asleep.

He snapped awake with a jerk to find her gently jostling his shoulder. He looked up at her, apologizing profusely to her bemused smile. She told him she was the one who ought to apologize. "Here you are, tired after a long day, and I'm keeping you up with my gab."

Saddened, he rose and followed her to the door. She waited for him to reach her and open it, then turned around to face him before passing through. "Tomorrow at the usual time?" During the months he was home, Mrs. Motley drove him to confession on Wednesdays, after which they went out for lunch.

His spirits lifted somewhat, Mr. McTeer said he'd be ready at eleven forty-five.

She gave him a last light embrace, the arm around his neck gone so quickly this time that the feathery sensation hardly had time to register. Because he was a gentleman, he watched from his open doorway as she crossed the street, which was silent save for the echo of distant expressway traffic. When Mrs. Motley opened her front door, she turned and waved. He waved back feeling more than a little humiliated.

CHAPTER FOUR

Cleaning the Slate

The next day, at a quarter till noon, Mr. McTeer, in a light gray suit and red bow tie, walked with his brisk, cane-assisted stride from the front stoop to the driveway where Mrs. Motley was parked after having completed most of her Wednesday errands.

The wind had shifted overnight to the northeast, bringing a low ceiling and cooler temperatures. Both he and Mrs. Motley were in trench coats, she with her tan beret and he with one of those gray woolen Irish slouch hats. A good night's sleep had rejuvenated his spirits, and the two talked pleasantly during the short drive.

Mr. McTeer attended Seven Sorrows Catholic Church, which was located on the west side of the neighborhood and a few blocks south of Diamond Foods. (The Seven Sorrows name was derived in part from a consideration of Mary praying at the foot of the Cross, where her tears mixed with the blood of Jesus for the salvation of the human race.) A brown-brick building set on a corner and directly across a narrow north/west street from the redbrick wall of the railroad yard, the church had a bell tower, a barn-like roof, and a high flight of front steps. Directly east was a two-story brown-brick building that housed the grade school Mr. McTeer's children had attended.

The church had an elevator, the entrance to which was on the west side of the building. Mrs. Motley parked there and waited until Mr. McTeer had pushed inside the ground-level glass door, whereupon she left to run the last of her errands. After the short elevator ride, Mr. McTeer, his hat off, tapped his fingers with holy water and entered the large nave which had two wide sections of blond-wood pews. With the overhead lights off the place was rather dim, the quiet broken only occasionally by the echoed noise of a handful of people, all women, who were kneeling in various spots among the pews.

The confessional curtain, off to the right side as you came in, was closed and Mr. McTeer took a seat nearby to wait. Though not nearly as large as many other Catholic churches in the city, Seven Sorrows was stylish nonetheless with stained glass and a small rosette window high above the altar and priest's perch. Mr. McTeer had become a member in 1947 when he'd converted to marry the woman who became Mrs. McTeer. The switch had infuriated some of his Baptist relatives back home in West Virginia, a few of whom severed ties with him in protest. He had never regretted his decision to switch, for although his initial reason for doing so had been to win a lady's hand, he came to see, after just a few years, that he had in fact gained his own salvation. He loved the Church—for the elegance of its ceremony and language, for the clarity and certainty of its tenets, for the order of its structure. He felt that this love had been returned a hundred-fold and nothing, not even "that Vatican II foolishness" as he called it, had ever shaken his faith. (The discontinuation of the Latin Mass had left him feeling like a person who comes home to find the house robbed. He had quit the Knights of Peter Claver for their—to his mind— enthusiastic support for stuff like guitar Masses, lay lectors, and the discouragement of praying Rosary during Mass.)

The confessional opened and out stepped Mr. Rogers, who had a bushy white mustache that reminded Mr. McTeer of a scrub brush. His children lived far away too, and his wife was in hospice. The two old friends exchanged nods as Mr. Rogers passed, Mr. McTeer noting that the other man, with bent posture and shuffling walk, didn't look too good himself.

The confessional was dark and outfitted with a cushy seat. Mr. McTeer confessed and Father Vader advised—the West Virginia accent in contrast to the priest's New England drawl. (Father Vader had come to Seven Sorrows in the early 1970s, before his hair had turned white and before the first *Star Wars* movie made his name an instant grin-producer whenever people were introduced to him.) Mr. McTeer told how he'd quarreled with his oldest son in a series of vitriolic letters they'd written each other over the past winter, the bone of contention being Mr. McTeer's refusal to loan his son more money. And there had been the birthday phone call he'd received in February from his oldest girl, who lived in San Francisco. Their talk had disintegrated into yet another round of recriminations, she telling him all that he had done wrong to her, with her live-in lover, who Mr. McTeer referred to as "that woman," getting on another extension and throwing in her two cents. He confessed that he'd wished for "that woman" to be dead, or at the very least deported back to Canada where she'd come from. Last but not least, there were all the lustful thoughts he'd had about Mrs. Motley. Father Vader, who had heard all these Motley-love confessions many times before from Mr. McTeer, instructed him to say the usual words of repentance.

"See you next week," Mr. McTeer said, rising, and Father Vader, sounding a bit distracted, replied: "God willing, God willing."

Mrs. Motley was waiting for Mr. McTeer at the side of the church. When he was in the car and belted, she asked cheerfully: "Ready?" And in the euphoria that always overtook him immediately after confession, he enthusiastically replied: "Ready."

CHAPTER FIVE

Happy, then Sad, then Happy at Logan's Diner

L ogan's Diner was on the drag a couple of doors west of Vernon Paiger's ward office. A Parkland institution for decades, Logan's had a black-and-white color scheme with classic diner furnishings like cylindrical-based stools along the Formica counters and booths set perpendicular to the high windows that fronted a small parking lot. The place was always crowded at midday, half with folks on their lunch hour, half with retirees for whom the trip to Logan's was the high point of their day.

The air was thick with the smell of frying meat and loud with music from an oldies R&B radio station when Mrs. Motley and Mr. McTeer entered. Hellos and how-you-dos were offered all around, including from the grill where a dark, bearded man wearing a white chef's pullover and check pants was flipping burgers. This was the current owner and grandson of the diner's founder, who was known in the neighborhood as Logan III.

There was only one available booth, at the west end of the diner, and Mrs. Motley and Mr. McTeer headed there. Being the first any others had seen of him in a while, he was stopped every step by someone. Like a politician working a crowd he slowly made his way, smiling and glad-handing, or waving to someone who was out of reach; and like a dutiful political spouse, Mrs. Motley followed closely, offering her own softer hellos.

When they made it to the west booth, Mr. McTeer helped Mrs. Motley off with her coat and hung it on a wall hook. She kept her beret on and sat facing the doorway. After Mr. McTeer was uncoated and de-hatted, he sat across from her, enjoying the contrast of the beret with her silvery white hair and the look of her pink blouse and pearl earrings.

Logan III called to them from across the counter: "The usual?" They both nodded yes. Whenever they lunched there, Mr. McTeer had the patty melt on rye with no onions and Mrs. Motley the tuna salad stuffed in a fat tomato.

While waiting for their food, Mrs. Motley apologized for having not asked him the night before how his children were doing. To this Mr. McTeer emitted a derisive snort.

She asked what had happened and he told her, in much greater detail than he had with Father Vader. Mrs. Motley listened with rapt attention, looking appropriately concerned. He talked through most of their meal and had just told her of his strong suspicion that his Florida daughter had wanted him to leave a month ahead of schedule, when the bell over the diner door jingled, followed by a roar of hellos.

Mrs. Motley glanced over and Mr. McTeer stopped his talk and leaned out the booth. At the break in the counter directly across from the door stood a rotund young man with a mustache and chin patch, dressed in a dark beret, glasses, and a gray tweed jacket over a black turtleneck sweater and denim jeans. This fellow was Airy Tarmore, a great-nephew of Vernon Paiger and a neighborhood precinct captain. With the beret and chin patch, his appearance reminded some old timers of Dizzy Gillespie, who had passed away that previous January.

Even with the diner as noisy as it was, Airy's loud voice was easily heard: "Hey, Logan. I'll take two cheeseburgers, one a regular and the other an Alderman's Special. And by the way, could you please make sure there aren't any rodent droppings on the burgers like the last time I was here."

Laughter erupted from all over, and Logan III, a few feet away and in the process of making cuts in a club sandwich, jabbed the long knife at Airy, who hopped back toward the door with mock fright on his face, which got more laughter.

Airy then peered around the diner with a pointed finger. "You all are my witnesses," he said. "My life was threatened by the owner of this establishment." Then to Logan III he said in a haughty tone: "I'm bringing you up on charges, my friend."

"Oh yeah?" Logan III replied. "Then where is Vernon going to get his special burgers?" (The special in question was a cheeseburger topped with chunky peanut butter and sliced beets.)

With a smile Airy said: "Oh yeah, I didn't think of that. Okay, forget the assault charge. I don't want to lose my job. We all know how *touchy* my uncle is."

More laughter. From childhood Airy had been a wiseacre who possessed that rare talent of being able to insult people to their face and make them laugh. He was well liked in the neighborhood, especially for his willingness to make light of his uncle. One person not enamored of him, however, was Mr. McTeer. When Airy, after chatting with folks near the door, caught sight of Mrs. Motley and headed toward her, Mr. McTeer frowned.

He greeted the older people warmly, for he was a former student of Mrs. Motley's and a past running buddy of Mr. McTeer's son.

In his best Eddie Haskell voice, Airy said: "Mrs. Motley, you're looking especially lovely today. So tell me, when are you and I going to go out on a date?"

Mrs. Motley's admonishing look was belied by the playful light slap she gave his arm.

"I'm serious," Airy said. "I know that I used to be your *student*. But that was years ago. We're even both wearing berets! Plus, I have the whole turtleneck sweater, chin patch, snazzy sports jacket look going on." He tugged lightly at the end of one of his jacket sleeves and wiggled his eyebrows. "Very Left Bank, don't you think?"

Mrs. Motley gazed at him over the top of her glasses. "*That* will be enough, Airy."

His voice still playful but now respectful in tone, he said: "Oh, I'm just kidding, Mrs. Motley. You know you were always my very favorite teacher."

Her gaze still holding, she said flatly: "That's what you say to *all* your former teachers."

And Airy replied, "Well, yeah, but when I say it to you, I really mean it."

Mrs. Motley burst out laughing. Logan III, holding a takeout bag, hollered: "Airy!"

"Well, see ya," Airy said, "I gotta go give *Der Kommissar* his grub." He bade Mrs. Motley and Mr. McTeer a good afternoon and walked away.

Mr. McTeer sat back in his seat with his arms crossed, looking glum. Mrs. Motley gave him a playfully chiding look, but he remained cross.

"That has to be the twentieth time he's done his ask-me-out routine," she said. "It's a joke."

"Well, it's a bad joke. It was insolent and disrespectful."

"Airy has always been silly."

Careful to keep the level of his voice between the two of them, Mr. McTeer leaned forward. "Yes. And why has he always been that way? Because when he was growing up his parents never gave his backside a good hiding. That's what's wrong with young adults today: they have no sense of propriety."

"I can't believe you're letting Airy Tarmore's joking ruin our day," she said, hitting him with her bemused smile. And just like that, all was once again a calm sea at their table.

CHAPTER SIX
A Confrontation

L ater on, Mrs. Motley and Mr. McTeer parted in his driveway in good spirits. Inside his house, after hanging up his hat and coat, he plopped down on the gray couch, sending up flurries of dust. He closed his eyes with the intention of being there only a few minutes, but he was soon asleep. About twenty minutes after that, the doorbell awakened him.

Wiping a trail of spittle from the corner of his mouth and grabbing his cane, he went to the door. Through the door's window he saw a tall, goateed stranger looking at him.

"Yes?" Mr. McTeer said.

The stranger smiled, his large white teeth within the dark frame of the goatee, and just like Mrs. Motley six weeks before, Mr. McTeer recognized the face immediately.

"Hello, Mr. McTeer," the toothy mouth said. "Could I speak with you?"

Although Mr. Powell had told him of Stew Pot's enlarged size, Mr. McTeer was not prepared for the muscular mini-giant standing before him. Stew Pot was, as usual, in denim overalls with another of his white T-shirts underneath. He had a Bible in his hand and Mr. McTeer assumed it was the one Mrs. Motley and Mr. Powell had spoken of.

Standing as straight as a man can manage while leaning on a cane, Mr. McTeer looked up into Stew Pot's eyes and said crisply: "What do you want?"

Stew Pot announced that he had come to deliver an apology for transgressions committed against Mr. McTeer and his family. Despite the promise of brevity, the apology took nearly two minutes. Stew Pot didn't cite any transgressions in particular, probably because there were so many. Back in the day there had been a number of thefts from the McTeer garage—a power mower, a pair of bicycles—with Stew Pot the prime suspect. In addition, he had, during his freshman year of high school, pursued Mr. McTeer's oldest daughter, the one who was presently residing in San Francisco. It eventually got back to Mr. and Mrs. McTeer that a romance was going on, which for the daughter produced the desired affect—Mr. McTeer going ballistic. Her mission accomplished, she dropped Stew Pot immediately after. Stew Pot, in typical young man fashion, retaliated by telling everyone at Parkland High that he and Miss McTeer had engaged in sexual intimacies, the acts consisting of the sort that, according to Stew Pot, only a prostitute or someone with a prostitute's morals would ever agree to perform. Mr. McTeer had gotten word of this as well and went after the skinny boy, Mr. Hicks and Mrs. Motley's husband having to restrain him at the driveway.

All this was going through Mr. McTeer's mind as he listened to Stew Pot ramble about his new well-being. By the time he was done, Mr. McTeer's jaw was clenched in all its bulldogged-ness. Stew Pot seemed not to notice, which only made Mr. McTeer angrier.

Mr. McTeer was ready to tell him goodbye, when the younger man's face grew serious. "Something else I'd like to speak with you about. It concerns Mrs. Motley."

"Mrs. Motley?"

"Yes. As you may or may not know, Mrs. Motley befriended me when I first came home." Stew Pot raised the Bible. "I cannot tell you how much that has meant to me. True, earlier today when I saw her headed to her garage, she did seem a bit reserved. I imagine it had something to do with the small role I played in driving the lesbianite from our midst. Mrs. Motley is forgiving to a fault, even to those who don't deserve it."

"So what is your point?"

"My point? I care deeply for Mrs. Motley and what people say about her as much as I do my own mother. Therefore, I must register my objections to the inappropriate appearances that have taken place between you two."

Mr. McTeer's emotions raced in several directions—surprise, anger, and fear.

"It's inappropriate," Stew Pot continued, "for you two to be in a house alone. Last night, from my second-floor window, I just happened to see Mrs. Motley bring you over a plate. That in itself was well and fine, but you shouldn't have enticed her into your house."

With his face and posture strong, Mr. McTeer began: "How dare you—"

"How dare me? How dare *you*. Last night I was so worried I went to my downstairs front window, which luckily is in direct line with your picture window. I trained my field glasses on you both. You nodded off before anything wrong could happen and Mrs. Motley, no doubt remembering herself, went quickly home. I'm glad I saw that, because if anyone should raise a question as to what transpired, I can say—"

Mr. McTeer stepped back and slammed the door.

"Hide from me if you want," Stew Pot called out angrily, "but you can't hide from your obligations to the memory of your wife. I imagine she's looking down from Heaven in shame at the way you behaved last night. God willing, Mrs. Motley will find her way to the guidance of Brother Crown. Until that blessed time when she's finally walking in The Light, I'm making it my job to see that nothing places the reputation of that grand lady in jeopardy. Good day to you, sir!"

CHAPTER SEVEN
Mr. McTeer's Side of the Matter

Before Stew Pot made it to the sidewalk, Mr. McTeer had gone to his picture window and lowered the blinds, whereupon he retreated to his bedroom. There, in the small, dimly lit room paneled with knotty pine, he sat sideways on the mattress.

Over the course of his life he'd experienced fear for his safety on more than a few occasions—with angry White men back home, under fire during the war, and as a bus driver working in some of the toughest neighborhoods in Chicago. And on every occasion he had, in his own eyes, stood tall. But not this time; for while others might see slamming the door in Stew Pot's face as defiant, he knew he had done it out of fear that Stew Pot might get physical with him, which he would have been helpless to stop because he was an old man who couldn't stand without leaning on a cane.

And yet it was not the being very afraid that bothered Mr. McTeer. Life experience had taught him that his being afraid was simply the workings of a rational mind that realized the potentially dire consequences of a situation.

There was only shame if one didn't stand his ground, if one ran away; or if one slammed a door closed because he felt his resolve crumbling. That's what had happened just now. And even after the danger was gone he had retreated, back into this room he slept in because he was too weak to make trips up and down stairs, the sort of thing most people did without even thinking about it. This room, with its old blue polyester curtain and the knotty pine paneling and old bedspread, was shabby. The whole pitiful first floor was shabby. How it must repulse the fastidious Mrs. Motley, he thought, to step into such a crowded, dust-ridden hovel. And of course he was the shabbiest thing of all; a shabby old man no better able to defend himself than could a young child.

An Amtrak train hummed past, the motion lightly vibrating the window glass. Mr. McTeer smelled the pungent, dusty odor of this place, of his life, and told himself that his weakness was why Stew Pot had been so bold. Back in his day, he would not have hesitated to take Stew Pot on, despite the man's size. In the army he'd bloodied more than a few faces of larger fellows who thought short, slight, and bespectacled McTeer was easy pickings. (Never happy about wearing glasses, he found his current eyesight even more of an embarrassment, forcing him to wear these large, thick lenses that so magnified his eyes that he knew he must resemble Mr. Magoo.) At the front door just now, Stew Pot had known he was facing a weaker adversary. A weaker adversary is why Airy Tarmore had spoken to Mrs. Motley that way; as if he, Mr. McTeer, were not even there. That's why his son felt free to write him so disrespectfully.

And he also knew that he could not tell Mrs. Motley what had happened at the front door. If he did, she'd confront Stew Pot, despite her aversion to such things. She'd do it out of loyalty to him, her shabby friend. And if that happened, whatever chance there was of her becoming his wife would be gone, for Mrs. Motley was of the old school and she'd never have a man she had to protect. And the thought flashed through his mind of getting a gun and shooting Stew Pot, but just as quickly he knew he couldn't. He'd shot men to death during the war and it was not an experience he ever wanted to repeat.

Later that evening in the cramped kitchen, Mr. McTeer gazed through the microwave window at the plate of leftovers. After much thought he had decided that the best way to strike at Stew Pot was surreptitiously, which most likely would arise from some unforeseen circumstance he'd have to take quick advantage of.

CHAPTER EIGHT

Springtime for Parkland; Mr. McTeer Seizes His Opportunity

O ver the next four weeks in Parkland, spring continued to unfold in its usual fashion: daytime grew ever more temperate and the leaf green ever more abundant. With weather too warm for central heating but not hot enough for air-conditioning, businesses on the drag kept front doors propped open with wood wedges, and when folks ran into friends on the street or in a parking lot, they stopped to chat at length instead of hurrying off after only a few words like when it was cold. Pickup basketball games at parks and playgrounds increased, and the baseball and softball leagues kept the park diamonds busy Friday nights and Sunday afternoons.

Reggie Butler made himself some extra money by hiring himself out to older owners of older houses like Mr. McTeer and Mrs. Motley, who needed storm windows taken down and window air condition-ers put in place. Mrs. Motley always looked forward to such times, glad to again have a young man to fix lunch for. Because Reggie and his grandmother needed the money, Mrs. Butler voiced no objections to his odd-jobbing at Mrs. Motley's, or to the obvious pleasure it gave him to do so. Mrs. Motley, who he had liked as a teacher, was as ador-ing as his own grandma, but not nearly as stern. He also liked the interior of the four-square with all that polished wood furniture and old family photographs.

In spring, yard fanatics were of course in their glory, luxuriating in the feel and smell of planting and pruning and fertilizing and trim-ming and cutting and watering. (Mrs. Motley took to her backyard gardens wearing an old white dress shirt of her husband's and an equally old pair of khaki slacks. She had leather gloves and sneak-ers blackened by years of faithful service, and a conical hat like field hands wear in East Asia, the straw dome another overseas present from her son.) Even Stew Pot got into the act, digging away the weeds in his front yard and parkway, and then laying down sod. (He and his mom—Mrs. Reeves seen now in only close-neck, ankle-length dresses and head scarves—continued offering cheery hellos to everyone they met on the street, the greetings receiving unenthusiastic responses from just about everyone, including Mrs. Motley.)

Because of his bad leg, Mr. McTeer confined his gardening to first-floor window boxes on his house. With the weather better, he again enjoyed reading poetry on his back porch and chess games with Mr. Powell on a card table in the driveway. During this time, no opportunity to mount a counteroffensive against Stew Pot presented itself, which he found frustrating. Finally, on Memorial Day, he got his chance.

The weather was silky smooth: sunny and warm with low humidity. Mr. McTeer and a couple of other immediate neighbors hung US flags on wood poles alongside their front doors, the only holdover from the old days (before the tumultuous 1960s) when nearly every home had flown a flag on Memorial Day and July 4. (In defiance of her stars-and-stripes neighbors, Mrs. Butler displayed a Black Power flag at her house.)

Late that afternoon, Mrs. Hicks had family and friends over for a barbeque. Being on the north side of the street, the house completely shaded the adjacent backyard summerhouse where the adults arranged themselves in lawn chairs around a circular, black metal table. The Hicks's three sons-in-law (all candy-bar brown and slender bodied) and Mr. Davenport were very excited about the Chicago Bulls' playoff victory over the hated team from New York. The game had been played earlier that afternoon, and by four o'clock these beer drinkers were quite jolly. The Hicks's grandchildren (thirteen in all, between the ages of four and fourteen) retrieved a croquet set from the basement and noisily went about arranging the hoops and sticks on the lawn that extended from the patio to the back end of the yard. Soon they were swinging and yelping, and from other nearby yards rose clouds of smoke as others set to barbecuing. The Memorial Day barbecue ritual was going on across the neighborhood, the breeze carrying the smell of roasting meat which got into everyone's hair and clothes.

Mrs. Hicks kept rosebushes—all pink—in beds set along the white picket fencing that bordered three sides of the yard. Mrs. Motley complimented Mrs. Hicks on the flowers, and that began a horticulture conversation. Mrs. Hicks (sporting a black wig that day), Mrs. Mot-

ley, the Hicks's three daughters (all gingerbread colored and Ruben-
esque), and the sons-in-law took turns describing their garden battles
against blights and insects. With only his flower boxes, Mr. McTeer
had little to contribute to the conversation. He was sitting beside Mrs.
Motley with his back to the kitchen doorway, feeling left out and re-
sentful. Though he didn't see himself as one who had to dominate
every conversation, he felt it was rude of the others to embark in talk
that left him on the outside listening in.

Mr. Davenport announced he needed to stretch a bit, and carrying a can of beer, he walked some steps away to the side of the yard
that adjoined Mr. McTeer's property. Mr. McTeer, out of frustration as
much as anything else, got up and followed him.

When he got to the fence, Mr. Davenport was stroking his mustache with a thumb and forefinger. One sniff of the surrounding air
told Mr. McTeer why his neighbor had moved from the patio. He
didn't want to embarrass Mr. Davenport, but by that point he was too
close to veer away without appearing to be offended by the flatulence-
sweet air. The best Mr. McTeer could do was step upwind, to Mr.
Davenport's right.

"I'm afraid it's a bit gamey here at the moment, Mr. McTeer. Sorry."

"That doesn't make me any never mind," Mr. McTeer said. "I spent
months riding around in a tank. Believe me, I smelled men passing gas
plenty of times."

Mr. Davenport chuckled, only to have his mirth cut short by the
sight of Stew Pot. Mr. McTeer's driveway ran parallel to the Hicks's
fence, providing a clear view of the street. Both men saw Stew Pot step
through the two-flat's doorway with a garden hose.

"Does he ever wear anything but overalls, T-shirts, and brogans?"
said Mr. Davenport.

Mr. McTeer heard the slight slur in his friend's speech. The
younger man's yellow shirt tail was loose from his blue jeans, and
strands of hair hung over his forehead.

Stew Pot connected the open end of the hose to the spigot beside
the two-flat's front door. After turning the little wheel and adjusting
the nozzle, he watered his narrow yard, the cone of spray catching the
sunlight and creating a rainbow.

Mr. McTeer muttered a curse.

"At least he fixed up that yard," said Mr. Davenport.

"Yard or no yard, it doesn't change anything."

"That's true." Mr. Davenport took a sip of beer. "Man, I would do anything to get him back in prison."

And like that, Mr. McTeer saw his opportunity. "You know, Mr. Powell told me how you took charge when Stew Pot first came back, calling the block club meeting, getting folks organized."

A smile faintly appeared at the corners of Mr. Davenport's mouth. "Well thank you, Mr. McTeer. I appreciate that."

"As block club president, you're our commander. We look to you for leadership."

"Well, I try to do right by my neighbors. Although I sometimes feel that as president I've failed. Stew Pot has been home coming on four months and we're no closer to ridding ourselves of him than we were in March. We've been hoping to catch him in some sort of violation of his parole, but so far no luck."

Mr. McTeer paused so as to not seem too eager, and then calmly said: "Maybe he needs to have his cage rattled a bit."

Mr. Davenport peered at him curiously. "Whatcha mean?"

Mr. McTeer shrugged nonchalantly. "Stew Pot likes to yank people's chains, maybe it's time someone yanked his, put a little needle under his skin."

Mr. Davenport released a mischievous laugh. "Now *that* would be fun."

"That it would," said Mr. McTeer.

"But what could we do to rattle him?"

Mr. McTeer coughed. "Stew Pot seems to be awfully enamored of his two-flat. But new lawn or no new lawn, I bet the building has plenty of code violations."

"You want to call the city on him?"

"No. Just let him think we're going to call the city, then let his imagination do the rest."

Mr. Davenport grinned and nodded his head slowly. He then fixed his eyes on Stew Pot. "I think you may have something."

Mr. McTeer, seeing how close Mr. Davenport was to the line of departure, gave him a gentle but nonetheless surefire nudge over that line. "What are you thinking of, Commander?"

Still gazing streetward, Mr. Davenport said, "I think I know how to yank old Stew Pot's chain. But I'm going to need a paper and pen."

CHAPTER NINE

Mr. Davenport on the Attack

Mr. Davenport went to the patio and asked if anyone had something to write with. Mrs. Motley, ever prepared, produced a small spiral notebook and a ballpoint from her purse.

Armed and ready, he went to the gate of the backyard walkway. Mrs. Hicks asked him what was up. Mr. Davenport smirked and said: "Just exhibiting a little leadership."

Mrs. Hicks, of course, had no idea what he was talking about, and as soon as he was out of sight, she said to those around her, "He's drunk." The sons-in-law thought this was very funny. Their wives cut looks at them, which only made the men laugh harder.

At the fence Mr. McTeer watched Mr. Davenport saunter away, moving out of the shaded section of the walk that ran alongside the house to the area beyond that was sunlit. Mr. Davenport stopped at the curb and stood with hands clasped behind his back, staring at Stew Pot, who had since moved to watering the grass on his parkway.

Stew Pot noticed him and said hello. Although Mr. McTeer could not see in great detail at a distance, his hearing was fine. He moved to the picket gate. Both Stew Pot and Mr. Davenport had strong voices, and he heard them from the otherwise quiet street.

"So, you watch the basketball game today?" asked Mr. Davenport. "The Bulls won."

Stew Pot shot him a serious look. "No, I did not watch it."

"What's the matter? You don't like basketball?"

"I have more important things to do, like keeping myself walking in The Light."

"It was a great game."

"The only thing great is God. Folks need to do less worshipping of jocks and more worshipping of the Lord. All those people paying money to crowd themselves into a stadium to watch grown men run around in their underwear and sweat, when they ought to be crowd-ing together to worship our Lord and shout His praises."

"Your new lawn looks in good shape," said Mr. Davenport.

"Thank you."

"What kind of shape is the rest of the place in?"

"Pardon me?"

"What kind of shape? That paint around the windows still looks pretty shabby."

"I plan to get to it and to other things as well. It's just going to take some time."

"The city has building codes, you know."

"And exactly what do you mean by that?"

"Oh, nothing," said Mr. Davenport, and he unclasped his hands and brought his arms forward, revealing to Stew Pot the pen and small notebook. Making a show of looking the two-flat over, Mr. Davenport began writing.

"What are you doing?"

In a nonchalant tone, Mr. Davenport replied: "Just taking notes for future reference."

"Reference for what?"

Mr. Davenport didn't answer. From the gate Mr. McTeer saw him step sideways until he was in front of the driveway. There, he raised himself on tiptoe and craned his neck as if trying to obtain a better view of something. Then he started writing again.

"I *said*, what are you're doing, Mr. Davenport?"

Mr. Davenport kept on writing. Suddenly he stopped and looked up at the second floor of the two-flat and did a double-take (which Mr. McTeer knew was playacting) as if he had just noticed something seriously amiss. Stew Pot looked up in search of what might possibly be wrong there. Then he turned back to Mr. Davenport who was now slowly shaking his head and writing furiously.

"I demand to see what you're writing."

Mr. Davenport kept scribbling.

Stew Pot dropped the hose and took a step forward.

Mr. Davenport made a show of ending a sentence with an exag-gerated flourish.

Stew Pot stopped.

Mr. Davenport held the spiral pad up, shook it at Stew Pot, stuffed it in his back pocket, then headed toward the Hicks's walkway. Stew Pot, his face angry, took a few sideways steps of his own, which is when he noticed Mr. McTeer.

Pointing at the gate, Stew Pot said to Mr. Davenport, "Did *he* put you up to this?"

Mr. Davenport turned around. "Mr. McTeer has nothing to do with this." Gesturing with a thumb at his own chest, he said: "I am the block club president and I intend to do my duty. I'm watching out for my block. It's me, Stew Pot—me." And then he turned again and walked out of the sunlight and back into the shady section of the Hicks's walkway.

Mr. McTeer watched Stew Pot hurriedly turn off the nozzle and spigot, the whole time snatching anxious glances across the street. As Mr. Davenport approached the gate, he held up the pad for Mr. McTeer to see. On it he had written in sloppy printing: *Who's afraid of the big bad wolf? Who's afraid of the big bad wolf?*

Mr. Davenport waited until he was out of Stew Pot's sight before breaking into laughter. He held an upturned palm to Mr. McTeer and said: "Don't leave me hanging."

Mr. McTeer slapped him five, although not enthusiastically, which Mr. Davenport didn't seem to notice. All this got the attention of the others sitting around the patio table.

"What are you two up to?" asked Mrs. Hicks, as if she were speaking to teenagers.

Mr. Davenport began to do a bad Cabbage Patch dance. "I *busted* a move."

"You need to drink some coffee," said Mrs. Hicks.

"I don't need any coffee," he countered happily. "What I need is another beer." And he marched over to a cooler where a few unopened beers sat at the bottom of the ice cube–laden water. He opened the dripping can, giggling.

"What is wrong with you, Davenport?" asked Mrs. Hicks.

After taking a long pull, he wiped his mouth and said nothing was wrong. "In fact, I never felt better in my life."

Later that night, lying in his bed, Mr. McTeer told himself, as he had done several times since the late afternoon, that he had not expected Mr. Davenport to be so aggressive with Stew Pot. And then, as he'd also done several times since that afternoon, he said to himself scornfully: *What did you think was going to happen?*

Mr. Davenport had been drunk, and he, Mr. McTeer, had played to his ego with all that *Commander* foolishness. Worse yet, he had been perfectly aware he was taking advantage of Mr. Davenport. But because of his own anger—over his wounded pride, over Stew Pot even suggesting that Mrs. Motley would ever do something improper—he had not been able to stop himself.

And even worse than that, when Mr. Davenport had told Stew Pot,

"Mr. McTeer has nothing to do with this," he himself had experienced an overwhelming sense of relief. This relief was a lighter version of the sort he'd experienced as a combat soldier, when after a battle he found himself still alive with a thankful realization that was in no way diminished by the death of a few friends. It was a thank-God-I'm-safe relief. The relief he had felt during the war had produced a tremendous guilt, as he in fact felt guilty right now in his bed. While the guilt over what he'd done with Mr. Davenport didn't dilute his current sense of relief, it did produce in him a profound self-loathing.

So, thanks to Mr. Davenport he had managed to hit Stew Pot back—a minor hit, really—without his beloved Mrs. Motley knowing, or putting himself in trouble. Mr. McTeer winced but could not shake from his mind the sight of Mr. Davenport moving boldly down the walkway, like some gung-ho soldier headed into his first battle, high on bravado, brimful with self-confidence, and ignorant as to the true magnitude of the danger he's allowed himself to be talked into.

BOOK IV

Stew Pot vs. the Davenports

CHAPTER ONE

Clown or King?

When Mr. Davenport returned home from Mrs. Hicks's Memorial Day party, he sat at the dining room table with his wife and daughter. While those two ate wedges of pan pizza, he told them, in happy beer-breath manner, of his confrontation with Stew Pot.

When he was finished, he sat with an arm over the back of his chair looking very pleased with himself. His wife, at the other end of the table, took a sip of her martini, made with sweet vermouth which gave it a golden color, and said matter-of-factly: "Great, now you've put yourself on Stew Pot's hit list. That's just what we needed."

A tall, lean woman with a long face, angular nose, and shoulder-length hair parted down the middle, Mrs. Davenport narrowed her heavy-lidded, sleepy-look eyes. She turned from Mr. Davenport's frown to their daughter, her spitting image, sitting midway down the table, and said: "Hear that, Delphina? Your daddy picked a fight with Stew Pot. I guess now that he's run Erma off the reservation, he can start in on us."

"I—or I should say we—are made of way stronger stuff than Erma. Furthermore—"

Delphina angrily tossed her napkin on the table. "Stew Pot, Stew Pot, Stew Pot. That's all I ever hear around here!" She then got up and stalked off.

As the girl stomped up the carpeted stairs, Mrs. Davenport said: "She's right. Lately, the only thing you ever talk about is that Bible-toting fool. Del's sweet sixteen party is in three weeks and you've hardly said a word about it. In two years she's off to college. And *that* will be that." The *that* she was referring to was the never-spoken-of-but-mutually-dreaded scenario of the two of them alone in the house with no daughter to give their cohabitation any sense of purpose.

Mrs. Davenport returned to her pizza and martini. Not wanting to provoke any more of her cutting looks or comments (which never failed to infuriate him and deeply hurt his feelings), Mr. Davenport left the table and built himself a tall scotch and water, then headed to the backyard deck to sit and mull in the twilight.

That afternoon the look of genuine fear on Stew Pot's face had been sweet for him to see, and Mr. Davenport floated the hopeful thought that Stew Pot, like a schoolyard bully who retreats the first time he's seriously challenged, might cease with his aggressions, since he now had to realize that he, Mr. Davenport, was a man to be reckoned with.

He took a sip of his drink and looked out over the long yard, the lawn and flowers under the haze of an amber lamp attached to an alley telephone pole. Something caught his attention off to his left, something in the shadowed corner of the yard where a juniper shrub stood ten feet high. He squinted in an attempt to make out what the movement was, but could discern nothing, and a blip of fear passed through him, along with the thought that his wife had been right, that he had placed his family in peril. Staring down that fear, he told himself that this time he wasn't backing down the way he had, in his opinion, done so many times before in his life. "This time," he said softly, "I will not falter."

CHAPTER TWO

The Stew Pot Chronicles

A week later, folks gathered for the June block club meeting in the air-conditioned chill of the Davenport living room. This meeting was marked by the first-time attendance of Mr. Glenn, the man who'd bought Erma's house. (Mrs. Davenport was again a no-show, while Delphina was in her customary seat by the front door taking the minutes in longhand.)

Mr. Glenn's auto repair shop was a few doors from Logan's, so everyone at the meeting knew of him. He'd been raised in the city, was divorced and in his early thirties. Rumor had it he was quite the ladies' man, although no one ever spoke of his dating any Parkland women. That evening he arrived wearing a black silk pullover, gray slacks, and black loafers; the first time the others had seen him in anything other than grease-monkey coveralls.

When Mr. Davenport introduced Mr. Glenn, the newcomer stood and acknowledged the polite applause with a slight bow. He was, in the opinion of more than a few females there, as good-looking a man as Erma Smedley was a woman, what with his wolfish grin and slanted nostrils. His hair was shaved close on the sides and back, and that silk pullover fit his tapered torso quite nicely. During the applause Mrs. Hicks, who was wearing a chestnut wig that evening, leaned over to Mrs. Motley and whispered: "He cleans up *real* good." Mrs. Motley acted like she didn't hear, but at the same time had to suppress a grin. Mr. McTeer, sitting on the other side of Mrs. Motley, heard it too. Not surprisingly, he didn't find the comment at all amusing.

The meeting adjourned around nine, with a few folks settling on the screened front porch for after-meeting drink and conversation. Along with Mr. Davenport, there was Mr. Glenn, Mrs. Powell, Mrs. Motley, Mrs. Hicks, and Mr. McTeer. Those last three sat on a suspended porch swing and the others on folding chairs arranged in a loose semicircle facing the swing. The only illumination came from a streetlamp filtering through the trees. The sound of their talk was accompanied by the up close rattle of ice cubes (everyone had liquor, save for Mrs. Motley, who sipped a tall orange juice and tonic) and the distant noises of children still outdoors playing.

As had happened so many times since March, the subject of Stew Pot soon came up and Mr. Glenn asked: "How'd he get that name?"

With a chortle Mrs. Hicks said: "Nobody knows. That's what his momma called him the first day they moved here, and what everyone has called him ever since—although after he was a teenager she took to calling him Gerald."

Mr. Glenn then asked how long Stew Pot had lived on the block and Mrs. Motley explained he and his family had moved there in the spring of 1968. "It was about a month after Dr. King was murdered and they had all that rioting on the West Side. The boy was about nine at the time. I looked out my living room window—it was a warm and sunny afternoon and I saw a man walking to the two-flat in what looked like a khaki janitor's uniform, with a small woman in an orange pantsuit and a skinny boy walking behind him.

"That evening I went over with an apple pie I had baked as a welcoming gift. Mrs. Reeves answered the door, still wearing the orange pantsuit. I remember there was music from a blues record coming from somewhere inside; real-gut bucket. Anyway, I introduced myself and welcomed her to the block. I remember saying, *I hope you and your family like apple pie*, more as a perfunctory thing because who doesn't like apple pie? And you know what she said?"

Mr. Glenn shrugged.

"She says, *My husband and I don't eat apple pie. Apples give him gas, and I don't like the taste of fruit pies.*"

Cutting in, Mrs. Hicks said to Mr. Glenn: "Can you believe that? Don't eat apples. Don't eat fruit pie. Who ever heard of such a thing?"

"And then," Mrs. Motley continued, "Mrs. Reeves said, *Stew Pot will eat it.* And my first thought was, *She's going to feed my scratch-pie to a dog?* And then she said, *But my son loves apples any way he can get them.* That's when she nodded over her shoulder, and I looked past her through the open doorway to the first-floor living room. There was the boy I'd seen earlier, asleep on a low stack of moving boxes with his thumb in his mouth."

"Who lets their kid sleep on boxes?" Mrs. Hicks said.

Mr. Glenn then asked: "Has Stew Pot always been bad?"

"Yeah, pretty much," replied Mrs. Hicks.

"Not always bad," Mrs. Motley said. "*Problematic* might be a better term."

"She's just being nice," said Mrs. Hicks. "Take it from me, he was evil. He used to sit in front of the two-flat on a kitchen chair. Little bucket-headed boy looking at folks all weird, like he was sizing them up."

"And how Mr. and Mrs. Reeves used to fight," said Mrs. Motley. "He'd come home drunk and start playing those blues records and then he and she would have at it; usually her accusing him of running with other women and him denying it."

"Yeah, Mr. Reeves was no great shakes," said Mrs. Hicks. "So it's not all that surprising Stew Pot turned out bad. We found out later he wasn't a janitor. He worked for an exterminator, and he liked to take photographs. He had a dark room in his basement where he made prints from pictures he took with a thirty-five millimeter camera."

"So what happened to Stew Pot's father?" asked Mr. Glenn.

"Oh, he died," said Mrs. Powell, "about three years after the Reeves moved in. He had a heart attack, I believe."

"The ambulance came for him on a Sunday evening," Mrs. Motley explained. "It was the middle of summer. Back then ambulances weren't the boxy things like today; they were modified Cadillac station wagons. Anyway, these White men wheeled Mr. Reeves from the two-flat on a rolling stretcher and put him in the white wagon. He was in the hospital for a few days, but he never recovered.

"I remember how when the ambulance pulled away, Mrs. Reeves was on her walkway and Stew Pot a few feet behind, asking: *They're going to bring him back, right, Momma?* It was after that that the boy started acting wild. Up to then he'd been a quiet, though not very studious child. But after his daddy passed he got into it with teachers and classmates. I had to send him to the principal's office a number of times."

"It was after his father died that Stew Pot started taking pictures," said Mrs. Powell. "He used his father's camera that he equipped with a telephoto lens and he began following people around, taking shots of them when they weren't looking. Like a spy."

"How'd you know he was doing that?"

"Because sometimes folks caught him at it," replied Mr. Davenport, who'd been waiting for the story to progress to the time when he himself had arrived on the block. "One day I come out of my doctor's office over in Morgan Park and who do I see but Stew Pot, standing across the street and snapping my picture."

"Of all the stuff Stew Pot did as a child" said Mrs. Motley, "following folks with a camera riled my husband the most. He used to grumble about Stew Pot and that camera."

"So his daddy died and Stew Pot got evil, is that it?" said Mr. Glenn.

Mr. McTeer chimed in angrily: "Plenty of folks lose their parents early and don't get evil." After a couple of silent moments Mr. McTeer continued. With hands resting on the curve of his upright cane, he leaned forward toward Mr. Glenn. "See that house directly across the street?" Mr. Glenn and the others glanced over at the redbrick Georgian. "Two of my best friends used to live there. Their names were Mr. and Mrs. Deckerdrill. They were very good people.

"One autumn day Stew Pot is walking down the block—he was sixteen by then—and he sees the Deckerdrills' granddaughter reading a book on their front steps. Now, she was a pretty girl, twelve at the time, with pigtails and the same cute overbite as her grandma. So anyway, Mrs. Deckerdrill comes to the screen door and sees Stew Pot talking all slick-daddy to her grandbaby, so she tells him to leave. Stew Pot starts cursing her—right there on her own front steps! Later on she tells Mr. Deckerdrill. Now ole Deck didn't take any mess off anybody. He wasn't any bigger than me, but he was tough; used to amateur box back in his youth. The next day he sees Stew Pot walking down the street with that first dog of his, the one he called Hitler."

"Hitler?" said Mr. Glenn.

"Yes, Hitler," Mr. McTeer confirmed. "Deckerdrill comes out of his house carrying a tire iron and tells Stew Pot that if he ever says so much as *boo* to his granddaughter or wife again, he'll put that tire iron upside Stew Pot's head. Stew Pot's dog started growling and Mr. Deckerdrill said he'd tire iron the dog too.

"Back then, the Deckerdrills, who were both retired, drove to Mississippi every winter to visit relatives. They'd leave right after New Year's and return around Valentine's Day. The winter after the run-in with Stew Pot, they go south as usual. Well, while they're gone, someone gets into their house and turns off the furnace. No heat, dead of winter."

"The water pipes burst," said Mr. Glenn.

"Yes sir," snapped Mr. McTeer. "They come home and their house is ruined. There's water damage all over the place, ice floes on the floors. And what was worse, because the police said there was no sign of forced entry, the Deckerdrills' insurance company refused to make good on their policy. They claimed it was possible negligence on the Deckerdrills' part; said they must've accidentally left the furnace off."

"And Stew Pot did it?"

Her voice full of incredulity, Mrs. Hicks said, "Of course Stew Pot did it! Who else around here was good enough at burglarizing to get in and out without leaving a trace?"

"So what happened to the Deckerdrills?" asked Mr. Glenn.

"They did the only thing they could do," said Mr. McTeer. "They sold the house for what they could get for it. They wound up in some retirement home out in the suburbs. Mrs. Motley and I used to visit them. It was pitiful seeing those two. It wasn't that their new place was bad, although it was small. But it wasn't their *home*. They were both gone within a couple of years of moving out there. If any two folks ever died of heartbreak, it was them. I'll *never* forgive Stew Pot for that."

"Like I said before," said Mrs. Hicks, "he was evil. Sixteen and messing with a child."

Now Mr. McTeer told the story of how Stew Pot had defamed his daughter, and Mrs. Motley told of the burning of her garage. Then Mrs. Powell told about what had happened between Stew Pot and Erma Smedley's aunt.

"One day Erma's aunt caught Stew Pot peeing in the alley behind her house and she yelled at him. She used to let her cat out on that screened porch when the weather was warm. Stew Pot must have gotten ahold of the cat from there. Come the next day, Miss Smedley opens her letter box and finds the cat's head inside."

"Lord," said Mr. Glenn, "and Stew Pot was never arrested for any of this?"

Sounding exasperated, Mr. McTeer said: "He was never caught with anything incriminating. If he had been, don't you think he would have been arrested?"

"How'd he wind up in jail?"

"He got caught burglarizing an apartment up on the North Side," said Mrs. Powell.

"Lincoln Park," added Mrs. Hicks. "He broke into a place with a White woman asleep in it. So he's coming out her building's front door with her jewelry and other valuables, and a cop car, answering a call about a loud party down the street, of all things, comes rolling around the corner. Cops see a young Black man walking around at two in the morning, especially up there, carrying a pillow case full of something, they're going to stop him."

"And that's not all," said Mr. McTeer, "They found . . ."

"Go on," said Mrs. Hicks, "we're adults."

Lowering his voice, Mr. McTeer continued, "Stew Pot left semen on the woman. They charged him with sexual assault as well a burglary. The jury found him guilty on both counts. That's why he got such a long sentence."

"Dag," said Mr. Glenn, "I knew he was a piece of work; didn't know he was that bad."

"Yes, he's that bad," affirmed Mr. Davenport. "The other day at Mrs. Hicks's party I tweaked his nose." He was about to say more, but he caught a worried look from Mr. McTeer which he took as a warning to not tell.

"How'd you tweak his nose?" asked Mr. Glenn after a moment.

"It was no big thing," Mr. Davenport said. "But do you now see the danger he poses?"

Nodding his handsome head, Mr. Glenn said he sure did see. "It sounds to me like something needs to be done about that man—and the sooner, the better."

CHAPTER THREE
Sixteen Candles

Two weeks after the block club meeting, at around seven on a clear Saturday evening, guests for Delphina's sixteenth birthday party began arriving. Those from the neighborhood came on foot while those from outside Parkland arrived in cars driven by older relatives who unloaded their cheerful cargos in front of the Davenport house. The few who were old enough to drive alone showed up with their stereos blasting bass-thumping music.

The invitations had stipulated formal dress attire and all the guests complied. A chubby deejay in a white button-down shirt and loosely knotted tie stood behind his setup near the backyard patio, the music causing heads to bob as people munched hors d'oeuvres and sipped punch.

The dinner went smoothly, the teenagers getting a kick out of sitting at the round tables with white cloths under a rented tent with a parquet floor. It was fun having adults in red vests serve their plates and fill their glasses. A number of girls said it was like those fancy dinners you saw on shows like *Dallas* and *Dynasty*. The food fit their idea of fancy too. No fried chicken or collard greens. That evening they got prime rib, grilled asparagus, sautéed green peppers, and saffron rice.

Mr. and Mrs. Davenport ate their supper out of sight in the dining room and did not come to the backyard until dessert: a large devil's food sheet cake with chocolate icing, and tart raspberry filling between the layers and around the sides.

The cake was set on a covered folding table on the patio with the lit candles arranged in the shape of a star. Mr. and Mrs. Davenport stood on either side of Delphina, the guests huddling close around on three sides. As they sang happy birthday, Delphina, in her pastel-blue dress, clasped her hands in joy just below her chin. It was the first backless dress her parents had ever let her wear and she was swept with the feeling that her life was finally, at long last, beginning, for now she could drive alone and go on dates without a chaperone. And when the singers reached "*Hap-pee birth-day, Del-fee-nah!*" it was just all too much and she felt tears welling.

When the guests noticed this, they smiled. Her father placed a hand on her bare shoulder. Earlier that evening, when she'd come downstairs in her dress, he'd said she had never looked so beautiful, and she'd felt a bubble of guilt for the harsh things she'd written about him and her mom in her diary, and the way she groused about her folks to friends.

One of the boys standing at the back yelled: "Come on and blow out those candles, Del! We want some cake!" And everybody laughed, including Delphina, as she wiped at the tears with the backs of her wrists. And her dad kissed her on the cheek, and her mom kissed her on the other cheek, and somebody shouted: "Del! Del! Del!" And the rest of them picked it up and then they were all chanting: "Del! Del! Del!" and she leaned over the candles, the flickering orange light sending a fluttering reflection across her smiling face, the light sparkling off her diamond-stud earrings (a present her mother had given her earlier that day) and off of the pearl necklace that had once belonged to her grandmother.

Delphina extinguished the candles with a long blow, bringing whoops and applause as the smoke wisps plumed upward. Her father then said it was time for her big present. He reached into his pants pocket and took out a pair of car keys and dangled them in front of her. Delphina began jumping up and down in place, going: "Oh! Oh!" She took the keys, turned to the guests, held them aloft, and jingled them with glee. The guests clapped, her girlfriends already envisioning chauffeured trips to the mall, while some of the fellows imagined the exciting possibilities of backseat sessions with Delphina in a secluded spot of the forest preserve.

"Where is it?" she asked excitedly. Mr. Davenport nodded at the side gate, and before you knew it they were headed out the yard. In front of the house was a blue two-door coupe. (During the dinner, Mr. Davenport had driven it over from its hiding place in Mr. McTeer's garage.) The car was six years old and nothing fancy, but there were no dents or rust spots anywhere and it had a CD player and new tires. Delphina climbed inside, put the key in the ignition, and gunned the engine, which brought another whoop from the crowd.

She got out, threw her arms around her father's neck, and kissed him all over his face. She had to wipe her eyes again before leading the throng back, saying how she couldn't believe she had a car, she just couldn't believe it!

By that time, the caterers had removed the tables and chairs. The parquet floor was quickly filled with people dancing, the crowd driven there by the opening chords of that summer's most popular song. Even Mr. and Mrs. Davenport got into the act, moving awkwardly with the music, much to the delight of Delphina and her friends. Then, before they wore out their welcome, her parents returned to the house. The music and dancing continued. Guys took off their jackets and loosened their ties, and girls occasionally hooked a forefinger at the edge of a dress top to get themselves some cooling air, the fellows getting excited seeing all that female sweat.

CHAPTER FOUR
The Life of the Party

As soon as Delphina's parents left, one of the guys retrieved a bottle of vodka from his car and jacked the punch. Four songs later, Delphina and a few guests were on the deck cooling off with the pumped-up juice, when someone said: "Who's he?"

The birthday girl looked past the crowd on the dance floor and saw Stew Pot standing in the alley by the low chain-link gate. His dog was with him and he was glaring at the party, his thick arms folded across the bib of his denim overalls, the leash wound around his left hand.

It should not be hard to imagine the anxiety that shot through Delphina at this point.

"Oh God. What is he doing here?" she wailed.

Reggie Butler, feeling brave after two quickly consumed cups of the jacked punch and eager to get into Delphina's good graces, said: "You want me to go get rid of him?"

And Delphina said: "Yes. Get him away from here before my father finds out."

Reggie led a squad of three guys to the gate, the angry set of their faces and their determined strides catching the attention of some of the dancers. It was a look those dancers had seen before at other parties and get-togethers, the look that said someone was about to get in somebody's face.

With the music going, those not near the alley couldn't tell what was being said over there by the gate, but the gestures made it clear that the conversation was not friendly. Stew Pot still had his arms crossed, as did the three guys standing directly behind Reggie.

In the manner beloved by bad-boy wannabes the nation over, Reggie spread his arms wide, then flopped them to his sides. Onlookers saw Stew Pot's mouth move, his white teeth showing in his sullen face. Reggie started motioning at Stew Pot with his right hand, using the ever-popular pointed-forefinger-perpendicular-thumb gesture, after which he clasped his hands in front of his crotch and cocked his head, as if to say: *Whatcha got?*

They saw Stew Pot mouth something else; meanwhile, Delphina had recovered herself and was now marching toward the gate. The rest of the folks on the deck followed her.

When she got there, the squad of four stepped aside for her. The other people trailing behind came to an abrupt halt. Folks from the dance floor began drifting over, and as they got closer they were able to make out what was being said.

"What do you think you're doing?" said Delphina.

"Witnessing for Christ, that's what."

"Well witness someplace else!"

"I go where God directs me," said Stew Pot. "Tonight He's directed me here. And I can see why. Look at you, dressed like a harlot. You ought to be ashamed of yourself. All of you should be ashamed of yourselves. It's like Sodom and Gomorrah out here, all this wild and sinful dancing."

From the crowd came catcalls, wisecracks, and profane suggestions.

"Go ahead and laugh," Stew Pot said. "You'll be laughing out the other side of your mouth come Judgment Day; which, by the way, may come sooner than you think."

Catcalls, wisecracks, and profane suggestions came again; this time more numerous, and louder. Delphina, standing at the gate, felt the collective body heat of the crowd on her bare back. Their closeness gave her confidence and she again told Stew Pot to leave. This was seconded from all over the crowd, their voices washing past Delphina's shoulders and arms. This wave of noise fazed Stew Pot not one wit. He stood defiantly with his left hand on his hip and still gripping the leash of the now pacing dog. He used the other hand to point at them.

"Heed Proverbs fourteen!" he shouted. "*God scorns the wicked! But the upright enjoy His favor!*" The catcalls and whatnot grew even louder. "*The heart knows its own bitterness,*" he continued quoting, "*and no stranger shares its joy!*"

The crowd surged forward yelling for him to leave, go away, get out. But he continued quoting Proverbs. "*The house of the wicked will be destroyed, but the tent of the upright will flourish!*" This last line he delivered with a wagging forefinger.

The crowd began booing like rowdies at a ball game. The dog began leaping at Stew Pot's side and barking. Stew Pot raised his right hand high with three fingers upright.

"Isaiah three! *For Jerusalem has stumbled, and Judah has fallen! Because their speech and their deeds are against the Lord! Defying His glorious presence!*"

"Booo!"

"*Their partiality witnesses against them! They proclaim their sin like Sodom!!*"

"Boooooooooooo!"

"*Woe to them! For they have brought evil upon themselves!*"

"BOOOOOOOOOOOOOOOOOOOOO!!!!!!"

Someone lobbed a punch cup into the alley, and the dog leaped at the fence in response, causing people in the first row to spring back and bump into the people close behind them, which caused those folks to bump into the people behind them. No one noticed at first that Delphina was sobbing. They also didn't notice that the music had stopped. (The chubby deejay, not sure exactly what the problem was but fearful it might lead to serious trouble like at some other parties he'd worked, had by then run to the kitchen where the caterer's people were peering out the window. "I think someone better call the police," he said, "it looks like they're about to riot.")

At the fence, Stew Pot was continuing to quote from Isaiah, his left hand jerking on the leash to keep his dog from leaping the fence as the crowd jeered.

"*Woe to those who are heroes at drinking wine! As the tongue of fire devours the stubble and as dry grass sinks down in flame, so their root will be as rottenness, and their blossom go up like dust! For they have rejected the law of the Lord of hosts! And He stretched out his hand against them and smote them! And the mountains quaked and their corpses were as refuse in the midst of the streets!*"

There was rustling at the back of the crowd, people being forced aside, the split moving forward. With his wife behind him, Mr. Davenport pushed to the fence and stood beside the anguished Delphina. He took her in his arms and asked her if she was okay. She threw her face against his chest and kept sobbing.

With one arm around her shoulder, Mr. Davenport pointed at Stew Pot with the other and told him in loud and profane terms that he had better leave immediately. "I called the police. You hear me? The police!"

"I'm the one ought to be calling the police," Stew Pot said, "what with all the racket these children are keeping up this evening. You ought to be ashamed of yourself, Davenport, letting your daughter walk out of the house looking like that! Why don't you put her on the stroll and complete the job?"

"Daddy, please make him stop!" screamed Delphina. Mr. Davenport made like he was going to open the gate, but the dog leaped in his direction and Mr. Davenport stopped.

Mrs. Davenport, on the other hand, seemed ready to throw all caution to the wind. Cussing a blue streak, she squeezed past Delphina's back and put a shoe toe through a square space formed by the chain link, looking like she intended to climb over the top rail.

"Such language," said Stew Pot snidely. "Like mother, like daughter, I see."

Suddenly, off in the far distance they heard a siren. Everyone quieted down and looked toward the west, Stew Pot and the dog included.

"Now we'll see what's what!" said Mr. Davenport triumphantly.

Stew Pot moved his gaze across to the crowd, making eye contact as he went. Then he swept the air violently with his free arm.

"You people had better get yourselves right with the Lord." He gave the leash a tug and he and the dog started off toward the west end of the alley. The crowd yelled more catcalls and profane suggestions.

The siren sound got louder. Those closest to the fence leaned over and watched Stew Pot move away, a handful getting off a few last insults. When he turned out of the alley the siren was very near, on the next street north. Through a gap made by a driveway across the way, they could see 128th Place. They watched the approach of the flashing blue lights as the squad car zipped by and continued east and through the viaduct over there, obviously on the way to some other emergency, the siren growing distressingly faint.

CHAPTER FIVE

A Woman's Touch

A squad car did eventually arrive at the Davenports' house, but not until an hour later. By then the yard was deserted and all was quiet. The two officers, both Black women, got out of their white car and spoke on the sidewalk to Mr. and Mrs. Davenport who'd been waiting on the front porch. After patiently listening to the angry tale of woe, the older of the two officers, who was as light as Erma with a sandy-colored head of curled hair, said that while the Davenports' distress was understandable, no one had been assaulted, no threats had been made, no property had been damaged or trespassed, and nothing had been stolen—in short, no crime had been committed.

The officer, whose nameplate read JARPER, said she and her partner would talk with Stew Pot. Mr. Davenport asked if they were going to arrest him and Jarper said: "Not unless he does something stupid."

With the Davenports watching, along with a few other neighbors, from their porches and stoops, the officers drove down to the two-flat. As they strolled up the walkway, loud barks could be heard from inside.

Jarper banged on the front door and shouted: "Chicago Police!"

They heard footsteps coming down the stairs and the unmistakable sound of dog claws clicking on floorboards. A man's voice asked who was calling. Jarper repeated that she was Chicago Police and told him to lock his dog away from the door. The barking stopped.

Several moments later, Stew Pot opened the door wearing a pair of cut-off sweatpants. He wore no shirt, his chest broad and well defined in the glow of the light above the door.

"What can I do for you, officer?"

"I understand you decided to crash a party tonight."

Stew Pot's downward gaze moved to the younger officer, who was darker and shorter, with a button nose and hair tied back in a bun.

"I was doing some witnessing for Christ this evening, yes."

"You realize you ruined what should have been a wonderful evening for that girl?"

"Some things are more important than parties. Tonight the Lord told me to go to those young people. Like those sinners dancing around Aaron's calf, they were—"

"Enough," said Jarper. "You'd better watch your step. I get half an excuse to run you and I'll run you. I'll run you faster than it takes a roach to get from here to there. Understand?"

"The only rule I obey is—"

"*Understand?*"

Stew Pot frowned and said he understood. Jarper then pointed at him. "Remember, a word to the wise is sufficient."

Jarper was driving the squad car and after a U-turn at the railroad embankment, she stopped again in the middle of the block. She got out and told Mr. and Mrs. Davenport that she was sorry, but there was nothing more that she could do. "If he starts anything else tonight, call." And then she was back in the car and she and her partner were gone, leaving the Davenports to fend for themselves.

CHAPTER SIX
The Summer of Their Discontent

The next few weeks were tense at the Davenport house. In the opinion of mother and daughter, there was a direct connection between what Mr. Davenport had done on Memorial Day and what Stew Pot had done at the party. "You just couldn't leave well enough alone, could you?" Mrs. Davenport said. "You just had to go and light a fire under that half-wit. Well, I hope you're satisfied." Delphina had plenty to say too: "The most important day of my life—*of my life!* Ruined! And it's all your fault!"

Mr. Davenport fought back with vigorous assertions that he would not tolerate being disrespected in his own home. Neither woman paid him any mind. Neighbors living on both sides of the family reported hearing, through an open window or doorway, snatches of rancor, Mrs. Davenport shouting that she was "sick and tired of your neighborhood grandstanding!" and Mr. Davenport responding just as loudly, "I will not apologize for defending my family!" and Delphina declaring in high decibels that her life was over: "I'm the laughing stock of Parkland! I might as well move to China!"

That last declaration was inaccurate. Most Parklanders saw Delphina in a sympathetic light. As for Stew Pot, most of Parkland-at-large shifted him from the weird-but-harmless category to the crazy-dangerous-hot-list, which is where folks on his block said he should have been all along. Now when Mrs. Reeves made smiling hellos during street encounters with neighbors on her way to or from work, most cut her a perturbed look. Stew Pot's happy greetings received the silent treatment too, only with angry expressions. Neither seemed at all fazed by these reactions. They continued to meet and greet folks with smiles and observations on what a blessed day it was, even if it was raining to beat the band. Their seemingly impervious attitudes only made the folks on their block madder, in addition to leaving them feeling a little helpless.

Interesting as the party blowup was, after a fortnight passed, it was pushed from the forefront of local conversation by the joys and events of June. The Bulls, to the delight of just about everybody, won the league championship for the third year in a row. School let out for the summer and the weekdays now had plenty of kids on the streets and at the park swimming pool. Mr. and Mrs. Davenport worked summer school, as did Mrs. Hicks. Delphina enjoyed frequent ride-arounds with girlfriends and playing the boy field while considering steady date offers from a pair of neighborhood fellows, neither of whom was Reggie Butler. Mrs. Motley, as she did every year, commemorated her wedding anniversary by visiting her husband's grave in the shady confines of Eden Rest Cemetery and having a single glass of champagne in the apple-green dining room. The rumors about Mr. Glenn were proven true. Young and slender ladies were seen shamelessly leaving his house early on Sunday mornings for their cars; a different femme each week.

Folks on the block kept an eye out for Stew Pot, some of them checking the street or alley before leaving home so as to avoid encountering him or his mom. What they could not see was that Mrs. Davenport was now spending all her evenings and nights in the Davenports' rec room basement, listening to Al Green in the dark while sipping martinis and smoking. Mr. Davenport would sometimes come to the head of the basement stairs and listen, before returning to the master bedroom upstairs, which was down the hallway from Delphina's bedroom. The girl was spending every evening behind the closed door, either talking on the phone or writing furiously in her diary, where for the past two years she had documented the thoughts, words, and deeds of herself and her parents.

CHAPTER SEVEN
Bombs Bursting in Air

Chicago is pretty strict about who can and can't put on firework shows. However, just across the Cal Sag from Parkland was a rough-and-tumble, predominantly White suburban hamlet (wedged between the more prosperous and diverse towns of Riverdale and Posen) which was far more lenient with fireworks permits.

For thirty years the hamlet had been the sight, courtesy of Vernon Paiger, of a Fourth of July fireworks show. (It was so grand that hardly anyone from those parts ever bothered with the city's lakefront fireworks extravaganza, which back then was held on July 3.)

The explosives were set off across from Parkland's Flipper Park (named for the first African-American to graduate West Point), which extended from the railroad yard for three blocks along the Cal Sag's north bank. Parklanders gathered there, as well as folks from Morgan Park, Blue Island, and Calumet Park. Residents from south of the Cal Sag gathered mostly along a road that paralleled the channel on the south side.

Some folks got to Flipper in the late morning to barbecue and make a day of it, with most others arriving in early evening with blankets and quilts. There were no high trees along the Parkland bank, so anywhere you sat you had a clear view.

Mrs. Motley gave Mr. McTeer a ride over. After parking Ingrid behind a stand of trees that lined the north side of the park, they walked through the tree area to a bench at the very back of the open space. During the hour and forty-some minutes before the show, they were passed on either side by loud and jolly streams of people, and they nodded and called hellos to any familiar face. This included the Davenports, out on their first family excursion since the party disturbance. Mr. Glenn was there too, as were Mr. and Mrs. Hicks and their daughters, sons-in-law, and grandchildren, and Mr. and Mrs. Powell. Mrs. Butler was not in attendance—like Thanksgiving, she considered the Fourth of July "the White oppressor's holiday." Reggie was there, though, having positioned himself near the bank and within easy sight of Delphina and her parents.

As the evening sky went from pink to pale blue to black, the park became more and more crowded. The hum of voices was punctuated here and there by the sound of firecrackers snapping in the distance, while out on the channel there was the low rumble of small motor-boats lazily circling.

Now, while it was true that Vernon never forgave anyone who crossed him, one of the things people liked about him was that he was no glory hound. Most politicians, if they paid for a fireworks show, would have forced folks to listen to at least a little blather. But Vernon didn't do that. He didn't even get on a microphone and say a brief hello to get applause. He never said anything at a fireworks show, for which those in attendance were most grateful. He did attend the events, always finding a place in the stand of trees behind and to the side of Mrs. Motley, which allowed him to see her on the bench without her seeing him.

At 9:05 p.m. the show started, the air high above the southern bank of the Cal Sag becoming all starburst and thunder, the explosions turning the mass of upturned faces different tints—pink, then green, then orange, then blue, then hot white, then pink again, and so on; one thunder piling atop another, and soon the air was smelly with cordite, and people "oohed" and "ahhed" in appreciation. And Mr. McTeer, who had seen big explosions at a much closer range than this—white phosphorous explosions, orange fireballs—sat beside Mrs. Motley on the park bench, not enjoying the show that much. When he and his wife were raising their children, he had come every year because they had wanted to come, and he came now because Mrs. Motley wanted to. And as he took sideways glances at her smiling, upturned face changing colors with every *ka-boom*, he told himself that this was one of the reasons he had fought in the war, why he had killed people: so that folks like his family and Mrs. Motley could blissfully watch a fireworks show without having their enjoyment sullied by disturbing memories of friends, enemies, and civilians blown to smithereens or burned to a blackened crisp by the flash and thunder of a much meaner sort.

Ahead and above them in the sky, the blasting went on and on, the thunder so close you could feel it in your chest, the cordite so thick now you could taste it. And Vernon Paiger, from his place amidst the trees, gazed ever so often at the bench where Mrs. Motley and Mr. McTeer were sitting, and he could tell by the occasional flinch of Mr. McTeer's shoulders what the other veteran was thinking; and he himself thought wryly: *With all this blast and boom, all that's missing are the blood-curdling screams.*

The thudding and thumping were heard all over the neighborhood, eddying down the mostly deserted residential streets. The length of the show provided the perfect situation for a stealthy person to do what he needed to do, like dislodge a window air conditioner, enter a house, and photograph certain sensitive items. Then, leave everything back in its proper place, so that the victims, upon their return home, would have no idea that anything untoward had happened, feeling for one last sweet night that they were safe and secure.

CHAPTER EIGHT
Extra, Extra, Read All About It

The next morning all of Stew Pot's immediate neighbors found that someone had left them an overnight delivery in their mailbox or mail slots: a stapled, photocopied thirteen-page excerpt from Delphina's diary. The handwriting was quickly recognizable as the same easy-to-read script used to record the block club minutes.

In the all-too-familiar the-world-revolves-around-me tone so favored by young diarists, Delphina wrote of her plans for college, where she intended to . . . *drink and stay out late and smoke weed and have sex if I feel like it*. She stated clearly her feelings for Mr. Glenn, who she described as *tres fine*, and her scheme to *drive to his shop wearing a top that's tight and cut low. That ought to get his attention.*

It had been unfair the way her parents made her life so difficult, she wrote, forcing her to wait until she was sixteen to date:

> . . . *ruining my life, telling me I had to invite that dweeb Reggie to my party, even though neither of them like Reggie or his crazy grandmother.*
>
> *Daddy all the time telling me sex is for marriage and marriage only, that any other kind is bad, and Momma tapping a forefinger on her wedding band and saying to me, "Sex is best when it has a ring around it."*
>
> *The very idea of them lecturing me is ridiculous. Daddy has those dirty magazines inside his tool box in the basement workroom. I know what kind of nasty stuff men do when they look at those sorts of pictures. Not to mention that time back when I was eleven and Daddy was down in the basement and I was at the top of the stairs in the kitchen and he didn't know I was there and I heard him say into the phone, "Hi there, baby," in a voice all cutesy-poo. And I knew he wasn't talking to Mom because she was at the hairdresser's. I lifted up the kitchen receiver and listened. Daddy was talking to that skinny buck-toothed Mrs. Coles from church who used to be married to the old principal at Parkland High School. Mr. Coles finally di-*

vorced the heifer and she moved to Florida with their five ug-motious kids. But before she did, she and Daddy were sneaking around doing the nasty. They talked about it on the phone that day. The sort of nasty stuff pictured in those magazines of his. AND EVEN AFTER MOMMA FOUND OUT SHE DIDN'T DO ANYTHING! SHE JUST GOT DRUNK EVERY NIGHT FOR A MONTH! SHE GOT DRUNK JUST LIKE SHE ALWAYS DOES WHENEVER SHE GETS UPSET!

The reason I know Momma found out about Daddy and Mrs. Coles is because I overheard them in their bedroom late one night when they thought I was asleep. Momma said, "I AM NOT A WHORE! I AM NOT ONE OF THOSE SLUTS YOU STARE AT IN THOSE MAGAZINES! HOW DARE YOU ASK ME TO DO THAT? GO ASK THAT SKINNY WHORE YOU RUT WITH IF YOU WANT SOMEONE TO DO THAT!"

Which is why her telling me about when "sex is best" is just a joke. SHE DOESN'T EVEN LIKE SEX! WITH OR WITHOUT A RING AROUND IT! I thought drinking lots of liquor was supposed to make a woman loose! Apa-rant-lee, not in her case.

There then followed another paean to Mr. Glenn that went on for two pages, after which Delphina shifted to the subject of neighbors she didn't like.

I hate being surrounded by all those dry balls at the block club meetings with their wrinkled faces and old people smell. Especially that Mr. McTeer with his funky-as-a-monkey cologne and Mrs. Motley with that lilac water she uses. Mrs. Powell wears way too much perfume. Momma says it's because she has halitosis and her breath stinks so bad she tries to cover it with the perfume. Well, somebody needs to tell Mrs. Powell that strategy ain't working because her breath could knock a maggot off a garbage truck. Then there's Mrs. Hicks. After every block club meeting Momma says you can tell where Mrs. Hicks was sitting because there's always bits of food scattered around on the carpet and it smells of her stinky feet. Momma said Erma Smedley was a perverted red bone who deserved to lose her house and that Mrs. Butler is the evilest person she ever met.

Delphina filled some four pages with negative comments her parents had made over the years about this or that neighbor, totaling nearly half the households on the block. But when Mom and Dad see these *people, they smile and act all friendly, because, they're—HYPOCRITES!!!!!!!!!*

Up and down the block folks frowned and shook their heads somberly as they read. Mrs. Motley did her reading over a cup of coffee in the yellow kitchen. Mr. McTeer did his at his dining room table, after which he crumpled the pages into a ball. Mrs. Powell read hers on her living room couch. She was in tears by the time she was through, which is how Mr. Powell found her when he got home from work around seven that morning.

That Stew Pot was the culprit behind the photocopying and deliveries, no one doubted for a second. He had somehow managed to get into the Davenport's house, most likely during the fireworks show, and filch Delphina's diary. They figured the photocopying had been done at an all-night convenience store with a coin-operated copy machine.

Around seven fifteen, Mrs. Motley called and told Mr. Davenport he ought to check his mailbox. "I think Stew Pot has done something." (Delphina had a separate phone line to her room, so she didn't hear any ringing.) Mrs. Motley called again fifteen minutes later and told Mr. Davenport he needn't worry on her account, that she knew from her own experience the teenage tendency to exaggerate. Mr. McTeer called not long afterward saying much the same thing.

Others however were not so understanding.

An angry Mr. Powell called Mr. Davenport not long after Mr. McTeer. Mr. Powell said that Mrs. Powell was "devastated." He cut Mr. Davenport off in mid-apology and told him he wouldn't have to worry about his wife's breath anymore because he and she had set foot in the Davenport house for the last time. Mrs. Hicks called minutes later to say she had heard and seen some cruel things in her time, but what she had read that morning took the cake. Mr. Davenport tried to explain, but Mrs. Hicks was having none of it. "What kind of daughter are you raising, anyway?" By seven fifty, ten angry calls had been lodged. And as people walked past or rode by the Davenport house on the way to work, all of them, the sympathetic as well the angry, wondered what was going on that morning behind the orange drapes of that Dutch Colonial.

CHAPTER NINE
All Fall Down

Standing over Delphina in her bedroom where everything was some shade of blue, with his wife there behind him, Mr. Davenport, in a white dress shirt and tan slacks, accused Delphina, who was sitting on the side of the bed, of carelessly leaving her diary somewhere, on the backyard deck maybe, where Stew Pot could get ahold of it.

Just moments before, he and Mrs. Davenport had burst into the room and awakened their daughter. She had at first looked bewilderedly at the photocopy, now she was crying and saying that she always kept her diary locked in her night table drawer.

He ordered her to get the diary. She stood up, retrieved her keychain from atop her dresser, and unlocked the drawer. To the surprise of all three, the diary was right where Delphina had last left it.

Mr. Davenport snatched the book and hurriedly thumbed pages. When he got to the place he was looking for, he stopped. His wife, dressed for work as well in a dark skirt suit and white blouse, moved alongside him. She and their daughter watched his eyes shift back and forth between a photocopied page and the white leather-covered book.

He shook his head slowly, thumbed forward and checked another page. After comparing some more, he slammed the diary closed and turned to Mrs. Davenport.

"It's a copy of Delphina's diary all right. I told you he didn't forge her handwriting." He turned back to Delphina. "You realize what you've done? You've destroyed us. We're ruined."

Mrs. Davenport said Delphina wasn't to blame, that this was all Stew Pot's fault.

"Stew Pot wouldn't have been able to do anything if she hadn't written this drivel," said Mr. Davenport. To which Mrs. Davenport angrily responded that Stew Pot would never have made them a target "if you hadn't decided to mess with him." Mr. Davenport told her to not start with all that again, and then returned his attention to Delphina.

"You ungrateful little fool. Your mother and I sweat and slave to give you everything and this is how you repay us, by humiliating us in front of everyone."

Mrs. Davenport called for him to stop, but he ignored her.

"Writing in that book like some foul-mouthed tramp, like some streetwalker."

"I said stop it!" Mrs. Davenport shouted. Her husband still paid her no mind and continued after Delphina, who sobbed and shook her shoulders with each admonition and accusation, as if his words were physical blows.

"I swear to God, in all my life I have never met anyone as self-centered as you. It's a good thing your mother and I *didn't* have any more children because no telling how they would have turned out with a big sister like you setting an example."

"I'm sorry, Daddy—"

"A simple sorry ain't gonna do it this time, Missy. You can forget about going away to college. Your little brown butt is staying right here in Chicago where your mother and I can keep a close eye on you. And as for that car, you've seen the last of it. I'm selling it tomorrow. And you can forget about dates—with anyone—for a good, long while. And the same goes for parties. I don't care if the event is chaperoned by the Pope. And I better not see you anywhere near that Mr. Glenn. You're not walking into this house with your belly swollen from carrying some fool's piglet. You're grounded until I say different. And if you don't like it, you can leave! You can pack your bags right now, you wretched little—"

"I said STOP!" screamed Mrs. Davenport, and catching her husband by surprise, she snatched the diary out of his hand. He made a move to snatch the book back, but she clutched it to her chest. Mr. Davenport demanded to know what she planned to do now. In a fierce voice Mrs. Davenport said she was going to burn the diary. "This has to be destroyed."

She then stalked out of the room. This took Mr. Davenport by surprise too, and it was a couple of seconds before he lit after her, leaving Delphina standing by the bed.

"That's evidence!" he shouted. "That's evidence of what Stew Pot did!"

Delphina heard feet thumping in the hallway and then her mother yelling, "No!" Moving to the doorway, she saw her parents near the top of the stairs in a twirling tug-of-war over the diary, elbows flying and feet moving in an ugly tango as they bumped against the walls, mouthing grunts and snarls and spittle.

And then just like that, her father, with his back to her, pulled the diary free. Her mother, with suddenly no resistance to counter her straining in the other direction, stumbled slightly before regaining her balance. She lunged for the book and he, cuddling his precious and hard-won treasure, swept his free arm to fend her off. The arm caught her off-balance in the chest. She pinwheeled backward, and fell over the top step and out of sight. A cascading series of thumps followed, the sounds filling the space where she'd been standing, with the last thump the loudest.

Delphina screamed, then screamed again, for she knew her mother was dead, dead at the foot of the stairs, crumpled like a rag. Her father, after a moment of frozen shock, stepped to the head of the stairs, looked down, and after an intake of breath loud enough for Delphina to hear, headed down and out of sight, still clutching the diary.

Taking tentative steps, Delphina moved after him.

When she reached the stair top she took a terrified look.

Her mother was not dead.

On the landing below she saw her mom pull herself to her feet, slapping away her dad's offered hand of help as she did so. Stepping back into the living room, she didn't appear to have broken any bones; however, in her topsy-turvy down the stairs, Delphina could see that her mom had suffered some injuries. One noticeable wound was a nasty rug burn on her left cheek. The skin was scraped raw, leaving an irregular pink spot the size of a quarter below the left eye; the pink in sharp contrast to the brown face. Her mom's bottom lip was bleeding too, and her right shoulder had apparently been hurt. She raised and lowered the right arm as if she were trying to alleviate pain, the movement causing a ripped seam, where the dark right sleeve met the body of the suit jacket, to open and close like a mouth.

Mrs. Davenport extended her left arm to Mr. Davenport. "Give me the diary."

From a new position midway down the stairs, Delphina said, "Momma, you all right?"

Without taking her eyes off her husband on the landing, Mrs. Davenport said she was fine. She again demanded that she be given the book. The fear that she might be hurt must have zapped Mr. Davenport's anger, because he now spoke in a calm voice, explaining why the diary had to be kept.

Through nearly clenched teeth filmed with blood from her injured lip, Mrs. Davenport said: "I want it burned. I want it gone. Do you hear me?"

"Dear, don't you see—"

"I want that filth out of here. I don't want to see it. I don't want it to exist."

"But we're going to need it."

"For what!"

"So we can make our case against Stew Pot—"

"My God, is he all you care about? What's the matter with you?"

Mr. Davenport said nothing was the matter, and calmly went back into his explanation of how the diary would be needed when they called the police to have Stew Pot arrested for breaking and entering.

Mrs. Davenport clasped her left hand in her hair and began shaking her head. "I can't listen to this anymore. I can't listen, I can't listen, I can't—"

Suddenly there were footsteps on the screened front porch, then someone pounding on the door, then a man's deep, deep voice shouting: "CHICAGO POLICE!"

CHAPTER TEN

The Rules Are the Rules

Standing beside Mr. Davenport in the sunlit first-floor powder room, a lanky police officer with a basso profundo voice explained to Mr. Davenport why he was going to jail. The officer used a modulated version of the basso profundo, the rich and resonant tones sounding like something you'd expect to hear coming from the stage or the pulpit. Nut brown, with a mustache, taller than Mr. Davenport by a good three inches, the officer's face was a set of lengthy features: a long wide-nostril nose and a long forehead. The brass nameplate on the cop's sky-blue blouse read, LAMPTON.

"Well, here's what we have," the hatless officer said matter-of-factly. "Neighbors on either side of your house heard you and your wife in another loud argument in the kitchen." Lampton nodded toward the adjacent room where the doorway to the backyard was standing open. "Later on, a woman screams. Out of concern, your neighbors call us. We get here and find your wife with ripped clothes, a facial contusion, a busted lip, and maybe a sprained wrist."

For the second time since Officer Lampton had walked him into the powder room to talk, Mr. Davenport said that while it was true his wife had fallen down the stairs, he had not meant to push her.

"I understand, Mr. Davenport, but as far as we're concerned, it doesn't change anything. See, if you hadn't hit her with your arm, she wouldn't have fallen. It doesn't make any difference that you didn't mean it. Your actions caused her to go down the stairs."

"But my wife isn't pressing any charges," said Mr. Davenport, and he pointed in the direction of the living room where three other officers, Lampton's partner and a female tandem from a second squad car, were talking with Mrs. Davenport and Delphina.

Lampton calmly explained that her not pressing charges didn't change anything either. "There was a time, Mr. Davenport, when if we answered a domestic situation and the couple looked like they'd settled down, and no one was bringing any charges, we could use our discretion as to whether we made an arrest, but not anymore. Nowadays, if we come and see that a woman's been injured in any way, or if a man in the home has threatened her, be it verbal or physical, the guy goes."

Mr. Davenport's face collapsed into despair and he sounded as if he were about to cry. He opened his mouth to speak but no words came out.

"I'm sure you feel it's unfair, Mr. Davenport, but those are the rules." Lampton then explained that per regulations, Mr. Davenport would have to be handcuffed. Mr. Davenport began to weep. "Not in front of my neighbors, not in front of my neighbors."

Bending over a little, Lampton spoke softly into Mr. Davenport's ear: "C'mon, now. You don't want your family or neighbors to see you this way. Stew Pot might well be out there watching, don't give him the satisfaction."

That last comment seemed to have an effect. Mr. Davenport wiped his eyes. Lampton stepped behind him and said he was going to put the handcuffs on. Mr. Davenport began breathing hard. When his hands were lightly cuffed behind his back, Officer Lampton said: "Remember, you have to stay frosty for your family." He then called to his partner. This guy was a White fellow, lanky too but not as tall, and much younger, twenty-five or so, with red hair, very pale skin, and freckles.

When the redhead arrived at the powder room, Lampton told him to stay with Mr. Davenport while he broke the news to the wife and daughter. (Mrs. Davenport and Delphina had asked the other three officers a number of times what was going to happen to Mr. Davenport, to which they had received no real answer.)

Delphina began crying when Lampton explained the situation.

"Can I bail him out?" asked Mrs. Davenport.

"Of course," said Lampton. "You come down to the station with the bail and he'll be home before lunchtime." This mollified her somewhat. Delphina came over and hugged her. Lampton went back to the powder room.

Moments later he and the redhead returned with Mr. Davenport between them. The two women officers, both with brunette ponytails and summer tans, followed.

While Delphina sobbed into her mother's chest, the quintet stepped across the shaded porch and out into the bright morning. On stoops and nearby porches, a few adults and children watched, while still more stood at a respectful distance on the sidewalks. They saw the cops lead a distressed and handcuffed Mr. Davenport to a squad car where he was guided into the backseat. With Lampton driving, the white squad car cruised up and then out of the Davenport driveway before slowly moving to the intersection. The second squad car did the same. When the cars were gone, the neighbors looked back to the Davenports' house. The orange front door was again closed.

CHAPTER ELEVEN
Game, Set, Match

Mrs. Davenport decided she did need her wrist examined, after having first turned down the police offer to call an ambulance. The subsequent hospital trip delayed her arrival at the police station with the bail money, leaving Mr. Davenport waiting in the 26th District lockup fearing that she wouldn't show.

When she finally arrived in her husband's car with her right wrist wrapped in an ACE bandage and a smaller round bandage on her left cheek, the desk sergeant, who had large ears and a small, almost girlish mouth, gave her that disdainful look cops tend to use when a woman bails out the man who hurt her. Mr. Davenport drove the short way home and found out, when they got to the house, why Mrs. D had not driven her own car.

Delphina was in the passenger's seat of Mrs. Davenport's gunmetal hatchback, the rear of the vehicle piled high with suitcases and duffel bags. Standing at the curb, Mr. Davenport made plaintive gestures with his hands, but his wife walked away shaking her head. He followed her to the driver's door of the hatchback. She slammed the door closed as he reached her open window. He shouted for her not to go and she shouted back that it was no good for Delphina (who was crying again) to be in Parkland right now.

"Just for once," she said, "can't you think of anyone but yourself?" And Mr. Davenport made a grab inside the car, maybe for the keys in the steering column, but remembering what had happened that morning, he stepped back and watched helplessly as his wife and daughter rode off. And when they were out of sight, he suddenly looked this way and that to see if anybody was watching. The only witnesses were Mrs. Powell and Mrs. Butler, the first from her screen door, the other from the sidewalk in front of her house.

Moving quickly to get away from what he knew were angry eyes, he went inside and found three messages on his answering machine.

One was from Mrs. Motley asking if there was anything she could do, and were Delphina and Mrs. Davenport all right. Another message, a long one, was from Mrs. Butler, telling him that she was calling, as was her right as a block club member, for an emergency meeting to be held at her house where she intended to present a motion that he be replaced as president. She had already spoken with a number of neighbors, and she assured him she had more than enough votes for the motion to carry. She said she also intended to place her name in nomination for president, and that she had enough votes for that too. The final message, also long, was from Mr. Coles, the ex-husband of the woman Mr. Davenport had had the affair with. Although Mr. Coles, or Dr. Coles as he insisted on being called, had left Parkland High and gone onto bigger and better things as a district superintendent, and although he had remarried (to a woman much younger than himself), he apparently still harbored some resentments. Dr. Coles informed Mr. Davenport that in light of his arrest on a battery charge, it really wasn't proper for him to be teaching impressionable teenagers; therefore, he, Dr. Coles, was notifying him informally (the written notification would be mailed by day's end) that he was suspended from all teaching duties, effective immediately. Of course, Dr. Coles went on to say, Mr. Davenport had the right to a formal hearing with the district review board, but given the board's busy schedule, such a hearing would probably not be possible until November.

Later that afternoon, Mrs. Motley and Mr. McTeer visited Mr. Davenport in his living room. Out of their worry for his saddened state, the white-haired and beak-nosed Father Vader was summoned from Seven Sorrows. It was Father who convinced Mr. Davenport to call his younger brother, who lived in New Buffalo, Michigan, and ask him to come and stay for a few days. This brother, who was clean shaven and not as stocky as Mr. Davenport, arrived that evening.

Meanwhile, at Mrs. Butler's house, a raucous block club meeting took place. Mrs. Butler's motion to remove the absent Mr. Davenport as president passed, but just barely. Her attempt to become president failed, and by more than just a few votes. Mrs. Hicks, whose name was placed in nomination by Mrs. Motley and seconded by Mr. McTeer, was the surprise compromise winner. The voting was by secret ballot and Mrs. Butler was so angry with the outcome that she demanded a recount, which she got. But it didn't change anything.

Parkland being Parkland, all sorts of wild stories were bandied about: Mr. Davenport had punched Mrs. Davenport in the nose. Delphina had *given* Stew Pot her diary because she was having an affair with him and was pregnant with his baby, which is why her momma got her out of town. Mrs. Davenport had had an affair with Dr. Coles after his ex-wife's affair with Mr. Davenport, and he dumped her, and so on and so on and so on.

It wasn't until lunchtime the next day that word made it around that Mr. Davenport had left with his brother to stay in Michigan for a while, causing some to wonder if Stew Pot would do another victory performance, this time outside the Dutch Colonial. He didn't.

BOOK V

Stew Pot vs. Mrs. Hicks

CHAPTER ONE

Christmas in July, Let Us Now Praise Unfamous Men

Mrs. Hicks was what one Parkland clergy called "a holiday Christian"—that is, a person who very much enjoys the celebratory aspects of Christmas and Easter, such as tree decorating, coloring and hunting boiled eggs, receiving presents, and parties, all while giving little if any thought to the person these observances are supposedly honoring.

Of course, if said clergy had ever made that charge to Mrs. Hicks's face, she would have happily corrected him by saying that she was in fact no Christian at all, holiday or otherwise, a perspective that was in no way a hindrance for her when it came to indulging in some of the pleasures listed above. Mrs. Hicks especially went in for Christmas-centered party giving, so much so that once a year was not enough for her. Every July, in the dead heat of summer, she decorated a tree (a white one with pastel-blue ornaments and little pink lights) and hung a string of multicolored lights around her front door, and had folks over for a big meal and gifts. The present giving was for family only, with herself as the sole buyer of goodies and her grandchildren as the only receivers, the dispensing of the wrapped gifts a task she merrily carried out while wearing a Santa hat and sipping a beer.

These July yuletides were a dream come true for Mrs. Hicks's grandkids and a bane for some immediate neighbors, who every July had to explain to their own little ones why there would be no mid-summer tree decorating or toy getting like at Mrs. Hicks's house.

With her chestnut wig slightly askew, Mrs. Hicks sat on a lawn chair with other celebrants that Sunday evening in her backyard sum-merhouse, the area bathed in the gentle glow of pink and white Italian Christmas lights strung below the slanted roof.

Sipping from the beer she had seasoned with a dash of salt, she looked on at the other adults around her, a gathering that included not only her husband, daughters, sons-in-law, and nearby neighbors—

the Powells, Mrs. Motley, and Mr. McTeer—but also her brother and sister. (There was a strong resemblance between her and her siblings: similar gingerbread coloring, broad-nose faces, and stocky bodies; the major differences were that her divorced younger sister, who still went by her maiden name of Shaw, had a full head of hair, while her widower brother had a wide white mustache.)

All the adults there had some sort of libation, Mrs. Motley again the only non–alcohol drinker with her orange juice and tonic, this one spiced with a splash of grenadine. At the moment Mrs. Hick's oldest daughter was holding forth with a story about a woman from her church. Mrs. Hicks, who had no interest in this, let her attentions drift elsewhere.

When Mrs. Motley accidentally knocked a paper napkin from her lap and into the air, Mr. McTeer, who was sitting next to her, grabbed the napkin in midair and presented it back to her in a manner Mrs. Hicks thought rather gallant. This little side-play, which the others there missed, caused Mrs. Hicks to smirk and gently shake her head, for although she had great affection for them both, she thought they were quite possibly two of the silliest folks she'd ever known.

Once, on a sunny autumn afternoon a few years before, over coffee in the yellow kitchen, Mrs. Hicks had asked Mrs. Motley straight out why she and Mr. McTeer "didn't just do it and get it over with."

Mrs. Motley had frowned and then explained that she and Mr. McTeer could never be more than friends because neither was willing to be intimate outside of marriage, and marriage for them was impossible since Mr. McTeer would only marry a woman who was Catholic and she could not see herself converting "at such a late stage in the game."

Mrs. Hicks had then asked: "And if he'd marry you *without* your having to convert?"

And Mrs. Motley had said: "What would we do on Sundays, he going off to one service and I to another? That's no sort of marriage, least not one that either of us would want. Besides, I would always know he was making a concession. I could never ask him to make such a sacrifice."

Under the pink and white lights, Mrs. Hicks took another sip of her salted beer and gazed at Mrs. Motley, taking particular notice of her white hair pulled tightly back in a bun and her slender lower legs set at a sideways angle out of the low hem of a blue skirt, the ankles crossed in ladylike fashion.

Mrs. Hicks preferred her own style of sitting, like now, with her sandaled feet planted square on the ground. As a young woman, sitting the way Mrs. Motley was sitting had caused her no amount of discomfort, but she'd done it anyway out of a reluctance to buck conventional fashion. Now that she was older and thick-bodied, she didn't care about fashion, conventional or otherwise, and she sat the way she liked and dressed the way she liked—roomy men's slacks and roomy men's shirts. She hadn't worn a dress or a slip in over twenty years and her only bow to societal expectations was her brassiere and wig.

Mrs. Hicks was happy with her existence. Her girls were all alive, plump-bodied, and healthy. None of the daughters were living at home and yet none had moved from the neighborhood, giving her easy access to her baker's dozen set of grandchildren, who were all healthy and happy too. Best of all, none of her daughters had ever come to her weeping and wailing about their husbands drinking too much, or doing drugs, or chasing other women (or other men), because her daughters had followed her example and steered clear of flashy guys with charming smiles and big ideas. They had chosen men like their father (who at the moment was sitting next to her clicking his dentures and contributing nothing to the conversation), men who were what Mrs. Hicks called "solid everyday men," the sort who were happy for a job to go to in the morning and grateful for a family to return to at night.

The skinny brown men her daughters had chosen were the sort of men a woman could depend on, the sort of men who could manage what Mrs. Hicks called "the long haul," men who were "the backbone of the race." Her pet name for her own husband was Brother Backbone, a moniker she used only when they were alone.

She glanced at him and smiled as he patted a red bandanna across his wide forehead, his body thick beneath his sleeveless white T-shirt, a roll of waist hanging over his belt.

Mrs. Hicks placed a hand to her mouth to cover a light belch while her middle daughter reminded her oldest daughter that the woman from church she was talking about had once had a crush on Mrs. Motley's son in grade school, the girl showing her affection by chasing him around the schoolyard and hitting him in the head with a rock.

The oldest daughter laughed and said she'd forgotten all about that, and off she went, relating her own version of the event. She had a thick head of hair held back with a blue plastic headband, and with one of her plump arms she demonstrated how the pigtailed girl, who was now one of the somber pillars of her church, had reared back in preparation for tossing the rock. Mrs. Motley laughed along with the others over there, and as the young woman kept talking and talking, Mrs. Hicks observed that her oldest daughter (who had surprised everyone in the family by becoming a Christian and a member of Hill of the Lord, the neighborhood's most hard-line church) still had not learned how to let anybody else get a word in edgewise.

Ten minutes later, the oldest daughter was still going strong when her youngest son, a bespectacled seven-year-old named LeShawn, came rushing around the corner of the house and up to the screen door calling: "Grandma! Grandma! Come look!"

"What is it, child?" asked Mrs. Hicks.

The boy pointed in the direction of the gate and said: "Stew Pot and his mother are out front kneeling in the street!"

CHAPTER TWO
A Most Unwelcome Intervention

After making the short trip down the walkway alongside the house to the front yard, the adults saw that LeShawn wasn't exaggerating. Stew Pot and Mrs. Reeves were kneeling in the middle of the street and directly in front of the Hicks's home, with heads down, eyes closed, and hands clasped chest-high in obvious prayer. Exactly what the prayer was, no one in the front yard could make out because the two kneelers were speaking softly.

Mrs. Hicks's sons-in-law ordered the children, who were now grouped at various points along the sidewalk, to go to their grandparents' backyard. "Right now!" The kids did so, glancing over their shoulders as they filed away with their toy trucks and dolls and battery-operated cars.

On a couple of porches on either side of the street, other neighbors were out watching. One of these folks in the distance called out that the police had been summoned.

Not knowing exactly what else to do, folks stared at Stew Pot, who had Mrs. Motley's Bible under one arm, and Mrs. Reeves as they continued. The pair's lips moved and their heads lightly bobbed. Then they heard Stew Pot exclaim: "Amen!"

He and his mom opened their eyes and stood up.

Mrs. Hicks, no doubt feeling the effect of the three beers she'd consumed, asked: "What do you all call yourself doing now?"

Stew Pot dusted off the knee areas of his overalls. "My mother and I were praying for God to not punish those innocent children for your blasphemy."

This produced, as one might expect, a number of angry responses from the children's parents, and Mrs. Hicks's middle daughter had to grab hold of her husband's arm to keep him from stepping toward the street.

Placing her hands on her hips, Mrs. Hicks said: "What are you talking about, fool?"

Stew Pot pointed toward the Cape Cod where a multicolored string of lights was arranged around the pink door and the white tree was aglow in the picture window.

"In case you haven't heard," declared Stew Pot, "Christmas is on December 25th, not July 25th. How dare you celebrate the Savior's birthday out of order."

Mrs. Hicks heard someone behind her, it sounded like her brother, shout: "What difference is it to you? Mind your own business!"

Mrs. Reeves, wearing another of her ankle-length dresses, a brown one that matched the scarf on her head, kept shifting her eyes with trepidation between her son and the group in the Hicks's front yard. Paying her worries no heed, Stew Pot continued.

"When I see my Savior disrespected during December month with the sort of gaudy pagan trappings of lights and trees and tinsel that folks like so much, that's bad enough. But to see such cheap and tawdry display done out of the calendar's chronological order, as if the birthday of Christ the King is like Mardi Gras or Saint Patrick's Day, some debauchery that can be celebrated anytime folks want to, well, that's just too much."

The ensuing retorts from the front yard were cut short by the sight of a squad car, its blue lights flashing, moving in their direction at a moderate speed.

Mrs. Reeves grasped her son's arm and took a step as if to begin a retreat, but Stew Pot held his ground, giving her hand a reassuring pat.

The cops got out of the car. It was Officer Jarper and her partner, the same cops who had come to the block the night of Delphina Davenport's party.

Standing by the open door of her car, Jarper gestured with a raised hand for Stew Pot to step over. He did so, leaving his mom, who began nervously rubbing her hands.

Jarper had to look up at him, as Stew Pot was a good deal taller, but the way she held her body, square-shouldered, the way she tilted her head slightly to the side with a slight squint, made her appear somehow not so short.

"What are you and your mother doing in the street?"

"We were praying because—"

Jarper cut him off by making a T formation with her hands. Stew

Pot shut up. Then she pointed a forefinger at him. "From here on, you keep your praying out of the street."

"Officer, I have the right—"

"Not in the street, you don't. Now we talked about this once before. You want to give me a reason to run you? Go on ahead, give me one."

Stew Pot mashed his lips and said nothing.

Jarper told him to go home. She and her partner, along with the other onlookers, watched Stew Pot touch his mother lightly at her elbow and walk her back to the two-flat.

When the door closed behind them, Jarper walked to the parkway in front of the Hicks's house. Her shorter partner joined her. Jarper asked who lived there and Mr. and Mrs. Hicks stepped forward to the curb. Jarper asked what had happened and husband and wife began speaking at once. Jarper raised a hand palms-up and said: "One at a time."

Mr. Hicks let his wife speak. With alternate pointing between the two-flat and the front of her house, she explained what had occurred.

"Okay," said Jarper when Mrs. Hicks was done, "I see your point. But here's my advice to you: leave Stew Pot be. Every time one of you all starts in with him, one of you gets hurt. Don't rise to his bait. Unless he's doing something criminal, leave him alone. I'll tell you what my momma used to tell me about dealing with folks like him: *Never argue with a fool, 'cause a fool don't know the difference.*"

CHAPTER THREE
Lights Out

Around six the next morning, the day already sunny and humid, a wigless and robed Mrs. Hicks came to her front door to retrieve her newspaper. That's when she discovered that a dozen or so of the outdoor Christmas lights were broken, the shards scattered around and under the folded paper. Careful not to step her bare feet past the threshold, she held the screen door open with one hand, bent over, and lifted a sheared piece from the ground. She grasped it gingerly, the way you might do with a flower petal. She then inspected the piece closely, the green side in contrast with the white-coated inner side.

She looked back at the low step, and something else caught her eye, something shiny. She bent over again and picked this item up. It was a pellet, copper and round. She straightened and rolled the thing between thumb and forefinger. It was a BB pellet. She looked down, and upon closer inspection noticed among the other shards another pellet, and another, and another, and another.

Mrs. Hicks gazed angrily up and down the street, as if the culprit might be somewhere in sight. The final home her eyes rested on was the two-flat, and with her mouth in a grimace, she stepped inside.

She immediately awakened her husband. It took her nearly a minute to make it clear to a groggy Mr. Hicks what had happened. He threw on his robe and came downstairs. While he was at the door, Mrs. Hicks got on the living room phone and called Mrs. Motley, who phoned Mr. McTeer, who phoned another neighbor.

Before ten of seven, everyone on the east end had been notified. There was absolutely no doubt in any of their minds as to the identity of the shooter, although no one had actually seen Stew Pot with BB gun in hand, which is what Mrs. Hicks was forced to tell the police when they arrived around seven fifteen in response to her six thirty call.

By then Mrs. Reeves had left for her job and Mrs. Hicks and her husband were washed and dressed for work, she wearing a chestnut wig. (Although the regular school year was over, the grade school was still open for the summer term.) The couple met the officers on the front walkway, exiting the house via the side doorway so as not to disturb the evidence on the front step. Next door Mr. McTeer was standing on his stoop, and across the street Mrs. Motley was there on her front porch.

The officers answering the call were the same two who had been the first to arrive at the Davenports'. While his red-haired partner stood quietly by, Officer Lampton, in his basso profundo loud enough for Mr. McTeer to hear, explained to Mrs. and Mr. Hicks that since no one had seen Stew Pot do anything, there wasn't much that the police could do. When Mrs. Hicks asked about searching the two-flat to see if there was a BB gun anywhere about, Officer Lampton said Stew Pot possessing such a device, which was not considered a firearm, was not enough to link him to the crime. There were no ballistic tests for BB guns, Lampton said, which meant there was no way to prove for sure what air gun had actually fired the pellets.

"We'll go have a talk with him," said Lampton, and the two cops set off across the street.

Mr. and Mrs. Hicks went back inside their house where they peered through the picture window, hoping, hoping, hoping that something dramatic might occur at the two-flat's front door that would end with Stew Pot being led away in handcuffs.

They saw Stew Pot answer the door, dressed in his T-shirt and overalls. As the conversation transpired, their emotions moved from hope to puzzlement to consternation. From the manner of Lampton's easygoing hand gestures, the interview did not appear to be particularly harsh; in fact, from where the Hicks's were standing, it looked downright friendly. At one point they saw Lampton turn to his partner and, smiling, say something that caused the red-haired younger man to laugh. Finally, they saw Lampton pat Stew Pot gently on the shoulder before turning from the two-flat with a cheerful wave of the hand.

When the cops reached the curb, a gray sedan pulled to a stop in front of the Hicks's place. Two cops in plainclothes—blue jeans and sneakers, white T-shirts beneath black bulletproof vests—stepped out. These two guys were Black, the driver a tall ginger-colored fellow as large as Stew Pot who had small round ears that stuck out noticeably from his block of a head. The four officers met on Mrs. Motley's parkway where they conversed for a bit, Lampton and his partner still all easygoing, the two tactical officers squinting and looking angry.

When the confab broke up, Lampton and his partner returned to their squad car, which was parked in Mr. McTeer's driveway. The plainclothes men went back to the sedan, made a U-turn at the embankment wall, and headed west. The squad car followed.

CHAPTER FOUR

Mrs. Motley Reports

t was a furious Mrs. Hicks, with her husband watching from inside the screen door, who swept the shards and pellets into a dust pan. Mr. McTeer and Mrs. Motley came over from their respective perches, he in a blue dress shirt, black bow tie, and gray slacks, she outfitted in a white cotton summer dress with a pale green flower print. Pausing to lean on the handle of the upturned straw broom, Mrs. Hicks let her friends know just how she felt.

"You want to tell me what that was all about?" she said, gesturing with a fist at the two-flat. "Stew Pot attacks my home and all the cops do is stroll over and have a friendly chat?"

"I don't know about that," said Mrs. Motley. "It may have looked that way, but it sure didn't sound friendly from where I was standing."

This was met with curious looks all around. Mrs. Motley answered by saying that from her porch, she had heard Officer Lampton's deep voice clear as day when he told Stew Pot that he knew it was he, Stew Pot, who was responsible for shooting out the Christmas lights, just like he knew it was he who had broken into the Davenports' house. And although he couldn't prove either transgression, Lampton was not worried, because he knew that sooner or later the police were going to catch Stew Pot for something. Because sooner or later, Lampton said, he was going to make a mistake—a zig when he should zag, a bob when he should weave—and then they'd get him.

"You can't beat the long arm of the law of averages," Lampton had said, smiling. "I know you, Stew Pot. You just like messing with folks. The only difference between now and before you went to prison is that now you're messing with folks in the name of God.

"You can't help yourself," Lampton had continued jovially. "You have to mess with people. It's just in you. It's just who you are."

"With all due respect, *officer*," said Stew Pot, "the only thing in me is the Holy—"

"Quiet now," Lampton interrupted calmly. He then returned to being jovial. "As I said, it's in you. You'll keep messing, eventually make a mistake and we'll get you. I can see it like a flatland farmer can see an approaching storm on the horizon.

"Oh yeah, you're definitely going back to prison. And when you do, you can hang out again with all your—*boyfriends*. And don't even try to tell me you didn't have a few." (It was at this point that the red-haired cop laughed.) "I bet when you first went inside, back when you were all slender and beardless, with no gang affiliation for protection, they must have been fighting each other to see who got the first crack at you. Of course, now that you're all buff and everything, maybe this time you'll get to be the punker right from the start, instead of being the punkee.

"Well, you have a good day there, Stew Pot, and remember—we're always watching."

When Mrs. Motley finished her account of Lampton's monologue, Mrs. Hicks was somewhat mollified. Mr. Hicks asked through the screen door what had transpired on her parkway. Mrs. Motley explained that the taller of the two plainclothes had said, while nodding at the two-flat: "I want me a piece of that chicken. And I'm going to get it too."

Mr. McTeer then asked if the big plainclothes copper was one of the Mance boys. And Mrs. Motley said yes, and Mrs. Hicks said she thought she had recognized him.

The Mance family was another Parkland legend. For the generation now in their thirties and forties (several who'd been Mrs. Motley's students), there had never seemed to be any middle ground. Three Mances were cops, two with the state and this one with the city. Another Mance was in Stateville doing a life sentence, with another doing fifteen-to-twenty in a federal pen out west. There was a Reverend Mance in Milwaukee and a couple of drug-addicted Mances who had wandered off to parts unknown.

The Mance they had seen that morning had a reputation around Parkland as a hard case. (He had been a three-letter man at Parkland High School.) Most cops did not want to pull duty in the neighborhoods where they were raised (unless there had been some radical shift in the area's demographics) because it ran the risk that one day or night they might have to arrest someone who had been a childhood pal, or a former teacher, or former love interest, or whatever. This Mance did not seem to have a problem in that regard. Over the seven years he'd been patrolling the area, he'd arrested, with no apparent remorse, a number of folks he'd been on friendly terms with as a kid.

On the low step in front of Mrs. Hicks's house, Mr. McTeer said that if Mance had Stew Pot in his crosshairs, then Stew Pot had better watch out. And Mrs. Hicks added: "We can only hope they take care of him soon. But I'm still mad about my lights, real mad."

Sounding concerned, Mrs. Motley asked Mrs. Hicks what she intended to do.

"Don't know," answered Mrs. Hicks, "but I'll think of something. I'm going to think on it good and hard."

CHAPTER FIVE

'Tis the Season to be Jolly

And think Mrs. Hicks did. Earlier she had called the grade school to say she would not be in that day. After dumping the shards and pellets in the trash can, she and Pinky walked Mr. Hicks all the way to his shop. When she got home later that morning she still had not come up with what she thought was a suitable response to Stew Pot. In the summerhouse, she took off her wig and sat bareheaded with a cup of coffee, staring off into space in an attempt to come up with a plan.

As so often happens in such situations, the right idea came when the mind was not consciously searching. It was midday and Mrs. Hicks was in the kitchen making a sandwich when all of a sudden the solution came to her.

She made phone calls to all her daughters and by late afternoon they and the sons-in-law, per her instructions, had arrived with all the necessary supplies. They immediately set to work, and the rest of that afternoon and early evening the brick Cape Cod was a frenzy of activity. They had pizza delivered and worked through supper, and the whole time they joked and chortled as neighbors looked on, some of them joking and chortling too when they saw what Mrs. Hicks and her family were up to. And when Mrs. Reeves arrived home from work around six and stopped stock still in front of Mrs. Motley's house and stared across the street with another look of trepidation, a number of people laughed. (Mrs. Motley and Mr. McTeer were not among them.) And when Mrs. Reeves went inside and moments later returned with Stew Pot, who stood in the doorway glaring at one and all, they laughed some more, with a few even letting loose with hoots and hollers after Stew Pot slammed the door.

Later that evening, when the sun was close to setting, Officer Jarper and her partner, on routine patrol, just happened to be rolling south on Honore. As they passed 129th Street, something caught Jarper's eye.

She stopped the squad car, backed up, turned left, and drove toward the railroad embankment.

When the squad car arrived at the Hicks's Cape Cod, Jarper and her partner got out, though neither moved from the car. The entire front of the Hicks's home—yard as well as house—was festooned and crowded with all manner of lighted Christmas decoration. It was like those houses featured on TV during the holiday season where homeowners trick-out their homes: lights upon lights upon lights that cast a multicolored glow across the immediate surroundings.

The strings of lights affixed to the brick walls of the Hicks house seemed to be crisscrossed almost as thickly as the ivy vines on Mr. McTeer's home. The lawn featured two illuminated manger displays, three standing Santas, two Santas in sleighs pulled by reindeer, and more lights strung like rows of barbed wire.

Sitting in lawn chairs by the low front step and wearing sunglasses were Mr. and Mrs. Hicks, who acknowledged the officers with a nod and a raise of their beer cans.

Jarper stepped toward the curb. She gave the house a good once-over; the colored lights reflecting off her silver badge, as they did off the windows and the white sides of the squad car.

Smiling, Mrs. Hicks called out cheerfully: "What do you think?"

Jarper nodded her head slowly. "I see you decided to take my advice."

Mrs. Hicks laughed and said: "It took us a good while to get them all up, but it was worth it. Let's see Stew Pot shoot out all these lights. If he does, he'll be at it all night."

That's when Jarper's partner called from the car: "Check this out."

Jarper turned around to see Mr. Glenn, Reggie, and four other residents of the block approaching on the other side of the street. Despite the heat they were wearing Santa hats and wool scarves and toting sheet music. The group stopped in front of Mrs. Motley's house and gathered together, with Mr. Glenn facing them and holding a pitch pipe.

Jarper shot Mrs. Hicks a curious look and Mrs. Hicks answered by saying that she had suggested to Mr. Glenn that some appropriate music was in order.

Jarper glanced at the group in front of Mrs. Motley's, then back at Mrs. Hicks.

"I sure hope you know what you're doing," Jarper said.

And with that she returned to the squad car. When she reached the door she shot her partner a rueful expression over the top of the car. Her partner shrugged and then the two women got back inside. Jarper made a U-turn at the railroad embankment, while on the sidewalk Mr. Glenn blew on the pitch pipe. And as the squad car headed back west the officers heard the singers as they started up:

Deck the halls with boughs of holly.
Fa-la-la-la-lah, la-la-la-la.

CHAPTER SIX

Hail, Hail, the Gang's All Here

The next morning, when Mrs. Hicks went to get her paper, she was not greeted by the sight of any glass shards or pellets at her front door. However, Stew Pot did make his feelings known. He had obviously been watching in wait, and when Mrs. Hicks stepped out, again wigless and robed, he came out of his doorway and down his walkway.

"I know you think you've insulted me with all your—decorations!" he shouted from across the street. "But you haven't insulted me. Like most disbelievers, you think that when you mock the Lord's way you're mocking the faithful. But you're not! You're just mocking God. And God don't like being mocked."

Mrs. Hicks, standing behind her mob of decorations that cast shadows across the grass, greatly enjoyed hearing his anger, since it proved that she had succeeded in getting under his skin. Smiling, she called back: "And a sweet good morning to you."

For the next couple of weeks nothing of any note happened. Mrs. Hicks, feeling she had made her point, took down the decorations. Not surprisingly, this did not mollify Stew Pot, who gave her hard looks whenever they encountered each other. (It was now Mrs. Motley warning Mrs. Hicks to be careful with Stew Pot.) Then, on the second Saturday in August she, Mrs. Hicks, had the honor, as block president, to lead the 129th Street and Honore contingent in the annual Parkland Founder's Day Parade.

A few words need to be said about this, because the Founder's Day Parade was a sore point with a number of other Blacks in the city. The second Saturday in August was also the date of the annual Bud Billiken Day Parade. Started in 1929, the event was a joint creation of the founder of the *Chicago Defender* newspaper and the paper's managing editor. (Back then the *Defender* was arguably the most influential African-American publication in the country.) Referred to by some as the nation's oldest such parade, it traveled for a mile-plus, from 39th Street to 51st, on a South Side avenue that had once been South Parkway and after 1968 was renamed Martin Luther King Drive.

Back in the days when Blacks from the city's established inner areas derisively called Parkland "the country," most of them had not cared that Parkland held its own little to-do on August's second Saturday. However, since the neighborhood had grown in affluence and prestige, Blacks from other parts of town came to see Parkland's insistence on continuing to hold its celebration the same day as Bud Billiken as proof positive of Parkland's snobbery. And as if that weren't bad enough, Parkland people insisted that *their* parade had first been held in 1898 (a church band of two trumpets and a trombone providing musical accompaniment for three dozen marchers), which meant that Parkland Founders' Day was in fact, the oldest such African-American celebration of its kind.

Parade day of '93 was sunny, but not too hot. Folks lined the sidewalk on the southern side of the drag, three deep in some spots, while a few groups of neighborhood teenagers watched from perches on the guardrail across the way on the forest preserve side.

The parade featured the Parkland High School marching band. Resplendent in their navy-blue and maize uniforms with old-fashioned white spats, the band fancy-stepped down the road with their polished brass horns gleaming. There was a float carrying Miss Parkland, a dark and lovely teenager, surrounded at lower seating by her court. There were clowns on tricycles, and men and women on horseback, members of the Parkland Cowpokes Club who sported cornball Hollywood versions of Old West outfits: shirts with rhinestones, hand-stitched boots, and ten-gallon hats. There was the Tuskegee Airmen's Club which arranged private airplane rides for kids and the Parkland VFW, which included Mr. McTeer, the old lions carrying flags and wearing black campaign hats.

There were floats sponsored by the neighborhood's larger churches—Seven Sorrows, Parkland First Baptist, and Allen A.M.E. People representing smaller churches like Wesley-Allen and Hill of the Lord made their way on foot. Mrs. Motley and the other seniors from her church were the last such group to pass in review, the dozen of them walking abreast and carrying a waist-high banner that read: *THE OLD GUARD.*

As always, Vernon Paiger was there, riding in the backseat of a white convertible, the bald top of his peanut-colored head gleaming, his owlish eyebrows scrunched low over his sunglass-covered eyes.

However, the absolute hit of the parade, everyone agreed later, was the 129th and Honore group. Like every year for the past ten, they wore period costumes tracing the years from Parkland's inception to the 1970s. But this time, in addition to that, they rode in vehicles to match the era of their costumes. The folks in bonnets and straw hats and calico dresses and overalls came in a horse-drawn wagon, the folks in early-twentieth-century clothes rode in a Ford Model T (pulled by a modern vehicle), the folks in Roaring '20s gear rode in a boxy vintage sedan, and so on and so on, right up to Mr. Glenn driving a pale green Gremlin and wearing disco clothes. (The block club had him to thank for the vintage vehicles, which he'd arranged through contacts he'd made from years of working car repair and attending antique auto shows.) All in all, it was a very good day for the 129ers. Until they returned home, that is.

CHAPTER SEVEN

Sign o' the Times

To make sure that Stew Pot didn't try to pull anything while everybody was away at the parade, a number of residents from the block had arranged for a relative or friend to stand guard and keep an eye out.

This had been Mrs. Hicks's idea. She had not wanted her fun at the parade to be spoiled by worrying about Stew Pot. She had left her brother, the white-mustachioed Mr. Shaw, on duty at the Cape Cod with orders to position himself in the living room while Pinky, a dependable barker at the first sign of trouble, kept watch out back.

This was in the days before everybody and his brother had a cell phone, so it wasn't until residents of the block returned home in the late afternoon that they found out about what had occurred in their absence.

It was Mr. McTeer who noticed it first. Mrs. Motley pulled her car into his driveway to drop him off, along with Mr. and Mrs. Hicks. After he exited the front passenger's seat, Mr. McTeer glanced over at the two-flat. Something there caught his eye, a large square over the front door. It had something written on it in black, but from that distance he couldn't make it out.

"What's that?" he said, pointing.

Mrs. Hicks, exiting from the backseat on his side, followed the direction of his arm. "It looks like some kind of sign," she said.

Moments later the four were standing in front of the two-flat. Set above the front door was a wooden square (five-by-five was Mr. McTeer's estimate of the footage), its white-painted surface carrying a black print message:

LET ALL WHO PASS OR ENTER THIS HOME BE INFORMED THAT THIS IS A <u>CHRISTIAN HOME</u> AND THAT THOSE WHO RESIDE HERE STRIVE NOT ONLY TO WALK IN THE LIGHT <u>EVERY DAY</u>, BUT

*ALSO TAKE AS THEIR LIFELONG DUTY THE RESPONSIBILITY TO
PREACH THE LORD'S WORD AND SPREAD HIS SACRED MESSAGE
INTO EVERY CORNER OF DARKNESS—NO MATTER WHERE IT
MAY BE, NO MATTER WHOM IT MAY OFFEND—FOR THE TRUTH
IS THE LIGHT, THE ONLY PATH IS THE LIGHT.*

—Brother G.X. Reeves, Counselor

Before any could respond, Mr. Shaw called out to them. They turned to see him walking quickly in their direction. "You see that?" he said. "You see it?"

When he reached them he told how earlier that afternoon he had been in the living room watching the ball game when he heard a loud pounding. "I went to the picture window and there was Stew Pot, up on a ladder and swinging a silver hammer. He must have used those big nails they make for hammering into cement."

The other four now noticed the dark circles of the nail heads, one in each corner of the sign.

"I waited until I saw him and his momma leave before I came over to read it," Mr. Shaw continued. "That was around three o'clock. I haven't seen them since." Then gazing at the sign again, he added: "Disturbing, isn't it?"

"I'll say," said Mr. McTeer. "Not so much by what it says, as by its tone."

"I agree," said Mrs. Motley. "The tone is very confrontational."

"Like a declaration of war," Mr. McTeer observed, "only without a stated enemy."

"Right," said Mrs. Motley, "which means his enemy could be anybody."

By early evening everyone on the block knew of "Stew Pot's sign," as it immediately came to be called. Neither he nor his mom had returned home by then and a number of people walked over to read the sign for themselves. Afterward they gathered in small groups across the street or down the way to discuss what this might mean. A few folks including Mr. Glenn and Reggie found the sign amusing, but most people's reaction was similar to that of Mrs. Motley and Mr. McTeer.

"Sounds to me like Stew Pot plans to spring something on us, something big," said Mrs. Powell as she stood at the street end of

Mr. McTeer's driveway with he and a few others. It was then that Mr. Hicks saw Stew Pot and Mrs. Reeves coming up their backyard walkway from the alley. Before anyone could do anything they were inside, but only minutes later they reappeared at their front doorway. Stew Pot took a step out, then pointed up at his sign with a triumphant look on his face.

Mrs. Hicks glared at him. Stew Pot proceeded to do the same and the two stood like that for some seconds, looking like a parody of movie gunslingers facing off on the main street of some Wild West town. The standoff was ended by Stew Pot returning inside with a sneer before locking his door.

Appearing triumphant herself, Mrs. Hicks turned back to the others. "Guess I showed him." And again Mrs. Powell said she thought Stew Pot was planning something big, and this time Mrs. Hicks replied that if Stew Pot tried catching them by surprise, it would not last long, "because I plan to keep an eagle eye on him."

CHAPTER EIGHT

Nearly Captured By the Game

The following Monday, Mrs. Motley, Mr. McTeer, and the Powells left for their annual vacation to Michigan, where the Powells had a lakeside summerhouse. As for Mrs. Hicks, with summer school finished, she could now monitor things across the street full time.

She made frequent peeks from behind pulled shades, but saw nothing unusual until that Wednesday afternoon. The roller-coaster that is summertime Chicago-area weather had by then shifted to sweltering, the sort of heat and humidity that cause weather forecasters to warn people about not tanning or exerting themselves outside, the sort of heat that keeps folks off the street and outdoor basketball courts as empty as in midwinter.

Around two that afternoon a large pickup truck pulled to a stop in front of the two-flat. The truck was white and had *MENO'S NURSERY & LANDSCAPING* printed in large green letters across the side doors of the cab. Two White fellows in dark T-shirts and jeans got out. Despite the deserted scene, both of these guys looked around cautiously, as if any second they expected to be ambushed by enemy forces lying in wait.

The driver, flat-faced and wrinkled with a potbelly sagging over his jeans, glanced at a yellow sheet of paper he held in his hand and pointed at the two-flat. He walked around the front of the truck and toward the building. His partner, who was much shorter and thinner with a Roman nose, followed close behind; the guy continuing to anxiously check the immediate area.

Across the street a wigless Mrs. Hicks stood at her living room picture window behind the slightly parted curtain. The address written on the door below the name of the landscaping business was from somewhere in nearby Beverly, and she chalked these anxious fellows up as White people who viewed venturing into Parkland a dangerous mission.

Mrs. Hicks sneered at the sight of this. With a Black-owned land-scaping businesses in Parkland, and another in Morgan Park, she saw no reason why Stew Pot should be hiring White folks.

Because of the two men's dark hair and tanned skin, Mrs. Hicks would have pegged them for Italians even without the name on the truck. The guy with the yellow sheet rang the doorbell and moments later there was Stew Pot standing in the doorway. For the first time she saw him in white painter overalls, which made his body seem even darker than before.

After a brief conversation Stew Pot went back inside, leaving the doorway open. The two White men returned to the rear of the truck and let down the flatbed door. They began taking out pots of plants. All of the flowers were white, and even from that distance Mrs. Hicks recognized them as begonias.

The driver pulled two shovels off the back off the truck and the other guy grabbed a small rusted wheelbarrow. After pulling on black-ened work gloves the men began digging in the narrow rectangular yard in front of the two-flat.

Although it took them only about twenty minutes to plant the flowers, and though they were in the shade cast by the building, be-cause of the intense heat and humidity, their faces and arms were shiny with perspiration when they were done.

Mrs. Hicks watched the entire time. From her first-floor vantage point she could see that the flowers were arranged in some sort of pat-tern, but she couldn't tell exactly what.

The older of the two landscapers rang the doorbell again and Stew Pot soon appeared, this time with his dog. The men took a step back from the door and Stew Pot and John the Baptist moved forward. With one hand grasping the leash, Stew Pot looked down at the planted flowers. The two White men stood to his right, alternating their gaze between Stew Pot and the dog. After a bit of this, Stew Pot nodded his head and pointed at the two-flat. Mrs. Hicks saw the older fellow nod his head and then Stew Pot and the dog went back inside.

The door closed and the two men went back to the truck, the driver looking perturbed and the younger guy looking downright an-gry. They got in the truck, and after a slow U-turn at the embankment, headed back down the street.

Something told Mrs. Hicks to stay put, and after a couple of minutes her hunch paid off. The front door of the two-flat opened and out stepped Stew Pot and the dog again. This time he headed off down the street and out of her sight.

Letting the curtain fall again, Mrs. Hicks stood pondering what to make of this. Stew Pot having flowers planted? Eager to get a close look, she put on her black wig, leashed up Pinky, and left the house.

As she reached the two-flat, up on the railroad embankment an Amtrak train flew by in a silvery blur. She took no notice of it, so transfixed was she by what she saw in the front yard. There, in stark white contrast to the rich green of the surrounding grass, were three flower beds, each shaped like a cross. The parts of the beds representing the upright sections of the crosses were about three feet long, with the traverse sections about half that length. The beds were set in an arched arrangement, the center cross a bit higher than the ones on either side. Even the nonbelieving Mrs. Hicks saw the arrangement of crosses as a reference to Mount Calvary, and the recognition caused her shoulders to give a single but definite shudder.

Mrs. Hicks could not have told you why the flower bed crosses made her feel such dread, or why she stood there watching for nearly half a minute before she was overcome by the thought that Stew Pot was watching her.

Her head snapped upward and she scanned the front windows of the two-flat, top and bottom, but she didn't see anyone. She looked at the front door, no one there either. Relieved, her attention was taken by the sound of men's voices. With the poodle at her side she stepped toward Mrs. Motley's house and peered down the gangway. The space was wide enough for her to make out part of the cab of the nursery truck in the alley behind the two-flat. So the men hadn't gone, after all! Now they were working in Stew Pot's backyard. But working at what?

From her position at that end of the gangway, all she could see was the backyard walkway and anything in the alley directly in line with it. She thought about just opening the gangway gate, walking down there, and having a look. But how would she explain her presence to the two Italians? And what if they told Stew Pot when he returned?

Mrs. Hicks very much wanted to know what was going on in that backyard, but she didn't want Stew Pot to know she had found it out. She thought about sneaking down Mrs. Motley's walkway on the west side of the house, but then just as quickly she decided against that idea. Because of the position of Mrs. Motley's back deck, Mrs. Hicks knew she'd have to walk all the way into the yard to get a good look at Stew Pot's yard, and the men would be sure to see her. She could always lie and say that she lived there, but again she worried that the men might tell Stew Pot about her when he returned—after all, they were White men, and to her mind there was no telling what they might or might not do, especially nervous types like these fellows. If they told Stew Pot some woman had come looking from the backyard next door, Stew Pot would be sure to ask for a description since he knew Mrs. Motley was away from home. Worse yet, what if Stew Pot came back and caught her spying, in either the walkway or Mrs. Motley's yard?

Mrs. Hicks wiped a hand across her already wet brow. Her only option, as she saw it, was to walk to the end of the block and then back down the alley. Having the men see her in the alley or having Stew Pot catch sight of her in the alley was, to her mind, much different than him catching her in Mrs. Motley's yard. The alley was public property and therefore a perfectly legitimate place to be walking one's dog.

Mrs. Hicks glanced at her wristwatch. Stew Pot's dog walks usually took at least an hour, but in this heat he might cut it short. Giving the leash a light tug, she and Pinky headed down the block.

When she reached the mouth of the alley behind Mr. Glenn's house, she paused and tried to look nonchalant as she peered down the shaded narrow lane. The landscaping truck was at the other end. The two men were nowhere in sight.

She gave the leash another light tug and stepped off. The closer Mrs. Hicks and her dog got to Stew Pot's yard, the more apprehensive she became, and she attempted to buck herself up by scolding herself for being a fraidy cat.

When she reached the apron of Mrs. Motley's closed garage, the smell of fresh earth coming from the pots of plants in the truck bed competed with the faint stench coming from nearby garbage cans. Mrs. Hicks stopped at the corner of the garage and held tightly to her poodle's leash as she listened to the voices coming from the Reeves's yard.

"What'd I tell ya? Didn't I say this job was gonna be something goofed up?" From the higher tone of the voice she assumed this was the younger man talking.

"Quit whining, okay?" a deeper voice said. "Sooner we're done, sooner we leave."

"Goof job," the first man muttered.

"You wanna keep it down? He might be in the house listening."

"Like I care. I ain't afraid of him—or that mutt."

"Surrrre you're not. And I guess that look of stark-raving terror I saw on your face when that front door opened and he walked out with that monster was my imagination."

"Whatever. First crosses on the front yard and now this."

"Like I said, quit whining."

"I hear ya, I hear ya. Tell you what, though, the next time the old man accepts a job for Boog-aloo-ville, he can come and do it himself."

The men's words incensed Mrs. Hicks, her desire to see what they were doing momentarily forgotten in the heat of a stronger desire to march over to Stew Pot's back gate and give those two what for. Boog-aloo-ville indeed!

Just then her poodle let out a yelp. She straightened with a start and snatched a look at the yard, realizing the men must surely have heard the sound. Her dog, which had been facing Stew Pot's place, was now turned around in the opposite direction. Mrs. Hicks looked back over her shoulder and felt her gut tighten as she saw Stew Pot and his dog coming fast down the alley.

The pair was halfway there when the pit bull bolted forward, pulling the leash taut. Stew Pot had to plant his feet and yank the dog backward.

Pinky, in what some might call an act of foolish defiance, began to yelp as if warning the larger dog to back off. It lurched forward and Mrs. Hicks nearly lost her balance before she was able to plant her own feet and tug her little animal back. This excited Stew Pot's dog all the more and it began barking and jerking about, rising up off its front paws.

Stew Pot stood behind looking like somebody engaged in a tug-of-war. Mrs. Hicks had a much easier time controlling her pet, pulling it close to her as it continued yelping. She picked the tiny dog up in the crook of her right arm, admonishing it to "shush." She had to look down to do this, and when she glanced back up, she saw that Stew

Pot was slowly letting his dog get closer while he took short steps behind it.

Her mind raced for a way to escape. Behind her was the railroad embankment. She didn't want to go into the yard with the two White men and she knew Mrs. Motley kept her back gate locked.

She sensed movement behind her and she turned back and saw the two White men standing at the Reeves's back gate. They both had red bandannas tied around their heads and their black T-shirts were soaked with perspiration. She had no idea how long they had been there. Their eyes met hers, but only momentarily before they gazed past her, which in turn brought her eyes back to Stew Pot and his dog. The two were closing fast, the pit bull barking and Stew Pot's right arm shaking as if any second he was going to lose control and let the leash go.

That's when Mrs. Hicks noticed the gate of the yard across from Mrs. Motley's garage. It had a low chain-link like the two-flat with no lock on the latch. With her barking poodle still under her arm, she stepped over, opened the gate, and went into the yard, the hinges squealing as she pushed it closed. She reset the latch, and with the defiant poodle warm against her side, she quick-stepped down the back walkway of the Georgian. When she reached the gate at the other end of the yard, she began to panic because she could tell from the sound of the barking that Stew Pot's dog was now directly behind her in the alley.

Trying to keep her yelping poodle under control with her right arm, she fumbled at this gate latch with her left hand. Any second now she expected to hear the hinges of the back gate squeal, followed by the sound of the pit bull's nails clicking rapidly across the walkway. She finally managed to undo the latch and stepped through, then reset the gate. Looking down the walkway she saw that Stew Pot was still in the alley, his dog looking as if it were trying to leap over the gate. She also saw that the two White men had retreated to the cab of the truck.

With his wide smile showing white in his dark face, Stew Pot shouted to her cheerfully over his dog's racket: "Where you going, Mrs. Hicks? Anything I can do for you? Can I *help* you with something? No need to rush off. John isn't going hurt you." And then Stew Pot yelled: "In Jesus' name!" And just like that, the dog immediately calmed down. It stood without a sound at Stew Pot's side, the leash slack. "Hallelujah!" he called out, and the dog sat on its haunches as if he'd said, Sit.

Seeing the actual control Stew Pot had over his dog infuriated Mrs. Hicks. A warm sensation washed over her heated face and rivulets of perspiration stung her eyes. She drew her free hand across her wet nose and wiped her palm on a pants leg.

"John the Baptist isn't going to hurt no one," Stew Pot said, still smiling. "You don't have to walk all the way around the block. Come on back through the alley."

Caught between the urge to curse and the fear of what that dog might do to Pinky, Mrs. Hicks tried to muster a retort, but for some reason, when she opened her mouth her bottom lip began to get that tingling feeling like when the dentist gives you Novocain and you can feel the numbness coming on. She spat across the gate to the walkway. From his place in the alley, Stew Pot tilted his head to one side and, still smiling, wagged a forefinger.

"Come, come now, Mrs. Hicks, is that any way to act?" Then he brought that wagging hand down to the back gate as if he were going to unlatch it. Mrs. Hicks turned and stepped down the rest of the gangway to the sidewalk on 129th Place. Stew Pot's laughter echoed after her as she put her poodle down and headed toward Honore.

Thinking fast, she decided to walk an extra three blocks west and another block north to 128th Place. There she would go east, entering her backyard by way of the alley behind her house, just in case Stew Pot was lying in wait for her and Pinky somewhere between Mr. Glenn's house and the east end of the block. This long way around would be a bit of a walk, especially in this heat, but it was safest; besides, she said to herself in a low voice: "I'm a strong Black woman. I'm not weak when it comes to heat."

CHAPTER NINE

Bereft, Bothered, and Bewildered

By early evening what had happened to Mrs. Hicks was all over Parkland. At Diamond Foods, Keisha the cashier heard the following exchange between two neighborhood women:

"She's in intensive care over at St. Francis."

"What in the world happened?"

"She was out walking her dog this afternoon and fainted. Just fell right over on the sidewalk. Doctors are saying she had heat stroke. And that's not all. When she went down she hit her head on the sidewalk. Right now the doctors aren't able to tell how bad off she is because she's still unconscious."

"Where'd they find her?"

"About four blocks from her house, over on Longwood. Somebody there looked out their front window and saw her lying facedown on the sidewalk with Pinky barking a blue streak."

"What in the world was she doing walking that dog in all this heat?"

"Nobody knows. And no one will until she comes to."

Of course, no one said what was on all their minds: namely, that Mrs. Hicks coming to was not a given; and that even if she did, with her age and all, consciousness didn't mean she'd be out of danger— kidney failure, lung distress, brain damage, all were possible.

That evening Mr. Glenn made a call to the Powells' vacation home, and by late morning the next day, they and Mrs. Motley and Mr. McTeer were at St. Francis Hospital in Blue Island, the four traveling there directly from the expressway.

Mrs. Hicks was still unconscious, so after a visit with the relatives on hand—Mr. Hicks, the two oldest daughters, and Mr. Shaw—the Powells took Mr. McTeer and Mrs. Motley home.

Mrs. Motley spent much of the rest of the day preparing food— fried chicken, potato salad, coleslaw, a ham—in anticipation of the family gathering later on at the Cape Cod. It was during this time that she also discovered the large white-blossom flower bed in the

Reeves's backyard. It was shaped like a cross, set in the middle of the yard, the vertical section of white begonias at least seven feet long and the horizontal traverse at least five feet. The flowers looked brilliant in the sunlight; however, just as with the smaller beds in front of the two-flat, which she had also noticed, seeing the plants arranged in such a manner was unnerving to her. (With no neighborhood person save Stew Pot knowing what had transpired in the alley, nobody in Parkland made any connection between the flower beds and what had happened to Mrs. Hicks. The two landscape workers, after Mrs. Hicks left with Pinky, had exited the truck to nervously finish their task as fast as possible, before rolling out of the neighborhood with no idea that anything amiss had happened to that lady and little white dog.)

While Mrs. Motley was preparing the food, the oldest Hicks daughter phoned. In an excited voice she told Mrs. Motley that her mother had come out of her coma. Following some preliminary checking by the doctors, her mom showed no immediate signs of neurological problems from the head bump she'd received.

Late that evening the family did gather at the Cape Cod. They were all, with the exception of Mr. Hicks, famished. Despite urgings from some of the others, he said he didn't want anything to eat. They tried to tease him, telling him they needed help eating all the food, but he said he was just not in the mood. (Other folks on the block had the same idea as Mrs. Motley. The Hicks's refrigerator was by then crammed with bowls and dishes and platters of food.) So as Mr. Hicks sat quietly in the living room sipping a beer, the others had their fill, the oldest and youngest daughters making frequent references to how great it was that their mom appeared to have no brain damage.

Mrs. Motley, with a white apron tied over a sleeveless blue dress, had just managed to wedge the last extra container of food into the fridge when the Hicks's middle daughter stepped in, nodding on her way out the back door for Mrs. Motley to follow.

Closing the door behind her so as not to let in the heat which was still very much in effect despite it being sundown, Mrs. Motley joined the middle daughter in the summerhouse, which was faintly illuminated by a pole lamp out in the alley. The warmth felt pasty on the skin and from various homes nearby they could hear the heavy humming drone of air conditioners.

The middle daughter tapped a cigarette from a pack and lit it with a plastic lighter, the flame making a flickering glow on her round gingerbread face. Like her sisters, her jaws showed her dimples even when she wasn't smiling, and like her sisters she favored blousy tops that hung untucked over loose slacks.

Mrs. Motley did not comment on the smoking, which the middle daughter had, after much effort, weaned herself from some years before. Instead, she stood with her hands in the pockets of the apron, a few feet behind and to the right of where the middle daughter was sitting on a lawn chair.

This daughter was the plumpest of the three sisters and, to Mrs. Motley's mind, the most practical. When she spoke now, she did so with the no-nonsense tone of someone who had seen it all and done it all as an emergency room nurse.

"Mom's kidneys have shut down," the young woman said flatly, "and more than likely, they're going to stay shut down."

There were a few seconds of silence, during which time Mrs. Motley resisted the compulsion to ask something silly like, *Are you sure?*

The middle daughter blew out a stream of smoke. "I had to get out of there," she said, nodding at the house. "My sisters, who both heard the same thing I heard the doctor say this afternoon, are acting like Mom is gonna skip out the hospital in a couple of days. I swear, those two are champions when it comes to burying their heads in the sand. Mom is going on dialysis. The hope is that her kidneys will come around eventually. But like I said, that's not going to happen, which means she'll be on dialysis the rest of her life."

Mrs. Motley asked about the possibility of a transplant.

"Older people aren't usually the best recipients for successful transplants. They often have other age-related illnesses. Mom has high blood pressure and a family with a history of heart disease, so that'll probably rule her out." After taking a long drag and blowing a heavy smoke stream, she dropped the butt on the cement floor and mashed it out with the heel of her white running shoe. She stared out across the yard to the alley for a few seconds, then said: "I am so angry, Mrs. Motley."

"About you mother not getting a transplant?"

The middle daughter began turning the lighter around in her other hand. "No. Not because of that. I'm angry because things are never going to be the same around here again. I think of how a few weeks ago we were all having fun here in the summerhouse, before Stew Pot and Mrs. Reeves started cutting up in the middle of the street, that is. And little did we know that would be the last time we'd all be together and happy like that."

"Well, I'm going to pray for your mother," said Mrs. Motley. "You know, miracles do sometimes happen."

Speaking over her shoulder, the middle daughter said flatly, "They call them miracles because they usually *don't* happen."

With no rancor in her voice Mrs. Motley replied, "Nonetheless, I'm going to pray for your mom anyway. I'm going to pray for my best friend."

The young woman lowered her head. "I'm sorry. I was rude to speak that way."

Mrs. Motley told her no apology was necessary.

They were quiet for a little bit, then Mrs. Motley asked: "And no one has any idea what she was doing walking around?"

The middle daughter said that when her mom regained consciousness, she had been groggy and confused. "She had no idea why she was even in the hospital. She was probably delirious when she passed out. She has no memory of even waking up yesterday morning, let alone this afternoon. I don't hold out any hope she'll ever remember. What difference does it make? We have other things to worry about— like Dad. We're going to have to start taking turns coming over here and looking after him. You saw him this evening. When have you ever known my father not wanting to eat?"

"I can help with that," said Mrs. Motley.

"I wasn't fishing for help, Mrs. M."

"I know you weren't. I live right across the street. I can help whenever you need. You and your sisters have your own children and they need you. There are other people on the block who'll help—Mr. McTeer, Mrs. Powell."

"Well, thank you, Mrs. Motley. I appreciate it, because Dad is going to need some helping. He can't take care of himself. Don't get me wrong, I love my dad. A person couldn't ask for a better father; but he hasn't so much as lifted a dishcloth, broom, or mop in all the years he's lived in this house. He went from being taken care of by his mother— may she rest in peace—to being taken care of by my mom. For all my mom's bluster, when it came to the fair division of domestic labor— well, let's just say June Cleaver had nothing on her."

Mrs. Motley chuckled. "You're not telling me anything I don't know. Your mom may have had others fooled, but she didn't fool me." Then, in a voice of self-recrimination, she exclaimed: "Oh my goodness, what is wrong with me? Talking about her like she's already gone."

Speaking evenly, the middle daughter said: "Well, in a way she is. I'm afraid there's a big part of her that's gone forever."

CHAPTER TEN
And So It Goes

Mrs. Hicks stayed in the hospital another week before they let her go home. So that she would not have to negotiate stairs to get to and from a bathroom, her family removed the dining room furniture and installed a rented hospital bed.

Many Parkland neighbors, from the block and beyond, as well as colleagues from the grade school, came by to visit. Many of these visitors filed oral reports with friends and relatives, the gist being that Mrs. Hicks looked bad and sounded worse. She was only able to speak slowly and just above a whisper. Her gestures, on those rare occasions when she used them, were languid.

The task of walking Pinky fell to Mr. Hicks. He was seen every morning and evening waddling bowlegged down the street, the little dog trotting along beside him. When people encountered him, they of course asked after Mrs. Hicks. Trying to sound as optimistic as possible, he responded that she was working hard at getting her strength back.

Three times that first week home Mrs. Hicks was helped into her clothes and out of the house and into a minivan that took her to the hospital and her dialysis treatments, which lasted between three and five hours. (As the middle daughter had predicted, it was determined that given Mrs. Hicks's age and overall condition, a transplant was not a viable option, so the dialysis treatments would have to continue and the family explored the possibility of getting her a portable machine that she could use at home.)

The next week she went back to the hospital for more tests and returned after a couple of days, looking none the better. Her three daughters, who took turns spending nights at their parents' house, were relieved of weekday cooking, housecleaning, and laundry work by Mrs. Motley and Mrs. Powell. Mr. Hicks continued walking Pinky; however, that second week folks he encountered noticed the distinct smell of whiskey on him. He spent his mornings sitting at his wife's bedside, reading the newspaper to her in a low voice.

Mrs. Motley visited every day, whether she had cooking and cleaning to do or not, and tried to be cheerful, relaying any neighborhood gossip she had heard because she knew Mrs. Hicks enjoyed such talk. The last week of August, Mrs. Hicks improved some and was able to get around to the living room couch to watch TV.

On Sundays Mrs. Hicks's family was at the Cape Cod. If the weather wasn't too hot, while the kids played in and around the house, the daughters sat with their mother and Mrs. Motley in the summerhouse. Mrs. Hicks had already lost a significant amount of weight and her wigs sat a little loose on her head. She would sometimes talk for short spells, in that almost whispery voice. She never spoke of what had happened the day of her heat stroke, her memory of that apparently erased for good. Her daughters kept an eye out for her every need: "You feel like having a glass of water?" "You want to go inside now, Mom?" The oldest and youngest daughters kept their spirits up by reminding themselves that the doctors and dietician had told them that with proper care their mother could one day make it back to being close to what she had once been, but that would take time, lots of time, and they must be patient.

BOOK VI

Stew Pot Attacks

CHAPTER ONE

Stew Pot Lodges a Complaint

On the early afternoon of September 1, a sunny Wednesday, Mr. Bird, the mailman, was making his deliveries to the east end of the block when Stew Pot opened the front door of the two-flat and called out to him.

Mr. Bird had just delivered the mail to Mrs. Motley's house. With nowhere to run or hide, he had no choice but to wait by his mail cart on the sidewalk as Stew Pot quickly approached. He had a long sheet of white paper in his hand. His pit bull, Mr. Bird was relieved to see, was nowhere in sight.

Without so much as a hello, Stew Pot said: "I have something to discuss with you."

Mr. Bird thought of saying that he had no time to talk, but figured Stew Pot might take umbrage at such a flimsy excuse. So Mr. Bird asked him what he wanted.

"I need you to sign your name."

"Sign my name, to what?"

"To my petition." Stew Pot raised the sheet and Mr. Bird saw that it had many numbered lines, all of which were blank.

"What's that for?"

"It's to protest an act of blasphemy by the Parliament of World Religions."

"The what?"

"The Parliament of World Religions conference. Didn't you read about it in the paper?"

Mr. Bird said he hadn't and Stew Pot proceeded to explain how the conference, an international gathering of religious representatives, had convened the day before at a Downtown hotel.

Although still nervous, Mr. Bird's curiosity was piqued. "What in the world do you have against a conference of religions?"

Stew Pot scowled. "Because they're anti-Christ, that's why. There is only one religion, all the rest is blasphemy. For a batch of so-called Christian leaders to take part in such a thing is an outrage, as if one following is as good as another. They're even allowing pagans to take part in the conference. Rabbis and mullahs are one thing, but pagans?"

"*Judge not, and you will not be judged,*" said Mr. Bird, employing one of the few Bible passages he recalled from childhood Sunday school classes.

"This isn't about judging," said Stew Pot, "it's about defending the faith. So, will you sign my petition?"

"Well, actually, I can't."

"Why not?"

"Because postal service workers are not allowed to do so while on duty."

"Oh really?"

"I'm afraid so."

"Whatever. I'm going to walk Parkland and get names for my petition. I'll knock on every door if I have to. This outrage won't go unchallenged. I will *not* be still."

CHAPTER TWO

Parkland Responds, Stew Pot Responds

lthough Stew Pot did not knock on every Parkland door, he did knock on more than a few. Leaving his dog at home, he traversed the neighborhood for much of that afternoon. He not only went to homes, but to businesses too. Most of the people Stew Pot spoke with declined to sign his petition (some angrily), but nearly three dozen did put pen to paper. Some were regulars of neighborhood drinking establishments who, with grins and smirks, scribbled on the petition sheet, amused at the sight of Stew Pot in a saloon. (It wasn't until he got home and checked the page closely that he saw that some were gag signatures—*Huckleberry Hound, Janet Jackson, Whoopi Goldberg.*)

Among the legitimate signatures, the most surprising name by far was that of Reverend Fennoy, the hard-line pastor of Hill of the Lord. When word of this got around the neighborhood, more than a few members of his congregation were embarrassed, none more so than the Hicks's oldest daughter. (Over the next couple of days, the middle daughter teased her older sister once too often about what the reverend had done, which led to a heated argument.)

Fennoy, when asked about his action, used a modified version of "The enemy of my enemy is my friend" as a rationale. As for many of Parkland's other religious leaders and more conservative laypersons, though none said so out loud, they were in basic agreement with the petition's sentiment, their feelings for Stew Pot notwithstanding.

Stew Pot's efforts alerted the neighborhood residents to an event most had overlooked. Reviewing news accounts from the previous few days, they read with interest the stories of how the Greek Orthodox delegation walked out of the conference to protest the pagan inclusion. While trolling for signatures, Stew Pot told people he was going to personally deliver his petition to the conference, but no one knew if he actually did.

What they did know was that while making the neighborhood rounds, Stew Pot had more than once grumbled about not receiving a single signature from his block. At some point during this process, someone mentioned that Father Vader from Seven Sorrows was a conference attendee. To this Stew Pot responded menacingly: "Oh, is that so? I wonder what my papist neighbor has to say about that."

The next day Mr. Bird was confronted by Stew Pot again, this time at the two-flat's front door. As Mr. Bird told folks later, Stew Pot asked his opinion of people who did not renounce blasphemers. Mr. Bird gave a "to each his own" response and Stew Pot said: "Early yesterday morning, before I spoke with you, I saw Mr. McTeer and Mrs. Motley once again leave off with the Powells. I'll bet anything that Mr. McTeer, in anticipation of my action, arranged for the getaway so he and Mrs. Motley could avoid signing my petition.

"Well, Jesus sought no escape from the Cross and we should seek no escape from our obligations as Christians. If Mr. McTeer can't find his way to the duty, then maybe the duty will have to be brought to him."

When Mr. Bird asked Stew Pot exactly what he meant by that, Stew Pot said with a smile: "The Lord works in mysterious ways."

CHAPTER THREE

Let's Get Away From It All

As Stew Pot said, that Wednesday morning Mrs. Motley and Mr. McTeer had gone away again with the Powells. In the roomy brown sedan they rode east through coastal Indiana—past Whiting and Hammond and Gary and Michigan City—and then north a much shorter distance through the Michigan Harbor Country—Michiana and Grand Beach and New Buffalo—their drive ending at the lakefront community of Union Pier.

The Powells' vacation house was a small white stucco cottage at the lake end of a row of similar white cottages. There were three snuggly bedrooms, one bath, and a patio on the west side. Lake Michigan could not be seen from the patio (although the waves were quite audible) because a thick stand of trees and brush stood between it and the beach. The shore was accessed by way of a sandy trail that curved downhill through the densely shaded area and then, like the mouth of a cave approached from the inside, presented a grand panorama of sandscape and water.

The Powells had bought the cottage in the early 1950s, and a few years later Mrs. Motley and her husband, along with Mr. McTeer and his wife, purchased cottages of their own in a nearby wooded area just down the road. The three families, sometimes joined by Mr. and Mrs. Hicks and their daughters, spent many a summer weekend, and a fortnight at the end of every August, at Union Pier. But that had been awhile ago. When their spouses had passed, Mrs. Motley and Mr. McTeer sold their respective cottages, neither feeling the need for a vacation house with no one to share it with. They still liked Union Pier however, which over the years had become home and haven for a diverse and artsy crowd. For a week every August they joined the Powells up there, spending their time reading, barbecuing, strolling the lake, playing cards, sleeping late, and enjoying local restaurants and crafts stores.

Not wanting to get away from his normal work/sleep schedule, in the afternoons Mr. Powell took long naps and his wife joined him. Mrs. Motley and Mr. McTeer, to give their hosts some alone time, took themselves to the beach where they sat side by side on lawn chairs facing the water. (If it was raining, they strolled beneath big umbrellas along the nearby roadways.)

On those sunny days, with poetry books in hand, Mr. McTeer wore a straw hat to the beach, the kind with the round upturned brim that's frayed at the edges. Mrs. Motley wore a straw hat too, hers featuring a wide, neat brim tilted slightly down. Beside him she'd kick off the deck shoes of her rather large feet—10 double-E—and work her toes idly in the sand. It was the sort of casual behavior she had always allowed herself at Union Pier, and which Mr. McTeer had always enjoyed.

At Union Pier Mrs. Motley wore no ankle-length pencil skirts or blouses buttoned high. At Union Pier she wore Bermuda shorts and loose cotton tops with the shirt tails out. The shorts revealed her skinny, blotchy legs, and though Mr. McTeer knew she was self-conscious about her gams, he thought them still attractive in the way they had retained the lines of muscular definition along the calves. As for himself, he kept his lower half hidden with baggy linen pants, his reasoning being that no one wanted to see his withered leg. He kept his top covered too, in Hawaiian shirts, because he was even more self-conscious about his chest with its small but noticeable breasts.

Mrs. Motley never brought Bibles to the beach, preferring to read paperback murder mysteries, which, like the casual clothes, was an indulgence she only allowed herself on vacations. Mr. McTeer didn't know why she only read mysteries—Ruth Rendell and P.D. James were her favorites—on vacation, and he didn't ask. Why did she do any of the things she did? Why did she occasionally, while beach reading, suddenly twist her pursed lips to one side? Why did she occasionally dig a big toe in the sand with a slow, circular motion? Why did she, once or twice while sitting there, turn to him, and from behind her sunglasses (which he felt made her look years younger) ask him: "You all right?"

At some point she'd get up without a word and stroll down to the wet sand. Standing with her back to him, she looked out to where the sky-blue vista and the deeper-blue vista met in flatline on the horizon (*Thinking of what?* Mr. McTeer wondered), and as the incoming rolls splashed and lapped around her narrow ankles, she held her blotchy arms akimbo, with her blotchy-backed hands splayed at her sides, and the breeze lifted the tail of her shirt away, as if raised by an invisible hand sympathetic to his desires, and he got a tantalizing glimpse of her lower back. After ten minutes or so she would return without a word and sit back down with her Ruth Rendell or P.D. James, her wet feet coated with sand, and the breeze would send silvery wisps of her hair in lazy movement about her head, because at Union Pier she kept her hair in a loose bun that she pinned in the morning and never bothered with the rest of the day. On the beach her only hair attention was to every now and then tuck a strand behind her ear—and oh, what all that did to him.

On the third night of their second stay that summer at Union Pier, which was the night before they were to return home, Mr. McTeer lay in the dark on a lumpy mattress in a room smelling heavily of damp wood. As with every night there, the sound of the waves had strong competition from Mrs. Motley's snoring in the next room.

Mr. McTeer's "vigor" (as he called it) was at full attention and he reminded himself to keep his hands idle, for he'd definitely want his vigor come morning. In the years that he and the other three had been coming to Union Pier, he'd learned to rise before Mrs. Motley and make his way to his bedroom door. He would stand there with the door parted just wide enough so he could watch Mrs. Motley exit her room, which she always did in a bathrobe and house slippers—with her silvery hair *down*. The mane would be all over her shoulders and upper back, which to his mind made her look even younger than when she wore sunglasses. Why this thrilled him he did not exactly know. Maybe it was because he was aware that since her husband's death, no one had seen her in bathrobe and slippers with her hair down—*except him*. Or maybe, since he knew they'd never be married, these surreptitious glimpses through the gap were as close as he'd ever come to the sort of visual intimacy that husbands had routine access to. (He also realized the peeking was the sort of thing an objective observer might judge creepy, but he could not help himself.)

That next morning, a cloudy Saturday, Mr. McTeer stood at his slightly parted door for nearly half an hour before Mrs. Motley, in a rust-colored robe and brown slippers, finally appeared. She had an armful of toiletries—hairbrush, toothbrush, toothpaste, shampoo, etc. His breath caught, as it had the previous two mornings, watching her pass the Powells' closed door, the ends of her silvery mane lifting slightly. She was almost at the bathroom threshold when the toothpaste tube fell, hitting the terra cotta floor with a clack.

"Shoot," she said softly, and made a bend to retrieve it. But as she did so, the shampoo bottle slipped. She straightened, secured her armload, and entered the bathroom.

Mr. McTeer let his breath go in high excitement. She would have to return for the toothpaste, which meant he'd get a bonus look. And sure enough, after some clattering about in the bathroom, she came back out. With her back to the bathroom doorway she bent over, and as she did so her hair draped past her jaw lines, and lo and behold, the loose top of her robe parted—the invisible hand at work again?— and he was able to see the wrinkled plane of her chest and the small rounded contours of what he knew no one, save her husband and doctors, had ever seen! And oh man, was the vigor with him now!

Moments later, as he listened to the shower running, Mr. McTeer wished that he might again enjoy intimate sights of Mrs. Motley without having to wait another year for the opportunity, a most pleasing thought for him because the only way he could see such a thing happening was if he and Mrs. Motley were married, and he made another wishful prayer that Mrs. Motley relinquish her resistance to becoming a Catholic, which he felt wrongheaded of her—on a spiritual as well as a personal level.

The drive home later that day was uneventful, Mrs. Motley in the backseat behind Mr. Powell, her hair again in a tight bun and her body in another low-hem dress, while Mr. McTeer sat beside her in dress shirt and slacks. They reached the east end of their block in the early afternoon. Mr. Powell parked in Mr. McTeer's driveway, and as he was getting out of the car, the Hicks's middle daughter emerged from next door. Mr. Powell was struck by the pensive look on her face, and his first thought was that Mrs. Hicks had taken a worse turn.

When the middle daughter got to the driveway, she pulled a folded sheet from the pocket of her stretch pants and held it out for Mr. McTeer to take. "It's from Stew Pot," she said. "Copies were left in everybody's mailboxes this morning. It's about you, Mr. McTeer; and you too, Mrs. Motley."

CHAPTER FOUR
With Every Secret Thing

THE BURNING BUSH
A journal of truth and righteousness
Our motto: One God, One Savior, One Way

PUBLISHER'S MANIFESTO
The only way to Salvation is by walking in <u>The Light</u>*. To do that, one must ask for forgiveness and do penance for one's sins. However, before one asks for forgiveness, one must first admit one's sins, and it is not likely that one will admit to transgressions carried out in secret. Therefore, in an effort to assist God in His* HOLY MISSION *to bring all sinners into* <u>The Light</u>*, this newsletter will cast the withering power of* HOLY LIGHT *on any and all acts of secret sin. In doing so, transgressors will have nowhere to run, nowhere to hide, and will be left with no choice but to stand before their neighbors as sinners, before God as sinners, which is the first step toward salvation. The truth is* <u>The Light</u>*. The only path is* <u>The Light</u>*.*
—*G.X. Reeves*

THIS ISSUE'S BIBLICAL QUOTE
James 4:7 Submit yourselves therefore to God. Resist the Devil and he will flee from you.

THE BURNING BUSH HAS LEARNED . . .
The Burning Bush has legally obtained personal papers written by Mr. McTeer. As no doubt many have observed, Mrs. Motley frequents his home at all hours of the day with doors and windows closed. He insists their relationship is "platonic." Well, that may be true for Mrs. Motley, who we all know as an honest woman of the highest order; however, just the opposite is true of Mr. McTeer. His writings, reproduced below, are in the form of poetry, which as we all know is nothing more than a tool Satan uses to ensnare the innocent and the ignorant. As with wine, its sweet taste camouflages numerous corrupting influences.

The original handwritten notebook page has been photocopied to verify its authenticity:

TO MY SWEET LADY M, WHO LIVES ACROSS THE WAY

LOVELY, IN THE WAY SHE SPEAKS,
GENTLE, IN THE WAY SHE SEEKS
TO EXTEND HER FORGIVING LOVE
TO THAT FOOL WHO GIVES HER
REASON UPON REASON TO FLEE
AWAY FROM HERE, AWAY FROM ME.
IN THE UNDENIABLE LIGHT OF DAY I DREAM
OF HER LYING BENEATH MY BEDROOM BEAMS,
THIS CEILING, THIS FEELING,
SO INTIMATE, SO PROXIMATE,
PANT AND PINE, PELT AND PURR,
THE SMELL AND SIGHT AND SOUND, OF HER.

Mr. McTeer might just as well have titled his verse "The Betrayal of My Dead Wife's Sacred Memory." I suppose such drivel is all we can expect from a man who won't even make a token protest when his priest openly consorts with nonbelievers. Mr. McTeer claims some "fool" is causing Mrs. Motley to want to flee. Maybe the real reason she wants to get away is that she realizes, at some level, that he is trying to corrupt her with all that "pelt and purr" he's so excited about. Although he does not explain exactly what he means by that phrase, it certainly sounds salacious, like something straight from the Devil, who Mr. McTeer has obviously not fled from.

Now that we know what's going on in Mr. McTeer's nasty mind, we must let him know that such behavior is not acceptable in our community. We must pray that he will admit the error of his ways, and beg God not only for forgiveness, but for the chance to do penance.

Again, let me state that in no way do we cast any aspersions on Mrs. Motley, who we all know to be of impeccable character, though perhaps questionable in her choice of confidants.

The Burning Bush will be released on an as-needed basis. This is necessary to keep those who would seek to interrupt its distribution from laying the sort of traps that a regular publishing schedule would be vulnerable to. Until the next time we communicate, Peace to all of you that are in Christ.

CHAPTER FIVE

Some Neighborhood Opinions,
at Craig's Barbershop and Elsewhere

S o what did Mr. McTeer do when he read Stew Pot's newsletter?"

"Mrs. Butler said Mrs. Powell told her that Mr. McTeer marched over to the two-flat and pounded on the door, demanding that Stew Pot show himself."

"So what did Stew Pot do?"

"He didn't do anything, he wasn't home; neither was his momma."

"So then what happened?"

"Well, after they managed to calm him down, Mr. McTeer said this time Stew Pot had outsmarted himself because that poem had been in a box in the rafters of his garage—"

"He didn't deny it was him who wrote the poem?"

"No he didn't. I guess he was too worked up to think about lying. Anyway, Mr. McTeer said that Stew Pot must have broken into his garage and gotten the poem. Remember the police couldn't charge Stew Pot for printing up that stuff from Delphina's diary because they couldn't prove it was him who'd gotten in the house or copied the excerpts."

"I see where you're going. This time Stew Pot admitted in writing it was him who obtained the stolen item, which meant McTeer had him cold on breaking-and-entering."

"Well, that's what Mr. McTeer thought."

"What do you mean that's what he thought? He called the police, right?"

"Oh yeah, he called them, and they came after a while."

"Uniforms or tactical?"

"Uniforms, a couple of White boys. Anyway, Mr. McTeer shows the sheet of paper to the cops and tells them the only way Stew Pot could have gotten it was by breaking in. So they—McTeer, Mrs. Motley, the Powells, the Hicks girl, and the two cops—march up the driveway to the garage. There was no sign of forced entry anywhere. It's at this point they see Stew Pot across the street, coming home with his dog. The cops call for him to halt, tell the other five to wait by the garage, and cross the street. Not taking any chances with that dog, the cops make Stew Pot tie the leash to a light pole. That's when they put the cuffs on him."

"Stew Pot give them any guff?"

"Nope, peaceful as a lamb as the cops walked him to the squad and put him inside."

"I didn't hear anything about Stew Pot going to jail."

"That's 'cause he didn't go. The cops come back to the garage, right? And they tell Mr. McTeer and the others that Stew Pot says he got the poem from Mr. McTeer's garbage. So Mr. McTeer tells the cops that no way was that box in the garbage. So the cops say, 'Let's go see,' and they and Mr. McTeer go to the alley, and sure enough, there the cardboard box is in the garbage can, right where Stew Pot said it was. It was full of a lot of old papers, most of which were damp from being rained on.

"So the cops then ask Mr. McTeer if he was sure he hadn't maybe tossed the box out and forgotten he'd done it. And that's when Mr. McTeer got mad again. He starts yelling he's not some addled-headed old man who can't remember when he throws stuff away. And the cops are saying, 'Calm down, calm down.' And Mr. McTeer is pointing at his right knee and saying: 'Does this look like the leg of somebody who could climb a ladder to get a cardboard box down from the rafters of a garage?'

"And the cops keep telling him to calm down, and the other four start talking angry in support of Mr. McTeer—actually, Mrs. Powell said it was the Hicks girl who was doing most of that—you know how she can get. So anyway, the cops say they're going to have to let Stew Pot go because there's no proof he actually took the box from the garage. 'There's no law against rifling through garbage cans,' one of the cops says, and the Hicks girl snaps at the cops and says: 'What does Stew Pot have to do before you all will arrest him?' And the cops then get ticked off and all pink in the face, and one of them snaps right back that they can't just go around arresting people with no evidence."

"Huh! That's a good one. I can recall a few times when they've done just that."

"Can't we all. Anyway, upshot is, the cops go back to the squad car and let Stew Pot go. By that time, Mrs. Butler said she and some others came down to that end of the block to join those who were already watching from the houses. The cops waited until Stew Pot and his dog were inside, then they came back and told Mr. McTeer they were sorry, but under the circumstances, yadda yadda yadda. And then they left."

The above telling at Craig's Barbershop was delivered by someone who'd spoken to Mr. Glenn, and was an accurate account. However, it will probably come as no surprise that the tale, in making neighborhood rounds, sprouted embellishments: the cops drew their weapons and threatened to shoot the dog; a cop cursed the Hicks's middle daughter; the cops found other poems in the garbage that were far racier than what Stew Pot had distributed. One thing all reports got correct was this: after the cops left, Mrs. Motley and Mr. McTeer retired to their respective homes and did not reappear for the rest of the day.

With the "true" nature of their relationship now out in the open, as it were, many assumed the two would lay low for a while, but no. The following morning Mrs. Motley drove Mr. McTeer to Seven Sorrows, as always. When he walked in he didn't avert his eyes when his gaze hit upon someone else's, an apparent lack of shame that disappointed conservative parishioners who up to then had counted Mr. McTeer among their number. (They'd also disapproved of Father Vader attending the conference.)

Mrs. Motley was subjected to similar scrutiny at Wesley-Allen, but as the lusted-for and not the luster, she drew no harsh feelings. Before service, the other Old Guards were supportive by making no mention of Mr. McTeer. After service, Reverend Wilkins took her briefly aside to ask if there was anything he could do, as if Mrs. Motley had lost a loved one or something. Although she appreciated his concern and said so, at the same time she felt this was another example of his tendency to go overboard, like with that invitation to have Stew Pot and his mom come to Wesley-Allen, an offer that, in light of recent Stew Pot events, she knew was now an embarrassment to the reverend.

Normally Mrs. Motley and Mr. McTeer had lunch at Logan's following church, and it was here that their routine changed. The Hicks's youngest daughter, on duty at her parents' place, was in the pink living room when Mrs. Motley parked in Mr. McTeer's driveway. To her surprise, Mrs. Motley didn't drive away after Mr. McTeer exited. Instead, she got out of her car and went inside with him, causing the youngest daughter to softly say: "Well, look at that." And she thought of how later, when her mom woke up, her mom would get a laugh when she told her how Mrs. Motley and Mr. McTeer had decided to maybe enjoy a little "afternoon cha-cha-cha" instead of lunch at Logan's.

CHAPTER SIX
The Blues and the Anything-But Abstract Truth

After picking up Mr. McTeer from Mass, Mrs. Motley had said matter-of-factly that there was something important she needed to discuss with him. He asked her what it was and she said she didn't want to start the conversation in the car, which was his first indication that something else was bothering her besides the revelation of his poem. (The day before, after the cops had gone and everyone had returned to their homes, he had phoned her and apologized profusely.)

When he and Mrs. Motley entered his living room after returning from Seven Sorrows, he offered her a drink—a glass of water or a cola—but she declined, his second indication that something was seriously wrong. He left the round-top front doorway open and she sat at the end of the couch nearest the picture window. Figuring it was good strategy not to crowd her, he sat at the other end.

In an attempt to head off whatever was bothering her, Mr. McTeer launched into another round of apology for his "indiscrete behavior." After nearly a minute of this, Mrs. Motley raised a hand for him to stop, which he did in midsentence.

Then she asked: "When did you write that poem?"

Eyes magnified by those thick lenses, he blinked hard. "I wrote it a long time ago."

She asked him how long and he rubbed a hand over his mouth, took the hand away, and said he had written the poem in 1972. She then asked if he'd written any other such poems and he said yes. Sounding irked, she said: "I assume Stew Pot has them as well."

"No, no, he hasn't. The one he stole was the only one I kept."

There were a few moments of silence, then she asked: "Did your wife know?"

Mr. McTeer looked crestfallen and Mrs. Motley's eyes went into a pained squint.

"How she must have hated me," Mrs. Motley said.

Mr. McTeer insisted that wasn't true. "When she discovered the poems, I made it clear that you had done nothing to provoke my affections. I told her it was all my doing—all my fault."

Mrs. Motley responded heatedly: "How could she *not* hate me? When I think of the times I sat with her when she was dying. Me thinking I was a comfort, when in reality . . ."

"No, that's not true. In her last days, she said—and I've never told this to anyone—she said she hoped you and I would always remain good friends."

Mrs. Motley folded her arms across her chest. "What you don't know about women is a lot. She said she wanted us to remain friends, as in, don't become man and wife."

From the look on Mr. McTeer's face it was clear that this interpretation of his wife's deathbed comment had never occurred to him. He was still reacting to this jolt when Mrs. Motley asked another question: "What did you mean by, *that fool who gives her reason upon reason to flee*? Who was the fool? Not Stew Pot, he was a boy."

Mr. McTeer's shoulders slumped and he gazed mournfully at the ceiling.

Mrs. Motley lost her temper: "Stop with the fidgety delays and tell me the truth!"

With eyes on the carpet, Mr. McTeer said that her husband had loved her very much, which was one of the primary reasons that he'd felt so guilty over his own feelings for her—and here she cut him off with a curt: "The issue is not *your* feelings."

He made a quick apology and continued: "He loved you, it was just that sometimes, when in the company of other men, after he consumed a whiskey too many, he liked to boast about intimacies with you. He never gave details, until one evening . . ."

"From your reticence, I can assume he was explicit."

"Yes," said Mr. McTeer. "I remember at the time that it struck me as so odd that he would do such a thing. It was as if he were trying to impress me and the others in some way, trying to convince us of something about himself."

"Convince you all of what?"

"I don't know. But what you must know is that I took him aside and told him if he ever wanted to set foot on my property again, he'd better not repeat such talk."

"So he said this to more than just you yourself?"

"Yes."

"Who else?"

"Mr. Hicks, Mr. Powell, Mr. Deckerdrill. We were playing cards in my garage."

Mrs. Motley rested her forehead on a raised hand. "Oh my Lord."

"No, you don't understand. After your husband went home that evening, I swore the others to secrecy. I'm sure Deck kept his word, and that Mr. Hicks and Mr. Powell have kept theirs. I've never spoken of it to anyone. I was so angry with him. It was later that night that I wrote the poem Stew Pot stole."

Mrs. Motley raised her head, folded her arms again, and met Mr. McTeer's eyes. "After my son was born, following a very, very difficult pregnancy and labor, I was advised it would be dangerous, life threatening in fact, for me to have another child. I was scared. Those things they fitted women with back then were not one hundred percent effective. I didn't feel like I could take the risk. I had a baby son to care for, but I also loved my husband. And I didn't want to . . ."

Mr. McTeer leaned forward and said he was the last person she had to explain herself to, and in an attempt to ease her feelings, he said her husband's loose talk probably had to do with the trouble she and Mr. Motley had been going through at the time.

Mrs. Motley's face froze in stunned bewilderment for a couple of seconds. Then she said anxiously: "What are you talking about?" And Mr. McTeer, realizing too late his mistake, and with the sickening knowledge that there was no way for him to close the can of worms he had so foolishly opened, met her eyes again.

"The day after I took him aside, he came over and apologized to me privately. He said he was under a lot of stress because you two were having trouble."

Her voice catching in her throat, Mrs. Motley said: "What sort of trouble?"

"Again, I don't know."

"What do you mean you don't know?"

"I didn't ask for details. And if he had tried to offer any, I would have stopped him."

"Are you sure you heard him correctly?"

"Of course I'm sure. A man says something like that, you don't mishear it."

"He never said anything to me about any *trouble*. How long did this trouble last? Did he ever say?"

"No, he never did."

"So it might never have ended?"

"That's possible. I have no idea. But surely you have no doubt that he loved you?"

Her voice breaking, Mrs. Motley said, "I just don't understand. My marriage was in trouble?"

CHAPTER SEVEN

Mrs. Motley's Side of the Matter

That evening, reading by lamplight on the blue couch, Mrs. Motley perused Psalms and got particular comfort from Chapter 139: *If I take the wings in the morning and dwell in the uttermost parts of the sea, even there Thy hand shall lead me and Thy right hand shall hold me* . . . However, when she lay in bed that night in the dove-gray bedroom, faceup in the dark with an arm over her eyes, her thoughts continued tumbling with the worries that had plagued her since her conversation at Mr. McTeer's house. She had always known her husband had not enjoyed working at her dad's insurance company where the partners of the firm, after her father's death, made him feel, he said, "like some interloper, no matter how hard I work." She had always known her husband had not liked living in this house (although she had told him plenty of times she would move if that's what he really wanted, just like she'd told him she'd support his leaving the firm if that's what he really wanted); however, she had always believed he had enjoyed being married to her; that he'd been a loving and understanding husband, if not particularly attentive in most areas, a notable exception being his aforementioned efforts in their lovemaking. (After her doctor had told her of the dangers of her having another child, she'd told Mr. Motley about her fears of intercourse: there had been no outrage on his part.) But now, to find out that for years he had not been happy, with her having not the slightest inkling that anything was wrong; knowing that caused her stomach to dully ache, as it had done off and on since her exit from Mr. McTeer's house. Had there been another woman in her husband's life? Had he contemplated leaving her? Mrs. Motley knew she would never know the answer to those questions. What she did know now was that one of her most cherished beliefs—that her marriage had been comfortable for her husband—was shattered forever. For her, that was far worse than finding out what her husband had revealed to Mr. McTeer and the other men, although the thought of that brought an ache to her stomach too. (It was baffling to her as well. The sort of bawdy behavior Mr. McTeer attributed to her husband was nothing she had ever seen her husband do.) And what had those men thought of her over the subsequent years when their families had socialized—at card parties, barbecues, picnics on the beach at Union Pier? Had the men thought of her doing that, an act that despite her husband's bragging had been anything but fiery—done always in the dark and under the covers, him lying nearly stock still as if he were concentrating on something, a single muted groan on his part at the end followed by a trip to the bathroom by her for tooth brushing. (There had been no reciprocity by him, partly because the thought of him doing such a thing had never occurred to her, and partly because his intimate finger-plucking was so satisfying she had no complaint in regards to her own pleasure.) And what effect, she now wondered, had knowing of her intimacies had on Mr. McTeer's feelings for her? She knew that if asked, he'd deny it had played a significant role. But the fact remained that for all these years he had known. How could it not have factored into his thinking? While on her knees saying her prayers she had forgiven him for leaving that poem where Stew Pot could get his hands on it and again make her the hot topic of the Parkland Gossip Line. On her knees she had reminded herself it was Stew Pot's fault the poem had come to light. And then, suddenly, her thoughts shifted to Mrs. Hicks. If she were her old self, Mrs. Hicks would surely ask, *Embarrassment aside, how do you really feel about Mr. McTeer loving you for all these years?* And then the guilt she'd felt over what Mrs. McTeer must have thought on her deathbed pounced again, and Mrs. Motley wondered if she'd ever forgive herself for that.

CHAPTER EIGHT

Mr. McTeer's Side of the Matter Yet Again

Mr. McTeer was awake too. Wearing his night clothes, he sat at his dining room table in the ambient light coming through the doorway to the kitchen. He sipped a finger of whiskey from a lowball glass, his second since he'd gotten up from bed after futile attempts to fall asleep.

He was now certain that Stew Pot (oh, what he wouldn't give to have him dead) had set into motion a series of events that had destroyed any chance he might have had with Mrs. Motley. The revelation of the poem and the ensuing neighborhood spectacle it would make of her was bad enough, but to learn of her husband's indiscreet talk? He doubted she would ever get out of her mind what she imagined he and the others had been imagining her doing in *their* minds. And if some modern types wanted to call that being uptight, they could go ahead and do so; but Mrs. Motley was who she was. (On that last point, though he would never have said it to her, he could not help but feel that their current troubles could have easily been avoided if she had only let go of her refusal to come to his Church. If she'd only done that, they'd be married by now, and some long-ago love poem would have not been of such consequence.) And finally, there'd been his slip of the lip about her husband saying he and she had been in trouble. Mr. McTeer knew Mrs. Motley would forgive him for all of this, because that was also who she was. But forgiving was one thing, forgetting was something else.

CHAPTER NINE

A Not-So-Long Goodbye

L ate the next morning, Mrs. Motley came over to sit with Mrs. Hicks a spell. Upon entering the dining-room-turned-sickroom, she looked down and greeted her old friend with a: "So how are you doing today, old girl?" Mrs. Hicks, who had lost more weight, frowned and said in a raspy voice: "Better than some, worse than most, I suspect."

They talked for a good little while, the two of them alone while the smallish, sad-eyed day nurse, on her first day on the job, took a break in the summerhouse with cigarettes and a romance novel.

Mrs. Motley told how she had gotten some great news. The day before, her son the army sergeant major had called from Fort Sill to tell her that he and his ex-wife were negotiating the details of a marital reconciliation and that the two of them and Mrs. Motley's granddaughter would be coming for Christmas. "I'll finally get to show my grandbaby the house and her family legacy." And Mrs. Hicks said that was wonderful. And after that the subject of Mr. McTeer came up (it had nothing to do with Stew Pot's newsletter, for Mrs. Hicks's family had not told her about that) and Mrs. Hicks asked: "When are you going to quit torturing that poor man and marry him?" And Mrs. Motley said: "Now, now." And Mrs. Hicks opened an eye and said in a playful scold: "For someone who's so smart, you can be real stupid sometimes." And Mrs. Motley wagged a finger at her just as playfully and replied: "I'm going to let you get away with that because you're sick." And they both chuckled, after which Mrs. Hicks's face grew serious. With eyes closed again she said, the way someone might comment on a bad movie they were watching: "This is so boring." And Mrs. Motley knew that Mrs. Hicks was not talking about the conversation they were having. And when Mrs. Hicks asked, "You're not mad at me, are you?" Mrs. Motley knew what she meant by that too, and she said no, she wasn't mad. "I know how you hate being bored." With her eyes still closed, Mrs. Hicks said: "We had some good times, though, didn't we? Didn't we have fun?" And Mrs. Motley grinned, sort of, and said: "Yes, we did. We had ourselves a real good time."

A little later on, after calling for the nurse, Mrs. Motley kissed the top of Mrs. Hicks's head, her lips pressing against the dry scalp and wisps of hair while Mrs. Hicks gave her wrist a weak but heartfelt grasp.

The middle daughter, on lunch break from the nearby clinic where she worked, came in as Mrs. Motley was leaving. The two spoke on the sidewalk, Mrs. Motley saying, in an effort to be positive, that Mrs. Hicks had been in a teasing mood that morning.

Not too long after that, Mrs. Motley was washing off a plate in the yellow kitchen after a lunch of tuna salad and tomato when the front bell rang. She went to the screen door to find the middle daughter there, biting lightly at her bottom lip. Without any preamble or hysterics she said: "She's gone." Mrs. Motley took first one deep breath and then another, then asked the young woman if she wanted to come inside.

The middle daughter said no, but that she would like to sit outside. The two stepped over to the wooden swing suspended by chains from the porch ceiling and rocked gently as they overlooked the otherwise quiet and sunlit street.

Calm and dry-eyed, the middle daughter said: "It happened just a few minutes ago. I was having a sandwich by her bed and we were chatting and then I went into the kitchen to get some more pop, and when I came back from the fridge she'd taken her leave. I checked her neck and wrist for a pulse and then got my stethoscope just to be sure. I put it to her chest. Didn't hear so much as a peep."

CHAPTER TEN

A Death in the Family

L ate that afternoon, after the EMTs had come and gone, Vernon Paiger's petite sister, the director of Paiger & Paiger Mortuary, arrived at the Hicks's house with her driver and assistant, a big, froggy-eyed guy that folks in the neighborhood called LaBear.

LaBear parked the black hearse at the end of Mr. McTeer's driveway and after a short time inside they reappeared with a white-sheeted bundle atop a rolling platform—LaBear pushing the head end and the alderman's sister pulling the other. They deposited the remains behind the tinted windows of the hearse and LaBear, in dark suit and sunglasses, went back to the wheel to wait while the alderman's sister, whose name was Mrs. Clark (she was divorced), returned to the house with her clipboard and checklist.

So they wouldn't have to sit staring at the now empty hospital bed, the daughters, Mr. Hicks, and Mrs. Clark retired to the summerhouse and sat at the circular metal table.

Mrs. Clark, who had her brother's peanut coloring along with lots of freckles on her face, as well as short, reddish-colored hair, immediately found there was a serious dispute within the family. The oldest daughter very much wanted their mother's funeral service to be held in a house of worship, in Parkland if at all possible. The middle daughter wanted no such thing on the grounds that Mrs. Hicks hadn't been a member of any church. To have her service presided over by some holy man, the middle sister said, was not what their mother would have wanted. The youngest daughter said she would do whatever their father wanted, and here he surprised his children by saying, as he wiped tears from his eyes, that maybe a church service wouldn't be such a bad idea.

Hearing this, the oldest daughter, as relieved as she was surprised, announced that the family had made its decision. The middle daughter, as angry as she was surprised, sat with her arms folded over her broad chest and a scowl on her face.

Mrs. Clark, trying to be as diplomatic as possible, said that having a service for Mrs. Hicks in a church might present some problems, especially in Parkland. For instance, Hill of the Lord, the oldest daughter's church, had strict rules about funerals: only someone who'd been a member in good standing could have services there. Other neighborhood churches like Parkland First Baptist, and Parkland Presbyterian, and Allen A.M.E., either had the same rules as Hill of the Lord or the stipulation, like Seven Sorrows, that the deceased be a person who'd been baptized in the church's faith or denomination.

Mrs. Hicks struck out on both those counts, and at this point in the discussion the middle daughter interjected that she didn't know why the oldest daughter would consider having their mom's service at a place where, at best, she'd be looked upon as an outsider, to which the oldest daughter responded sharply: "We're talking about Momma's soul!"

To this the middle daughter flung a dismissive wave of the arm.

"I was wondering," the oldest daughter then said to Mrs. Clark, "if you, or perhaps your brother, might intervene on our behalf?"

Again, being as diplomatic as possible, Mrs. Clark said she would see what she could do. "But I'm not making any promises." Mr. Hicks and the middle and youngest daughters thanked her while the middle daughter said: "Frankly, I think it's humiliating for our family to have someone calling around the neighborhood begging people to let us have a service for our mother, as if Momma were some wretch in need of their pity. But don't mind me; obviously no one cares what I think. Go on, Mrs. Clark, and make your calls."

Later on that evening, Mrs. Motley and other folks from the block brought prepared foods to the Cape Cod, enough to keep Mrs. Hicks's family, immediate and extended, fed for a week. Folks stayed and sat and ate and commiserated with the daughters and their husbands and their children, and their aunts and uncles and cousins, the neighbors and friends crowding the first floor of the house. (The sons-in-law had by then moved the hospital bed from the dining room to Mr. McTeer's garage.)

Mrs. Hicks's grandson LeShawn was like a brave little soldier, some said later, shedding no tears and saying calmly that his grandma was "with the angels now," and that "God has called her home." His mom, the oldest daughter, beamed with pride over this. Meanwhile,

236 † Bedrock Faith

the middle daughter's kids, a pre-teen girl and a teenage boy, looked sullen, particularly when LeShawn was making one of his comments, and at one point their mom took them aside and said quietly that LeShawn was just aping blather he'd heard at Hill of the Lord.

Around seven thirty the phone rang yet again—there had been many incoming calls from folks expressing condolences—and the oldest daughter answered. It was Mrs. Clark calling from Paiger & Paiger. Holding a hand over her free ear to block the noise from the voices around her, the oldest daughter asked if she had anything to report on her search for a church, to which Mrs. Clark responded: "I have good news."

CHAPTER ELEVEN

Say Amen, Somebody

The good news had come from Reverend Wilkins. Upon receiving a call from Mrs. Clark that evening, he had, without hesitation, said that the family would be more than welcome to have Mrs. Hicks's service at Wesley-Allen.

The wake was that following Thursday at Paiger & Paiger, the cars filling the adjacent parking lot and for blocks, all the available curb-side spaces. The wake went off without a hitch, if such an expression can be used to describe an event of that sort. Over the course of the evening, well over three hundred people made their way down the dark carpet hallways of Paiger & Paiger to pay their respects, a group that included the alderman. With his owlish eyebrows, bald pate, and beaky nose, he stood at the back of the visitation room alongside his sister. There he nodded in response to the acknowledgments of constituents passing by, and spoke briefly with several of them.

Folks filed past the bronze casket where Mrs. Hicks was outfitted in a royal-blue pantsuit. The loose outfit, gaunt face, and mortuary makeup caused her to appear hardly anything like what folks remembered her looking like when she was alive. Her family, sitting in the first row of chairs, managed to make it through the evening without crying, so busy were they conversing with people.

The next morning, which was overcast and breezy, seventy or so folks filed into Wesley-Allen for the service, sitting themselves in the dark pews on either side of the center aisle. Two microphones were set on the raised but not very high area at the front of the church. One mike was affixed to the reading light of a wooden podium located on the right side (if you were facing front) and the other to a pole on the left which was not far from the organ where a short gray-haired man, one of the newcomers Reverend Wilkins had brought in, played the sort of tuneless dirge so common to wakes and funerals.

The daughters, their husbands, and Mr. Hicks sat in the first row to the right of the aisle, with the grandchildren and Ms. Shaw in the second row, and other relatives—a few cousins and a couple of aunts—in the third row. Mrs. Motley was in her usual aisle seat in row four with Mr. McTeer at her side, with the Powells and Mr. Glenn to the right of them. Mrs. Butler was there too, as was Reggie. (Mrs. Hicks's brother was not in attendance because he didn't think he could make it through the service.)

Mrs. Hicks's closed casket was below the podium, surrounded by flower arrangements. Reverend Wilkins, in his black robe, stood at the podium and in a brief invocation, called upon the Lord to "aid and guide us so that we may keep to Your righteous path."

He then recited the twenty-third Psalm, which everybody knew by heart. They all joined in halfway through the first sentence, their collective voice filling the room.

> . . . Surely goodness and mercy shall follow me all the days of my life;
> and I shall dwell in the house of the Lord forever.

The reverend looked out over the gathering and began his remarks by reviewing Mrs. Hicks's life and accomplishments. "She was a good wife, mother, grandmother, sister, aunt, and cousin. She was a good neighbor, coworker, and longtime member of our community. She will be missed."

A few calm amens were voiced to that, and the reverend nodded his head in recognition. He then launched into his sermon, speaking of how, in tough times, "we often pray to Jesus to come to our aid, to help us, to spare us from the pains and sufferings of this world. But that's not what Jesus is about. Jesus is not here to save us from any and all harm, but to assist us, to be a rock of comfort, if you will. And that comfort comes from the knowledge that, because we have given ourselves over to Him, no matter what is happening right now, no matter how bad things are right now—better is coming."

This produced a few more amens.

"That's what I say to Mrs. Hicks's family this morning. The comfort of Jesus comes not from sparing us from pain, because pain in this life is inevitable, but from giving us the knowledge that glory awaits us—if we believe in Him as our Lord and Savior."

The amens notwithstanding, many listeners felt the reverend was treading a thin line. They all knew that the middle daughter, and her husband and children, and Mr. Hicks, did not practice the faith as he described it. Therefore, by the rationale he spoke of, they would receive no comfort from the prospect of any coming glory, *and* since Mrs. Hicks had not believed, that meant no glory was in store for her, either. While many there agreed with him in principle, they did not know if that principle was the sort of thing you threw in family members' faces at a funeral. And as if to confirm such concerns, there in the first row sat the middle daughter with shoulders stiff while the oldest daughter, right next to her, nodded her head in agreement to the reverend's words.

Reverend Wilkins went on for a good little while, sailing back and forth between talking of the coming joys for believers—"*Thou dost guide me with Thy counsel, and afterward, Thou wilt receive me to glory*"—and how nonbelievers had better get themselves right before it was too late: "*For we must all appear before the judgment seat of Christ, so that each may receive good or evil, according to what he has done in the body.*" Some people sitting in the first pew row on the left-hand side of the aisle said they saw the middle daughter shoot her older sister several harsh looks during all of this.

When the reverend was finally done, everyone sang "My Savior Walk with Me," after which it was time for others to make remarks. The announcement of this by Reverend Wilkins caused Mr. McTeer to fidget.

Although Mr. McTeer was very happy that Mrs. Motley had agreed to drive him to the service and sit beside him (despite their troubles of the week before), at the same time, he could not help his irritation at the service itself, which he felt terribly mundane. He also didn't like the practice of these Protestant funerals where folks grabbed microphones and proceeded to hem and haw their way through ill-prepared remarks.

The youngest daughter made her way to the microphone. She was noticeably shorter than her older sisters and had to lower the mike before talking. Speaking on behalf of her family, her voice faltered only a couple of times, and she ended her remarks by thanking those people who'd helped her family with acts and words of kindness. "We shed tears at moments like these because we're sad for ourselves, because our loved one will be terribly missed. Which I guess is the best thing you can say about someone when they pass."

When she was finished, Reverend Wilkins asked if anyone else wanted to speak.

The next three speakers fulfilled Mr. McTeer's worst fears. First Mrs. Powell, then Mr. Powell, then Mr. Glenn came forward. All three did plenty of the hemming and hawing and rambling. After they were done, Mrs. Motley came forward. When she reached the microphone she took a folded sheet of paper from inside her black suit jacket. Unfolding it, she glanced around at her audience. "I wrote this as a letter to Mrs. Hicks's daughters," she said.

"Dear girls, although your mother and I both grew up in Parkland, she was a few years behind me in school and I did not really meet her until the day your family moved to our block some thirty years ago. I brought over a cake; I remember it was chocolate. I also remember that it didn't last very long once you three—and your daddy—got sight of it."

That produced laughter, with the loudest coming from the daughters, though none of them actually remembered the event.

"It was spring and the leaves were budding. Little did I know that in your mother, I was not only gaining a new neighbor, but a person who'd become my best friend.

"The next day your mother returned the cake stand along with a pie she had baked. And when I returned the pie pan she invited me in for coffee. And over the next few months she invited me on trips to the hardware store, or the plant store, or the department store, on the grounds that she needed my advice on what she planned to purchase. At first I didn't know what to make of her reaching out to me like that, but after a while I didn't care because I found that I enjoyed her company so much.

"You were all kids back then, just as my son was, and over the years your mother and I saw our children grow not only into adulthood, but into the kinds of people we could not only love, but respect. I cannot tell you how many times your mother related to me how proud she was of you, and the men you married, and the families you've created.

"When my son went to Vietnam and I worried night and day, your mother was a great comfort. When my husband died, she was a bulwark for me throughout that trying time.

"I know, and she knew too, that a lot of people, seeing us together shopping or having lunch, thought us an odd pair. I once asked her, early on in our friendship, why she had reached out to me. She said she just decided that she wanted to be my friend. She said, *I decided I was going to work on you because I noticed, at the first few block club meetings I attended, that you were a little aloof and standoffish.*

"Of course," Mrs. Motley grinned, "I'd have preferred she call me quiet and reserved."

She paused as people chuckled and laughed.

"That was your mother, she spoke her mind. But at the same time, she was not mean. You know how some people who say they speak their mind use that as an excuse to justify hurting other people's feelings? Your mother was not like that.

"Although I know my loss is not nearly as deep as yours, I shall miss her terribly."

With a hand across her chest, the oldest daughter mouthed a silent *Thank you* to Mrs. Motley, who paused at the first pew and placed a hand on Mr. Hicks's shoulder. As she walked back to her seat, Mr. McTeer kept his eyes fixed on her, the white silk of her blouse brilliant against her black jacket and skirt, the white of her hair brilliant against her butterscotch skin. When she sat down next to him, he wanted to give her lower arm a discreet squeeze, but with all that had happened recently between them, he did not feel he could take such a chance.

The reverend asked if anyone else wished to speak.

That's when a deep, all-too-familiar voice sounded from the back of the church: "I have something to say."

CHAPTER TWELVE

Bull in a China Shop

Everybody sitting in the pews turned halfway around and saw Stew Pot standing there at the back end of the aisle. He had apparently slipped in while others were speaking and had waited out of sight in the anteroom.

Before anyone could say anything, he strode forward. He was wearing a white dress shirt, navy-blue tie, and dark gray slacks that looked a tad small for him, the polyester material taut across his muscular thighs. The heads of the crowd turned as if synchronized, their gazes following his brisk movement.

The middle daughter leaned to her older sister and in a whispered hiss said: "Do not let him speak!" The oldest daughter was just sitting there looking at Stew Pot, and did not quite get what her sister had said. "What?" The middle daughter leaned closer and grabbed her older sister tightly by the wrist and hissed louder: "I said, don't let him speak!" But by then Stew Pot was already ascending the two steps of the raised area at the front of the church.

The oldest daughter was not sure exactly what to do. Could you prevent someone from speaking at a funeral if there'd already been an open call for remarks? The idea of causing a scene at her mother's service terrified her even more than the idea of Stew Pot speaking. She glanced at Reverend Wilkins in the hope that he might give some signal as to what she should do, or better yet, intervene himself; but he looked as unsure as everybody else. She heard her husband mutter a curse and felt a yank on her arm. She looked back at the middle sister, who stage-whispered: "Do something!" which is when Stew Pot set himself before the microphone, adjusting the pole higher.

"I'd like to say a few words about Sister Hicks," he began, giving no indication that he was aware of the glares coming at him from various points of the room. He smiled, showing off the large white teeth inside the goatee. "I stand before you today a sinner. The crimes of my youth are well known to everyone in the neighborhood. Some may even question whether I have the right to speak at the service of a woman like Mrs. Hicks. I can understand such hard feelings." Stew Pot punctuated his comments with light jabs of a crooked forefinger. "But I ask you to be merciful to me, for I am heartily sorry for my youthful misdoings."

That Stew Pot was speaking before people in a church was for many attendees bad enough; that he was going on about himself—as if folks had come out that morning to see him—was almost too much. He looked grotesque to them in his too-tight pants, his white dress shirt with faint yellow stains at the armpits, his tie that hung only three-quarters of the way down his front, and his scuffed black brogans.

From Mrs. Hicks's relatives came looks that could have peeled paint, while in other sections of the room people engaged in whispered commentary. Meanwhile, Reverend Wilkins, who seemed to have regained his sense of authority, fixed Stew Pot with a hard gaze.

"No longer am I haughty of spirit," Stew Pot continued. "I'm humble of spirit. In Proverbs twenty-nine, verse twenty-three, it says: *A man's pride shall bring him—*"

Reverend Wilkins interrupted him by clearing his throat into the podium microphone. Some people grinned at seeing Stew Pot stopped cold, standing there with his crooked finger held in front of him, giving the reverend a puzzled expression.

The reverend then said dryly: "I believe your reason for coming forward was that you had something to say about Mrs. Hicks."

This produced several laughs. Stew Pot lowered his hand and nodded to the reverend with the sort of grin that suggested acquiescence.

"I guess I got a little bit carried away there," said Stew Pot.

"So it would seem," Wilkins said. "*Do* you have anything to say about Mrs. Hicks?"

"Yes sir, I do." Stew Pot gestured toward the bronze casket with his left hand. "I think it's altogether fitting that Sister Hicks's service is being held in this humble house of worship. She was a woman who had no time for the fancy or frilly. She was a no-nonsense woman."

He moved his gaze just past the Hicks family's outraged expressions to the folks seated elsewhere whose faces were merely furious. "Mrs. Hicks was a humble woman—just as this house is humble. She was down to earth—just as this house is down to earth. She was solid and unpretentious, just as this house of God is solid and un-pretentious. Not like some of the fancy edifices you see being built these days by money-grubbing preachers out to make themselves rich; places where the congregations host pastors' days and all that sort of thing; where folks listen to the so-called pastor dressed up in his expensive suits, and showing off his shiny rings and expensive wrist-watches. Such churchgoers think being holy doesn't require any work on their part. They think Jesus has already done the hard work. They think all they have to do is sit and pray and drop some discretionary cash into the collection plate once a week, or help with a church bake sale or some other kind of fundraiser that is done in the name of God, but does not serve God. Just puts more cash in the money-grubbing pastor's pocket . . ."

So effective was Stew Pot's address that a few people found them-selves involuntarily nodding their heads in agreement with his points before catching themselves.

"*Our* ends will correspond to *our* deeds," said Stew Pot." It's not enough to just pray. How many times have you given of yourself with no thought of getting anything in return, because you realized that do-ing God's work is its own reward? *That* is true humility. *That* is a true search for Christ. Mrs. Hicks was always searching, always seeking, always looking to find out what was on the other side of the fence, as it were, and now she will be with her own special angel of light, which is her just reward for the searching deeds she has done in her body."

There were only a few people in the church, none in the first three pews, who were familiar enough with the Scriptures to discern the meaning of Stew Pot's last comment. Mrs. Motley was one of those few, and when she heard this, she let forth with a hushed "*Oh my Lord.*" Mr. McTeer, seeing the stricken look on her face, touched her shoul-der and she turned to him. He asked softly what was wrong as Stew Pot continued talking about Mrs. Hicks being with her angel of light.

Inside the book holder attached to the back of the pew in front of them was a Bible and a hymnal. Mrs. Motley took out the Bible, a Revised Standard Version, and quickly went to Second Corinthians. When she got to page 915 she pointed to the top right-hand section of the page, to verse 15.

Mr. McTeer had to bend forward a bit to read. It was the passage Stew Pot had just quoted, but there was a sentence from the middle of the passage that he had omitted: *And no wonder, for even Satan disguises himself as an angel of light.*

Now it was Mr. McTeer who had a stricken expression. He looked back to the front of the church. Apparently Reverend Wilkins also did not care for Stew Pot's latest line, because his eyebrows were scrunched and his lips frowning.

"As we sow, so shall we reap," said Stew Pot. "And for those of us who perform special deeds, there will be an angel of light waiting for us, with a light as bright as—"

Reverend Wilkins cut Stew Pot off again: "Sir, are you an ordained minister?"

This time Stew Pot's expression was not the supplicating grin of before. As soon as he caught sight of the reverend's face, he assumed a serious look of his own.

"No sir," Stew Pot said, "I am not ordained, although I read the Scriptures daily without fail and I have committed many passages to memory. While in prison for my sins, I had nothing but time, which as it turned out was a blessing because—"

"Yes," snapped the reverend, "you told us all about that. But I'm going to have to stop you because only ordained ministers may deliver sermons in this house."

"I was simply saying a few words on behalf of Sister Hicks. Words I might add, that sorely need saying."

Mutterings rose from the first two pews as the Hicks family, no longer able to contain themselves, gave voice to their anger. From somewhere behind Mrs. Motley and Mr. McTeer, someone said: "Sit down!"

"You were giving a sermon," said Reverend Wilkins. "I know a sermon when I hear one. Only ordained ministers may deliver sermons here. You, sir, are not ordained."

"I am simply speaking the word of God," replied Stew Pot with a faint smile that convinced no one there of his good will.

"And I say," Reverend Wilkins countered, "that I am pastor here and you must take your seat. Or better yet, leave."

From several locations came angry calls for Stew Pot to sit down. Mr. Hicks began to weep and the youngest daughter, who was sitting beside him, threw her arm around his shoulders. In unison her sisters, her husband, and her two brothers-in-law stood up, forming a solid wall of fury.

"That's it!" the middle daughter said, pointing a finger up at Stew Pot. "Leave! And I mean *now!* I don't want to get crazy in here, but I will if you don't take your worthless self out!"

Stew Pot gave her a contemptuous look. "Such malice, such spite. And at your mother's service, no less. You ought to be ashamed of yourself."

The wall of rage at the front pew exploded into shouts and gesticulations. From around the room came catcalls, one of them shouted by Mr. McTeer.

The middle daughter stepped forward. "I know you. We all know you! We know what you are!"

"*You* know nothing at all," Stew Pot sneered.

From all over came more shouts and catcalls.

"I command you to leave my house!" said the reverend into his microphone.

"*Your* house!" said Stew Pot with equal vehemence. "This is not *your* house! It's God house! You don't even know your role. You have no idea what your job is!"

"AND I SAY LEAVE!" cried the reverend.

Nearly everyone was now on their feet, some leaning forward at the waist over the pew backs. The middle and oldest daughters and their husbands moved forward near the set of steps, yelling and gesturing while the youngest daughter sat rocking the still weeping Mr. Hicks in her arms.

"I tried to be polite to you, Reverend, when I spoke earlier," Stew Pot said into his microphone, "but when you challenge my right to witness for the Lord, you're attacking *Him.* And when someone attacks my Savior, then I take off the kid gloves!"

Stew Pot pointed an outstretched arm at the reverend, his forefinger like a blunt blade. "You are a false prophet! You worship on Sunday, not on the Sabbath as the Bible teaches! You have spent your life leading men, women, and children astray, teaching as the gospel the precepts of man! And God has—"

Suddenly Stew Pot's microphone went dead. He tapped it with his forefinger, but there was no sound. The old man organist had snuck to the wall behind him and yanked the cord from the socket.

"I don't need electronic amplification to witness!" Stew Pot shouted. Then, just like that, he threw up his right arm and ducked out of the way as something dark went sailing over his lowered head. One of Mrs. Hicks's cousins from the third row, a fifty-something woman wearing a dark-feathered hat, had grabbed a nearby hymnal and flung it at Stew Pot. Unfortunately, because of Stew Pot's quick reaction, the hymnal missed its intended target and kept right on going at a high rate of speed toward the organist, who was on his way back to the organ bench. His reflexes were not nearly as quick as Stew Pot's, and the book hit him a glancing but nonetheless hard blow against his forehead. He wobbled and then fell.

A number of people who saw this cried out and the oldest daughter dashed by Stew Pot to the fallen man and bent over him. The church quieted. Some people stood on tiptoe among the pews in an attempt to get a better look, while others left their places and headed up the aisle and then the short set of steps. Stew Pot now stood with his back to the church, his view of the organist quickly blocked by the bent backs of a dozen or so people crowding around the old man. As a result, he did not see the middle daughter come up alongside him and give him a powerful shove. Caught off guard, he stumbled back, almost falling down the steps before managing to regain his balance.

"I said get out!" the middle daughter shouted.

The contemptuous expression returned to Stew Pot's face. "Lucky for you I don't fight women."

He then stumbled forward from another shove, this one given to him from behind. He got his balance again and turned around to see who'd done it.

"I'm a man, why don't you fight me?" It was the oldest daughter's husband. His jaw was fixed in a clench and his hands tightened into fists.

The folks still remaining in the pews went to tiptoe again while the folks bent over the organist gazed over their shoulders. Though not as muscular as Stew Pot, the oldest daughter's husband was just as tall, and from the way he was glaring, he looked like he was ready to throw dukes with the Devil himself.

"I don't fight in the Lord's house," Stew Pot said.

"We can step outside if you want," snapped the oldest daughter's husband.

Stew Pot looked around at all the staring faces, then back to his challenger. "I did not come here to fight. I came to witness."

From somewhere in the crowd a woman shouted: "Why don't you witness your butt on out of here!" which produced numerous calls of agreement.

The oldest daughter, looking fearful, pushed through to her husband's side, clasping an arm around his tense arm, obviously terrified of what might happen.

"Let me pass!" Stew Pot said. And the folks near him made a hole and made it wide. He strode down the aisle and again the heads rotated as if synchronized, following his progress. He turned around at the end of the aisle and shouted back at them: "You are all serving the Lord in vain! Heaven and earth shall pass away, but my words shall not pass away! Jesus the father! Jesus the son!" And then he left.

CHAPTER THIRTEEN
The Return of an Old Friend

After Stew Pot was gone, someone called 911 for an ambulance. By then the organist was sitting next to the bench. He said he thought he was okay and you could tell he was embarrassed at all the fuss being made over him. Although he protested, the paramedics took him to the hospital anyway, just to be on the safe side.

It was decided to dispense with any further service and just head over to Eden Rest for the burial. The Hicks daughters asked their father, who by that time had composed himself, if he was up to going. Still sitting in the first pew, he nodded his fuzzy gray head.

"I'm going to bury my Lovey today," he rasped, using his pet name for his wife.

As usually happens immediately after a church function, there was some milling about out front. Folks stood in small groups talking over the events they'd just seen, many using these moments to shape how they would retell things later to family and friends.

It was while the alderman's sister and her attendees were passing out orange-glow FUNERAL windshield stickers that someone asked: "Is that Erma?"

The folks looked toward the middle of the block. It most certainly was Erma. She was closing the driver's door of a red car, and she was not alone. There was someone in the front passenger's seat. No one recognized the person, but what was perfectly clear, even from that distance, was that the passenger was a blond White woman.

Word of Erma's presence passed from conversation cluster to conversation cluster and talk of Stew Pot stopped as folks turned to get a good look. Although her hair was noticeably shorter, Erma looked pretty much as folks remembered. Stylishly decked out in a black skirt suit with a black blouse and high black boots, she approached along the street next to the other parked cars. She stepped to the curb between the back end of the hearse and the nose of one of the black Paiger & Paiger limousines. With a tepid smile she nodded to those closest to her and they nodded back. Mrs. Motley pulled her close for a smiling hug and then Mrs. Powell gave her one too.

Mr. McTeer did not smile, and Mrs. Butler said nothing, both looking like they'd just swallowed dill pickle brine. Similar expressions were in evidence on a number of other faces, including that of the oldest daughter who was standing with her husband and children a few feet from Erma.

Why the oldest daughter did what she did next would become the subject of numerous conjectures over the coming days and weeks, with most people citing the stress caused by her mother's death and Stew Pot's carryings on at the service.

"What are *you* doing here?" said the oldest daughter. The anger in her voice caused the smile to melt from Erma's face and a wave of anticipatory tension to charge through the others.

"I just wanted to pay my respects. When I read the death notice in the paper—"

"You should have sent a card," the oldest daughter said, "instead of showing up here at my mother's service parading your perversion in front of my children!"

And just like that Erma threw her arms around the oldest daughter's bountiful body, hugged her, and said: "I'm so sorry for your loss." Erma then let her go and hugged the other two Hicks daughters, who both gave her a sincere thank you.

That's when Mr. Glenn stepped forward and took both of Erma's hands in his. Not immediately remembering who he was, she looked curious at him and then brightened when she recognized him. He asked how she was doing and she said she was actually doing quite well, and then Mr. Glenn surprised everybody by asking her if she wanted to come by the house so she could show her friend where she used to live. Erma smiled like the Erma they'd known so well, and she said she'd love to as long it wasn't any trouble. Mr. Glenn said it was no trouble at all.

Erma went back to her car and the rest dispersed to their vehicles, with the Hicks's immediate family getting in the two limousines.

At windy Eden Rest Cemetery, set on a high bank above the Cal Sag (where the dead relatives of many in attendance were buried), folks got a good look at Erma's gal pal. The couple stood at the back of the crowd, though some paid more attention to them than to Reverend Wilkins speaking at graveside where the bronze casket sat before Mrs. Hicks's weeping relatives.

The blond White woman was wearing a red flannel shirt and jeans (*Now isn't* *that* *just typical*, a few of the onlookers snidely thought) and was the same height as Erma, with her feathered hair cut even shorter. Later that day, as details of the dramatic events were reported by those who'd attended the service and burial, there was a strong difference of opinion over who the blond White woman most resembled. Some of the older folks said she favored Kim Novak, and other older folks said she looked like Ann-Margaret, while one old meanie posited that both groups were wrong: "Kim Novak? Ann-Margaret? Uh-uh. No way was that heifer *that* attractive."

BOOK VII

The Neighborhood Strikes Back

CHAPTER ONE

Turning Point

The next day it was all over Parkland what had happened at Wesley-Allen and Eden Rest and how Mr. Glenn had given Erma and her honey a tour of Erma's old home. Some were not happy about this. Mr. McTeer and Mrs. Butler, finding common ground in a shared bigotry, were among those who voiced the strongest objections, causing the youngest daughter, who was liberal about such matters, to comment: "Those folks are just mad 'cause Erma came back to Parkland looking fit and happy. If she'd shone up looking sad and miserable, they'd have been delighted."

Per usual, there were various Parkland Gossip Line elaborations: Stew Pot had thrown a Bible at Reverend Wilkins; Erma and her lover had exchanged a kiss at the burial service in front of God and everybody; the oldest daughter had spit at Erma in front of the church.

Folks were still talking about all this the next day. A constant in the conversations was an outrage over what Stew Pot had done. This included Mrs. Motley. That day, wearing her conical straw hat, she was working with her gardens (which were in all their late-summer splendor: crowds of colors and petal curvatures) when Stew Pot exited the back door of the two-flat with his leashed dog.

He gave Mrs. Motley a cheerful hello, as if nothing had happened the day before. From where she was kneeling with gloves and a trowel, Mrs. Motley's eyes narrowed.

"I no longer wish to speak with you," she said. "Please do not make living next door to you any more distasteful than it already is by trying to converse with me. "

"Mrs. Motley, let me explain."

But she simply returned to her digging. Appearing truly crestfallen, he walked away with his dog.

Over the next few days, when other immediate neighbors saw Stew Pot on the street and he greeted them, they acted like he wasn't there. When they encountered Mrs. Reeves in her comings and go-ings, some folks took the opportunity to let her know exactly how they felt: "You need to talk some sense into your son." She responded by looking worried and hurrying off.

In Parkland-at-large, Stew Pot also greeted people cheerfully as if nothing had happened, like it had been somebody else who had dis-rupted Mrs. Hicks's service. Everyone thought this was really weird, and they indulged themselves by ignoring him too. As satisfying as giving Stew Pot the cold shoulder was, some people insisted that more needed to be done. So widespread was this talk that a number of cops in the 26th District started a pool as to when someone would make the first attack on Stew Pot.

Those who bet sooner rather than later won the pool. On the Sun-day night after Mrs. Hicks's service, someone threw a rock through a rear window of the two-flat. The next night someone threw a rock through one of the windows overlooking the two-flat's gangway.

Both times Mrs. Motley was awakened by the barking of Stew Pot's dog, and both times whoever had done the deed was gone by the time she got to her window. The night after the second attack, Stew Pot left his dog in the backyard unchained. There were no disturbances that night and most people assumed the dog's presence would bring an end to any more moves against the Reeves's home. They were wrong.

CHAPTER TWO

A Bump in the Night

The second Saturday night after Mrs. Hicks's service, at around two a.m., Mrs. Motley and other neighbors living near the two-flat were yanked from their sleep by the loud barking of Stew Pot's dog. An hour or so later, after the police had come and gone, Mrs. Motley, in nightdress, robe, and slippers, sipped coffee in the yellow kitchen with Mr. McTeer and the Hicks's youngest daughter, who were also in nightclothes, robes, and slippers.

Mrs. Motley was at one end of the table with Mr. McTeer on her right and the youngest daughter, who'd spent the night at her father's, on her left.

"So there I was," Mrs. Motley said in a voice that revealed her fatigue, "sound asleep, when the dog woke me. Then I heard a car out in the alley roar away."

The youngest daughter said she'd heard it too. She hadn't been able to sleep and had gone to her parents' summerhouse to sit in the night air for a while. "I heard the dog barking and stepped to the side fence and looked down your driveway, Mr. McTeer. That's when I realized the barking was coming from Stew Pot's place."

"Yes," said Mrs. Motley. "I looked out my back window upstairs. The Reeves's gate was open and the dog was in the alley barking at a dark car. I couldn't tell exactly what kind of car because I could only see the tail end; the rest of it was blocked by my garage."

"Then suddenly the vehicle took off and the dog went barking after it."

"Did you see what kind of car it was then?" asked the youngest daughter.

"No," said Mrs. Motley. "Like I told the police later, it was moving too fast. Anyway, at this point I see the back light go on next door and Stew Pot step out in just a pair of baggy basketball shorts and those brogans. He was carrying a baseball bat. He stepped off the porch, and at the same time, further down the alley, I heard the car stop and its tires screech. Then the engine gunned in reverse and I heard a bump sound. The car crunched to a stop again, and then the engine gunned again and roared off. I heard the tires screech in the distance, I imagine from the driver doing a high-speed turn out of the alley."

"Then what happened?" asked Mr. McTeer.

Mrs. Motley took a sip of coffee. "Stew Pot trotted down the alley with the bat. He wasn't gone long. When he got back he was carrying the dog in both arms, so he must have left the bat down there. I could tell right away the dog was dead. It was limp and its head was lolling over the crook of his arm and its mouth was hanging open with its tongue out. That's when Mrs. Reeves came out on the porch in her robe. She gasped when Stew Pot reached the back steps. He set the dog down and squatted next to it, rubbing a palm over its side."

"How long did it take the police to get there?"

"Not long. I don't know who called. The first car there was unmarked with the flashing light on the dashboard. It stopped in front of the open gate and one of the policemen who got out was that big fellow, Mance."

"I could see down the two-flat gangway that police were in your alley, Mrs. Motley," said the youngest daughter. "That's when I knocked on Mr. McTeer's door."

"Oh, I see," Mrs. Motley said, before continuing. "So Mance and his partner walked to the back steps and asked Stew Pot what happened. They spoke casually, like it was no big deal. Still rubbing the dog, Stew Pot said: *They killed my dog.* Then he stands up and tells them what I just told you: somebody opened the back gate and the dog ran out, and that person got back in their car and drove a ways down the alley with the dog in pursuit, then stopped and backed the car over the dog. Mance asked why the dog was in the yard, as if he didn't know that rocks had been thrown through the Reeves's windows. When Stew Pot explained what had happened, Mance and the other officer just smirked. I thought Stew Pot might lose his temper, which they were probably hoping he'd do. But he didn't.

"That's about the time a squad car showed up and parked behind Mance's car. Later on, a uniformed officer—a White woman—came to my back door asking if I'd seen anything. She didn't act particularly concerned and I have a sneaking suspicion the police aren't going to put a lot of effort in getting to the bottom of this."

Mrs. Motley leaned forward and massaged her forehead with her left hand. Mr. McTeer asked if she was okay. Mrs. Motley took her hand away and sat up.

"I dunno. I never cared for Stew Pot's dog, but to just run it over like that . . ."

"Don't tell me you feel sorry for that mutt," said the youngest daughter.

"It's not that. A dog acts in whatever way it's trained."

"Want my opinion?" asked the youngest daughter (who had never been a big fan of dogs, including her mother's). "I say goodbye to bad rubbish."

"I agree," said Mr. McTeer.

CHAPTER THREE

Ding-Dong, the Dog Is Dead

The following day Stew Pot buried his dog behind the two-flat in the rear corner of the yard near the alley. He had bundled it in an old sky-blue blanket, the shrouded body lying on the grass beside him as he dug, perspiration coating his head and neck and glistening in the sunlight. When he finished, he eased the bundle into the deep hole.

Observing from a kitchen window, the thought came to Mrs. Motley that Stew Pot had probably felt as strongly for his pet as Mrs. Hicks had for hers. It did not please her to have such a sympathetic Stew Pot–related thought, but she could not deny it, just as later on that day, when she was out in the neighborhood, she could not deny her negative reaction to the way people happily asked for details about the killing of the dog, and the way they laughed when she told them of how Officer Mance and his partner had been so cruel.

Such elation had spread all over the neighborhood. A few of Parkland's harder souls—smart-mouth teenagers mostly—had fun teasing Stew Pot when they saw him: "Hey there, Stew. So how's the dog?" Several cops, pulling their cars to a slow roll alongside him as he walked, made similar jests. In all these confrontations Stew Pot stared back at the jokesters for a second with a blank expression before continuing on his way, laughter dancing in the air behind him.

CHAPTER FOUR

Shine On, Shine On, Harvest Moon, Up in the Sky

The Parkland Harvest Moon Festival was held the first weekend in October, as it had been for the previous thirty years. The fest was set up in the large parking lot directly west of the commuter train station and featured the usual carnival fare: a moderate-sized Ferris wheel, a merry-go-round, and games of skill involving the tossing of tennis balls or bean bags for the honor and glory of winning cheap-quality stuffed animals. For consumption there were lots of fried and grilled meats, sugar-loaded snacks and soft drinks, and lots of beer.

A stage was erected on the west side of the lot with speakers stacked either side and a banner reading PARKLAND HARVEST MOON set above it. The music began at noon both days and ran till ten at night. Some performers were acts hardly anyone had ever heard of, like Wide Load and Windjammer, while others were one-time big names reduced to working the street-fair circuit such as Who Loves You, Baby? and Vic Vegas.

Harvest Moon drew folks from all over the far South Side and southern suburbs, the crowd kept more or less under control by armed off-duty cops who patrolled the mass in bright yellow T-shirts with SECURITY printed in big purple letters across the backs.

The best place to people-watch the mob while avoiding the aromatic overload of grease, candy corn, beer, and perspiration, was to stake out a place on the long commuter train platform. This was technically against the law, but the folks there—Mrs. Motley, Mr. McTeer, Mrs. Powell, Mr. Hicks, and a few other folks from the neighborhood—had been doing so for so long that nobody said anything.

The platform sitters came on the Saturday evening of the festival with lawn chairs and picnic basket suppers. They lined their seats in a single row down the middle of the platform, which allowed room for folks stepping on or off a train to get easily by.

The October after Mrs. Hicks's passing, with the sun setting behind the silhouetted roof and treetops of neighboring Blue Island, the sitters did that plate-balance-on-the-lap thing and chatted and ate their potato salad and fried chicken. (For Mr. Hicks, it was the first excursion out of the house since his wife's service.) They helloed to passersby they knew coming from or going to the festival, and someone commented, as someone always did, that certain things never changed, in this particular case referencing the squads of teenagers all about with their giggling and loud talk and horsing around, which got the conversation rolling, as such observations always did, with memories from their teenage years in the neighborhood. Back then there wasn't a block that didn't have at least a few vacant lots where folks grew corn and cabbage and onions and carrots to supplement their larders. Back then, at this time of year, those fields would be bare for the first time since spring and they'd all go to the Parkland Fall Cotillion. The dance hadn't been held for some years, which was too bad, they said, because it had been such fun. And there had been hayrides in horse-drawn wagons, and much later in the fall, the curbside burning of leaves that sent smoke wafting through the nearly naked tree branches and turned the air hazy and thick with a not-unpleasant burnt smell. And wasn't it too bad, they said, that the city wouldn't let you do that anymore?

CHAPTER FIVE

Brother Crown

That night the crowd hit critical mass around nine p.m. and a couple of sitters were talking about going home when a southbound train glided to a stop with its bell dinging. The doors parted with a sigh and out of the last car at the north end of the platform stepped Stew Pot carrying a suitcase, Mrs. Reeves in a dark blue scarf and ankle-length dress, and a man none of them had ever seen before.

The stranger was pale, like vanilla ice cream. He was taller than Stew Pot but slender, dressed in a milk-white three-piece suit complete with matching shoes, shirt, socks, tie, and handkerchief. Topping the outfit off—literally—was a white wide-brimmed fedora. The hat shaded the pale face from the platform lights, but not so much that they couldn't make out his wide nose and full, pale pink lips.

The three waited at the north end of the platform as the train, which had temporarily blocked the festival from view, pulled away, its bells dinging until it cleared the crossing.

With a sneer, Stew Pot made a sweeping gesture toward the festival crowd. "See?" he said to the albino man, loud enough that the platform sitters heard him over the female jazz singer on the distant stage. "What did I tell you? Sin as far as the eye can see."

The albino man didn't say anything, just nodded his head in apparent agreement.

The trio set off down the platform. Stew Pot and his mom kept their faces forward, avoiding eye contact with anyone. The albino man, however, nodded and smiled as he passed by the gawking faces. He stopped in front of Mrs. Motley, who was in the middle of the sitting row, and turned his back to the festival goings-on. Stew Pot and his mom, obviously surprised by this action, stopped too.

To the platform sitters, the combination of the stranger's native sub-Saharan features and vanilla skin was unsettling. On closer inspection of his suit, Mrs. Motley and the others noticed that the jacket cuffs were frayed in a couple of spots and the outer sides of his shoes were scuffed. They also noticed the dull yellow of his teeth against the pink lips, and that he appeared to be in his fifties at the very least.

The albino man began walking in an easy circle, making eye contact with everyone, which included a handful of people waiting for a northbound train.

"Hey there, brothers and sisters, how're you all doing tonight?"

"Just fine," said Mr. McTeer sarcastically, "until about a minute ago."

The albino man kept smiling. "My name is Brother Crown. I'm here visiting with my friend Brother Gerald and his dear mother, and to speak the word of God."

"Church is tomorrow," said Mr. McTeer.

"That's true," smiled Brother Crown. "But it's never too early to get right with God. There's a war on, brothers and sisters, and your souls are the battleground. The Devil knows the only way he can cause God pain is to corrupt *you*." And here he extended an arm and pointed forefinger at the festival. Save for a few folks eating and drinking at nearby picnic tables, most festival-goers were unaware of him.

"The crucial question is," Brother Crown continued, "will you move from sin and into The Light? It just takes one step. Salvation is inches away. Put down that tobacco and take that step. Put down that liquor and drugs and take that step. Renounce sinful thoughts and deeds and take that step." (At that point, Stew Pot cut Mr. McTeer a look.) "Now, some people say, *But Brother Crown, that tobacco feels good, those liquor and drugs feel good, lustful thoughts and deeds feel good.* To which I say, of course sin feels good. The Devil knows he can't corrupt anybody by making them feel *bad.* Satan may be evil, but he's not stupid.

"There's only one thing to do: step into The Light. Jesus is waiting. He's got a candle burning in the window and a welcome mat at the door. But He can't take the step for you. I hope you all will take these thoughts with you this evening. Also, tomorrow afternoon at four o'clock I will be holding a prayer service in front of Brother Gerald and Sister Reeves's place. Any who want to join us are more than welcome. God bless you all."

He then stepped quickly past Stew Pot and Mrs. Reeves, who followed behind him. The sitters watched them disappear through the swinging doors of the station house and then, moments later, head east over the crossing and away from the festival.

When the platform sitters from Stew Pot's block returned home that evening, folks there were eager to share the news about the stranger who had arrived that evening at the two-flat with Stew Pot and Mrs. Reeves, only to have the sitters relate the even bigger news of what had transpired on the platform. And when Mrs. Powell told those gathered in front of Mrs. Butler's house about the prayer service Brother Crown had mentioned, Mr. Glenn got a wolfish grin on his face and said: "No kidding?"

CHAPTER SIX

A Pregnant Pause

The next day Mrs. Motley told folks she wanted no part of whatever was going to happen in front of the two-flat later that afternoon. By three thirty she was reading the Sunday paper away from the front windows in the apple-green dining room. (She read with great interest an account of a battle between US soldiers and militiamen in Somalia that had occurred two weeks before, and fervently hoped that the situation there would not escalate into anything requiring the deployment of her son, like with the Gulf War five years before.)

Though many on the block had spoken angrily about the prospect of the outdoor prayer service, most folks could not resist the urge to watch; this included Mr. McTeer and Mr. Hicks and the middle daughter. These folks were on porches and stoops or in their open doorways at four when Brother Crown walked out in his white three-piece suit, sans fedora, which revealed his bushy wheat-colored hair.

Stew Pot and Mrs. Reeves followed. Some minutes later, Mrs. Motley's phone rang. It was Mr. McTeer. In an urgent voice he asked if she was watching what was going on out front. She said no. "What's Brother Crown doing now, calling down the thunder or something?" And Mr. McTeer explained: "Crown isn't doing anything. It's Erma Smedley who's doing the something."

When Mrs. Motley got to her screen door she saw a red convertible sports car parked in front of the two-flat and Erma at the doorway in agitated conversation with Stew Pot. He, Mrs. Reeves, and Brother Crown were all dressed as they'd been the day before, but Erma was in a condition Mrs. Motley had never seen her in. Erma looked pregnant. A large protrusion bulged out in front of her, sheathed by a red pregnant-lady blouse. She also had on shades, green stretch pants, and dark flat-soled shoes.

"Our baby is due in a month, Gerald," Erma said loudly. "What are you going to do?"

Having seen a normal-sized Erma just several weeks before, Mrs. Motley knew that the pregnancy could not be real, that Erma must've placed a pillow prop under the blouse.

"Now listen here, Erma," Stew Pot said. "Stop this false and sinful talk right now."

"Oh, so now you don't want me to talk sinful. You liked it well enough when I talked to you that way in my bed. In my bed you liked sinful talk just fine."

"I don't know what you're up to," replied Stew Pot, "but you're going to have to leave. We're conducting a worship service here and—"

"And I'm tired of you playing the nut role like you don't know I'm carrying your child."

Stew Pot looked at Brother Crown with a she's-crazy expression. And that's when it hit Mrs. Motley. Stew Pot and his mom, who hadn't seen Erma after Mrs. Hicks's service, and who never talked to anyone, did not know there was no way Erma could be pregnant.

"Erma, I'm sorry you've gotten yourself in this sad state. I suppose one good thing is that you've obviously turned from the lesbianite ways you were indulging in before and you've decided not to slaughter your child with an abortion; however, I'm in no way—"

"Then what's your explanation," she snapped, "an Immaculate Conception? Are you saying I just imagined it was you grunting and sweating on top of me?"

Brother Crown, who was holding a large white-covered Bible, stepped forward and, waving an arm toward the open doorway of the two-flat, asked Erma to come inside. She answered by dropping her head and launching into a crying babble about how "Gerald" had sought her out after she moved away in shame, and he had brought her to the Lord, and he had gained her trust, and she had fallen in love with him, and he'd told her that he was in love with her too, and that their sleeping together would be a holy joining of their love, for each other as well as their shared love for Jesus.

Brother Crown stepped forward and embraced her. She mashed her face against his chest, careful not to press her big belly against him. He cooed to her that everything was going to be all right while patting her back with a pale hand. Stew Pot meanwhile looked as if *he* might start to cry, his pained gaze shifting back and forth between the embracing pair beside him, the neighbors bearing witness, and his mother, who for all the bewilderment that showed on her face, uttered not a word in her son's defense; a point that did not go unnoticed by Mrs. Motley.

Erma brought her face away from Brother Crown. He pulled a white handkerchief from inside his suit jacket and gave it to her. As she wiped under her sunglasses and sniffled, she said that Gerald had told her he wanted to get married, but when she told him about the baby he had changed; now she didn't know what she was going to do.

Stew Pot looked at Brother Crown, threw up his arms, and then let them flop to his sides.

Again Brother Crown asked if she wanted to come inside. Erma shook her head no. "What for? So my baby's father can deny him— *again*?" Then in a harsh whisper she said to Stew Pot: "You will *never* see this child." And before he could respond she turned and waddled back to the red car. When she reached the driver's door she shouted: "You'll never see him! That's right; the doctor says the baby's going to be a boy!"

Erma made a show of struggling to get back behind the wheel of the car. She made a quick turn at the railroad embankment and drove away. Back in front of the two-flat, Brother Crown had an arm around Stew Pot's shoulder and Mrs. Motley heard him say gently: "Let's go inside, Brother Gerald."

It was as they turned to go back that Stew Pot noticed her. He stopped, and with a look of hope on his face he called out: "Mrs. Motley! Mrs. Motley! You know me. Please explain to Brother Crown that I'm not guilty of what Erma has accused me of doing." Then he looked at Brother Crown and said: "Remember I told you how Mrs. Motley befriended me? She'll vouch for me now." He stared at her desperately. "Tell him, Mrs. Motley. Please."

"I have nothing to say," replied Mrs. Motley, and turned her back, leaving Stew Pot in disbelief, his hand reaching toward her as if he might pull her from behind the closing screen door.

CHAPTER SEVEN
Walk This Way, Talk This Way

Nothing was seen of the two-flat trio until the following evening. At around seven Brother Crown emerged, followed by Mrs. Reeves in a black scarf and dress, then Stew Pot, who was encased in a double placard getup like the kind you see men wearing in black-and-white photos from the Great Depression. The placards hung from his neckline to his knees, the boards connected at the tops by shoulder straps of twine.

Both boards carried messages printed in large black letters.

The front placard read:

> *I AM A SINNER, SEEKING*
> *HIS WAY BACK INTO THE LIGHT.*
> *I KNOW NOT WHAT THE FUTURE*
> *HOLDS FOR ME, BUT I KNOW*
> *WHO HOLDS THE FUTURE:*
> *THE LORD, THE LORD, THE LORD!*

The back placard read:

> *GOD BE MERCIFUL TO ME,*
> *A SINNER.*
> *PLEASE DELIVER ME. IT'S*
> *GOD'S WAY OR THE HIGHWAY.*

Moving from his living room couch, where he'd first spied the trio, Mr. McTeer went to his front steps; there, he glanced across his driveway and saw Mr. Hicks standing in front of the Cape Cod's front door.

Across the way on the Reeves's walkway, Brother Crown and Mrs. Reeves stood on either side of Stew Pot. Brother Crown spread a pale hand on Stew Pot's dark, bowed head. Brother Crown closed his eyes and Mrs. Reeves followed his lead.

Speaking loudly, as if he were in a theater, Brother Crown said: "Dear Lord, watch over Brother Gerald in his hour of need. Hear his plea for forgiveness, which he makes willingly and for all to see. Help him find the way back into The Light—"

And Mrs. Reeves, in a surprisingly loud but still squeaky voice, said: "*Back into The Light, Lord.*"

"For you are the power—"

"*The power, Lord.*"

"And the glory—"

"*The glory, Lord.*"

"You *are* the Great I Am—"

"*You are great, Lord.*"

"You are the wheel inside the wheel—"

"*The wheel of wheels, Lord.*"

"You are Alpha *and* Omega—"

"*You are everything, Lord.*"

"Hear Brother Gerald's plea—"

"*Hear him, Lord.*"

"So he can get back into The Light—"

"*Into The Light, Lord.*"

"In your Holy name—"

"*Your holy name, Lord.*"

"Amen."

"*Amen.*"

The three then headed west. Folks on the block later learned they marched over to the main drag where they strode up and down the street in silence. They drew comments from folks crowded in the doorways of saloons, or who stopped on the sidewalk to gape, or who slowed down in cars with heads craning out the window.

As evening hit eight thirty, they were still at it. Airy Tarmore, on duty in the ward office, watched impassively while across the street at the forest preserve, a group of local lads that included Reggie Butler sat on the guardrail pointing and laughing at the trio. (The police saw them too. Around eight forty-five, Officer Mance and his partner were flagged down by a do-gooder citizen who said he'd just heard that Stew Pot was causing a disturbance over on the drag. And ho-ho-ho, folks said later, were Mance and his partner disappointed when they rolled up on those three, only to discover they were simply walking down the street.)

By a quarter past ten the trio was still walking their walk, to everyone's amazement. By then some bar flies, a little further along in their drinking, made snide—and in a few cases profane—comments. None of the three responded. Their refusal to rise to any bait must have surely dismayed Officer Mance and his partner, folks said. Those two swung by the main drag every now and again in the obvious hope that some drunk might say something to cause Stew Pot to throw a punch, giving them cause to haul him in.

The trio headed home around eleven thirty, and every night that week they strolled the drag. By Thursday night the novelty was long gone and most folks didn't pay the Holy Three (as one local smartmouth named them) much mind. No one stood making wisecracks from the doorways of saloons, although a drinker was heard to say that one good thing about Stew Pot's marching around was that for a few hours a night at least, they could all rest easy because they knew for sure where he was.

CHAPTER EIGHT
Who's Your Daddy?

The following Friday afternoon, in a packed Parkland High School gymnasium, there was a noisy pep rally for the homecoming game the next day. Per longtime neighborhood tradition, Reggie Butler and other seniors on the football team enjoyed an evening barbecue in the forest preserve, followed by some light nighttime beer drinking in a secluded section of the woods.

Reggie arrived at the back gate of his home around eleven thirty, well ahead of his grandmother's midnight curfew for Friday and Saturday nights. There was a high wooden fence around the backyard and as Reggie, wearing his dark blue wool jacket with the maize leather sleeves, approached the gate by the brick garage, Stew Pot, like a ghost suddenly making itself visible, stepped from the alley's shadows and blocked Reggie's path.

Though surprised and a bit scared, Reggie was also emboldened by beers. Speaking sharply and with no slur he said: "What do you want?"

Stew Pot calmly explained that they needed to talk.

Even more sharply, Reggie replied: "Yeah, about what?"

Still calm, Stew Pot said: "Now listen, son, there's no need to get angry."

In a condescending tone Reggie said: "I'm not your son—okay?"

When Stew Pot responded, "Yes, you are," Reggie at first didn't grasp his meaning.

"Yes, I'm *what*?"

"You heard me," Stew Pot said gently.

There followed several seconds of silence, Stew Pot's calm gaze fixed on Reggie's face, before Reggie realized what the older man had actually meant.

With his voice rising a couple of octaves to a near falsetto, Reggie said: "Have you lost your natural mind?"

Stew Pot, cool as an ice floe, said: "Your mother and I—"

For Reggie, the subject of his mother—who he had no direct memory of—was a very raw nerve. He grabbed Stew Pot firmly by the bib of his overalls. "Don't you dare talk about my mother."

"I don't believe in physical violence," Stew Pot said evenly, "especially against my own flesh and blood; even when the flesh and blood is obviously intoxicated from drinking in the woods with wayward boys and slut girls."

Pushing Stew Pot away, Reggie snapped: "I'm no flesh and blood of yours."

"You can say all you want, Reggie, but it won't change the facts: your mother—may God guard her wherever she is—and I were intimate. You are the result of those intimacies. It's time you knew it. It's time everybody knew.

"Erma's calling me out as the father of her baby was a lie, and as a result I may lose my chance for an assistantship in which I would have traveled with Brother Crown around the country and Canada spreading the word about The Light. I asked God, *Why is this being done to me?* And then I realized, in the humble humility of deep prayer, that I was being punished not for what I'd done to Erma, but for what I'd done to your mother—seducing her and then not making up for my sin by marrying her.

"God sent Erma to do what she did and stayed Mrs. Motley's tongue so that I'd be punished, *and* so I'd have the opportunity to confess and atone. In the next issue of *Burning Bush* I'm going to confess everything I've confessed here tonight. And if you let me, I'll be a good father to you and help get you into The Light."

Reggie blurted that Stew Pot had better keep his trashy rag to himself.

Stew Pot chuckled. "Everyone doubts the value of my journal. Even Brother Crown says the publication is unwise. But he'll eventually see its value. God bless you, son."

Reggie watched Stew Pot walk down Honore. Feeling more anxious than he'd ever felt in his life, he told himself that at all costs he had to stop Stew Pot from publishing his lies. How he would accomplish such a thing he didn't at the moment know, but he had to find a way. He had to be strong, for himself and for his grandma.

CHAPTER NINE

Be True to Your School

The next morning, dozens of round folding tables were set up in the Parkland High cafeteria, draped with white cloths, and the walls of the wide, high-ceilinged room were festooned with navy-blue and maize bunting and balloons.

The annual homecoming pancake breakfast began at eight a.m. The attendees were mostly alumni over forty, with the food served by current students wearing white full-length aprons. By eight fifteen the place was noisy with gab and the air heavy with the aroma of maple syrup and fried sausage.

Vernon Paiger was there like he was every year. After finishing his meal he got up and worked the room, shaking hands and saying hellos, which hardly anybody minded since most were lifetime friends and acquaintances who appreciated all he did for the ward. For instance, a few years prior, Vernon had been instrumental in getting an athletic field built across the street from the high school, which meant that folks attending the homecoming's morning activities didn't have to get in their cars and drive from Parkland to some other part of the South Side for the game, then haul it back to the neighborhood for the post-game festivities. (That morning, while doing his rounds of glad-handing, the alderman spent significant time at Mrs. Motley's table where he merrily chatted with her and the others sitting there.)

After eating, the group strolled down the hallway, their voices echoing off the polished hard-tile floors, glazed brick walls, and high ceiling with its banks of fluorescent lights. They moved past the inlaid trophy case by the main entrance where individual and team awards were displayed, the ribbons and statuettes won by Parkland students in various state and national scholastic competitions. (There was another, much smaller trophy case for athletic awards. Not because such endeavors were looked down upon at Parkland High, but because few of its athletes had ever won anything.)

The group filed through the main doorway of the assembly hall where a large mural depicting Parkland's first settlers stretched across some thirty feet of wall space above the double-door entrance. The painting featured a regiment-sized group of grim-faced dark brown men, women, and children in straw hats and bonnets traveling on foot, wagon, and horseback through fields of high grass. The people in the painting's foreground were at the crest of a ridge, with the rest trailing behind in diminished size, reminding one of depictions of the Israelites leaving Egypt, what with the painting's low sunlight casting the backs of the people's bodies in deep shadow. A dramatic, if not particularly accurate account of how the neighborhood had first been settled.

Inside the auditorium, which was still outfitted with rows of wooden seats, people were welcomed from the stage by the principal, a short brown man with a shaved head who was wearing a dark suit. (He had reportedly been glad to see Mr. Davenport go.) The football team was up there too, under the bright overhead lights, sitting in rows of folding chairs behind the principal, their dark blue game jerseys with maize numbers worn over dress shirts and ties. Off to the side were the cheerleaders—girls in white skirts and blue sweater tops, and a few boys in blue polo shirts and white pants. The band was in the orchestra pit, decked out in their blue jackets with high collars, double rows of brass buttons, and maize epaulets.

After the principal was done with his remarks, which were thankfully brief, the cheerleaders came forward, and as they'd done at the pep rally the day before, they commenced to prance about and chant with megaphones and pom-poms:

Give me a P! Give me an A! Give me an R! Give me a K!
L-A-N-D, L-A-N-D, L-A-N-D—hey!
PARKLAND! PARKLAND! PARKLAND ALL THE WAY!

After a few minutes of this and other cheers, the audience stood, and the players stood, and the crowd sang the Parkland fight song, accompanied by the band:

Parkland, sweet Parkland,
We stand tall, for the sable and gold,
We're strong, we're tough, we're bold.

We're the raven pride, of the far South Side
Loyal through and through,
Parkland, we love you!

The song, which some current Parkland students found lame, had been written by Mrs. Motley's maternal grandfather and she sang it with great gusto. The alderman, two seats away and to her left, also sang for all he was worth, while occasionally glancing at her.

After the song was done (followed by much whooping and clapping), those players in their senior year were introduced individually by the principal. Tradition called for the senior, after he was recognized, to step to the podium and say a few words.

For Reggie Butler, sitting in the first row of players, this was something he'd been looking forward to for years. He'd first attended an alumni rally as a little boy, and he'd been dazzled by the players on the stage who had seemed like giants to him.

Even though football was not his best game, and even though the school's basketball coach had strongly urged him not to risk a future college scholarship by playing football, Reggie had gone out for football anyway. That morning, his grandmother, who had not been wild about his playing football either, was at the homecoming assembly for the first time. (She'd passed on attending the breakfast.)

Mrs. Butler was sitting in the front row on the other side of the aisle from Mrs. Motley and wearing another of her black ensembles. She did not take part in the singing of the fight song, she didn't even stand up, but when Reggie stepped to the podium mike in his number 85 jersey, she got a big smile on her face.

Reggie himself did not look all that happy, despite this being his big moment. Speaking like he had a lot on his mind, he said: "Uh, it's great to be up here as a senior. I want to thank my grandma for helping me to get here. Go Parkland."

As he returned to his chair, folks clapped briefly, as they did for each player, and a few of them around Mrs. Butler saw her wipe at her eye. Normally this would have been a point folks would comment on later, but it was not, because when the clapping ended after Reggie's remarks, one person continued on.

The noise came from the auditorium entrance, the doors of which were still open. Folks turned to see who it was and saw Stew Pot. Before anyone could do anything, like yell for security, Stew Pot pointed at Reggie and shouted: "That's the way to do it, boy!" And then, just like at Wesley-Allen, he turned and was quickly gone.

Later that afternoon, the Parkland Pirates lost to the Morgan Park Mustangs 32-20, the third season in a row that Pirate footballers had gone down to defeat at the hands of their archrivals from up the road. Parkland backers took the loss philosophically, telling themselves as they left the stadium that at least the contest had been fairly close, unlike the 52-0 shellacking they'd suffered the year before.

After the game, when folks crowded places like Logan's and Sonny's tavern and Minton's Pool Hall, Stew Pot's name came up more than a few times. This continued in the evening at the homecoming dance, and later that night in the forest preserve where kids gathered for beer and weed and making out.

Eventually someone at this last gathering asked Reggie why Stew Pot had clapped and cheered for him at the assembly hall. Reggie, again in his blue and maize letterman's jacket, gave the same answer he'd given folks several times earlier that day: "How should I know? The man's crazy."

Reggie then nodded to his girlfriend, a short and perky Parkland junior who had pursued him for nearly a year with all manner of flirting, and who had finally won him when Delphina moved away. The two rose from the log where they'd been sitting and walked away to find a private spot for tongue-tag and inside-the-underwear groping.

Reggie got her home—their shirts and jeans properly rebuttoned—before her eleven thirty curfew. On the way to his house he reviewed his plan of action. That afternoon, after the game and before the homecoming dance, he'd hidden all his preparations in the garage, a place his grandma seldom entered since she had no car. He told himself that Stew Pot, with his threat of the night before, had left him no choice. He, Reginald Demetrius Butler, was going to have to take care of his business and put a stop to Stew Pot's residence in the neighborhood once and for all.

CHAPTER TEN
The Fire This Time

That night Mrs. Motley had one of her fire nightmares, which she hadn't experienced in some months. From her dream position of being faceup in her bed and unable to move, she looked toward the ceiling where the flames throbbed as if keeping time to a heartbeat. The fact that her mind realized it was all a dream didn't make the nightmare any less terrifying.

At first the flames sounded like bedsheets fluttering thickly in a strong wind, but then she became aware of another sound, some sort of noise that was both faint and urgent. There was a snatch of sound, then it was gone, then it was back, and then it was gone again. The dream flames continued to throb and move closer. The thick fluttering sound grew louder too, as did the other noise until her mind knew it was just below the surface of her perception, tantalizingly close. What was it? And then suddenly, the other, lower noise clawed its way into the dream full volume—

BEEP! BEEP! BEEP! BEEP! BEEP!

Mrs. Motley raised herself, her initial grogginess cut short by an acrid intake of breath which scoured the back of her throat. She began coughing and took in another smoky breath. In an instinctive move to get away, she rolled to her right and fell to the floor.

BEEP! BEEP! BEEP! BEEP! BEEP!

Down there on hands and knees she finally found fresh air. She gulped a breath. Her nose was running and her eyes were tearing. She reached for her house shoes at the side of the bed and, while remaining on hands and knees, struggled to get the slippers on.

BEEP! BEEP! BEEP! BEEP! BEEP!

High above her head was a cloud bank of smoke. She frantically reached for her glasses on the night table, but in her haste she knocked them to the floor. She began reaching around in a panic for them, whimpering as each grab came up empty. She heard a siren in the distance and began desperately sweeping the floor with her right hand, bumping against the glasses, knocking them further away. Fortunately, she heard the frames clack against the molding below the window. She crawled quickly over, lifted the curtain, and by the dim light of the streetlamp, she was able to see them.

BEEP! BEEP! BEEP! BEEP! BEEP!

Mrs. Motley carefully put the glasses on. The bank of smoke was getting lower. Still on her hands and knees, she now had to duck her head to keep her nose in clear air. She looked over her shoulder, over the bed, and saw snatches of fluttering orange in the thin aperture between the bottom of the closed door and the floor. She moved back to the window and raised herself to her knees. She pushed the curtain aside and lifted the sash all the way. The screen was one of those old-fashioned models with a grooved, horizontal metal latch set below the bottom corner. You had to pull the latches inward to disengage the screen from the main window frame to raise and lower it and the storm window. The latches always got rough with grit, which made them hard to move. She kept trying and trying to budge the latches, the hard metal edges pinching and nicking her fingertips.

BEEP! BEEP! BEEP! BEEP! BEEP!

As she kneeled and struggled, the siren grew deafening outside and there were spinning red lights, the sigh of brakes, and then the siren faded out in a long drone.

Later, she would not remember screaming for help, only that the window screen had suddenly parted and two large hands in rough gloves grabbed hold of her under the arms and lifted her up and out, her face so close to the firefighter's plastic face guard she could see the chin stubble on his White man's face. Later, she did not remember climbing down from the porch roof on a ladder. She didn't remember being asked if there was anyone else inside or what she said in reply. She didn't remember the roof of the house caving in with a crash and blast of sparks, or the cries of astonishment from onlookers. She didn't remember getting oxygen on her front lawn, or being questioned by a female police officer while sitting in the open rear of an ambulance as an EMT bandaged her fingertips.

She did remember standing, too stunned to even weep, with Mr. McTeer and Mr. Hicks and several others at the head of Mr. McTeer's driveway, watching the firefighters across the street in their hard hats and long coats. The ones working the hoses waived the nozzles, causing the long arcs of water to twist in the air like dancing snakes.

BOOK VIII

Sense or Sensibility

CHAPTER ONE

Logan's Diner, the Morning After the Fire

S o Mrs. Motley is okay?"

"Yeah, but her house is totaled. The outer walls are standing to about where the second floor used to be, but everything else is pretty much a big burnt heap."

"So how long was she there at the end of Mr. McTeer's driveway?"

"A good little while. She didn't look too bad after the paramedics were through. Her hair was mussed and hanging over her face. First time anyone could remember seeing her hair anything other than pinned up. There were folks from every house on the street and surrounding blocks too, most still in their night clothes, standing and watching. Mr. Glenn said the smoke stink was so strong you could taste it. He said when he got home his clothes reeked of that burnt smell."

"So what did she do when she left the driveway?"

"She and Mr. McTeer and Mrs. Powell went to Mr. McTeer's front steps. It was while she was over there that she finally broke down, sobbing onto Mr. McTeer's chest."

"Did Stew Pot and that Brother Crown and Mrs. Reeves show up during any of this?"

"Yeah, but the cops didn't make any arrests. Turns out the Holy Three had an ironclad alibi, from the police no less. At the time the fire started, Mance and his partner were eyeballing the trio as they paraded past the bars over on the main drag."

"What did those three do when they got to the block?"

"They stood watching the fire like everybody else. A few times, sounding all worried, Stew Pot asked after Mrs. Motley; but as you know, everybody on the block is giving him the silent treatment. They didn't answer any question from Crown or Mrs. R. either.

"Eventually Stew Pot did make his way toward Mr. McTeer's house. When he saw Mrs. Motley sitting on the steps, he started calling to her: 'Mrs. Motley, Mrs. Motley!'"

"What she do?"

"She hopped up and dashed inside McTeer's house and stayed there all night."

"Really? Humph. I guess Mr. McTeer finally got his wish, huh? Anything else happen?"

"The arson cops and fire inspectors picked through the heap once it had cooled off enough. After the cops, firemen, and everyone else had gone, somebody threw a rock through the front window of the two-flat. <u>And</u>, at the crack of dawn, Vernon Paiger arrived at Mr. McTeer's house."

"Vernon? Who saw him? And what did he want?"

"Mr. Hicks's oldest girl said her dad was out walking his dog this morning early and saw Airy behind the wheel of Vernon's parked limo. She said her dad asked Airy what was up and Airy said his uncle was there to give Mrs. Motley her insurance check. She must've had a policy with Paiger Insurance, I guess."

"Hold on a second. Motley didn't have a policy with her daddy's old company?"

"Man, Vernon bought that firm years ago, and she must still have preferred-customer status because he didn't even wait for an official report as to the fire's cause before handing over her money. Now that's what I call service."

CHAPTER TWO

A Baker's Dozen

The thirteen wild Parkland rumors concerning Mrs. Motley's house burning down:

1. Stew Pot stood in the middle of the street laughing as the house burned.
2. Stew Pot predicted that Mrs. Motley's house would burn while walking the drag.
3. Mrs. Butler joked that the police ought to check and see if Mr. McTeer started the fire since it finally got him the chance to get Mrs. Motley into bed.
4. When Mrs. Motley got up and went into Mr. McTeer's house, he got up and went in right behind her and slammed the door closed without saying so much as a word to Mrs. Powell.
5. When Vernon came to give Mrs. Motley her check, he had to wait nearly ten minutes before Mr. McTeer came to the door pulling a pajama top over his head.
6. Vernon Paiger left Mr. McTeer's house in a huff.
7. The reason Mrs. Motley took so long getting out of her house is because she was running around her bedroom trying to gather up family heirlooms.
8. Vernon's younger brother Albert, who "ran" Paiger Insurance, got into a shouting match with Vernon over giving Mrs. Motley a check so soon.
9. Mrs. Butler said getting her house burned down served Mrs. Motley right for not being more helpful in the block's efforts against Stew Pot.
10. While everyone was standing in the street watching the fire, Mr. Glenn aimed at Stew Pot with a pointed forefinger, pistol gesture.

11. Brother Crown called the fire a Holy Blaze of Glory.
12. When Vernon gave Mrs. Motley the check, she cupped his face and kissed him on the lips.
13. While watching her house burn, Mrs. Motley shouted to Stew Pot: "Are you happy now?"

CHAPTER THREE

Various Sides of the Matter

Around ten that morning Mr. McTeer was awakened by a scream. From where he lay on the living room couch he struggled to his feet, put on his glasses, and went to his bedroom. Mrs. Motley was sitting up in the narrow bed. He asked what was wrong and in a panic she told him she'd had another fire nightmare, only this time the flames had spread over her face, feeling like a horde of insects leaving stinging razor cuts.

She begged him not to leave. He set his cane against the bedside and slid beside her. She fell into him and he smelled again, as he had on his front steps, the smoke in her nightgown and hair that mixed not unpleasantly with the scent of her lilac body wash. She looked up, her eyes slightly parted, and he kissed her mouth lightly and she kissed lightly back. Then she dropped her head and a few minutes later was back asleep.

Meanwhile, at the other end of the block, Reggie Butler was wide awake, as he'd been all night and morning. He was in his basement bedroom where the ceiling was low and the air funky from all the dirty clothes strewn about.

Lying on his back, wearing basketball shorts and a gray T-shirt, he closed his eyes and wished, for the umpteenth time, that he could make it be the previous night again, before he had listened on the stairway for the sound of his grandmother's snoring from behind her bedroom door, before he had put on gloves and a black-hooded sweatshirt, before he'd gone to the garage to stuff a rag in the neck of a juice bottle full of sloshing gasoline, before he'd snuck over to the alley behind the Reeves's place and lit the rag with a butane lighter and nervously swung his arm with way too much side-arm action, causing the flung bottle (its flaming wick like the blazing exhaust of a rocket) to miss the two-flat's roof completely and sail over the gangway and onto Mrs. Motley's roof, the gas exploding into a fireball.

If he hadn't seen it with his own eyes, Reggie would never have believed fire could move so fast. He had taken off in a panic down the walkway and through the open gateway to the alley. As he'd run toward Honore, he'd seen no one and had only heard his feet pattering the alley concrete, his labored breathing, and the crackle of those voracious flames. He changed out of the incriminating clothes in the garage. (While doing so he'd smelled the gas he'd dripped on them earlier.) Minutes after returning to his room, his grandmother, awakened by the fire sirens, knocked on his door.

When the two of them reached the east end of the block, Mrs. Motley's house was completely ablaze, the flames whip cracking into the sky, and he was sure he had killed her. But then he saw her sitting in the open doorway of the ambulance. At first, the relief of seeing her safe held his guilt at bay, but as the fire burned on, as if impervious to the arcs of water pouring on it, the guilt came back on him, and had remained with him.

As Reggie lay in bed thinking about all this, across the street Mr. Glenn was sitting on his screened back porch where the smell of burnt house, even at that distance, was still noticeable. In jeans and a sleeveless T-shirt, he had his bare feet up on a stool as he sipped a mimosa from a flute glass, a carton of OJ and a bottle of bubbly in a nearby cooler.

The way Mr. Glenn saw it, Stew Pot's parading around the main drag the night before with Brother Crown and his mom had been done in coordination with whoever Stew Pot had retained to torch Mrs. Motley's house. Why could the cops not see that? They ought to be sweating Stew Pot in an interrogation room right now.

Mr. Glenn took a sip from his flute glass. He saw that once again it would be up to him to get things accomplished, like when he had phoned Erma and persuaded her to take part in humiliating Stew Pot in front of Brother Crown. (Truth be told, it hadn't taken much persuading; Erma had been immediately hot for the idea.)

Mr. Glenn was proud of his actions, which he felt were an example of initiative and élan, traits that were sorely lacking in many of his immediate neighbors. He was even prouder of what he had done a few weeks earlier, when he'd backed a car over Stew Pot's dog, the mutt emitting a yelp upon the initial contact and nothing when he ran over it a second time to be sure. (He'd used a car that had been left in his shop a few days earlier that was scheduled for pickup by its owner the following day.)

Sitting in the shade of the porch, he told himself that the next move against Stew Pot should be directed against the man himself, and that ideally it should include everyone else on the block; a full-frontal assault with an overwhelming superiority of numbers.

An hour and some four mimosas later, Mr. Glenn was still out there, while down the street Mrs. Motley awoke for the second time that morning. Upon finding herself in the strange bedroom, she was initially buoyed by the thought that she was dreaming and the fire had been a dream too; but then she smelled the burnt aroma permeating her nightgown and the crushing reality of what had happened descended upon her again.

After collecting herself, she went to the living room and awakened Mr. McTeer, who was sleeping on the couch. Sitting beside him there, behind the pulled blinds, she told him it was best if she went and stayed with the Powells. They had more room, she said, and she didn't know how long it would be before she had a permanent home of her own. She couldn't very well have him sleeping on that couch indefinitely, now could she? Mr. McTeer nodded, and because she made no mention of the kiss, he made no mention of it. He then gave her the alderman's envelope, along with Vernon's message that she was to call him if she needed anything. And Mrs. Motley, surprised and relieved, said: "Can you believe this?" and clasped the envelope flat to her chest.

An hour after that, following her run to the mall, Mrs. Powell came to Mr. McTeer's with a blow dryer, toiletries, and women's clothes (shoes included). While Mrs. Motley used the downstairs shower, Mrs. Powell and Mr. McTeer sat uneasily in the living room. Mrs. Powell was still angry from the night before when, in her opinion, Mr. McTeer had taken advantage of Mrs. Motley's troubled state by not advising, after she ran into his house, that it would be better to stay with her and Mr. Powell.

After the shower Mrs. Motley emerged from the bedroom with her hair in its usual bun and dressed in a sage blouse, a dark skirt, and flat black shoes.

Because the blinds were drawn, when Mr. McTeer opened the door, it was the first daylight sighting Mrs. Motley had of the ruined house. "Oh my goodness," she said upon seeing the peaks and valleys of the walls that were blackened nearly to the porch line. The gangway between what had been her home and the two-flat was piled with blackened wreckage, with another pile of blackened rubble inside the mountain range of walls. But what really got her was the powerful burnt smell that permeated the air.

"You going to be okay, honey?" asked Mrs. Powell.

Nodding quickly, Mrs. Motley stepped into the warmth and sunshine.

CHAPTER FOUR

A Conversation of a Sincere and Searching Sort

As soon as Mrs. Motley got to the Powells', she called her son in Oklahoma. He took this bad news the way he'd taken the news of his father's death (which years before she'd also had to relay to him by phone), with a calm that was for her a little unsettling.

After assuring him she was okay, she told him the story of the house's destruction and her rescue, her voice breaking only a couple of times. (Her one major omission was not saying anything about spending the night at Mr. McTeer's.) When she finished, he said he'd see if he could get an emergency leave. She told him no. There was nothing he could do at this point since there was nothing to salvage from the wreckage. The Powells had told her she could stay for as long as she wanted and she had an insurance check in hand. That last statement momentarily broke his professional calm, causing him to ask in a voice of genuine surprise: "You got the money already?"

After she told him how that had come about, he reverted to his professional soldier form and said that maybe it would be best to tell his ex-wife and daughter to cancel their plans to visit Chicago for Christmas. Maybe they could come in the spring? Mrs. Motley, barely able to keep the panic out of her voice, said no to that. "Tell them to go ahead and come as planned." When he asked where they would all stay, she said she didn't know just yet, but that he should not worry. "I'll manage it. I'll figure something out."

"Are you sure, Ma? Christmas isn't that far away."

"I said I'll figure something out. You just make sure to get your family here for Christmas. Promise me you'll do that."

"Okay, Ma, okay. I promise."

CHAPTER FIVE
Cops Come Calling

Two plainclothes cops came around later that afternoon. They were the same pair who had earlier picked through the burnt rubble after the fire was knocked down. Now, in fresh clothes, they went house to house on Stew Pot's block and the blocks immediately south and north, talking to people on front porches and stoops.

Residents gave variations of two stories. A couple of folks living near Mrs. Motley, on her street and across the alley, said they'd glanced out a window and, seeing her roof ablaze, called 911. The others said they hadn't known anything was amiss until they heard the fire sirens. No one said they saw anybody. Just about everyone said Stew Pot had to be involved, though no one offered any evidence.

By then two things were clear to the investigators: the fire had definitely been arson, with the accelerant gasoline. The cops questioned Mrs. Motley first, she becoming weepy a couple times while sitting in the Powells' purple living room. The cops, both older White guys with moony faces, thick mustaches, and veined noses, were patient, saying that anything she could tell them, even the smallest thing, might be a big help.

She said she couldn't think of anyone but Stew Pot who'd want to burn her house. The cops questioned folks at the two-flat too, people on the block eagerly watching to see if Stew Pot would be led off in handcuffs. They were very disappointed when he wasn't.

CHAPTER SIX

The Police Side of the Matter

After the interviews, the arson cops returned their hefty selves to a gray sedan parked in front of Mr. Glenn's house. Gazing eastward down the block, they discussed the case.

"So what do you think?" said the cop behind the wheel.

"Well, at first," answered the other cop, "given that this Reeves guy admitted to Motley that he burned her garage, I of course was thinking he's our number one and that he used an accomplice—somebody he knew inside or some knucklehead from the neighborhood—who did the dirty deed while he and his mom and that albino were walking the street under the watchful eye of that sweetheart Mance."

"But now you think different," said the cop behind the wheel.

"Yeah. After talking to these people here, seeing the anger, the *rage* they have for this Stew Pot, my thinking now is maybe Stew Pot was the target. Somebody decided to burn him, somebody who didn't know what they were doing and who botched the job."

"Or maybe the albino set it up; I bet Stew Pot wasn't his only jailhouse disciple."

"That's a possibility too, and we can check that out. But here's another thing. If Stew Pot or the albino got someone to burn Mrs. Motley's house, what did they pay the torch with? A guy does that, he's going to want cash payment."

"One or both of them got the money from the mom," said the cop behind the wheel. "She looks skittish enough to do anything Stew Pot or the albino tells her to do. Or they hired a junkie willing to do it for a few bucks. Or they stiffed whoever they got to do it."

"All plausible," said the other cop. "And if so, we keep our ears to the ground and hope somebody talks to somebody who talks to somebody and we get a break. But I don't think that's it. It was a botched job. Just chalk it up to our old friend Mr. Gut Feeling."

"Okay, let's say we go in that direction. We do, and the list of sus-

294 † BEDROCK FAITH

pects grows as long as your arm; all the way across the neighborhood."

"That could be, but I wouldn't be surprised if our torch is someone we spoke with today, someone who looked us right in the eye and lied through their teeth. Here on this block is where our firebug lives. I can feel it."

"Okay, but these people get a hint we're angling one of them for this and there'll be a whole lot of hollerin' going on. This ain't the projects, this is Vernon Paiger's patch."

"I know where we are. We'll have to be patient as always."

"Okay," said the cop behind the wheel, "so where do we start?"

"We start by coming back tonight, see if anyone put anything interesting in the garbage."

"I hate fishing through garbage, especially when I ain't getting paid OT for it."

The other cop chuckled, playfully wagged a forefinger at his partner, and said: "Hey, you knew the job was dangerous when you took it."

CHAPTER SEVEN

A Telltale Heart

That evening folks came by the Powells' to visit with Mrs. Motley, forty-some people over the course of the evening—neighbors from the block, Old Guards, Reverend Wilkins, and other friends.

Mrs. Motley held court in the purple living room (which many of the neighbors thought a bit gaudy). To succeeding groups of concerned people, she told how thankful she was that she had made it out of the fire with nothing worse than a few bandaged fingers. Plus, her car had been spared. (In a reverse of what had happened in the fire years before, the garage was unharmed.) To a person, the visitors denounced Stew Pot. She responded by saying she hoped the police solved the case soon. She also said she'd heard about another rock being thrown through the Reeves's window and that she wanted no violence done out of consideration for her.

Reggie spent most of his time in the dining room, which was also done up in purple. Wearing his letterman jacket, he sat in a corner looking glum. When someone asked his grandmother what was wrong with him, Mrs. Butler shrugged. "Who knows? It probably has something to do with that little heifer he's been running with."

What Mrs. Butler did not say was that late that afternoon, she and Reggie had had an argument after she'd awakened him in his basement bedroom. He had demanded to know why they had to visit Mrs. Motley. "It's not like somebody died. You don't even like her. You're just doing it to try and win votes to be the next block club president. "

"Reggie Butler, I do not have time for drama!" she'd snapped. "Go wash up and get dressed!"

Later on, in front of Mrs. Motley at the purple couch, he'd lowered his eyes from hers and said in a rush, "I'm real sorry about your house," and stepped immediately away.

At one point during the evening, Mrs. Motley, on her way back from the first-floor washroom, passed through the dining room and gave Reggie a nod of acknowledgment. The boy's face went even more sullen and he got up from the chair without saying a word and escaped to the empty kitchen and out the back door.

Knowing a troubled child when she saw one, Mrs. Motley glanced at the living room where a new set of folks had arrived and were waiting for an audience. Partly out of curiosity and partly because she was weary of the condolences and questions, she turned around and walked to the back porch.

She didn't see Reggie in the yard or the alley or, looking to her right across Mr. Glenn's yard, on Honore. *How could he have gotten away so fast?* she wondered.

She turned to go back inside when she thought of the basement stairs. The Powells had a walkout basement and the steps to that door were under the back porch. Mrs. Motley went there, passing the barbecue grill where the white coals were still warm.

She peered down the short set of steps and saw Reggie sitting with his back to the basement door. He had the knees of his long legs drawn to his chest, his hands clutching them, and his head bowed.

Mrs. Motley stepped down, ducking a bit as her head neared the overhang of the porch. "Reggie?"

He didn't raise his head. He just shook it slowly

"What's wrong, child?"

He stopped shaking his head but still did not raise it. "I'm sorry, Mrs. Motley. I'm really sorry. I didn't mean it. I swear I didn't."

"You didn't mean what?"

He began shaking his head slowly again.

The ensuing flash of recognition hit Mrs. Motley so hard her knees went momentarily weak and she had to brace herself with a hand against the overhang. There she stood for a few moments looking down at Reggie, who continued to shake his lowered head. She saw him open his mouth as if to speak again, and moving a few steps closer, she said in a hissing whisper: "Hush!"

He looked up. He'd never before seen her so fierce—eyes squinted and hands clenched. However, the need to tell what he'd done caused him to try and tell again anyway. This time she slapped him across the face. "I said hush!" He stared at her, his jaw aching as Mrs. Motley took a step back. "Listen, we don't have much time," she said. "Folks will be wondering where I am and come looking. You are to tell me nothing, understand?"

He nodded yes.

"If you tell me nothing, then if anyone asks me, *Did Reggie Butler say he did something Saturday night?* I can honestly say, *Reggie never told me he did anything.* And you must say nothing to anybody."

"But Mrs. Motley—"

She put a finger to her mouth to silence him again. Then she stepped forward, bent over, and clutched his face, a hand on either side, her palms soft and warm. She brought her face close to his and he smelled the scent coming off her skin. Her brown eyes, looking very sad, searched his for a few moments. Then she said: "You have your whole life ahead of you. You can go to college, and if you study the way you have so far, you can have a life your mother threw away, and maybe your father too, whoever he may be."

Reggie tried to speak but Mrs. Motley shook his face lightly.

"My house is gone," she said. "Nothing will bring it back, including well-intentioned confessions. Understand?" He nodded. "You must tell no one. Not buddies, coaches, girlfriends, either now or years from now, because you never know who they'll blab to. People love telling. If Parkland has taught me anything, it's taught me that. Say nothing about this—especially to anyone with a badge; no matter how many times they ask, no matter how hard they try and make you feel guilty. My house is not worth your life. If it's punishment you seek, the burden of silence will have to suffice."

He told her he understood; however, later that night, in his bed, he wasn't so sure he understood anything. And that wasn't the only thing worrying him. There was still the matter of what Stew Pot might reveal in his newsletter, as well as the gas-stained clothes and shoes still in the garage. Thinking of that latter issue, he reminded himself that in the morning he'd better throw the clothes away before he went to school.

CHAPTER EIGHT

Mrs. Motley's Side of the Matter,
Mr. McTeer's Side of the Matter

Not surprisingly, Mrs. Motley did some serious praying that night. In the Powells' spare bedroom, kneeling before another strange bed, wearing a pink polyester nightgown Mrs. Powell had purchased (not the fabric she'd have chosen, but she wasn't complaining), she gave profuse thanks for her life which she knew she'd come close to losing. She prayed for Reggie too. The idea of him in the prison system, a Dante's Inferno from which he might never fully escape, had terrified her under the Powells' porch and it terrified her now. Yes, she loved her house, but she didn't want the boy sacrificed for it.

At the same moment, Mr. McTeer was sipping whiskey in his dimly lit dining room. In his poem he'd longed for Mrs. Motley to sleep under his roof. At Union Pier he had wished that it not take a year before he saw her in nightclothes again. Both desires had been granted. *And* he had kissed her (her breath somewhat sour, her lips soft). However, there had also been a price. For Mrs. Motley it was her house. For him it was the awareness that knowing how wonderful it was to kiss her was going to be a lot harder to live with than *not* knowing had ever been. In addition, he now strongly suspected that over the coming weeks Vernon Paiger, who had arrived so fast with that check, would make himself an indispensable help to Mrs. Motley, whether she asked him to or not. And she'd appreciate it, even if she refused to admit it to herself at first. And out of all that, might something like love emerge?

CHAPTER NINE
With Catlike Tread

I t was after one a.m. when the two arson inspectors, having advised the commander of the 26th District of their plans, returned to Stew Pot's block. In dark windbreakers and sneakers they searched the black garbage bins, thankful that Parkland did not have the nocturnal animal population so common to more central areas of the city.

They started at the Butler bin and found nothing out of the ordinary. They worked their way east, then back west on the alley's other side. They did their inspections quietly, keeping their long-handled flashlights aimed inside the bins so as to not give off beams that might be noticed. They moved the garbage bags and trash deftly, for they were old hands at this. However, after nearly an hour they'd found nothing of any use.

They were back at the bins by the Butler home and about to head over to the alley that ran behind the south side of the block, when the cop who hadn't been driving nodded toward the Butler garage. The vehicle door was set on the alley side and there was a row of square windows across the upper half of the door.

Aiming his flashlight through one of the panes, the cop peered inside. After a few moments of sweeping the beam around the floor, something caught his eye. He fixed the beam on it and after a few seconds said softly to his partner: "Well lookee here now."

CHAPTER TEN

Day's Disasters in Morning Face

Before the overcast dawn of the next day, the arson cops, operating on little sleep, drove back to the block in an unmarked white van. They checked to see if the stuff they'd glimpsed through the garage window—the clothes, the shoes, a gasoline can, and a cigarette lighter—were still on the garage floor. The items were still there.

They parked on Honore a few spots north of the alley entrance on the west side curb, which put them out of direct sight of anyone coming out the Butler's backyard.

From officers in the 2-6 they'd learned that Mrs. Butler worked mornings at the food pantry in Blue Island which she opened at seven, so they figured she'd leave home by six thirty at the latest. They'd also checked with Streets and Sanitation and knew the garbage pickup for the block was midmorning Mondays, which meant that if Reggie Butler wasn't completely stupid, he'd dump the incriminating items after his grandma left for work and before he went to school.

Without probable cause to look in the Butler garage the night before (at least not any a judge would have found proper), their plan was to observe Reggie throwing the items away and then collect them from the bin. With the incriminating items and Reggie in hand, they would question him. Without his grandma or a lawyer, they were fairly confident they could get a confession, what with Reggie being a never-been-in-trouble sort of kid.

That he was the one who had set Mrs. Motley's house on fire, the arson cops had no doubt. Neither he nor Mrs. Butler owned a vehicle, or even a power mower, so what was a gasoline can doing in their garage, along with a cigarette lighter and strips of rags?

The investigators were sure that the clothes and shoes would at the very least have traces of gasoline, and that the gasoline can and cigarette lighter would bear Reggie's fingerprints. Both were excited by the prospects of all this. Arson cases, when they were solved at all, usually took months, and in some cases years, to close. Only once in a blue moon did they get a situation like this: the kit and caboodle right there for the taking.

Their plan worked almost perfectly.

Inside the van the cops watched Mrs. Butler cross the intersection at 6:32 a.m. and head out of sight down 129th. They then made a bet as to when Reggie would appear. The driver cop (same as the day before) won this one. At 6:46, Reggie, in blue jeans, black sneakers, and an untucked red polo shirt, opened the tall wooden backyard gate and deposited a large black plastic bag in the garbage bin.

Giving him a few minutes to get back inside, the non-driving cop got out and dashed across the street. Opening the bin he checked the contents of the black bag, turned, and gave his partner the thumbs-up, then lifted the bag and trotted back to the van.

With the engine running they now bet as to which way Reggie would leave the house, front or back. This time the non-driver won. At 7:27, Reggie, wearing a green army-issue jacket and toting a backpack on one shoulder, approached the intersection.

The driver cop hit the gas, the other one holding his door ajar. The van screeched to a halt louder than they would have liked. Reggie took a surprised step back and the cop flung open his door and stepped fast around the front of the van.

Reggie's eyes bugged out and he was obviously scared. They had him slip his backpack to the ground and put his hands on the hood.

"What's wrong?" he asked.

They quickly cleared his pockets—a ring of five keys, a ballpoint pen, a wallet.

"What'd I do wrong?"

The driver cop pulled his hands behind his back.

"Tell me what's wrong."

The handcuffs were slipped on—cold and tight.

The boy's voice pleading: "Won't you please tell me what's wrong?"

The back door on the driver's side was opened and Reggie was guided to the dark maw.

Then there was another voice, a man calling from across the street: "What's going on here?" It was Mr. Glenn, drawn to his walkway by the screech of the van's tires.

Mrs. Motley and Mrs. Powell, drawn by screech too, were now standing on the Powells' walkway.

As he was gently pushed inside the van, Reggie looked over his shoulder and saw, or thought he saw, Mrs. Motley raise a forefinger to her closed mouth, the way she used to do when he was a kid at grade school and she wanted things quiet in her library.

CHAPTER ELEVEN
The Moment of Truth

Because neighbors had seen them, the arson cops changed their plans. They had originally intended to go to the 2-6 station to interrogate Reggie; now they headed to another South Side police house. They assumed that one of the nosey neighbors would call Mrs. Butler, and when she managed to get ahold of a lawyer, the first assumption she and the lawyer would make was that Reggie had been taken to the 2-6. Their hope was that when the lawyer called the 2-6, the desk sergeant would say in all honesty that there was no Reginald Butler there and no information as to where he was—which they hoped would buy them enough to time to get their confession. (This is also why they hadn't taken Reggie Downtown to the Bomb and Arson offices at police headquarters. After the 2-6, Downtown would've been the next place a defense lawyer would have looked.)

In the windowless and scruffy interrogation room of a station two districts away from Parkland, the arson officers, their windbreakers off and sitting across from a very rattled Reggie, spoke in voices of calm and reason. If there was an explanation Reggie had for why he had thrown away such incriminating items, the cops said they were ready to hear it; however, they had to be honest: things did not look good for him.

In an unhurried but direct manner they laid out everything they had recovered from the black plastic bag—sweatshirt, jeans, socks—all which carried the stains and smell of gasoline. They then pointed out to him that he had been caught red-handed disposing these items less than a block away from where, two nights before, a house had been set on fire with gasoline. They spoke as if one, and only one, conclusion could be drawn from all this, a conclusion that any reasonable judge or jury would invariably arrive at: whoever the clothes belonged to had set the fire.

"Those are your clothes, aren't they, Reggie?"

Being from Parkland, where many kids were book smart but few were streetwise enough to know that in an interrogation room you don't say anything besides "I want to speak with my lawyer," Reggie said: "Yeah, those are my clothes."

The cops then shifted gears, the driver cop asking if he was thirsty. When Reggie said yes, the other cop asked if he wanted a can of pop. Reggie, taking this as hopeful sign, said yes again, and the cop asked him what sort of pop he wanted, and Reggie named one, and the cop, acting as if he couldn't be helpful enough, got up and left, returning soon after with a cold can which he opened for Reggie and placed in front of him just like a waiter does in a restaurant. And as Reggie sipped, the pop feeling so good in his dry mouth, the cops explained that they knew he was a good kid, that he got good grades and was a good basketball player.

"We'll probably see you on TV playing in the Final Four someday," one of them joked; which Reggie also took as a good sign.

"You're an all right kid," said the other. "Not like some of the punks we have to chase around the streets. So we know you're not the kind of person to intentionally set out to hurt somebody like Mrs. Motley. She's such a nice lady. Of course, she's lost her house and everything in it. She's homeless, essentially; a retired old lady living on a pension. Now she has nothing."

The cops were then silent, giving that last point a chance to run around Reggie's mind. He lowered his head.

"You okay, Reg?"

Head still down, Reggie nodded. In his mind he could see Mrs. Motley's house blazing, but he also saw her face close to him when she had cupped his face in her soft hands under the Powells' back porch and told him not to tell anyone.

"You know," said the driver cop, speaking in a conciliatory tone, "she almost died in that fire. That's what the fire battalion chief told us the other night. *By all rights she ought to be dead*, he said. That's how close the person who set this fire came to killing that poor woman. Imagine what her nightmares must be like now."

As that punch hit Reggie, the other cop followed with the second blow of the combination, speaking in the way a kindly pastor might do with someone from his flock who'd come in for guidance: "You know, Reggie, when a wrong's been done and a person has the power to make amends, it's that person's responsibility to do so. You know what I'm talking about, right?"

Reggie, his head still down, nodded, and a tear fell onto the table.

It embarrassed him to be crying in front of these White men, and he knew that he had promised Mrs. Motley not tell anyone, but he had hardly slept the last two nights because of what he had done. He was so tired, and he so much wanted to tell someone, just to get it out, which might relieve this pressure that was building inside of him so bad that he felt like he might suffocate.

He began breathing hard, and the driver cop, in a voice that couldn't have sounded more sympathetic, said: "Is there something you want to tell us, Reggie? Get it off your chest? We're ready to listen." And Reggie's shoulders slumped and the cops continued to be patient in their nudging him to where they knew the decent and honest and good part of him wanted so desperately to go, and had probably been wanting to go since Saturday night. They had seen people in this situation before, of course, and they could sense he was almost there, seconds away maybe; once it was out, they'd have enough for an arrest and a search warrant for the garage to get the gas can and the lighter, which would seal it.

And then, in the quiet of their anticipation, there came a soft knock on the door.

With the silence so tense, the knock had the effect of a much louder sound, like someone hard-kicking the door. All three were startled. Reggie's head shot up and the cops, momentarily caught off guard, displayed angry faces. They quickly regained their magnanimous expressions, but saw that Reggie had noticed their anger, and they knew that the spell they'd worked so hard to build had been broken. They turned to the door behind them to see what moron had interrupted their interrogation.

The brown-haired head of a clean-shaven uniformed lieutenant, who had a bold chin and a nameplate that read O'REILLY, leaned through the space of the partially opened door. The driver cop was about to ask, while working to keep his fury in check, what this O'Reilly wanted, when the lieutenant, in his crisp white blouse and gold shoulder bars, stepped inside the room followed by a man in an impeccable dark blue, double-breasted suit. At first the cops thought the suit was a White man, so light was his complexion, but then they recognized the toothy smile they'd seen so often on TV. He was Scotty Woodbury, one of the best defense lawyers in town.

Speaking amiably, like someone who'd arrived late for a friendly poker game with pals, Scotty Woodbury said: "Hey there, guys. I need to speak with my client."

CHAPTER TWELVE
Mum's the Word

Reggie's conversation with Scotty Woodbury lasted a good little while, client and attorney taking turns whispering questions and answers in each other's ear. Despite having observed the room's recording device being shut off and despite being handed, per procedure, the device's key by the officers, Woodbury did not doubt that the authorities might still be somehow surreptitiously listening. (As it so happened, the two arson cops were left to cool their heels in the hallway, furiously wondering who among their so-called brother and sister officers in the station had sold them out, had let Reggie's people know that he was there.)

The police could question a person for three days before they had to let him go. After the conversation with Woodbury, the cops took Reggie from the South Side to Bomb and Arson, which at the time was located Downtown in the old police headquarters at 11th and State streets.

They questioned him again and again, but all Reggie did was read from the card Scotty Woodbury had given him: "My lawyer has told me not to talk to anyone about my case, to not answer questions, and to not reply to accusations. Call my lawyer if you want to ask me questions, search me or my property, do any tests, do any lineups, or any other ID procedures. I do not agree to any of these things without my lawyer present."

Despite it being obvious after day one that they were getting nowhere, the cops kept Reggie for the full seventy-two, which Scotty Woodbury, in his first conversation with Reggie, had predicted: "They'll do it as much out of spite as anything." Woodbury reassured Reggie that if the police really had a case against him, they would have already filed charges. "Technically," Woodbury explained, "you aren't even under arrest. You tell them nothing, they got nothing."

Three days later, Woodbury drove Reggie home through a late-morning downpour. As soon as Woodbury's car (a sporty navy-blue foreign job with license plates that read: *LE ADVOCAT*), pulled in front of the house, Mrs. Butler hurried out the front door and down the walkway where she threw her arms around Reggie's neck (the boy smelling sour after three days without washing), kissing his face. He returned her affections in kind, Woodbury keeping them dry with a red umbrella.

Moments later they were in the Butler living room, which had burnt-orange walls hung with African prints, carved wooden masks, and framed posters of Malcolm X, Angela Davis, Marcus Garvey, and Harriet Tubman. The three sat on a lumpy couch where Woodbury repeated what he'd told Reggie on the ride out to Parkland.

"The arson case involving Mrs. Motley's house is still ongoing. Now, some arson cops have reputations as slackers, while others are known to be vigilant bulldogs with the patience of Job. I have it on good authority that the cops who took Reggie are the latter variety, which means they're perfectly willing to wait years for Reggie to slip and say something to somebody who might later get in a jam with the law and, in an attempt to save themselves, spill whatever Reggie told them. Or if the arson cops suspect he's told someone something that might help their purposes, they'll have no qualms about putting the screws to that person in hopes that he or she will crack under pressure and betray Reggie. Save for me, neither of you should talk to anybody about anything having to do with this case. That includes each other. Reggie, the best way to protect your grandmother is to tell her nothing. Mrs. Butler, the best thing you can do for Reggie is to ask him nothing."

That night in his basement bedroom, Reggie felt claustrophobic, like the room had shrunk, a direct result of his experiences of the previous three days. Woodbury had told him what to expect. He'd be strip-searched. Central lockup stank. The place was overrun with roaches and rodents strolled about. The warning had helped, but only somewhat, when he'd had to bend over and spread his behind, when the roaches invaded his cell, when he'd seen scurrying shadows along the floor, and when the cops had kept him in an interrogation room for twenty-six hours at one stretch with no food or toilet breaks; and the dirty walls of that room had blood splatters, and his wrist had been cuffed to a metal bar (that arm still ached). Different cops, all White, had yelled and cursed at him. Woodbury had visited twice a day to keep his spirits up and on the drive home had said that things could've been worse: "County jail? Now *that's* bad."

On an intellectual level Reggie thought this was true, but on an emotional level it was as if he'd already been punished, because no matter how this all turned out, he knew those last three days would haunt him for the rest of his life.

CHAPTER THIRTEEN

What They Thought

When anyone asked Mrs. Butler about anything connected to Reggie's case, she said she couldn't speak on it because the cops, angry over their thwarted attempt to railroad her grandson, were determined to hang a charge on him. This satisfied most Parklanders since it played to their opinions of police attitudes toward young Black men. "You think the cops would've pulled such a stunt on a studious White boy from Mount Greenwood or Beverly?" one person opined.

As for Reggie, he just told people: "Can't talk about it."

Because he'd never been loquacious, his reply more or less satisfied everybody; however, he did notice, in the days immediately after his release, that folks looked at him oddly. He'd catch this out of the corner of his eye as he walked the school hallway or sat in class. Same for when he went in a store or sat in the barbershop. It was never a stare, more like a curious glance, like his ears had grown slightly too big or something, and he knew they were thinking that the only reason a person needed Scotty Woodbury was because that person had done something really bad, since bad people—gangsters, crooked politicians, etc.—were the only folks Woodbury ever seemed to defend. Reggie felt naked and exposed wherever he went in this neighborhood that up to then had been a safe haven for him. Anytime he saw police he got nervous, especially those in unmarked cars and vans. His girlfriend's father forbade Reggie to see her, forcing the couple to sneak around, an impossible trick in a place where everybody knew you and knew you weren't supposed to be together. So they snuck around outside of Parkland, requiring long bus trips and leaving and arriving separately. And even then, in some away-from-Parkland movie theater, let's say, he'd sometimes catch her looking at him odd, as if she were thinking: *I'm glad you're not in jail—but I know you did it.*

CHAPTER FOURTEEN

Mrs. Butler's Side of the Matter

Although the nights immediately after Reggie's return were not as troubling for Mrs. Butler as the nights had been immediately before, the immediately-afters were not easy. Around eleven p.m. she'd doze off on the lumpy living room couch while reading a book, only to awake with a start a couple of hours later with a sheet across her body that Reggie had placed there. After going upstairs to her bedroom, where the green walls were decorated with more African prints and masks, she'd lay awake in the brass frame bed for hours (à la Mrs. Motley), fretting over the events of the previous few days.

On that fateful Monday morning, Mr. Glenn (in spite of her anger at him for befriending Erma) had called the food pantry about Reggie being taken into custody. She'd immediately put that news together with his reluctance to visit Mrs. Motley the evening before, and had known in that instant he was somehow involved with the fire. Then later, after Mr. Glenn had driven her home, she'd received a surprise call from Airy Tarmore informing her that Scotty Woodbury was on his way to represent Reggie and that she was not to worry about the cost because Woodbury was offering his services pro bono. Airy called her again a couple of hours later and said she might want to make sure her garage doors were locked. When she asked what he meant by that, he'd only said: "You really ought to check." When she got to the garage and made the shocking discovery of the gasoline can and the cigarette lighter, she put the items in a burlap sack and phoned Mr. Glenn, who had gone on to his shop after dropping her off.

He was back within minutes. With trembling hands she'd given him the sack and told him to get rid of it, and he'd looked at her in a way that said he understood he was not to check inside. After that, there was the anguished three-day wait for Reggie's release.

That first day home, Reggie had been unable to look her in the eye for very long, which confirmed for her what his Sunday-evening behavior and the garage items had so strongly indicated. As for Woodbury's instruction that they not discuss the case with each other, that had been a sweet relief. Reggie didn't have to suffer through explaining his actions to her and she didn't have to suffer through hearing it.

On those sleepless nights, Mrs. Butler often clasped a hand over her eyes as tears dribbled down the sides of her face. Since her teens she had aligned herself against the Scotty Woodburys and Vernon Paigers of the world. (She was sure the latter had a hand in all this, though for the life of her, she could not imagine why.) To her mind, they were the sort of Negroes (she refused to honor them with the terms *Black* or *African-American*) who had no problem with America's bulldozer of racial oppression, just as long as White folks allowed them to stand on some lower rung of the bulldozer to grab the occasional coin that dropped from the driver's seat. The kind of people who were Johnny-at-the-doorway to buy this or that expensive car, while never once volunteering their time at places like her food pantry, for instance, where as the only full-time employee she was in constant need of volunteer help. It was disgusting to her that Reggie's freedom was owed to people like Woodbury and Vernon; and what was worse, that everyone in Parkland knew Reggie's freedom was owed to those scoundrels. No doubt her old enemy Mrs. Motley was enjoying this turn of events; assuming of course that the old ninny could break away from reveling in Vernon's attentions long enough to notice what was going on around her.

CHAPTER FIFTEEN
Have I Got a Deal for You

The Monday after Reggie's release was a flawless autumn day with the oranges, reds, and yellows of remaining tree leaves in beautiful contrast to the cloudless sky. In the early afternoon Vernon Paiger paid Mrs. Motley a visit. He sat on one end of the Powells' purple couch, his back to the open doorway, while she faced the bay window where through the panes she saw his shiny black limo parked at the curb.

Mr. Powell was still asleep upstairs (it was his day off) and Mrs. Powell, to give them privacy, had excused herself and retired to the basement.

As the faint sound of game-show chat and laugher wafted up the stairs, Vernon crossed his right leg over the other. His dark gray suit jacket was unbuttoned, revealing red bracers and the full length of a paisley tie. Mrs. Motley, meanwhile, in another Powell purchase, was wearing a purple dress that didn't quite fit her right. After opening pleasantries about how each was doing and the wonderful weather, he told her why he'd come.

There was a family across the street from him, he said—the Wilsons. The husband was a UPS deliveryman, the wife a receptionist. Did Mrs. Motley know them? Mrs. Motley said she did, having taught them both as youngsters. Vernon explained that the couple had recently been blessed with a fourth child, a healthy girl, giving them a matched pair when added to the two sons and daughter they already had. The three-bedroom ranch home they were living in was way too small and they didn't want to leave Parkland. Mrs. Motley said she certainly understood that sentiment, but what did it have to do with her?

Vernon said that the Davenports' Dutch Colonial, with its four bedrooms and three baths, would be perfect for the Wilsons. Unfortunately, the Wilsons had some credit issues at the moment, which meant they'd have to sell their house before they could buy a new one, by which time the Davenport house might well be sold.

Mrs. Motley said she hadn't realized the Davenport place was for sale. Vernon told her it wasn't on the market officially, but that it might be soon. He grinned at her surprised look and said there was a story behind all this. In north-central Minnesota, he explained, there was a small boarding school started by a former Chicago couple—a dentist and a public school teacher. The Smith School (for that was the couple's name) took in impoverished inner-city kids, about fifty in all, and educated them in a rural, clean-air environment.

Vernon said that over the years he had played a role in placing several children at Smith. Mrs. Motley asked what that had to do with Mr. Davenport and Vernon told her that a vacancy had recently and unexpectedly opened on the Smith faculty, a position Mr. Davenport was perfect for. He had told Mr. Davenport as much.

"You've spoken with Mr. Davenport?"

"Yes, I got ahold of him through his brother. Mrs. Davenport and Delphina are in Cleveland, though Delphina is apparently not happy there."

"You spoke with Mrs. Davenport too?"

"Just briefly, but that's not important; what's important is that if Mr. Davenport takes the Smith position, he'll have to do so soon because the school needs to fill the position right away. If he moves up there, he'll need to buy a home."

"And?"

"And you need a home. Although I'm sure the Powells are making things welcome and comfortable, you can't very well remain here indefinitely."

Mrs. Motley crossed her arms. "Go on."

"I was thinking. You have the insurance money. If you sold your old property, you'd have enough funds to buy the Wilsons' house right away with plenty of cash left over. Their ranch is a perfect size for you, and with only one floor there'll be no more climbing stairs. The house also has an attached garage, so no more walking through the cold or the rain getting to and from your car. The place is in good shape, a little rough around the inside edges—they have kids, after all—but nothing a crew of good workmen couldn't fix without too much trouble or cost. Living there would allow you to stay in Parkland, which I know you want to do.

"If you buy the Wilson place right away, they can buy the Davenport place right away, before it's even on the market, and then Mr. Davenport would have money to get a nice home with some land around it in Minnesota. He'd get a fresh start—leave all that unpleasantness with the Chicago public schools behind. And just between you and me, I strongly doubt he'll get the fairest shake at his review next month. Even if he's reinstated, the principal at Parkland High has already filled his position. Davenport will have to teach at another school in the city, and who knows where that might be. Chances are better than even it won't be as good a school as Parkland; not with a domestic battery arrest deal on his record, regardless of his wife not filing charges. He could well wind up in one of those places full of roughnecks where just getting through the day can be a trial. Of course, that's not to say he couldn't make a strong contribution in such a situation, but there's something else to consider."

"And that would be?"

"Well, and this is just the sense I got from talking to Mrs. Davenport. She might find Minnesota appealing. It's away from urban hubbub, a chance for a fresh start."

"Sounds like that was quite a brief conversation you two had."

"Brief, but substantive," said Vernon.

"I have to tell you, I don't think Delphina is likely to be any less homesick in the wilds of Minnesota than she is in Cleveland."

"I've actually been to that area a couple times, Mrs. Motley. It's quite nice."

She uncrossed her arms. "I assume there's a buyer ready for my property?"

"Yes, there is. My sister's boy Roland, he runs Paiger Construction, as you know. He's been rehabbing buildings and flipping them, making good money at it too, but it's time he branched out into home building, where the real money is. He could put two houses on your wide lot. I can assure you he'd give a good price."

"Just so I understand," said Mrs. Motley, "I rescue the Wilsons by buying their house and then they buy the Davenport's place. We get to stay in Parkland while the Davenports have the money to reunite anew in Minnesota. *And*, you and I are even."

Vernon shrugged. "This is no quid pro quo; if you don't like the idea, don't do it."

After a few moments of silence she said she'd need a few days to think it over. He said he understood and that he hoped that for now, she'd keep this talk between the two of them.

"As I'm sure you'll keep our phone conversation of last Monday morning private," she replied.

He stood to leave and complimented her on the purple dress.

Mrs. Motley said flatly: "I didn't buy it."

Vernon paused momentarily, the way folks do after a minor faux pas, then recovered by smiling and saying: "In any case, you wear it well."

CHAPTER SIXTEEN
Vernon's Side of the Matter

Driving west on 129th Place, Airy said: "You think she'll go for it, Uncle Vern?"

In the backseat Vernon nodded. "I think so. She'll be suspicious at first—after all, my reputation precedes me—but she'll do it. Folks usually do what's best for themselves."

"So you're pinning your hopes on Vernon Paiger's Theory of Blatant Self-Interest?"

"You say *self-interest* like it's a bad thing. Self-interest is just using good common sense, and our Mrs. Motley, kindhearted though she may be, is nobody's fool. This is a good deal for her all the way around."

"So how much did you gild the lily this time?"

"I didn't gild it at all. If Mrs. Motley were to find that even a small thing of what I told her isn't true, she'd assume I was lying to her about everything else."

"Like that you're madly *in luuuuvv* with her?"

"I didn't tell her that because that subject never came up. And I'm going to remember your mocking tone of voice the next time you come around mooning over some flighty girl."

"Point taken, Uncle Vern, point taken. So you mark today's conversation a success?"

"Yes, I do. I may not be able to write stirring poems like *some* people, but actions—like what I did with the check and what I proposed today—can, in addition to occasionally speaking louder than words, sometimes be more appealing than words."

CHAPTER SEVENTEEN
Mrs. Motley's Side of This Particular Matter

After Vernon left, Mrs. Motley leaned against the backrest of the couch and reflected on her dealings with him that week. The Monday before, after seeing the police take Reggie away and after Mrs. Powell left for the basement to tell her husband what had happened at the intersection, Mrs. Motley had waited until she was sure her friend was downstairs before dialing directory assistance for Vernon's number, which everyone in Parkland knew was listed under his late wife's maiden name. (A trailblazer of sorts, the alderman's wife had kept her original last name.) The flatness of Vernon's hello had blossomed into welcoming warmth when she identified herself. However, the voice then immediately shifted to businesslike when she told him why she had called. He'd asked if she knew why the police had taken Reggie and she said the officers were the two arson investigators from the day before, so it had to be connected with the fire.

Vernon had then asked what she wanted him to do and she said: "Get Reggie a lawyer as soon as possible—a good lawyer. Don't worry about the cost. You tell whoever you contact I'll pay the fee. I'll use the money from my insurance check."

He said such a sacrifice might not be necessary. "Let me make a few calls."

And Vernon had made some calls, and now this afternoon, his comment about quid pro quo notwithstanding, he'd come to collect on the favor he'd done (as well as the one involving the insurance check) by trying to arrange for her to move across the street from him. And what was she to make of this?

Gazing out the bay window at the tree leaves and sky, Mrs. Motley told herself that with Vernon Paiger, you always had the feeling that he was playing some angle, and that instead of being his opponent on the other side of the chessboard, you were in fact one of the pieces he was moving around. Could she trust such a man? How much of what he had told her that afternoon was actually true? Mrs. Motley believed the surface facts of his story, for Vernon was too crafty to tell lies that could easily be disproved. For instance, she did not doubt there was a faculty position available at this Smith School—but was it available because someone had resigned or died, or because of something Vernon had arranged? And whose idea was it for his other nephew to go into homebuilding, and from whom would the lion's share of the money for the purchase of her property come?

She'd known Vernon all her life, the way you know someone in the neighborhood who is not in your immediate circle. They had never socialized as adults until he surprised her, a respectful two years after her husband's death, by asking her to dinner. He'd been clear about his interest back then too, although not in a crude way. His polite directness had put her off because—and oh, here was the rub—it had reminded her too much of her husband who had, in his initial approaches, come at her in the same gentlemanly direct fashion. And finally there was this. That Monday morning when she had called Vernon, she had been fairly sure he would not dismiss her request. Had her confidence been because she knew there was an angle that *she* could play with *him*? And if so, did that make her no better than he? Mrs. Motley told herself she had no interest in any of Vernon's steamy romantic ideas. *But if this is true*, she wondered, *why am I even thinking about it?*

But think about it she did, along with the other things he'd said; for the rest of the day she thought about their conversation, and the next day, and the day after that, which is when she phoned Vernon and said: "All right, it's a deal."

He said his nephew would get a check to her within the hour and that his niece would draw up the contracts. Then she could pay the Wilsons in full and they could pay the Davenports in full. "No loans will expedite things. This is a good decision."

"Let's hope so," she said. "There's one more thing. Under no circumstances are the Davenports to know the details of our arrangement. Understood?"

"Understood," said Vernon.

BOOK IX

Decline and Fall

CHAPTER ONE

A Whiter Shade of Pale

The day after Mrs. Motley accepted Vernon's deal, a crew of men in hard hats, one operating a small steam shovel and another a backhoe, began clearing the site where Mrs. Motley's house had stood, the work unleashing clouds of black dust. Mrs. Motley did not venture down there to watch, though echoes of the cracking and grinding, which unsettled her, did make it to the other end of the block.

The crew was done three days later, leaving behind a neat square excavation that revealed the basement's dark concrete floor (added decades after the house was built) and the grayish stone walls of the foundation. It was so odd, folks said, to see an open view over there, with the empty teal garage and its black shutters and white-laced windows looking like a miniature prairie house behind the beds of now-forsaken plants.

As for the two-flat, the building's entire west side was now visible from a good distance. If you were standing on the opposite side of the street you could see the whole of that side from as far away as the Davenports' place midway down the block.

That first night after the crew finished, a Thursday, someone spray-painted ARSONIST in big white letters along the two-flat's west side. The news of this produced more than a few laughs in the neighborhood. The next day, Stew Pot covered the word with white paint, creating a large ivory rectangle on the bricks.

The next night someone again sprayed ARSONIST on the west-side wall, this time using black paint. It took Stew Pot three coats of white to cover that, which produced more amused responses, as well as many guesses as to who the painter might be.

The following night, Saturday, Stew Pot appeared outside just before midnight, wearing a dark windbreaker and carrying a folding chair and his baseball bat. In the walkway alongside his home he sat guard in the amber light of streetlamps, the bat across his lap.

A couple of early risers said they saw him out there asleep at the first light of dawn, chin resting on his chest, the bat askew on his lap. An hour later, with the two-flat shadowing the walkway from morning sunlight, someone else saw him start awake as if he'd heard a bell. He stood and stretched, the groan of his yawn loud enough to be heard a couple of doors away. Before going inside, with his hands clasped, he bowed toward Mrs. Motley's property as if offering his thanks.

No one knew what to make of that, which odd as it was, was nothing compared to what happened a bit later. Early that Sunday afternoon, east end neighbors raking leaves or trimming hedges in their front yards saw Stew Pot come out of the two-flat and walk to the now sunlit west wall. Using a metal tape measure and moving and stopping between the wall and the low chain-link fence that divided the Reeves property from what had been Mrs. Motley's, he made measurements on the wall, pulling the tape to an arm's length at times, holding it at horizontal angles, then at vertical angles, and occasionally standing with hands on hips and gazing upward, like he was searching for something up there, or was imagining how something up there might look.

He was in such a pose (having been out there around ten minutes) when a hatless Brother Crown came around from the back door. The two men spoke in low tones there on the side walkway, their shadows cast against the brown bricks as Stew Pot gestured at the wall with a length of tape measure, like a general with a riding crop explaining some battle plan on a map. Brother Crown listened with his arms folded across his chest, and appeared, to the surprise of onlookers, as if he was none too happy about what he was hearing—his pink lips mashed .

At one point Brother Crown slowly shook his wheat-colored, wooly haired dome in an obvious negative response to what Stew Pot was saying. This caused Stew Pot to increase the vigor of his gestures toward the wall, using his free hand as well as the tape measure. After about a minute more of this, Brother Crown turned abruptly around and walked back to the rear door.

Stew Pot went back to measuring, staying out there another fifteen minutes or so. When he went inside, witnesses left their yard tools and began discussing what all this might mean.

An hour later, word of this was still being bandied around the block when Stew Pot appeared again, this time carrying a big white plastic bucket, a paint roller on a long pole, and cotton drop cloths. He set these items on the side walkway and left, returning shortly after with an extension ladder that he had to lean against the wall at a steep angle because of the closeness of the chain-link fence.

The ladder's height allowed him to reach the upper areas of the wall, and a hook from one of the higher rungs allowed him to hang the paint bucket so he could easily re-soak the roller. He started at the end closest to the street. He had the upper half done by afternoon's end and the lower half by early evening.

When his work was completed he put the painting stuff away and at around nine p.m. came out again to sit guard on the folding chair with the bat across his lap.

In the whirlwind of talk that came in the wake of all this, his immediate neighbors were sure the white wall was preparation for some kind of display. Whatever it was—and this was the scary part—even that Brother Crown character seemed to think it was a bad idea. The neighbors did not doubt it would be something that Stew Pot felt would swing the tactical advantage in their war of wills back in his favor. And as it turned out, they were right; however, before he put that plan in play he had another trick up his sleeve, and when he pulled it, all the immediate neighbors, save one, were caught totally off guard.

CHAPTER TWO
Hear Ye! Hear Ye!

THE BURNING BUSH
A journal of truth and righteousness
Our motto: One God, One Savior, One Way

THIS ISSUE'S BIBLICAL QUOTE
Mark 9:23 All things are possible to him who believes.

THE BURNING BUSH SAYS . . .
Our heartfelt condolences go out to Mrs. Motley. We shall miss her close presence. Hopefully the foul arsonist who destroyed her home will be apprehended soon, especially since police have quit their perplexing pursuit of our innocent youth. We must also, once again, condemn Mr. McTeer. In his most appalling action yet, he took advantage of Mrs. Motley's confused state of mind immediately after her rescue by hustling her into his home. The very next day, her senses clear, she made good her escape. We of course give Mrs. Motley the benefit of the doubt in this regard, unlike certain gossips of the neighborhood. Although the loss of a beloved house is a great loss, she may one day look upon it as a blessing, for it has removed her from the close proximity of he who has striven so mightily to ruin her.

THE BURNING BUSH ANNOUNCES . . .
With Mrs. Motley's house gone an opportunity has arisen. With the west side of our home (which some have defiled with false accusations) now exposed to the general area, we feel it should be used for Holy purposes. In the coming days, as Brother Crown and I continue with plans for our coming evangelical sojourn to regions of the South, work will begin that will put our west wall into sacred service.

Peace to all of you that are in Christ.

P.S. FROM THE BURNING BUSH . . .

Reginald Butler is my son. I shall strive in the weeks and months ahead to make amends for the previous shirking of my responsibilities to him as a father. Amen.

CHAPTER THREE
With Paint and Purpose

Stew Pot's immediate neighbors were still recovering from their Monday-morning discoveries of the *Burning Bush* (a few gathered near Mr. Hicks's place before heading to work) when at seven thirty they received their second surprise of that clear, cool day: a trio of painters arriving at the two-flat in a battered blue pickup.

As three men emerged from the parked truck, onlookers immediately tagged the strangers as Hispanic, what with their dark hair, short heights, and deep olive complexions. These assumptions were proven true moments later when folks heard the apparent boss of the crew, who had a thick mustache, use Spanish when he instructed the other two, who were both clean-shaven with ponytails, to follow him to the front door. All three had a potpourri of multicolored paint spots on their work boots, and the white T-shirts they wore under white overalls contrasted sharply with the skin of their muscular arms.

Just as they reached the two-flat's front door, it opened and out stepped Stew Pot. A head-plus taller than the other three, he led them around the front corner of the building to the side walkway where he commenced pointing at various areas of the wall. The crew boss stood alongside him, gazing upward and nodding his head in understanding, while the other two remained silent.

As Stew Pot was going about giving these instructions, Brother Crown and Mrs. Reeves, in their usual attire, left the two-flat, also by way of the front door. They watched the men on the walkway and Stew Pot stopped his instructional talk to send a wave and a smile. Brother Crown returned Stew Pot's acknowledgment with the sort of rueful shake of the head a person might use when he sees someone about to embark on an unwise course of action. As for Mrs. Reeves, she kept her mouth shut and her eyes on the ground.

Brother Crown and Mrs. Reeves, both armed with Bibles, walked off—she for her job Downtown, he for nobody knew where—and Stew

Pot resumed giving his instructions. When he finished, he went back inside and the painters set to work. They threw white drop cloths over the walkway and then ascended their extension ladders. Like Stew Pot the day before, they set their ladders at steep angles because of the chain-link fence, which they used as a brace.

Those neighbors who were watching dispersed to relay the news to other homes on the block, and before long there were several groups of people standing on the sidewalks and nearby curbs, looking on from both sides of the street as the crew went about their business, drawing lines on the wall that formed the outline of large letters.

Eventually, most of these onlookers had to depart for work or school, and it was left to the block's handful of stay-at-homes like Mr. McTeer and the Powells and Mrs. Motley to continue the watch. It took the painters awhile to finish the trace work and begin painting, carefully filling the outlines in bold red. And when it became clear later that morning what the words on the white wall were, those watching realized that Stew Pot had managed to outfox the neighborhood yet again.

CHAPTER FOUR

The Sound and the Fury

In the wake of Mrs. Hicks's passing, there had been no block club meeting in September, so when folks crowded into the Powells' living and dining rooms for an emergency meeting the evening after Stew Pot's sign went up, many were concerned that there would be another row over who would be president. To people's surprise and relief, Mrs. Motley, who had spearheaded Mrs. Hicks's challenge of Mrs. Butler that past summer, made an opening proposal: since Mrs. Butler had finished second in the last election, she should be named president by a simple show of hands. The ensuing vote was unanimous in favor.

Mrs. Butler, who had arrived at the meeting looking tired, was for a few moments left speechless by this swift and unexpected turn of events. (So drained was she by the troubles of the past week, she had come to the meeting with the intention of making no attempt for the office.) To a round of applause she pulled herself together and stood with her back to the bay window nodding here and there in acknowledgment.

When the clapping had stopped she thanked folks for their support. She made no special thanks to Mrs. Motley, who did not seem bothered by the oversight.

With the potentially divisive issue avoided, the meeting then got down to what had brought them together that chilly evening. A number said that if Stew Pot wanted **IN JESUS' NAME** painted in huge letters on the side of his building, that was his business. (No one made mention that the wall was now graffiti-proof, since no Parklander was likely to deface such a display.) What had them riled, people said, was the small lettering that had been painted just below the word NAME:

THE FOLLOWING ARE LISTED FOR SHAME:
"Lesbianite" Smedley

"Wife Beater" Davenport
"Lecherous" McTeer
"Busybody" Hicks.

The small print had not been read by neighbors until late after-noon, after the painters left and Stew Pot and Brother Crown (in a quiet but argumentative exchange) had gone inside the two-flat with a worried-looking Mrs. Reeves bringing up the rear.

There was simply no need for that sort of thing, folks said, espe-cially the insult about Mrs. Hicks.

"But what can we do about it?" asked Mrs. Powell. And somebody said they ought to get some gas and do a little burning of their own, which got a couple shouts of support.

Mrs. Motley reminded folks that Stew Pot might be gone soon, off with Brother Crown on that traveling evangelical trip he'd referred to in the newsletter. The Hicks's youngest daughter, representing Mr. Hicks who was too upset to attend, said she would believe Stew Pot was leaving when he saw him exiting the two-flat with a suitcase. "Maybe burning him out isn't such a bad idea."

There were more shouts of support to that motion, and a small but spirited argument ensued with arm waving and pointing on both sides. Some merely watched, either in worry at the bizarre turn of the discussion or in irritation at what they saw as a waste of their time. Mrs. Butler had to call loudly for order three times before the arguers shut up.

"Nobody is going to burn out anybody. End of discussion," she said.

After a few moments of quiet, Mr. McTeer said, "Okay, fine; but if not that, then what?"

A number of ideas were then suggested, and after some debate, all were discarded. Either the suggestions were deemed too aggressive: spray-paint *ARSONIST* on the two-flat's front door and all its windows, nail a dead rodent to the front door, rip down the two-flat's telephone line, break a basement window and drop a running garden hose inside to flood the place; or they were thought too soft: sneak up with a small brush and paint over the offensive small print, or tape sheets of paper with the word *SHAME* printed on them all across the front and back of the house.

Finally, after some more fruitless talk, Mrs. Powell said what they needed was something that would let Stew Pot know, in no uncertain terms, exactly what they thought of him. It was then that Mr. Glenn, with his wolfish grin (looking as if he had been waiting all meeting for this dramatic moment), made a suggestion that they were all able to agree upon.

CHAPTER FIVE

Mrs. Butler's Side of the Matter Again

S tew Pot naming himself as Reggie's father was, in Mrs. Butler's mind, the final clue as to why Reggie had done what he'd done. She did not doubt that Stew Pot had first confronted Reggie with his claim. That was just the sort of stunt Stew Pot would pull. And her Reggie, confronted by that claim, had, in the impulsive tradition of his granddad, mom, and uncle, come up with a ludicrous scheme that had ended disastrously.

Early that morning, Mrs. Butler had shown Reggie what Stew Pot had written and the boy had not appeared at all shocked.

Suspecting that word of the claim would make it to Parkland High before the end of the school day, she told Reggie that Stew Pot was lying. (During his childhood he'd asked about his father's identity, and every time he did, she'd said she didn't know.)

Sitting beside him on his bed that morning, she had told him his mother had gotten pregnant while living in Oakland, California. She hadn't come home until she was three months along. Stew Pot had been in Parkland that whole time, ripping and running the streets with Reggie's all-too-easily-influenced uncle. "I don't know who your father is," she concluded, "but I know for sure it's not Stew Pot."

When she finished her explanation, Reggie had dropped his face in his hands, which she took as his realization that their current troubles could have been easily avoided if he'd only come to her with Stew Pot's claim before taking rash action.

The morning after the emergency block club meeting, Mrs. Butler sat in her galley kitchen waiting for the coffee to finish percolating. She was very worried about what would happen if the police got wind of Stew Pot's newsletter. If they did, they were sure to come to the same conclusion she had, which meant they'd redouble their efforts to get Reggie. (Back in her younger, civil-action days, she'd had more than a few run-ins with the authorities, and since then she was forever on the suspicion for things like phone taps, listening devices, and undercover agents.)

The coffee almost done, her thoughts wandered to what had happened at the meeting the evening before. She didn't know for sure what had prompted Mrs. Motley to make her proposal. Mrs. Butler suspected it may well have been the woman's guilt over finally realizing that she—Mrs. Butler—had been right all along, and that what had happened to the house was in part the result of Mrs. Motley's lack of vigor in going after Stew Pot from the start. Or maybe Mrs. Motley was just having too much fun, now that she had *two* men slathering attention on her. (Mrs. Butler would not have taken Mr. McTeer or Vernon Paiger on a bet; nonetheless, she found it irritating the way men were forever falling for modest-maiden types like Mrs. Motley, while giving a wide berth to any woman who showed even a modicum of backbone.)

Mrs. Butler bowed her head, but not to pray, for she did not believe in what she called "all that God nonsense." She told herself she must continue to have faith in herself and do what needed to be done, like the morning before when she told Reggie his mother had gotten pregnant in California when in fact she had been living wild up on the North Side. As far as Mrs. Butler really knew, Reggie's father could have been anybody from among his momma's plethora of paramours—Stew Pot, Mr. McTeer's son—*anybody*.

CHAPTER SIX

A Perfect Hatred

The following Saturday morning, Mr. Glenn went early to a suburban hardware superstore where he bought thirty wooden signs. Six inches wide by one foot long, each was a thin plank, looking not unlike the sort used for signposts—one end pointed and the other end flat. He also purchased thirty narrow, circular, three-foot-long sticks, several boxes of nails, black spray paint, and scads of letter stencils.

When he returned home he was joined on his back porch by the Hicks's middle daughter. With a portable radio tuned to a soul station and sipping mimosas, they happily went about nailing planks to posts. Reading from a list that immediate neighbors had given Mr. Glenn at the block club meeting, they applied the four-inch stencil sheets to the planks and spray-painted. They finished around lunchtime and stood side by side, observing their handiwork. The signposts were lined all around the porch screens and the back wall of the house, with each plank carrying a one- or two-word message.

Mr. Glenn and the middle daughter clinked their glasses to signify a job well done, which was the opinion expressed by many neighbors when, as planned, they gathered at three that afternoon in front of what residents (save for Mrs. Motley) still thought of as the Davenport house.

When everyone had a signpost in hand, they marched to the two-flat. They were silent at first, but as they neared the Hicks place someone began singing "We Shall Overcome" and others quickly took up the song. (Mrs. Motley and Mrs. Butler, in a rare moment of like-mindedness, both felt the situation inappropriate for such a hallowed song and did not join in.) At Mr. McTeer's driveway the group crossed the street.

There was a narrow strip of land between the chain-link fence and the rectangular hole of excavation. Some people, singing all the while, walked down this stretch for a bit before turning to face the two-flat's west wall. Others stopped on that part of Mrs. Motley's old front lawn that paralleled the two-flat's walkway.

Those singing raised their voices, their volume fueled by their collective energy and emotional release from finally confronting Stew Pot with direct action and not just angry words amongst themselves.

Before long, less than a minute, Stew Pot stepped out of the two-flat's front doorway. At first he had a near-smile showing as his gaze moved around the crowd. Mrs. Motley, standing near the sidewalk and a bit unnerved by the raw wound of the nearby gray hole and the sad and lonely sight of the garage, immediately realized that Stew Pot must've been thinking that a miracle had occurred, that they had come to join him as disciples of Brother Crown, who she now saw in the two-flat's doorway along with Mrs. Reeves.

At the end of the next chorus the singers stopped. No one said anything for a few seconds and Stew Pot moved closer, until he was steps from Mrs. Butler and Mr. Glenn, who were part of the front row of people on Mrs. Motley's old side of the fence.

Raising his arms and speaking pleasantly, Stew Pot said: "What's all this?"

Mr. Glenn smirked and replied: "We have something for you." Then he took his sign and, with a vigorous move, plunged the stick into the ground in front of him. The plank carried the word *LIAR!*

Stew Pot peered down at the sign and his face went to a scowl. Looking back at Mr. Glenn, he said: "What do you think you're doing?"

And Mr. Glenn, obviously enjoying himself, answered nonchalantly: "Making a statement."

And Stew Pot, his voice angry, asked: "A statement about what?"

And Mrs. Powell, in that front row and a couple of people to the left of Mr. Glenn, replied formidably: "It's not about *what*, it's about you!"

In a tone of innocence, as if he could not for the world understand why a person would say such a thing to him, Stew Pot said: "About me?"

Mrs. Powell, with her husband beside her, thrust her sign's stick into the turf with the same vigor Mr. Glenn had used. Her plank read: *BURGLAR!* She matched Stew Pot's ensuing glare heat-for-heat, and Mr. McTeer, standing to the right of Mrs. Motley, jammed down his own stick with a plank that read: THIEF! And Mrs. Butler pushed down hers that read: SPY! And then the rest began planting their signs, either in the strip of land by the fence or in what had once been the east side of Mrs. Motley's front yard: DOG! ARSONIST! DEADBEAT! HEATHEN! PEEPING TOM! MORON! PHONY! LOUDMOUTH! FOOL! MUSCLE-HEAD! HOME-WRECKER!

Stew Pot folded his arms across his chest, his face set in sneering defiance. "Do you really believe I'm troubled by such foolishness? I'm walking in The Light, people." However, his mood changed when Mrs. Motley planted her sign: FALSE PROPHET!

Stew Pot's face went to a scowl again. He marched over to her and said, "That really is not necessary, Mrs. Motley."

And Mrs. Motley countered, "Taking into account all you've done, it's absolutely essential."

And then Stew Pot said, "I still have all the respect in the world for you, Mrs. Motley, despite your sometimes questionable—"

And she cut him off: "Your respect is something I've neither asked for nor desire. It was unforgivable what you did to Erma, and the Davenports, and to Mrs. Hicks's family—"

And he then cut her off with: "All I've done since my return is try to educate you wayward people, get you to at least think about where you ought to be going, how you ought to be living."

This produced shouted insults from the crowd. Stew Pot stepped back and slowly swept a forefinger at the opposing faces while quoting from Psalms, choosing a passage Mrs. Motley usually skipped in her searches for solace: *"O that Thou wouldst slay the wicked, O God, and the men of blood would depart from me, men who maliciously defy Thee, who lift themselves up against Thee for evil!"*

Those shouting increased their volume and vehemence, causing Stew Pot to raise his volume and vehemence: *"Do I not hate them that hate Thee, O Lord? And do I not loathe them that rise up against Thee? I hate them with a perfect hatred!"*

Someone tossed an empty pop can, which bounced lightly off Stew Pot's chest. He threw his face skyward and raised his arms high. *"Oh Lord, my Lord, my strong deliverer, Thou hast covered my head in the day of battle. Grant not, O Lord, the desires of the wicked; do not further their evil plot! Let burning coals fall upon them! Let them be cast into pits, no more to rise!"* This produced still more shouting from the other side, with arms thrusting and fists shaking.

Stew Pot returned his eyes to the collected fury and pointed once again. "I *will bring distress on men*," he said, shifting now to the Book of Zephaniah, "*so that they shall walk like the blind because they have sinned against the Lord; their blood shall be poured out like dust, and their flesh like dung!*"

From somewhere a clump of turf, pulled from the lawn, sailed over and hit Stew Pot in the face. Some folks laughed as he swept with his hands to clear the dirt from his mouth, spitting out the last bits of earth before shouting: "*The great day of the Lord is near, near and hastening fast!*" He marched up to Mr. Glenn. The two were now so close, just a few inches of space above the fence rail between them, that they were splashing each other's face with spittle. Mr. Glenn suggested obscene acts Stew Pot could perform on himself and Stew Pot continued quoting Zephaniah: "*A day of wrath is that day! A day of distress and anguish, a day of ruin and devastation, a day of darkness and gloom—trumpet blast and battle cry!*"

It was at this point that Brother Crown and Mrs. Reeves hurried to Stew Pot, threw their arms around him, and tried to pull him back as he kept on yelling. "*Their goods shall be plundered, and their houses laid to waste!*"

Mrs. Motley, who had not shouted, realized Stew Pot was quoting Zephaniah out of order for what she assumed was his idea of maximum rhetorical effect. She also realized that this plan to confront Stew Pot directly had been a mistake. She had approved of it at the meeting, but seeing things now so completely out of hand, she regretted her decision. (As for Mrs. Butler, this was now her kind of game—freewheeling, rough-hewn. She screamed at Stew Pot that he was trash, had always been trash, and would never be anything *but* trash.)

The slender Brother Crown and petite Mrs. Reeves had no success in moving Stew Pot back. Mrs. Motley was certain that any second Mr. Glenn and Stew Pot would come to blows and the angrier people in the crowd would rush to Mr. Glenn's aide and Stew Pot would go down under the weight of violent punches and kicks which would continue until—what? Until he was beaten to within an inch of his life, until he was dead?

Which might have happened had not Mrs. Reeves, while still pulling desperately at her son, shouted in his ear: "Gerald, look!" Stew Pot glanced toward the alley where the front end of a dark sedan could be seen beyond the edge of Mrs. Motley's garage.

While the crowd continued yelling and gesturing, Stew Pot went silent and let Brother Crown and his mother pull him away. This had a calming effect on the crowd and one or two glanced at the alley and saw the front of the sedan. Soon the message "It's the cops" made it all the way to those standing near the sidewalk. Folks saw Officer Mance and his partner in sunglasses, jeans, and blue windbreakers standing by the two-flat's gate.

"Go on ahead with what you were doing, Stew Pot!" Mance called happily into the sudden quiet. "Don't let us stop you!"

Her voice desperate, Mrs. Reeves pleaded with Stew Pot to go inside. Though becalmed, he remained resolute before the now-quieted but still furious faces.

"Unlike the E'phraimites," he said, "I have not forgotten the miracles God has shown me. I will not retreat from the field."

Brother Crown, in a soft voice of reasoning, suggested that they go inside.

From somewhere in the crowd someone yelled: "Yeah, drag your butt inside and take your fool momma and that miserable excuse for a Black man with you!"

This re-enraged Stew Pot and he lunged forward, carrying Brother Crown and his mother, who still had ahold of him, forward too. Seeing this, the crowd stirred and grumbled.

Stew Pot pointed again with an extended forefinger, this time shouting: "None of you walk in The Light! The Devil's Den is in your future! Burning of the eyes, ears, nose, and throat! Burning hotter than the sun! Hotter than a thousands suns! *God gave Noah the rainbow sign. He said no more water, the fire next time!*"

Shouts came back for Stew Pot to go join the Devil right now, shouts called him a black this and a black that, the way some White folks will do when they want to be particularly vicious. Meanwhile, Mance and his partner watched, not moving, hoping the anger would blind people for the crucial moment necessary for a melee to ensue. Then they could call for backup, charge in, and after the mob had given Stew Pot a good beating, arrest him for assault along with Mr. Glenn, who Mance didn't like either.

Stew Pot gave a second lunge forward when Brother Crown, using a dancer's move, slid around and blocked him. Stew Pot stopped and then, just like that, Brother Crown slapped him across the face, making a sharp sound.

Folks in the crowd *oohhed* and *ahhed*. Stew Pot glared so fiercely that for a second some thought he might hit Brother Crown back; but then his expression softened just a little.

"That will be quite enough, Brother Gerald," said Brother Crown.

"But—"

"I told you," and Brother Crown pointed at the wall, "that such a display would only provoke anger. Didn't I tell you? It's just one of a number of bad decisions you've made. Disrupting that woman's service after I advised you by phone not to, publishing another so-called newsletter, and now this wall where you defame people."

"But Brother Crown, don't you see?"

"Yes, I see. I see you're headstrong and don't listen and can't be trusted to not throw gasoline on every fire. I'm afraid I simply can't have an assistant traveling with me on my evangelical missions who demonstrates such poor judgment."

Stew Pot's face went suddenly stricken. "What . . . what do you mean by *that*?"

"What I mean is that I do not think you will be suitable to accompany me on my national travels. For a two-year pilgrimage, I need someone I can depend on."

"But Brother Crown . . ."

At this point the good Brother stepped away and strode into the two-flat. Mrs. Reeves peered at him and then back at Stew Pot, then at the open doorway, then back at Stew Pot. Looking as if she had made a final decision, she stepped inside.

Stew Pot backed away from the fence and his opposition. He looked like a man who could not remember where he had set down the keys that he'd had in his hand only moments before. He fixed the crowd with a bewildered expression, then wheeled around and hurried for the doorway, hollering: "Brother Crown! Brother Crown!"

CHAPTER SEVEN
Wilt Thou Leave Me Thus?

The next morning Mr. McTeer was up early as usual. When he went to get his paper, he saw that at some time during the night, Stew Pot had removed all the signs. Back inside on his living room couch, he scanned the paper, set it down, and contemplated the prospect of another bittersweet Sunday with Mrs. Motley, wherein she would drive him to Seven Sorrows and lunch with him afterward at Logan's. While their talk would be pleasant enough, no angry words from her or recriminations, at the same time it would be carried out with what he could not help but feel was an emotional distance on her part, which had marked most of her behavior toward him since the revelation of the poem.

This line of thought was cut short by the arrival of a yellow cab in front of the two-flat. The driver, who Mr. McTeer saw in profile, appeared to be South Asian, for he wore a white turban and the end of his thick mustache was curled high. He waited with the engine running for only a little while before the front door of the two-flat opened and Brother Crown, with his white fedora set at what Mr. McTeer thought a jaunty angle, exited with Mrs. Reeves beside him. She no longer had a scarf on and she had a coat draped over one arm. Stew Pot followed, carrying two black suitcases.

The taxi's trunk popped and the driver, in a white dress shirt and dark slacks, came quickly around to the back of the car, getting there in time to take the suitcases from Stew Pot. The driver set the cases inside while Brother Crown opened the back curbside door. Mrs. Reeves and Stew Pot embraced on the parkway, his hugeness enveloping her petiteness. He bent over and she lifted herself to throw her arms around his neck. She said something into his ear and he nodded vigorously. She gave him a peck on the cheek and moved to disengage, but he pulled her tighter. He spoke something into her ear. Mrs. Reeves nodded vigorously in response.

Finally he let her go and she blew him a kiss, causing Stew Pot to tighten his lips in an obvious effort to hold back tears. Then she turned away and got inside the cab.

The driver by then was back behind the wheel. Brother Crown placed a left hand on Stew Pot's right shoulder and extended his other hand. The two men shook and then Brother Crown stepped around to the street side of the cab. After he was inside, with Stew Pot watching forlornly from the curb, the taxi slowly turned at the embankment wall and rolled out of sight. And Mr. McTeer remembered Mrs. Motley's telling of the scene from years ago when a young Stew Pot had watched the ambulance take his father away: *They're going to bring him back, right, Momma?* Which caused Mr. McTeer to think (the thought embarrassing him for its coldheartedness) that seeing Stew Pot again in such anguish was almost enough to make you feel sorry for him— almost.

CHAPTER EIGHT

Stew Pot's Fateful Fortnight

The second Monday after Mrs. Reeves and Brother Crown left, a chilly, sunny day, Mr. Bird was walking west, halfway down the block from the two-flat, when he heard Stew Pot shout after him. With a groan he stopped pushing his cart and turned to wait.

Stew Pot ran up to the jacketed and very nervous-looking mailman, shaking a sheet of paper high over his own head. "What is this?" Stew Pot demanded.

Mr. Bird said he didn't know what Stew Pot was talking about.

Stew Pot shook the sheet at Mr. Bird's nose. "I'm talking about this letter you delivered to me Saturday!"

"I still don't understand."

"Then read it!"

Mr. Bird gingerly took the white sheet and did as Stew Pot asked.

November 2, 1993

Dearest Gerald,

We were married in Atlanta yesterday afternoon. Unfortunately we will not be back for Thanksgiving as originally planned. Our pilgrimage work will keep us down here for a while. Assisting with the planning of our revival meetings, though they will be small at first, has been so very exciting. Quitting my job to do this holy work is the wisest decision I've ever made. Hopefully we'll be back by Christmas. Just pay the utilities and food out of the account I left at the bank.

With my deepest love and faith in our Savior,
Mother

When Mr. Bird was done reading, Stew Pot snatched the letter back. "Can you believe this? And after all I did for her! After all I did!" And with that Stew Pot balled up the sheet, tossed it to the ground, and stalked back to the two-flat.

Mr. Bird waited until the front door slammed before picking the ball up. He unfolded it and continued on. Before his route was done that day he showed the wrinkled sheet to a number of people, the first ones being Mrs. Motley and Mrs. Powell, who were both in the purple living room when he reached the end of the block.

After they had read the letter and Mr. Bird had gone, Mrs. Powell said: "His momma left with the man to travel around the country. What did he think they were going to do to pass away the idle hours, play cards?"

That evening and night around Parkland, many people made similar comments, greatly enjoying, for the second week in a row, a sad development in the life of Stew Pot Reeves.

Neighborhood talk of the letter lasted only twenty-four hours, however, because the next day, at around eleven a.m., Stew Pot walked into Sonny's Tavern and asked for a beer.

The bartender looked him up and down in surprise. "A beer?"

"You *do* sell beer here—right?" said Stew Pot.

The bartender, a white-haired retiree who worked the slower day shifts for the pension supplement and free drinks, did not want to rile the younger man. "I'm sorry. I didn't know you took liquor anymore. What kind of beer you want?"

Stew Pot placed his order, and as the bartender brought him the cold brown bottle, Stew Pot said that while he was at it, he might as well pour him a shot of bourbon. Stew Pot named his brand of poison and the bartender poured the amber liquid into a little glass.

The barman and the few barflies in attendance, other retirees with nothing constructive to occupy their days, watched out of the corner of their eyes as Stew Pot drank his shot with one gulp, followed by a wince and a cough. No one said anything to him, though he was there about forty minutes having himself two more beers and another bourbon shot before leaving.

He was then sighted waiting for a northbound bus, which he boarded at about noon. Some folks said they saw him return after dark around seven that evening.

The next day in the late morning he showed up at Minton's. This time the bartender was a woman who was short but mighty. As Stew Pot slid onto a barstool near the window, the gray-haired woman told him straight out that the first time he started preaching or what-have-you, he was gone. Showing not the least irritation, he said she had nothing to worry about. True to his word, he sipped his bottles of beer (four) and downed his shots of tequila (three) without a peep.

Like the day before, he took the bus north in the early afternoon and returned in the evening. Naturally, there was much talk about this around the neighborhood, with all kinds of speculation as to what it might mean and what Stew Pot might do next.

What he did was more of the same; for the next fortnight he was sitting at some neighborhood bar. Every time, he arrived in the late morning, stayed for about an hour, left on the bus, and arrived home after dark; sometimes well after dark. During these excursions he never spoke to anyone save the bartender when he ordered his drinks, and the bartenders were the only ones who spoke to him, and then just to ask what he wanted. Nobody else, not even the most smart-mouthed punter, wanted to mess with someone as big and temperamental as Stew Pot who was also liquored up.

Officer Mance and his partner, immune to such concerns, had fun baiting him from their car. As Stew Pot walked down the street, they rolled slowly alongside and told him they knew all along he'd go back to his old ways. They described various lewd acts his mom was doing with Brother Crown, and said that Crown had been after her all along and that he—Stew Pot—was a chump for not figuring out what that pale-face had been up to.

Try as they might, Mance and his partner never got a rise out of their nemesis.

During the second week of Stew Pot falling off the wagon, Mr. Davenport returned (alone) to move his family's things. His first day back lots of folks came by, interrupting him as he went about packing and dismantling. Even Mrs. Butler and Mrs. Powell came over to say goodbye to him amid the jungle of boxes and stacked furniture.

While away, Mr. Davenport had lost some weight and grown a goatee. Visitors commented that he seemed younger.

Looking happy, even with bloodshot eyes, he said he and his family were looking forward to living in the wooded and lake-bejeweled Minnesota countryside. The air was so clean up there, he said. On clear nights you could see the aurora borealis. Yes, the winters were cold, but it was a dry cold and in that way not as intense as the damp air of a Chicago winter.

The next afternoon around three, as moving men in green coveralls carted boxes to a long green trailer in the driveway, Mr. Davenport stood on the front lawn in a light coat and tan slacks, having a last chat with Mrs. Motley and Mr. McTeer. He spoke again of the wonders of north-central Minnesota, how the Smith School campus was located on grounds adjacent to the beautiful Lake Roosevelt. Their conversation stopped at the sight of Stew Pot across the street, strolling in the direction of the two-flat. Stew Pot stopped and fixed them with a flat stare, then turned his head and continued on his way.

The day before, folks had told Mr. Davenport what had occurred in the neighborhood since his leaving. Glancing at his old adversary's back, he said: "You see that look on his face? His eyes look lifeless, like a doll. That boy is going to snap; that is, if he hasn't already. Mark my words; he's going to do something. And when he does, it'll be something messed up."

The truck left for Minnesota that evening and Mr. Davenport shortly after. Two days later, on Monday evening, folks on the block thought Mr. D.'s prediction had come true when they saw Stew Pot doing something to the west wall of the two-flat.

He walked over to what had been Mrs. Motley's property carrying two white buckets. From the buckets he grabbed what at first looked like a half-inflated balloon, which he hurled across the chainlink fence at the wall. The balloon exploded in a paint blast of red. He then reached into the bucket for another, and then another.

When both buckets were empty, the white background and the large words were spotted with crimson splotches; some had uneven lines dribbling below them, the wall now looking like a bad mix of Jackson Pollock and Andy Warhol.

Those neighbors who saw this, which included Mr. McTeer, said later that what was particularly unnerving was the grunting Stew Pot emitted with every hurl, and how, after he had no more balloons left, he grabbed first one and then the other plastic bucket by the handle and flung them at the wall too.

Of all the neighbors, Mrs. Motley was perhaps the most bothered, for she did not believe this was the end of the messing up Stew Pot planned to do. "This sounds more like a beginning," she told Mrs. Powell.

Two days later she had proof she was right. When Mrs. Powell went to the stoop to get the paper, she returned not only with the folded *Sun-Times*, but also with the Bible Mrs. Motley had given Stew Pot.

"It was on the front porch," Mrs. Powell said as she handed the book over to Mrs. Motley, who was sitting with her morning coffee in the purple dining room. "What do you think it means?"

Mrs. Motley, rubbing her fingertips across the hard black cover, said she didn't know exactly. "But coming on the heels of what he did to his wall, it can't be anything good."

Later that day, which was exactly a week before Thanksgiving, in the cloudy midafternoon, Mrs. Motley was doing a crossword puzzle in the purple living room and Mrs. Powell was in the basement watching her soaps, when suddenly it seemed as if half the police cars in the 26th District were descending on the block. Mrs. Motley watched as white squads and dark sedans, with blue lights crackling flashes, came down the street at high speed. She heard noise out back and went to the room's archway and looked through the dining room to the kitchen window and saw police cars moving east down the alley as well.

After calling down the basement steps to Mrs. Powell, Mrs. Motley returned to the living room. She stepped down the walkway and looked east toward the flashing lights.

Mr. McTeer was home at the time. From his living room window he saw the police, some uniformed, some in jeans and windbreakers, park their cars along the curbs and in the apron of his driveway, before hustling to the two-flat with their weapons drawn. From the alley he glimpsed another group racing up the backyard walkway.

Officer Mance led the way to the front door where he pounded loud with a fist and shouted that it was the Chicago Police and that whoever was in there had better open the door—*now!* The cops must have heard someone approaching the front door because they stepped back a few feet with their pistols held in that double-hand clutch they use.

The door opened and there was Stew Pot, the top of his overalls undone so that the bib and shoulder straps hung from his waist.

Mance and his partner, their weapons aimed directly at Stew Pot's head, shouted for him to get down on the ground immediately. Even though Stew Pot did exactly as he was told, lowering himself to his knees and then lying facedown across the threshold, Mance kept yelling at him as his partner lowered a knee and planted it in his back. The partner yanked one of Stew Pot's arms backward and slapped a black handcuff on the wrist, then pulled the other arm backward and applied another cuff.

Screaming now and still aiming his pistol at Stew Pot's head, Mance demanded to know if anyone else was in the two-flat. A uniformed officer and Mance's partner dragged Stew Pot to his feet and away from the doorway, and Mance and a slew of other cops then poured inside the building shouting, their voices echoing through the doorway.

Stew Pot, with a flat expression on his face, was quickly taken to an unmarked car parked directly in front of his home and guided into the backseat. Two cops got in the front and two more wearing suits got in back, wedging Stew Pot between them. After a quick turn at the embankment wall the gray car moved quickly west toward Honore.

The vehicle passed Mrs. Motley and Mrs. Powell as they were making their way eastward. It went by so fast all the women saw of the backseat was the profile of the cop sitting to Stew Pot's left: a Black man with a mustache who stared straight ahead.

Of the remaining cops, some continued going in and out of the two-flat, always, it seemed, carrying something on the outbound trips—cardboard boxes, evidence bags sagging with items that none of the onlookers, which after a few minutes numbered half a dozen, were close enough to make out clearly. The other cops, about ten or so in uniforms, stood around in klatches talking.

Mr. McTeer came out of his house and recognized two from this latter batch, the pale red-haired White man and the tall Black man who had lead Mr. Davenport from his house the previous summer.

The Black cop, Officer Lampton, had played high school ball against Mr. McTeer's son, and although he had never met him formally, Lampton knew of the man, knew he was a combat veteran. Lampton had served in the military too, and like many veterans who have never seen combat, he was in awe of veterans who had.

Lampton waved when he and Mr. McTeer made eye contact, calling out in his basso profundo: "How you doing, Mr. McTeer?"

Mr. McTeer shrugged in response.

Lampton, who was jacketless with an open collar despite the chilly air, left the group he was talking with and strolled to the curb where he offered his large hand. When they shook, Mr. McTeer peered up at the taller man curiously, unsure as to how he knew him. That's when Lampton told him about having competed as a high school jock against the younger McTeer, causing Mr. McTeer to respond with a simple "Oh," as if it were no big deal. Lampton thought this an odd way for a father to answer, but made no show of his feelings. Before he had the chance to ask how his son was doing, Mr. McTeer nodded toward the two-flat and the officers coming in and out.

Lampton glanced over his shoulder at a uniformed sergeant and lieutenant, then said: "All we can tell you right now is that Stew Pot's been taken into custody. Of course, we don't roll out this kind of show for somebody jaywalking. And as you may notice, there are no arson cops around. And Stew Pot isn't in a gang, so it's not anybody from Gang Crimes."

Picking up on Lampton's drift, Mr. McTeer said, "And none of these plainclothes guys look scary enough to be Narcotics or Vice."

"Yeah," replied Lampton evenly, "that's true."

"Which kind of whittles it down to Violent Crimes? Which means Stew Pot raped or killed someone. Or maybe both?"

"Or maybe both," Lampton said.

BOOK X

Thanksgiving

CHAPTER ONE

Anatomy of a Murder

Stew Pot was charged with first-degree murder in the death of Megan O'Brien, who was found dead in her apartment just hours before his arrest. A forty-something school teacher who lived and worked on the North Side, it was her testimony that had been chiefly responsible for Stew Pot's earlier conviction.

The story led all the local TV news that evening. Using Stew Pot's given name, the broadcasts featured video of O'Brien's building, an orange-brick three-flat; the grade school where she taught; and a segment from a late-afternoon media conference where a jowly captain said that Stew Pot's arrest had come after detectives "found significant physical evidence in Ms. O'Brien's apartment connecting Mr. Reeves to the crime scene. Items from her home were later found during a subsequent search of Mr. Reeves's home."

That night, the local newscasts led with the same story. This time the reporters referred to her by her nickname, "Katie" O'Brien.

In Parkland public houses, the normally noisy joints were quiet as folks stared up at the high TV screens. These broadcasts reported that O'Brien appeared to have been strangled. There was a photograph of her, an enlargement of a smaller image, showing a woman with short reddish hair, an aquiline nose, and a faint smile partially revealing an overbite. There was video of colleagues crying on each others' shoulders, of the school principal, a Ms. Solorzano, who with a strained look on her face said: "Katie was loved by everybody." There was no footage of students, but a couple of student parents, a Ms. Gasca and a Ms. Jimenez, paused to dab at tearing eyes and spoke of O'Brien in equally glowing terms. After that there was video of youngish White adults who lived near O'Brien, none of whom had known her, and several of whom said: "You just don't expect that sort of thing around here." Reporters gave live feeds from the makeshift shrine in front of O'Brien's building: flowers, cards of sympathy—

352 † Bedrock Faith

some store-bought, some handmade—and burning votive candles.

Then, finally, a segment on Stew Pot: a summary of what had occurred between he and O'Brien years before, the clip from the earlier media conference video, and a mug shot of Stew Pot taken that evening with him looking eerily calm.

The next morning, local papers had the O'Brien story on page one and detailed how the day before O'Brien had not reported for work or called in sick. A worried colleague drove to her home and got the second-floor neighbor (who had yet to leave for work) to buzz her in. The two women went to O'Brien's third-floor flat where they found the door closed but unlocked and O'Brien's body in her bedroom. The reports also said that O'Brien was childless, lived alone, and was a native of Lake Forest and a product of Catholic schools. Between her two encounters with Reeves she'd been married and divorced.

In Parkland, folks reading these stories knew that reporters would likely be coming to find out about Stew Pot, and Vernon Paiger phoned Mrs. Motley.

"Having been Stew Pot's next-door neighbor," he said, "some of those news hounds are really going to want to talk to you. If you don't want to be hassled, you better make yourself scarce."

CHAPTER TWO

The Few, the Proud, the Fourth Estate

S tew Pot's bond hearing was held early that same afternoon.
In his T-shirt and overalls, he stood calmly in the windowless
shabby courtroom alongside the public defender assigned to
his case—a short, youngish-looking White man in a gray suit jacket.
To the surprise of no one, the portly brown judge ruled that Stew Pot
was to be held without bond.

This pro forma was over in less than three minutes, after which
the reporters in attendance set out for Parkland. Armed with pens,
narrow spiral notebooks and ID badges dangling from chains looped
around their necks, the reporters did a full-court press on the block
where Gerald Reeves had lived. Radio reporters toted tape recorders
and mobile phones for their numerous updates, while the chosen few
of TV with their coifed hair, expensive suits, and mugs familiar to everyone, went about their work accompanied by video camera jockeys
wearing athletic-style jackets with station logos and call letters across
the backs. (The newspaper photogs, operating as usual on independent command, took whatever images struck their fancy.)

Because it was a weekday, there weren't many people on hand to
speak with, and those who were home—Mr. McTeer, Mrs. Powell,
and a couple of others—gave reporters polite but firm no-comments.
(A family moving onto the block that day by the name of Wilson said
that since they'd never met Mr. Reeves, they had nothing to offer.)

Undaunted, the reporters set off across the neighborhood to homes
and businesses, asking folks about Gerald Reeves. Having a healthy
suspicion of reporters and their ilk, many of these people were closed-
mouthed too. However, a few did talk. Reporters soon found out that
nobody in Parkland called Reeves by his given name, and no one, absolutely no one they spoke with, had anything good to say about him.
No one said the usual stuff like he was a good kid who had fallen in
with a bad crowd, or that he was trying to get his life back together, or

that the cops were racist for so quickly settling on him as the suspect.

As Vernon had predicted, because Mrs. Motley's name was frequently mentioned by those who talked, some newsies circled back to her block and the Powells' house. There they were told by Mrs. Powell, speaking through the narrow space of the parted front door, that Mrs. Motley wasn't there and no, she didn't know when she would be back.

The reporters returned to their newsrooms most invigorated. Not only did this story have a *Native Son* angle (always an attention grabber), there were more intriguing aspects to it than you could shake a swizzle stick at. This Stew Pot (was that a great handle or what?) was like *Night of the Hunter*, that flick where Robert Mitchum plays a creepy Bible-quoting killer. Where were Stew Pot's mom and her husband? What of the lesbian he allegedly drove from Parkland? If he burned the Motley woman's garage like everyone said, why had the cops not interrogated him when her house was torched? And where was Motley? Some folks said she was romantic with Vernon Paiger! And there was the splattered wall, and someone had killed Stew Pot's dog, and on and on and on.

CHAPTER THREE

The "Ha-Ha" Welcome Wagon

As the reporters headed away for the day, Mrs. Motley sat inside the Wilsons' freshly vacated residence. She'd driven there in the midmorning, before reporters arrived on the block and shortly after she saw a yellow moving truck stop at the Davenports' old place.

The redbrick ranch had white trim around the windows and doors. After parking Ingrid in the attached windowless garage, it had been an odd sensation for her to step from the garage's gasoline smell directly into the house, which reeked of cleaning fluid from all the mopping and scrubbing that the Wilsons had done.

The connecting door opened into a galley kitchen that was a study in blue: royal-blue cabinets, counters, and fridge; sky-blue floor tiles and a pale-blue ceiling.

With her heels echoing in the empty place, Mrs. Motley carried a folding chair and a card table (borrowed from the Powells) which she set up in the living room. Feeling relatively safe behind the lowered window shades, she spent much of the afternoon perusing interior design magazines and writing detailed notes in a spiral notebook. She'd already decided the kitchen would have to be gutted, and she wanted crown molding in every room save the kitchen and bathroom. The hardwood floors needed stripping and revarnishing, and all the dings, scratches, and scrapes in the walls needed fixing. Since she had the available money, she also wanted a central air-conditioning system installed.

Around four thirty there was a knock at the front door. It was nearly dark by then and she flicked on the front-door light and looked through the peep. It was Vernon Paiger.

As soon as she opened the door he gave her a big smile. He was wearing a long black wool coat over a navy-blue three-piece suit, with oxblood dress shoes. Vernon gazed about the nearly empty room. "You manage to steer clear of our journalism friends?"

"Yes," Mrs. Motley said. "How'd you know I was here?"

"Saw the light was on in the window of the living room. I figured I'd come over and welcome you to the block. So welcome."

She thanked him and he, eyeing the card table, went straight over and began thumbing the pages of the spiral notebook.

"Elaborate plans, I see: crown molding, brand-new kitchen."

Mrs. Motley wanted to grab the notebook away from him. At the same time, she felt such a reaction was silly, and because she didn't want him to know he was having an effect on her, she chose the lesser of two evils and stood silent while he read the pages with what was for her an excruciating slowness.

He finally turned back to her and said, "So, you want to give me the nickel tour and show me what you plan to do with the place?"

Unable to think of an excuse for saying no, Mrs. Motley took him on a room-to-room tour, pointing out what she wanted done—a new ceiling light fixture put in there, white wainscoting done there, that room painted this color, this room painted that color.

When they were back in the living room Vernon asked: "Mr. McTeer been here yet?"

She said no. He asked about Mrs. Powell and Mrs. Motley said no again.

"So I'm the first person you've had across the threshold as a guest. I'm honored."

She gave him an arched-eyebrow look over the top of her glasses, which provoked a puzzled smirk in response.

"What? I *am* honored." He wagged both forefingers in the air like metronomes and said in a silly, sing-song voice: "I saw your house before Mr. McTeer."

She now fixed him with that slightly wide-eyed look Black women like to use to convey the message: *I am not amused.*

This made him laugh and he said: "I'm just trying to be playful and spontaneous. Not the stuffy old alderman I usually am."

"You need to work on it."

"If I worked on it, then it wouldn't be spontaneous. I'm just happy that for once I have a leg up on my rival."

"Mr. McTeer is not your *rival.*"

"Oh yeah?" said Vernon, still smiling. "Does he know that?"

She gave him another not-amused look, this one a little harsher.

Changing the subject, he said: "So Roland is coming over tomorrow, is he? He and his crew will have this place shaped up in no time."

"How does he feel," asked Mrs. Motley, "about the 'hole' in his schedule that allowed him to help me so soon? The last time he and I spoke, he didn't seem all that thrilled."

"I can assure you Roland feels just fine. Are you going to be hiding out here again tomorrow?"

Mrs. Motley said she would, just in case reporters came to the neighborhood again.

CHAPTER FOUR

The Sunday Funnies

The newspaper reporters did come out the next day looking for more info. They found a few tidbits, but got nothing from Mrs. Motley. Because hardly anyone had yet learned she'd bought a house, there were few knowledgeable mouths available to blab that information. So the day after that, Sunday, the reporters from local dailies had to make do without Mrs. Motley's help, the stories with leads like—

> *In the wake of the Thursday-morning homicide of Chicago school teacher Megan O'Brien, a story is emerging involving her accused killer, Gerald X. Reeves. That story is one of community unrest in the far South Side enclave of Parkland where Reeves had lived from the time of his prison release last March for the 1978 sexual assault of O'Brien, until Thursday afternoon when he was arrested by police at his Parkland home . . .*

> *From the time of his prison release this March for the 1978 sexual assault on Megan Katherine O'Brien, until police arrested him in connection with O'Brien's death last Thursday, Gerald Xavier Reeves has engaged, his Parkland neighbors say, in an escalating series of conflicts with other residents of the far South Side community . . .*

> *With its neat lawns and quiet streets, the far South Side neighborhood of Parkland appears as tranquil a place as any you'll find in Chicago; however, in the last eight months this normally quiet community has been rocked by turmoil involving Gerald "Stew Pot" Reeves, who police allege, killed Megan O'Brien, a Chicago school teacher who was found dead in her Lakeview apartment Thursday morning . . .*

The stories went on to detail, with only a few degrees of inaccuracy, what had been going on in Parkland the previous eight months.

(One story had Stew Pot disrupting Mrs. Hicks's service by banging a tambourine, another story had him preaching a long anti-gay sermon at Erma Smedley's house with a bullhorn, and still another had him threatening to sic his dog on people at Delphina's party.) There was stuff about the *Burning Bush*, and Stew Pot's witnessing, and his confrontation with the neighbors who'd marched on his home, with one newspaper account making reference to "Reeves's religious mentor, a mystery man known only to neighborhood residents as Brother Crown. According to many residents, Crown eloped with Reeves's mother last month and moved to Georgia. Neither has been heard from since Gerald Reeves's arrest Thursday."

The stories reported the widespread neighborhood belief that Stew Pot was behind the fire that destroyed his next-door neighbor's house, and that there was something fishy about the fact the police had not brought him in for questioning. That last point prompted the Chicago Police to release a media statement that the investigation of the arson case in question "is ongoing" and that Gerald Reeves had not been questioned because he had a verified alibi as to his whereabouts at the time of the fire.

These stories were read with great interest throughout the Chicago area, with some meanies from outside the tribe saying that Stew Pot was just another example of what was wrong with Blacks in general: "Even their best neighborhoods produce rapists and murderers." Meanwhile, brothers and sisters from other areas, who had long resented Parkland, took some solace in the thought that its people, for all their snooty attitudes, "aren't any better than anybody else."

In Parkland, the information that folks found far and away the most intriguing was the revelation (produced from reportorial investigation of recent real estate records) that Mrs. Motley had not only sold her property to Vernon Paiger's nephew Roland, but that she had also bought a house across the street from the alderman.

Armed with this new information, several reporters arrived at various times Sunday morning at the Powells' house. They had gone to church, but Mrs. Motley had decided to stay home. Standing in the doorway she told the reporters, politely but firmly, that she had no comment. She said the same to those journalists who called her on the phone.

CHAPTER FIVE

The Parking Lot of Diamond Foods, Early Sunday Afternoon

You read today's paper? That's a lot of money Roland paid Motley for that property."

"Roland didn't any more pay for that property than Scotty Woodbury came to Reggie's rescue on his own. Vernon paid for one and arranged the other. And he did it all for Mrs. Motley."

"How you figure?"

"From what I understand, only three folks saw Reggie taken into custody that morning: Mr. Glenn, Mrs. Powell, and Mrs. Motley. Of the three, which one do you think could get Vernon hopping to get Reggie a good lawyer?"

"I never thought of that."

"Take it from me, Mrs. Motley is mixed up in this Reggie business too. That she and Vernon are now thick as thieves shouldn't be a surprise since she's as secretive as he is."

"I suppose. I wonder if the cops have tried to beat a confession out of Stew Pot."

"They might not have had to. They said they found all sorts of evidence in his two-flat."

"Found it, or planted it after the fact?"

"You defending Stew Pot?"

"I'm not defending anybody. I'm just saying the police are the police."

"So what do you think Stew Pot's going to use for a defense?"

"Who knows? Maybe he'll claim it was his evil twin that killed that woman."

CHAPTER SIX
Two Letters

After the destruction of Mrs. Motley's house, Mr. Bird delivered her mail to the Powells' house. The day following the Sunday stories about Stew Pot, Mrs. Motley received two letters. (It was also the day of Megan O'Brien's funeral. There were midday TV reports of her tall and white-haired mother exiting a north suburban church with a grim-faced male relative by her side; her head tilted back and the pain on her face the very illustration of grief.) The letters came in standard white envelopes. One was thick with what seemed like several folded pages, while the other seemed to contain only a single sheet. There was no return address on either. Her handwritten name and the Powells' address were in black all-caps on the thick one and in blue script on the other.

Sitting alone that afternoon in the purple living room, Mrs. Motley used Mrs. Powell's gold-plated opener to slit open the top of the thick envelope. The pages were stapled in the upper-left-hand corner and the lettering was the same as on the front of the envelope.

As soon as she read the first lines her breath caught.

DEAR MRS. MOTLEY,
    I AM THE REAL STEW POT. AFTER SOME TWELVE YEARS OF CONFINEMENT AT THE HANDS OF THOSE TWO HOLIER-THAN-THOUS, I AM FINALLY FREE.

Mrs. Motley dropped the letter and stared down at it in near disbelief. Was this someone's idea of a joke? But the very next paragraph cleared that up.

I HAVE CHOSEN TO WRITE TO YOU BECAUSE YOU'RE THE ONLY ONE TO EXTEND ANY KINDNESS TO ME, EVEN IF IT WAS INTENDED FOR THAT GOODY TWO SHOES WHO CAME ASKING

362 † Bedrock Faith

FOR A BIBLE, AND LATER WALKED ON HIS KNEES ACROSS YOUR KITCHEN FLOOR PLEADING FOR FORGIVENESS. I SWEAR I DON'T KNOW WHO'S WORSE, GERALD THE SMILING NO-BACKBONE PUNK WHO WAS FOREVER GIVING THE CHEERFUL HELLOS, OR THAT SELF-RIGHTEOUS LOUDMOUTH, GERALD X, CONTINUALLY MAKING A NUISANCE OF HIMSELF.

A QUESTION THAT I'M SURE IS VERY MUCH ON YOUR MIND IS—DID I KILL MEGAN O'BRIEN? ANSWER: NO. THOUGH SHE CERTAINLY HAD IT COMING. SHE CLAIMED UNDER OATH THAT I SEXUALLY ASSAULTED HER THAT FIRST TIME. NOW I ADMIT I SEXUALLY RELIEVED MYSELF AS SHE LAY WITH EYES CLOSED AS IF ASLEEP. (AN ACT THAT DID NOT FOOL ME.) BUT I ATTEMPTED NO PENETRATION OF HER. STILL, AFTER TALKING WITH POLICE SHE CONCOCTED A STORY THAT I HAD SEXUALLY VIOLATED HER, RESULTING IN MY LONG SENTENCE DOWNSTATE.

EVERY TIME I THINK OF HER SITTING IN THAT COURTROOM LOOKING LIKE LITTLE BOW PEEP, I WANT TO PUKE. SHE WAS NOT LITTLE BOW PEEP, LET ME ASSURE YOU. I WILL NOT GO INTO GRAPHIC DETAIL ABOUT THE MASTURBATORY DEVICES I FOUND IN HER PLACE, BECAUSE YOU ARE A LADY. IF THERE'S DIVINE JUSTICE, AS GERALD AND GERALD X ARE ALWAYS CLAIMING, THEN O'BRIEN'S DEATH (WHOEVER KILLED HER) IS A JUST PUNISHMENT FOR HER LYING ABOUT ME!

TO REPEAT, BECAUSE OF MEGAN O'BRIEN I ENDED UP DOWNSTATE. I WAS ALONE, MRS. MOTLEY, WITHOUT A FRIEND ANYWHERE. AGAIN, BECAUSE YOU'RE A LADY, I WON'T GO INTO DETAILS OF WHAT WAS DONE TO ME IN PRISON. I WILL SAY THAT I WAS VIOLATED—REPEATEDLY. AS I SMELLED MY TORMENTORS' SOUR SWEAT AND BREATH AND HEARD THEIR ANIMALISTIC GRUNTS AND LAUGHTER, THE IMAGE OF MEGAN O'BRIEN WAS CLEAR IN MY HEAD AND I TOLD MYSELF THAT ONE DAY HER CRIME WOULD BE AVENGED. ALTHOUGH NOT NECCESSARILY BY ME.

THOUGH I TAKE NO CREDIT FOR O'BRIEN'S UNTIMELY END, I'M RELIEVED TO BE FREE OF HER, JUST AS I'M HAPPY TO BE FREE OF GERALD AND GERALD X. THEIR INCESSANT DEBATES—GERALD ARGUING KINDNESS AND UNDERSTANDING, GERALD X ARGUING FIRE AND BRIMSTONE—WERE A TORTURE TO LISTEN TO!

BUT THE LAST LAUGH WAS ON THEM, FOR THEY WERE OUTDONE BY AN EVEN CRAFTIER PAIR THAN THEMSELVES. I'M SPEAKING OF MY DEAR MOM AND GOOD OLD BROTHER CROWN. WHEN THEY SKIPPED OFF TOGETHER, THE SHOCK WEAKENED GERALD AND I WAS ABLE TO ESCAPE MY CONFINEMENT.

AND NOW, LET ME TALK A BIT ABOUT MY DEAR OLD DAD— LOVER OF GUT BUCKET BLUES, CHEAP WHISKEY, FLOOZIES, AND BEATING HIS SON. YES, THE VIOLATIONS I RECEIVED IN PRISON WERE NOT MY FIRST-GO-ROUND WITH BLUNT FORCE. (FEELING A LITTLE GUILTY, MRS. MOTLEY? ALL THAT WAS GOING ON NEXT DOOR AND YOU DID NOT NOTICE!) DURING ALL OF THIS ABUSE MOM WAS A GOOD WIFE AND RAISED NO COMPLAINTS. I'M SURE SHE FEARED DAD WOULD WHACK HER IF SHE DID. I GUESS I CAN'T BLAME THE OLD GIRL FOR LOOKING OUT FOR HERSELF.

MOM DID EVENTUALLY GET REVENGE. DAD HAS HIS HEART ATTACK IN THE LIVING ROOM. GERALD RUNS TO ALERT MOM IN THE KITCHEN. MOM COMES, FINDS DAD ON THE FLOOR GASPING FOR AN AMBULANCE. AND SHE CALLS ONE—AN HOUR LATER!

WHEN THE AMBULANCE GOT THERE, DAD WAS NEAR GONE. I CAN STILL SEE HIS OPEN EYES STARING OFF INTO NOTHING. NOW GERALD, AS YOU MIGHT EXPECT, THREW A FIT. "THEY'RE BRINGING HIM BACK, RIGHT, MOMMA?" HA! IT'S EARLY MORNING AND I'M WRITING FROM THE SECOND FLOOR FRONT ROOM WHERE DAD HAD HIS FINAL FALL. GERALD X IS IN THE KITCHEN MESSING AROUND AND MUTTERING SOMETHING ABOUT "5-32 AND 32." THERE ARE SOME OF O'BRIEN'S THINGS HERE. I SUSPECT GERALD'S HAND. (HE'S MOPING AROUND SOMEWHERE.) THE ITEMS ARE HIS LAME ATTEMPT TO PIN O'BRIEN'S MURDER ON ME. WELL, IF THERE'S ANOTHER TRIAL I WON'T HAVE ANYBODY LYING ON ME IN OPEN COURT, AND I WILL BE VINDICATED!

SINCERELY,
STEW POT REEVES

P.S. DO NOT LISTEN TO ANYTHING GERALD OR GERALD X SAYS! THEY ARE LIARS!

Mrs. Motley set the pages down, wondering if the letter was an attempt on Stew Pot's part to build some sort of insanity defense.

She opened the second envelope. The single sheet carried writing on both sides.

Dearest Mrs. Motley,

I can't tell you how painful it's been these last months to leave home full of the Lord's joy only to be met by angry faces and no knowledge of what Gerald X had done. Mom's letter sent him over the edge. He wanted to take off for Georgia to do Mom and Brother Crown harm. I had to stop him. Meanwhile, Stew Pot took advantage of my preoccupation with keeping Gerald X under control to regain his own freedom. I knew murder was going to be done one way or another. I had to make a choice, so I chose to keep Gerald X under control to save my mother and the man who helped bring me to the Lord. When I found myself in that poor woman's apartment, I grabbed a few items and took them home so that if the police did come, they would find plenty of incriminating evidence. After I saw that Stew Pot had written to you (and subsequently fallen asleep), I knew I had to hurry and write you so as to set the record straight. I intend to mail both letters. If you compare the two it will prove that Stew Pot is quite mad. I know you'll do the right thing and make sure they get to the proper authorities. That way, Stew Pot and Gerald X will get their just desserts. Although I don't know exactly how he did it, Gerald X was directly responsible for what happened to Mrs. Hicks. She is dead because of him. As I write this, I am in the front room where my father died. Two important notes: contrary to what Stew Pot claimed in his letter, it was he who took his own sweet time, over an hour, before telling Mom that Daddy had passed out. I am comforted by these words from First Corinthians which I'm sure you are familiar with:

> *"Behold, I show you a mystery; We shall not all sleep, but we shall all be changed, in a moment, in the twinkling of an eye, at the last trump: for the trumpet shall sound, and the dead shall be raised incorruptible, and we shall be changed. For this corruptible must put on incorruption, and this mortal must put on immortality."*

I will float above this, Mrs. Motley, as I floated above it when my dad did his worst, as I floated in prison and watched from a safe distance while *those cackling lost souls set themselves upon me. My father and the lost souls thought they were harming me, but they were not, for they did not know or see the true me. Stew Pot is not me, and Gerald X is not me. It was Gerald X who returned your Bible by the way, along with some other item, although he didn't say what it was. He may well have been lying, he tells so many lies. He is as likely a suspect for Ms. O'Brien's murder as Stew Pot. After Mom's letter, Stew Pot got him worked into a lather, telling him that Mom and Brother Crown had planned all along to leave him. It was also Stew Pot who, after getting himself good and liquored up, gave Gerald X the bright idea to go see if O'Brien was still teaching at the school where she'd been working at the time he first invaded her home. Unfortunately, she <u>was</u> at the same school. Because she took public transportation to and from work, it was not hard for him to follow and find the location of her new home. Thank you, Mrs. Motley, for all you've done and tried to do for me.*

Sincerely yours, and in Jesus's name,
Gerald Reeves

CHAPTER SEVEN
A Matter of Opinion

I t's bogus," said Mr. McTeer. He and Mrs. Motley were sitting on the couch in his living room where she had come soon after she finished reading the letters. Mr. McTeer had read them both and was now rendering his decision.

In white dress shirt, gray slacks, and red bow tie, he sat facing the picture window, his dark cane leaning against the coffee table. His bulldog jaw was set, the bottom lip somewhat pouted.

"I thought the letters might be phony," said Mrs. Motley from her place at the window end of the couch where she sat with her trench coat open. "But then I thought, *What if they're genuine?*"

Mr. McTeer's face went incredulous. "How on earth could they possibly be genuine?"

"I meant genuine in so far as indicating Stew Pot's mental state."

Mr. McTeer shook his head a couple of times. "No, no." He looked back at her. "It's a trick. I've read about this kind of thing, about how convicts read mental-patient case histories and become experts on the symptoms of disorders and fake them in an attempt to avoid prosecution. Obviously that's what Stew Pot has done here."

Realizing he was not convincing her, he softened his voice. "Stew Pot is playing upon your good graces. When he returned home from killing that woman he knew he was in big trouble and that he had to come up with some sort of strategy."

"Then why did he bring home incriminating evidence?"

"Maybe he was on some sort of high from what he'd done and took the stuff as a souvenir. I read that murderers sometimes do that. Or maybe this nut-wagon charade was premeditated and he went to O'Brien's house with the intention of taking some things to make his nuttiness look convincing. Whatever the case, there's no need for you to get mixed up in it." The softness in his voice gone, he leaned toward her. "Don't play the fool for him."

"Is that what you think I've been?"

"No, that's not what I think. It's just you have a trusting nature—"

"And my nature causes me to act like a fool—"

"I didn't say *that*. Look, you came here with letters from Stew Pot. You asked me what I thought. I've told you. If you didn't want my opinion, why did you come?"

After a moment of silence Mrs. Motley apologized. He forgave her immediately and they were silent again for a few more seconds.

"So you feel I shouldn't send the letters to Stew Pot's lawyer or the presiding judge?"

"Correct," said Mr. McTeer. "Why do anything that might help him? I say burn them."

A longer bit of silence ensued. Mr. McTeer could feel his temper rising, not just over the folly Mrs. Motley was contemplating, but over her dealings with Vernon and her moving away. He knew what people were saying behind his back, he knew they were laughing at him or, worse yet, pitying him. When she had phoned him saying she needed to see him right away, he had hoped that perhaps . . .

"So what are you going to do?" he asked, full of worry, feeling his control waning.

In a voice of fatigued frustration she replied: "I really don't know."

His next words were not spoken sharply, for sharpness of tone was not needed: "Turn in those letters and you *will* be a fool, and this time you'll have only yourself to blame. How could you think of coming to Stew Pot's aid, after all he's done to our friends? After all he's done to you? Why, the very idea is unthinkable, hideous."

Mrs. Motley did not get angry or apologetic. She looked right in his eyes, magnified by those thick lenses, and said evenly: "After all these years I don't even get the benefit of the doubt?"

In a voice just as even, he said: "You don't care what I think."

As soon as he spoke he knew his words were nonsense, but he was also thinking: *How much more of this am I supposed to take?*

Retrieving the letters from the coffee table, Mrs. Motley, still even-voiced, said she had better be going. Mr. McTeer did not try to dissuade her.

CHAPTER EIGHT
Another Matter of Opinion

That evening, after she told Mrs. Powell about the letters, Mrs. Motley called Vernon Paiger and asked if she could speak with him face-to-face that night on a matter of some urgency. He of course agreed. Feeling that it was impolite to call someone on such short notice *and* ask them out of their home, she drove to his place, arriving around eight forty-five.

Vernon's ranch-style house was larger than most. The front wall of taupe-colored brick stretched across three lots' worth of space. The double door of the attached garage was at the south end (to your left if facing the house) with a six-window turret set dead center.

Approaching the pine-green front door, Mrs. Motley wondered if nearby neighbors were spying. She rang the bell and glanced left toward the south corner of the block where a large dumpster for Roland's rehab crew sat at the curb in front of her new house.

The door opened and a smiling Vernon welcomed her in. His light blue dress shirt was open at the collar and his dark blue cardigan was unbuttoned.

As he took her coat and beret, Mrs. Motley was surprised by the room. Double the size of her old living room, it was illuminated by the muted light of brass table and floor lamps. The walls were yellow, the crown molding white like the ceiling, and the hardwood floor (accented with expensive-looking rugs) was a glossy dark brown.

Vernon gestured to a white couch that looked nearly as long as her car. He asked if she wanted anything to drink. Sensing his need to be hospitable but not wanting to stay too long, she chose something simple: "Orange juice, if that's not too much trouble."

Alone on the couch she gave the room a closer inspection. The couch faced away from the large picture window and toward a wide-bodied black-marble fireplace. If the gleaming poker and spotless hearth were any indication, it hadn't seen a fire in a while. Large paintings were set at strategic points about the room—all of them affixed to brawny frames, and all depicting wooded landscapes. The place smelled of leather, though no leather seating was anywhere in sight, and it all reminded Mrs. Motley of a museum.

After a few minutes Vernon returned with a silver tray and two tall glasses of orange juice. "I hope you don't mind if I take mine with a slug of vodka," he said as he set the tray down on the long coffee table. "My doctor allows me one full-bodied drink a day." He sat close to her, his dark pants legs crossed at the knee and inches from hers. She complimented him on the room and he looked about as if appraising it for the first time.

"It's my wife's doing. She was the design wiz. I've left it the way she left it."

They took sips from their glasses and Vernon asked: "So, what's the urgency?"

Taking the letters from her purse, Mrs. Motley explained how she'd gotten them. Vernon set his drink on the tray and pulled wire-rim glasses from his shirt pocket. He read in silence, his only visible reaction an occasional pursing of his lips.

When he was done he handed the letters back with one hand and removed his glasses with the other. "Are you sure Stew Pot actually wrote these?"

"No, and that's part of the problem. I don't want to be the butt of someone's practical joke. I also don't want to assist Stew Pot in some scheme to evade justice. However, if he truly is unbalanced . . . what would happen if that's true?"

"That would bring two issues into play," said Vernon. "The first is his competency to stand trial. Is he insane now? Does he know what he's charged with? Can he cooperate with his attorney? That could be determined at a competency hearing before a trial. The second is his mental state at the time of the crime. Can he appreciate his criminality? Can he not conform his conduct to the requirement of law? That's a defense. Whether he's nuts or not would have to be determined through a trial. Although I must also say that lawyers in Cook County don't often use insanity defenses in homicide trials because judges and juries have such negative reactions to that kind of plea."

Mrs. Motley said she hadn't known that. Vernon assured her it was true and added: "There's also the possibility Stew Pot's attorney might not be excited about the letters."

"Why not?"

"If the letters are genuine, we have Stew Pot admitting that he was in O'Brien's apartment the night she was killed, that he took items from her home, that one of his other 'personalities' may have done the deed. In reality, that other personality is he himself. Those letters are written confessions."

"So the prosecutors would want the letters entered?"

"Maybe they would and then again maybe they wouldn't. They might feel they already have enough to nail Stew Pot's hide to the barn door. These letters raise the possibility that he's crazy, which might nix their getting a death penalty sentence."

"You think they'll definitely ask for the death penalty?"

"Nice Irish girl is murdered and the accused is a Mandingo-type ex-con? Bank on it."

"So these letters won't do Stew Pot any good?"

"They might if Stew Pot's lawyer decides he's headed for a date with a fatal injection."

"So they might get him out of prison and into an asylum."

"That's no sure thing. Sometimes a defendant is uncooperative during a psych exam. They just clam up. In which case the shrink might say: *I can't determine anything from this person.* Also, in Illinois, judges and juries can find a person guilty but mentally ill. That means, *Yeah, we agree you're nuts, but you did it and you're still going to jail.* A person receiving such a sentence is supposed to get mental health care upon their incarceration, but the reality is, there's no guarantee as to the quality of such care, or even that they'll actually receive it."

Mrs. Motley paused a moment to take all the information in, and then asked: "Would I ever have to testify in court or give some sort of sworn statement?"

"You might be subpoenaed and asked to give testimony as to how you got the letters."

"So if I turn these letters in, there's no way to keep my part of it quiet?"

"I'm saying maybe yes, or maybe no. Look, Stew Pot's lawyer can order a psych exam anytime he or she wants. That can't be contested by the judge or the prosecution. If the exam determines that Stew Pot is crazy-eights, then what triggered his lawyer asking for the exam might never be an issue . . . So, what are you going to do?"

"From what you've said, these letters could either help Stew Pot or hang him. I just want to do what's right."

"That's highly commendable, though I imagine some people won't see it that way."

"You can say that again."

"Let me guess: you told Mr. McTeer about turning in the letters and he wasn't happy."

"No, he was not."

Vernon chuckled. "Imagine that, and him being such an understanding soul."

Mrs. Motley's voice went sharp: "I won't sit for that talk. Mr. McTeer is one of the most honorable men I've ever known and one of the best friends I've ever had."

"If you say so," said Vernon calmly, and here he leaned over their nearly touching knees, "but think about this: Why is it Mr. McTeer always has to have things *his* way? Why was he unable to see you are not the sort of person to let a man go to death row when you have evidence that might save him from it? Why could he not see that no matter how much you might hate Stew Pot, or hate the things he's done, you could never stand idly by as if you'd never received those letters?"

"There were other reasons for his anger," she said.

"I know, and how many of those reasons have to do with you deciding not to do something his way? Why does he always insist that it's you who must bend? After all these years, aren't you tired of always having to be the one to bend?"

"I didn't come here to talk about my relationship with Mr. McTeer, which by the way is none of your business."

"All right then, let's talk about your relationship with me."

"I didn't come here to talk about that, either. Besides, we don't have a *relationship*."

"Oh, is that so? Then why did you call me the morning Reggie Butler was taken into custody? It was because you knew I was a button you could push and get a positive response."

Mrs. Motley opened her mouth to protest but Vernon raised a hand.

"And why were you so sure you'd get a positive response? Because of what had already transpired between us since the destruction of your house. Since then I've made it clear in any number of ways, though none directly stated, that I still have strong feelings for you."

"So that business about wanting to help the Davenports and the Wilsons was just talk?"

"No. I was glad to help them. Sometimes helping the one you love dovetails nicely with helping people you merely like; or in the case of Mr. Davenport, don't like at all."

Mrs. Motley lowered her head into the palm of her right hand and, sounding very tired, she said: "What do you want from me?"

"I want to be your husband—what do you think?"

"I should never have come here."

He gave her a look that was part bemused, part gentle scold. "Oh, come on now. When it suits you—helping Reggie, staying in Parkland, asking what'll happen if you do with those letters what you know you must—you like having a *relationship* with me just fine."

"Please stop this, Alderman."

His voice showing a touch of irritation, he said, "Fine, back to your business at hand. Don't bother sending the letters to the presiding judge, he or she will just send them to Stew Pot's lawyer. In Cook County the only public defenders allowed to handle homicide trials for the indigent are on the Homicide Task Force. They're an elite group. Their offices are next door to the Criminal Courts building. The lawyers are in court during the mornings, so plan on trying to catch Stew Pot's attorney while in the hallway of Criminal Courts or at the Task Force offices in the afternoon."

CHAPTER NINE

Fretful in the Dark

Lying on her back later that night in the dark of the Powells' spare bedroom, Mrs. Motley admitted to herself that Vernon's point about her always having to bend had hurt, not only because she felt that, in regards to Mr. McTeer, it was more than a little true, but also because it described her marriage. Vernon! Had any woman ever been proposed to in such a fashion? And yet, if she were totally honest she could not deny that his unromantic tone had not been without its tenderness. He'd said flat out that she was the one he loved. And he had not said, "Marry *me*," or "Be *my* wife," but, "I want to be *your* husband."

Mrs. Motley then told herself she'd have to be crazy to live in that museum testament to his dead wife. And why was she thinking these things? And she was stung by the fact that this was the second time in a month she'd had to ask herself that question.

Not wanting to think of Vernon, she shifted her attention to Mr. McTeer, which did not make her feel all that much better. His current anger at her was most upsetting, and she did not look forward to telling him the next day, as she drove him to Seven Sorrows for confession, that she could not have lunch with him at Logan's because she had to go to 26th and California to run down Stew Pot's lawyer. If only there was some way out of that unpleasant prospect, she thought—if only, if only, if only.

CHAPTER TEN

On the Spur of the Moment

Mrs. Motley arose the next morning fully planning to go to Criminal Courts that afternoon, but while having breakfast with Mrs. Powell in the dining room, Mr. McTeer called with the news that Stew Pot's mother and Brother Crown had just returned.

Mr. McTeer spoke only to Mrs. Powell, who after hanging up told Mrs. Motley that the newlyweds had arrived by cab, that Brother Crown was wearing what looked like a black three-piece suit, *and* that Stew Pot's mom was bareheaded and decked out and in a red wool coat with the hem nowhere near her ankles.

Ignoring for the moment her disappointment that Mr. McTeer had not spoken to her directly, Mrs. Motley focused on a sudden premise, which quickly became an idea. As can often happen when a solution to a knotty problem comes in a flash, she was struck by how simple it was.

Mrs. Motley said she was going to the two-flat to give the letters to Stew Pot's mother. "She can go hunt down Stew Pot's lawyer, or burn them, or mail them to the newspapers. Whatever, the letters will be out of my hair and I'll have done my duty."

Mrs. Powell asked if Mrs. Motley wanted her to come along, perhaps they could get Mr. McTeer to join them. Knowing how he felt about the letters, Mrs. Motley said that she would go alone. "I don't want them thinking the block is marching on them again."

Minutes later, bereted and trench coated, Mrs. Motley knocked at the two-flat's front door. When Mrs. Crown answered, Mrs. Motley was initially taken aback by what she saw. The woman's hair had obviously been professionally done, with a sweep of dark tresses across her forehead. Her face, with evidence of strain at the corners of the eyes, had a touch of blush on her cheekbones. Her dress was forest green, cinched at the waist, with the hem just below the knees. Her pumps matched the dress.

After they exchanged hellos, Mrs. Motley said, because she felt it was only polite to do so, that she was sorry for all the trouble Mrs. Crown was going through. Mrs. Crown clutched Mrs. Motley's hands and in her squeaky voice launched into a profuse round of thanks, which ended with Mrs. Crown having to let go to wipe away a tear.

"I can't tell you what your consideration means to me, Mrs. Motley. I know most people on the block hate me."

Wanting to be comforting, but not wanting to lie to the woman, Mrs. Motley settled for offering up a weak, supportive-looking smile.

Mrs. Crown then apologized for not inviting Mrs. Motley in. "The police wrecked the place looking for things to incriminate Gerald. Why did they have to leave stuff all over the floor? Why did they have to rip open mattresses and pillows?"

Mrs. Motley kept her supportive smile going through all this, while at the same time feeling a growing dread. When she had first thought of her idea, she had imagined handing the letters over quickly with a very brief explanation and being on her way. Already things were taking longer than she'd anticipated, and aware that others would soon be leaving for work and school, she wanted to bring this meeting to a close.

Interrupting Mrs. Crown, Mrs. Motley said she had letters which she believed to have been written by her son the night of Megan O'Brien's murder. Mrs. Motley then took the letters from inside her coat and handed them over. As soon as Mrs. Crown saw the front of the thicker envelope, she said excitedly: "That's Gerald's handwriting. I'd know it anywhere."

Mrs. Motley tried to explain the letters' contents but had to stop because Mrs. Crown turned and called up the stairs behind her: "Royale! Come quick!"

Mrs. Motley now had to wait for Brother Crown to arrive. He came down the steps hatless and, just like Mr. McTeer said, dressed in a black three-piece suit.

When he got to the door, Mrs. Crown shook the envelopes in front of his face. "These are letters from Gerald. He mailed them to Mrs. Motley. She says they were written the night that woman was killed. These letters prove he's innocent. If he was here writing letters, then he couldn't possibly have been up on the North Side hurting anyone."

Brother Crown had a skeptical look on his face as Mrs. Crown, her face bright with joy, swiveled her head back and forth between him and Mrs. Motley.

"Let me take a look," Brother Crown said, and his wife gave the envelopes to him. As she and Mrs. Motley watched him read, Mrs. Motley knew that coming there like this had been a big mistake, for how could she explain to Stew Pot's mother that the best the letters could do was keep him from being executed?

Speaking eagerly, Mrs. Crown asked her husband: "This proves Gerald's innocence, right?"

Having obviously gotten the gist of the letter's meaning from the little he had read, Brother Crown shot Mrs. Motley a concerned, knowing glance. Then he said to his wife: "I'll explain it all in a bit, dear."

He reached for her to guide her further inside, but Mrs. Crown thrust her arms to her sides and closed her hands into fists. Shaking her head slowly she said: "I've got to pray."

And with that she brushed past Mrs. Motley and out onto the walkway. She looked up at the overcast sky, her face still showing delight. "I've got to pray out loud this morning." Then she turned to Mrs. Motley and extended an arm like someone reaching for help. "Will you pray with me, Mrs. Motley?"

As with her son eight months before at her kitchen table, Mrs. Motley felt she couldn't refuse the request without being rude. She stepped slowly over to Mrs. Crown, followed by Brother Crown.

The three formed a close circle and held hands. With her head bowed Mrs. Crown asked: "May I lead the prayer this morning?"

And her husband said: "Of course."

Mrs. Motley bowed her head and closed her eyes, one hand clasped in a small smooth hand and the other in a large rough one.

"Oh Lord," she heard Mrs. Crown say, "I come to you with thanks in my heart this morning. I'm grateful in my heart, joyous in my heart for Your love. The Bible says put your faith in Jesus, and there will be an answer. And the answer came this morning, Lord, through the hands of Mrs. Motley. Bless her, Lord, watch over her—so decent, so kind, so forgiving. She does not hate; she does not judge."

Mrs. Crown went on for close to another minute. After Brother Crown and Mrs. Motley said amen almost in unison, Mrs. Motley raised her head and opened her eyes and saw that they had been joined outside, in front doorways and walkways, by onlookers on both sides of the street. There was Mr. McTeer and Mr. Hicks and at least a dozen others.

They all saw Mrs. Crown hug Mrs. Motley tightly. And moments later, as Mrs. Motley was nearing the sidewalk, they all heard Mrs. Crown call from the doorway: "God bless you, Mrs. Motley, for coming to Gerald's aid in his hour of need!"

CHAPTER ELEVEN
Heart to Heart

Mrs. Motley fully expected Mr. McTeer to call her at the Powells' when she got back from the two-flat, but he didn't. After telling Mrs. Powell what had happened with the Crowns, Mrs. Motley thought of calling him, but feeling disappointed for the second time that morning about him not calling her, she decided against it.

Later, she drove to his house at the usual time for their Wednesday ride to Seven Sorrows, and as she waited at the curb, she wondered if he would show.

He did.

As soon as he was belted in, he asked: "What was all that about this morning?"

Driving west, she explained in brief why she'd done what she'd done.

Sounding cross, he said: "In the end it still comes down to the same thing—you helping Stew Pot."

Mrs. Motley explained that the best the letters could do was keep Stew Pot off death row. Again in brief, she told him what Vernon had said.

"You been talking to a lawyer?" asked Mr. McTeer.

She paused before answering yes, and he, suspicious now, asked who the lawyer was.

She paused again, and before she could speak, he sneered: "Vernon?"

She didn't say anything to that, which of course spoke volumes.

"So you went running to him, huh? Oh, I bet he just loved that!"

"I hate it when you act like this," she said.

"Like what?"

"Like *that*. Getting grumpy with everything I say."

They rode the rest of the way in silence.

While Mr. McTeer was inside, Mrs. Motley went around the

church to where a small cement grotto was located beside the school building. There she lit a candle for Megan O'Brien, bowed her head and said a prayer, then went back to her car to wait for Mr. McTeer.

When he returned after his session with Father Vader, Mrs. Motley said, "I'd rather we skipped lunch today. After this morning, I'm afraid I won't be very good company." He said okay and that he understood. The edginess of his earlier tone was gone, which she attributed to the gentler mood he always assumed after confession.

They didn't say anything else until they were parked in front of Mr. McTeer's house. With both of them looking straight ahead, he said: "I'm sorry for the way I spoke earlier. That was wrong of me."

She accepted his apology and he then asked if he could say something, and if she would wait until he finished his point before answering. He turned in his seat toward her and she did the same toward him.

"I think that you've been looking at the idea of joining the Church from the wrong angle. Instead of thinking of what you'll be giving up—Wesley-Allen, your friends there, etcetera—you should think about what you'll be gaining.

"I became a Catholic because it was the only way I could marry the woman I wanted to marry. But once I'd done so, become a Catholic I mean, I discovered a spiritual bounty. The first time I left confession, I felt a serenity unlike any I'd ever experienced. I know you're joyful in your faith, but my point is that the Church is offering a life even more joyous. You may think that impossible, but I'm telling you that it's true.

"You said you couldn't imagine a marriage with your spouse going to one church on Sunday and you to another. Well, neither can I. Join me and that won't be an issue."

Mrs. Motley blew a short breath. "The Church hasn't made an issue of this thing for years. We could alternate: one Sunday Seven Sorrows, the next Wesley-Allen."

He smiled at her indulgently. "I know what the Church says now, but that is not the Church I came in on. A marriage is not just between a man and a woman, it's between a man, a woman, and the Church; the three in unison."

Mrs. Motley didn't know what to say, so she said nothing and let him continue.

"We should be married properly and live here." He nodded at his house.

Suddenly spurred into voice, she said: "Here?"

Again he offered the indulgent smile. "I know it's no palace, but with a little sprucing up we could have it in good shape."

"It needs more than sprucing," said Mrs. Motley. "That carpeting has to go, the wallpaper too, the rooms painted, and that's just the first floor." He was about to answer when she added: "What about my new place? No stairs, plenty of room, central air."

Mr. McTeer, with a little less indulgence in his smile, said: "You're going to compare your feelings for a house that two months ago you hardly knew existed with my feelings for the house I've called home for nearly half a century? After your loss, I'd have thought you would understand my feelings better than anybody."

"But what about the stairs?"

"What about them?"

"We'd have to get one of those electric banister chairs so you could ride up and down."

Those eyes magnified behind the thick lenses took on an incredulous squint. "I'm not riding up and down the stairs like some cripple."

"But where would we—where would the bedroom be?"

"Where it is now."

And she, in a voice that was as incredulous as his expression had just been, said: "In that little room?"

And they were both then struck silent, he by the realization that she was making a fuss over issues of interior design because she could not bring herself to say the real reason she would not have him, and she thinking that as much as he wanted her, he also wanted everything else too.

Mrs. Motley looked away.

Mr. McTeer, summoning his last bit of courage, but not sounding all that confident, said: "Will you consider my offer?"

And she, still not looking at him, slowly shook her head yes in a way that did not inspire confidence.

He unbelted himself and got out.

CHAPTER TWELVE

More Advice from Vernon

That night, while Mrs. Powell was in the basement watching TV and Mr. Powell was off at work, Vernon called Mrs. Motley to find how things had gone with Stew Pot's lawyer. After hearing the details (Mrs. Motley leaving out the doorway conversation and walkway prayer), Vernon asked what Mrs. Crown planned to do. Mrs. Motley said she assumed she'd give the letters to Stew Pot's lawyer.

"But you don't know for sure?"

"No, not for sure. Did I do something wrong?"

"Well," he said, "by giving the letters to Stew Pot's lawyer, you could argue later, if you had to, that you made a good-faith effort to get items that might prove crucial evidence in a homicide trial to the proper hands. Giving the letters to another private citizen might be seen by the authorities in a bad light."

In an anxious voice Mrs. Motley asked: "Why didn't you say anything about that last night?" and Vernon, his voice showing just a touch of agitation, replied: "If you had asked me what I thought about you giving the letters to Stew Pot's mother, I would have told you. But you didn't."

Chagrined, Mrs. Motley apologized. "It's been kind of a stressful day."

"I would have thought getting those letters off your plate would have had you in better spirits."

Mrs. Motley was not about to tell him what had transpired between she and Mr. McTeer in the car, so she shifted gears: "Something about those letters keeps nagging at me, but I can't put my finger on exactly what it is. I feel like there's something I ought to have noticed that I haven't."

Vernon told her not to be too hard on herself and then asked about her Thanksgiving Day plans. She told him she was eating with the Powells. He asked if Mr. McTeer would be there too and she said,

"He's been invited," realizing as she said it that in the wake of what had happened with him earlier, she was now not sure if he would show.

She asked Vernon what he'd be doing and he said he'd be at his sister's "with the rest of the Paiger mob," which caused her to chuckle for some reason.

"So you think I should tell the Crowns they should give the letters to Stew Pot's lawyer?"

"Yes, that way you can always say later that you told them to do the right thing." She wondered out loud if she should bother the Crowns on Thanksgiving, and Vernon said: "Might as well. They're probably sure to be home."

CHAPTER THIRTEEN

And Everything Comes Too Late

After taking a bath and donning a blue flannel nightgown, Mrs. Motley sat in the Powells' back bedroom and perused her old standby, Psalms:

. . . My hope is in Thee. Deliver me from my transgressions . . . When my soul was embittered, when I was pricked in heart, I was stupid and ignorant . . . Nevertheless I am continually with Thee; Thou dost hold my right hand. Thou dost guide me with Thy counsel . . .

Though the reading lessened her blues about what had happened at the two-flat and with Mr. McTeer, it did not help with the nagging in her mind about the letters' contents.

Before her prayers she sat with the closed Bible and reviewed what she could recall: Stew Pot writing in the front room; Gerald doing the same; and Gerald X., who was furious over his mother leaving and had not written any letter, "in the kitchen messing around and muttering."

She went to sleep that night no closer to figuring out anything. The next morning at the dining room table while having breakfast with Mrs. Powell (the room already fragrant with the turkey roasting in the oven), Mrs. Motley gave a glancing inspection of the crossword puzzle clues from the day's newspaper. It was a few minutes later, while reading the obituary page (she saw no familiar names), that it came to her, the rhythm of puzzle clues reminding her of something from the second letter that Gerald X. had been muttering: "5-32 and 32."

The Bible Stew Pot had returned was on the dining room sideboard. Mrs. Motley knew from memory that the fifth book of the Bible was Deuteronomy. After reaching over for the book, she went straight to that section.

Seeing Mrs. Motley thumbing rapidly through the pages, Mrs. Powell asked, "You looking for something to read for the blessing later today?" Mrs. Motley didn't answer, her eyes focused on the pages she was snapping through, causing Mrs. Powell to wonder what was wrong with her friend now.

Mrs. Motley found Chapter 32, verse 32 at the top of page 164: *For their vine comes from the vine of Sodom, and their grapes are the grapes of poison.* She immediately looked up at Mrs. Powell's concerned face and said: "We have to go to Stew Pot's house right now."

"What in the world for?"

"I think Stew Pot has done something. We have to go right now." And with that Mrs. Motley was out of her chair, hurrying to the living room closet. Mrs. Powell followed after her, though not as quickly.

"What has he done?"

"I think he may have hurt his mother."

"How? He's in jail."

"Something he did before he was arrested."

"Shouldn't we wait for Powell? He'll be home before long."

"There's no time."

And then Mrs. Motley was gone into the overcast morning, not even bothering to pull the inner door closed behind her.

Mrs. Powell went and turned off the oven, grabbed her own coat, and wrote her husband a quick note which she taped to the glass of the storm door: *GONE TO STEW POT'S HOUSE.*

When she reached the sidewalk she saw that Mrs. Motley, her open trench coat billowing behind her, was about three-quarters of the way down the block, stepping as fast as she could with her bad knees. With no such affliction, Mrs. Powell was able to move at a much faster pace down the street, which because of the holiday had no one leaving for work or school. She arrived at the two-flat not long after Mrs. Motley, who had already begun pounding loudly on the front door with the side of her fist.

Mrs. Motley tilted her bare head toward the door and listened hard. Mrs. Powell came up alongside her and did the same. They heard nothing from inside. Mrs. Motley pounded several times with her other hand, after which they again tilted and listened. Again they heard nothing.

"Maybe they left early," said Mrs. Powell. "Maybe they're off witnessing somewhere."

Ignoring her, Mrs. Motley urged: "We have to go around and

check the back." And just like that she stepped around Mrs. Powell and headed to the gate of the walkway beside the two-flat.

As Mrs. Powell moved to follow, she heard a door open from across the way. She turned and saw Mr. McTeer standing on his stoop.

"What's going on?" he called.

Mrs. Powell shrugged and raised her hands palms-up, then turned and went fast through the open gateway. Down the walkway she moved, past the paint-splattered wall and the hole where the four-square had been, catching up to Mrs. Motley as she walked up the steps to the back porch.

When she opened the storm door, which flung on the hinges easily because the air cylinder was still broken, she found the inner door's window blocked by a sheet hung from inside. Mrs. Motley went immediately to the window near the door and was met by another sheet.

As if Mrs. Powell weren't even there, Mrs. Motley brushed past her to the steps leading to the second floor. She took the stairs slowly, Mrs. Powell right behind her.

The kitchen door window up there was uncovered. Mrs. Motley pounded. After more silence she put her face close to the glass, cupping her hands to either side. After a bit she stepped back from the door, her breathing a bit labored. "I don't see anything."

Mrs. Powell said again that maybe the Crowns had left early. Mrs. Motley went to another nearby kitchen window, which was also uncovered. Mrs. Powell saw Mrs. Motley cup her face there. After a few seconds of looking Mrs. Motley jerked back, slapped a hand over her mouth, and began shaking her head slowly from side to side.

Stepping gingerly, Mrs. Powell moved over and brought her face to the glass while Mrs. Motley, hand still on her mouth, backed away. The window was over the sink and directly in line with the passageway to the dining room. There, beneath an overhead light, a table was set with food and place settings. Mrs. Powell saw nothing amiss until her gaze lowered to the hardwood floor. Extending from somewhere beyond the edge of the passageway were the slender legs of someone lying motionless on the floor, the feet in a pair of forest-green pumps.

CHAPTER FOURTEEN

Minton's Pool Hall, the Following Sunday Afternoon

S o they found her in the upstairs dining room and him in the upstairs hallway?"

"That's what the papers say. The cops think he was trying to get to the telephone to try and call 911 when he passed out. Whatever poison it was, it hit them fast and hard. Stew Pot put it in the salt and sugar and flour."

"So now Stew Pot is up for three murders?"

"Yeah, they found containers of old poison his daddy had used in the basement. The cans had Stew Pot's fingerprints all over them"

"What's Mrs. Motley been doing the last few days?"

"With reporters running around here worse than last time, she hid out in that place she bought across from Vernon. I didn't see any quotes from her in any news stories."

"So is it true Stew Pot phoned her the night of O'Brien's murder and confessed?"

"No. He wrote her a letter saying he did."

"Says who?"

"Mrs. Powell. She was real upset right after seeing Mrs. Reeves lying there dead. After the ambulances and the police arrived, she and some others from the block were standing around talking in front of Mr. Hicks's house."

"Where was Mrs. Motley?"

"Talking to the police."

"So what did Mrs. Powell say?"

"She said that Stew Pot mailed Mrs. Motley an insane letter confessing to killing O'Brien and that Mrs. Motley gave the letter to Stew Pot's momma Wednesday morning. Then Thursday morning, Mrs. Motley got a vision of Stew Pot killing his mom."

"What did she do then?"

"When she joined the others in front of Mr. Hicks's house they asked if it was true what Mrs. Powell had said, and Mrs. Motley said Stew Pot had written her a letter."

"So now the police have the confession letter? That should seal the case against him."

"Hold your horses. Word is, the cops didn't find the letter when they searched the two-flat. I heard some folks say the police palmed the letter because they don't want Stew Pot dodging the death penalty on a psycho-plea, and some say his mother burned it because she thought it would for sure get him convicted, and a few, just a few now, are saying the letter never existed, that Motley made it up. After all, no one besides her is claiming to have actually seen it. Mrs. Butler says she's always believed Mrs. Motley was in love with Stew Pot."

"Butler must be drunk. Any word on how Mrs. Motley is doing?"

"She was at Wesley-Allen this morning. I hear she partly blames herself for what happened, says she should've realized earlier what Stew Pop was up to."

"And Mrs. Powell?"

"She and Mr. Powell were in church too. I guess Mr. Powell really needed to get himself some prayer after the scare he had Thursday."

"What scare?"

"You didn't hear? Powell gets home from work, sees flashing lights at the end of the block, then finds a note from his wife saying she's at Stew Pot's. Fearing the worst, he runs down the street yelling for Mrs. Powell. The paramedics had to give him oxygen. Later on, he said that ever since Stew Pot got back from prison last March, he's feared he would come home one morning to find that Stew Pot had done something to Mrs. Powell, and that even though Stew Pot was in jail, that fear was still in his mind."

"He and Mrs. Powell have Thanksgiving supper after all that?"

"Yeah, they did. Mr. McTeer came over there too, I understand."

"Did he try to play patty fingers under the table with Mrs. Motley? Heh-heh-heh."

"I don't know. What I do know is that Vernon came by on the way to his sister's, just to make sure, as he put it, that Mrs. Motley and Mrs. Powell were _okay_."

"Why didn't he just call on the phone?"

"You know the answer to that as well as I do."

"So even without that letter, looks like they have Stew Pot six ways to Sunday."

"So it would appear. At this point, a psycho-plea strategy might be the only thing keeping him from getting the death penalty."

"Man, I knew the boy was crazy, but I didn't know he was _crazy_. Poison your own momma? That is all kinds of messed up."

"Any word on when or where his mom's service is going to be?"

"Not yet. Maybe Reverend Wilkins will come through for her like he did for Mrs. Hicks."

"Think the authorities will let Stew Pot attend the service?"

"Probably. After all, he hasn't been convicted of anything—yet. I tell you this: if they do let him attend, wherever that service is, there'll be a crowd."

CHAPTER FIFTEEN

Rest in Peace

As it turned out, Brother Crown had family in Georgia. His body was sent there. These people had met Mrs. Crown only once (and were not impressed with her) and did not want to pay for burying her too. Though she had a few living relatives—a couple of cousins, an aunt, a grown niece and nephew—none had much money, so Mrs. Motley had Paiger & Paiger take care of her old next-door neighbor.

There was just a simple graveside service at Eden Rest. The media were denied access, kept at a distance outside the walls where they gathered on both sides of the gateway as the hearse, a white Cook County sheriff's van, and three cars carrying the small band of mourners rolled to a distant corner of the cemetery.

The attendees were Mrs. Motley, Mrs. Powell, a handful of Mrs. Crown's former coworkers from the Department of Motor Vehicles, three of the aforementioned relatives, and Stew Pot, who was escorted by armed Cook County deputies wearing navy-blue uniforms.

In an ill-fitting gray suit, he stood alone, temporarily uncuffed, by the casket poised above the freshly dug hole, while Reverend Wilkins, there at Mrs. Motley's behest, spoke the solemn words. The deputies stood directly behind Stew Pot, the brisk wind of the cold and sunny morning lifting people's coattails and, in the distance, causing the bare branches of the trees to slowly sway.

CHAPTER SIXTEEN

Miss B's House of Beauty, the Day after Mrs. Crown's Burial

I heard Mrs. Motley paid for that suit Stew Pot was wearing."

"I thought his lawyer bought the suit."

"I have it on good authority Motley bought it. I think Mrs. Butler's on to something."

"You're just saying that because you don't like Mrs. Motley."

"Well, if she wants folks to like her, she shouldn't be going 'round providing aid and comfort to murderers."

"Mrs. Motley said she didn't want the woman going into the ground like a pauper."

"Stew Pot is the reason she's in the ground! Funerals are for helping surviving relatives get closure. The only closure Stew Pot deserves is a noose around his neck. And I'm not the only one who feels that way. Mr. Hicks and his daughters are real upset with Mrs. Motley, and I don't blame them. There are times you can take Christian kindness too far."

"I saw Motley yesterday. She looks haggard; not surprising, all she's been through."

"What about that O'Brien woman's family, and Mrs. Reeves's other relatives, and Brother Crown's people in Georgia? They're the ones going through something."

"Weren't you the one saying last month that Mr. and Mrs. Crown were lame brains?"

"They were. But no one deserves to die like that. Stew Pot's arraignment is in a couple of weeks. You ask me, they ought to just do away with him and be done with it."

BOOK XI

Season's Greetings

CHAPTER ONE

Christmastime Is Here

I t'll probably be no surprise to learn that folks in Parkland made a big deal about Christmas decorating. Strings of lights were draped through hedges, around trees, over doorways, along rain gutters, and in some cases across rooftops. Save for those homes of a scattered handful of non-Christians—Nation of Islam, Jehovah's Witnesses, agnostics like Mrs. Butler—dwellings and front lawns were decked in lighted finery, which included the sorts of things Mrs. Hicks had crowded her lawn with in July—manger scenes, Santas on foot or riding reindeer sleighs, winged angels. (On the drag, businesses had holiday lights around display windows and wreaths hung on streetlamps.) Last but not least, in the picture windows of the homes there were trees that ran the gamut from real evergreens to fake trees that looked like evergreens to silver and white jobs that tried to make up in dazzle what they lacked in traditional appearance. At night, traveling the neighborhood streets was like passing through an extended carnival midway.

This was the sight Mrs. Motley's family entered the evening before Christmas Eve after a long drive from O'Hare Field. There was no snow, though the ground was wet from drizzle, which made the streets and sidewalks sheen with multicolored reflections.

Her son had come in dress uniform from Oklahoma, his haircut high and tight and his chest full of pinned paraphernalia—nameplate, combat infantryman's badge, double-rainbow row of ribbons. He was driving Ingrid, a chore Mrs. Motley had gladly turned over, she enjoying the unusual experience of riding in the front passenger seat. She was turned halfway to the left so she could face her son while also watching the backseat where her granddaughter and daughter-in-law-to-be-once-more were sitting.

The granddaughter, Alison-Jean, though thirteen, sat nearly as tall in her seat as Mrs. Motley. She had a head of bushy hair and the Motley features of heavy brows, front-tooth gap, and high forehead. Wearing a straw cowboy hat and red ski vest, she spent much of the trip gazing out her window. She'd been amazed at the amalgamation of tall buildings when they passed Downtown, as well as the length of the drive, asking at one point, her voice revealing just a trace of German accent: "Is all of this Chicago?"

Her mother was sitting behind Mrs. Motley. Joyce Williams (she had always kept her original last name) was coco brown with cat eyes that got her attention wherever she went. She had a short afro that Mrs. Motley thought mannish, even for a woman who had once been in the army and whose shape was a fulsome abundance of hips and thighs. (Joyce and Mrs. Motley's son had first met while serving overseas. After they divorced, she moved herself and AJ to Germany on the grounds that for all its recent history and culture of beer drinking, the schools were better and its streets safer—"You ever hear of drive-by shootings in Germany?") On the drive to Parkland, Joyce recounted the trials of the transatlantic flight: a German toddler "caterwauling nearly the whole way"; an African woman "changing her baby's diaper in the cabin and stinking up the place"; and behind she and AJ "a couple from India or wherever reeking like a spice rack. Don't get me started on the stewardesses."

Alison-Jean was impressed by all the neighborhood lights and decorations, making yummy hums as she craned her neck to look at this and that. Mrs. Motley's son asked Joyce (his voice so much like his dad's, Mrs. Motley thought) how the neighborhood compared to the holiday layouts from her hometown of St. Louis, to which she responded: "It's not bad."

As they pulled into the attached garage of the ranch house, Mrs. Motley began apologizing. "It only has one full bathroom—"

And here her son gently cut her off with a reassuring touch on the arm and a kindly, "I'm sure the place looks fine."

And it did too, in a generic, interior-design-magazine sort of way. The galley kitchen they entered, in a bow to her old place, was painted yellow with white wooden cabinets and a black-and-white checkered tile floor. As for the rest of the place, in an attempt to not try and recreate what could not be recreated, as well as in the interest of keeping the smaller house from feeling cramped, Mrs. Motley had kept the furniture to a minimum and the wall colors light—a streamline table and chairs in the peach dining room, a brown leather couch and club chairs in the eggshell living room.

Mrs. Motley's son made a big deal of the crown moldings and wood-slat window blinds. Joyce nodded in ho-hum fashion and mouthed, "Oh, that's nice," a couple of times. Alison-Jean said nothing.

The nearly six-foot tree, which had been delivered the day before, stood bare before the picture window. Mrs. Motley said she'd hoped they would be able to decorate it that evening, but Alison-Jean and Joyce said they needed a nap. (With the time difference between Chicago and Marburg, they'd been up nearly twenty hours.) Mrs. Motley's son, who was as tall as the tree, said he wanted to change into civilian clothes and go over to Minton's to meet with some old neighborhood running buddies and play some pool.

"We can decorate the tree tomorrow," he suggested. And so, a short while later, with the meal she'd prepared earlier in the fridge, Mrs. Motley sat on the living room couch with her Bible, reading by the light of a standing lamp, the house as cathedral quiet as it had been when she'd left for the airport earlier that day.

CHAPTER TWO

Trouble in Paradise

Joyce and AJ awoke three hours later and Mrs. Motley served them the meal she'd prepared—fried chicken, potato salad, greens, and rolls. They sat at the dining room table under a ceiling light with brass arms and little taupe-colored shades over the four bulbs.

AJ had never eaten collard greens. She made a face after taking her first forkful and didn't touch the rest. She liked the chicken, though.

They were at the living room end of the table. Joyce, still wearing the brown turtleneck sweater she'd arrived in, was to Mrs. Motley's left and AJ, in a rhinestone-studded denim shirt, was on her right. After prompting from Mrs. Motley, Joyce talked about her job, teaching American Lit at a German school. From the way she checked her wristwatch every ten or so minutes, it was obvious she was angry that Mrs. Motley's son wasn't there. AJ seemed to pick up on this, the child mostly keeping her own cat eyes on her plate.

In an attempt to take Joyce's mind off her son's absence, Mrs. Motley gave the two a rundown of what had happened in the neighborhood over the past nine months, sans the stuff about herself and Mr. McTeer. (In the three-hour wait for Joyce and AJ's flight at O'Hare, Mrs. Motley had given her son a similar rundown.) At first Mrs. Motley's ploy worked: however, by nine thirty her son had still not returned and Joyce flung her napkin down and said to no one in particular: "Where *is* he?" She then thrust away from the table and stalked off to the master bedroom, loudly closing the door.

AJ sat with shoulders slumped as if her mother's reaction was her fault. Mrs. Motley offered dessert—apple pie and ice cream—but the girl shook her head no and asked if she could be excused. Mrs. Motley said sure and AJ returned to the guest room across the hall from the master.

After taking care of the dishes Mrs. Motley lay on the couch to wait for her son. By eleven he still hadn't arrived and she began to worry. That's when Joyce, wearing a white T-shirt and gray sweat pants, paused by the couch on the way back from the bathroom.

"You seem to be taking this all very calmly," Joyce said.

Mrs. Motley shrugged. "Every year on his first night home, he changes clothes and runs straight to Minton's. So I guess you could say I'm disappointed, but not surprised."

"I have a good mind to put AJ and me on the first plane tomorrow back to Germany."

Mrs. Motley said nothing.

"From your silence I assume you don't care if AJ and I leave or not."

"I want what makes my son happy," Mrs. Motley said evenly. "If marrying you makes him happy, I'm fine with that. I was fine with it before, I'll be fine with it again."

"Well, there's some real doubt in my mind as to whether there'll be any marrying happening around here." Then she left, closing the door softly this time.

Around eleven fifty there was at last the sound of someone trying to open the front door, clicking the key around in the lock. When her son finally managed it and the door eased slowly open, he peeked inside, his expression going sheepish when he caught sight of her. She smelled whiskey and cigarettes on him as soon as he entered. She kept her face composed despite her strong dislike of both aromas and was relieved to find, when he bent over and kissed her forehead, that there was no perfume scent on him.

Making a point to keep any scolding out of her low voice, she asked what had taken him so long. Looking even more sheepish and speaking at an equally muted level, he said that at Minton's one thing had led to another with this old friend and that old friend and the next thing he knew it was coming on midnight.

She told him Joyce was angry. He made an *uh-oh* face and she said it might be best if he saw her before he showered. His face went curious and he asked: "How come?"

"Because you don't want her thinking there was a trace of some other woman you had to wash off before she got a sniff of you."

He then opened a wide smile that revealed his gap tooth and squeezed his eyes narrower, which made him look even drunker than he was. He nodded and tapped a forefinger to his temple. "That's what I like about you, Ma, always thinking." He kissed her lightly on the forehead again, turned his head, and she kissed his cheek. They whispered good-nights to each other and she watched him step softly around the corner to the master bedroom.

In the second guest bedroom on the other side of the living room, Mrs. Motley undressed and put on a nightgown. Prayers said and under the covers of a not-all-that-comfortable sofa bed, she listened for any sounds of conflict; yet she was so tired that she dozed off within minutes. So soundly did she go under that she slept right through the arguing that began a short while later.

CHAPTER THREE

A Truce of Sorts

The next morning Mrs. Motley got up early. While waiting for the others to awake she sat nervous in the peach dining room with her paper and coffee, wondering if Joyce would make good on her threat to cancel the reconciliation and fly home with AJ.

Her son appeared around seven in a maroon-striped robe over a green army T-shirt and shorts. Barefoot, he sat down as she poured him a cup of coffee. After a yawn and stretch he apologized "for all that racket last night." She asked what he was referring to and he explained about the argument he and Joyce had gotten into not long after he returned.

"So where do things stand now?" Mrs. Motley asked.

"Well, she hasn't got up and packed her bags, so for now it looks like she's staying."

Joyce arrived shortly after and made a point of saying a sweet good morning to Mrs. Motley and a flat hello to her fiancé. Much to Mrs. Motley's relief, he didn't rise to the bait by saying something cross in return.

Mrs. Motley got up to start breakfast. As she moved about the kitchen, the silence from the dining room was broken only occasionally by the rattling of newspaper pages being turned, which Mrs. Motley supposed was better than angry voices.

The smell of eggs, bacon, and pancakes roused Alison-Jean, who came to the table wearing a white bathrobe covered with musical notes and Miss Piggy house slippers.

After bringing out the food, Mrs. Motley had them all hold hands as she said a brief blessing. They commenced to eating and before long the tasty grub eased tensions somewhat. Sergeant Motley asked after old neighborhood friends and Mrs. Motley brought him up to date on some folks, taking care not to talk of them too long lest Joyce and AJ get bored. Toward the end of the meal she told her son she wanted him, at some point during his stay, to drive her car to her old garage and pick up her gardening items—a rake, a garden hose, a shovel, a bag of fertilizer, and so on—that she'd yet to bring to the ranch house. AJ said that she wanted to see where the house had been (which very much surprised and pleased Mrs. Motley), while Joyce called a truce of sorts: "I guess we should get started on the tree." (That very much pleased Mrs. Motley too.)

With Mrs. Motley the only one not in night clothes and a CD of Christmas standards playing on her new boom box (she had to ask AJ how the contraption worked), they dressed the tree with brand-new ornaments and lights that Mrs. Motley had bought earlier that week. While the mood between her son and Joyce could hardly be called cheery, as the process continued they were at least able to get themselves to a polite civility.

They finished around ten. Mrs. Motley didn't like tinsel, so there was none of that. There was a potpourri of Italian lights, cutesy animal ornaments—birds, bears, fishes—to go with the standard round shiny ones and a gaudy gold star at the top.

Mrs. Motley's son hummed the *2001: A Space Odyssey* theme as he raised the picture window blinds and the other three applauded. He then announced that he and Joyce had to drive to the mall to buy presents. AJ, sounding quite proud of herself, said she'd already done her shopping and her presents were safely packed in her suitcase.

"Give me a chance to change, Grandmother, and we can walk over to where you used to live."

CHAPTER FOUR
Walk with Me

O vernight the temperature had dropped significantly and Mrs. Motley was happy to learn that AJ had brought with her a red wool hat, a heavy black woolen sweater to wear under the red ski vest, and warm hiking-style boots. (Mrs. Motley thought the boots not very ladylike, ditto AJ's expansive and untamed hair that poofed out from under the red hat.)

They took a circuitous route to the old block, walking past the quiet high school. AJ hurried over to a first-floor classroom window to conduct a visual inspection and came away looking unimpressed.

Mrs. Motley, with a wool cap of her own (caramel) and a camel hair coat, told AJ about her various high school triumphs, and when the girl asked what the maroon-brick structure was across the street, Mrs. Motley told her that it was for American football, and that her father had played while a student at Parkland High. She then did her best to explain the North American version of the game, which actually involved very little kicking, and she realized after only a minute that she wasn't doing a very good job. When AJ asked what her father had done with the American football, Mrs. Motley said that part of the time he had run with it until an opposing player or players wrestled him to the ground, and that the rest of the time he'd chased after opposing players who ran with the football until he wrestled *them* to the ground.

They walked down the main drag past Logan's. When Mrs. Motley told her that's where she'd had her first date, AJ grinned and asked: "Was he handsome?" and Mrs. Motley, grinning too, said: "Handsome enough, I suppose." Mrs. Motley then asked AJ if she had a boyfriend back in Marburg. If the child hadn't been so dark her blush would have shown. She shook her head no. Mrs. Motley asked if there was a boy back there she *wanted* for a boyfriend. AJ shrugged as if she didn't know one way or the other. Mrs. Motley elbowed her arm. "Come on, what's his name? I promise I won't tell your mom or dad." After a few more steps, AJ said, her voice full of pubescent longing: "Otto."

And suddenly it hit Mrs. Motley that AJ's home of Marburg, Germany was quite likely as strong a place for her as Parkland was for she herself, and that taking AJ from the familiarity of the town and her friends, which included the dreamy Otto, to resettle her in Oklahoma might not necessarily be a thing the girl was looking forward to.

"Are you happy about possibly coming to live in America?"

AJ made a sour face. "I don't want to come if Mother and Father are going to fight like they did last night. I *hate* that."

Deciding to change the subject, Mrs. Motley told AJ she could visit her anytime she wanted. The girl said she wanted to go to where all the big buildings were that they had passed the day before, and where the big lake was, and she also wanted to go out west and see some real cowboys. Mrs. Motley said there were cowboys in Oklahoma, and AJ replied that her parents had told her that. Mrs. Motley then asked if she knew that there had been Black cowboys, and AJ said excitedly, "Really?" and Mrs. Motley assured her it was true and that if she wanted, they could go to the Parkland Public Library the following week to check out some books on the subject.

They approached Mrs. Motley's old block by way of Honore, walking past Mrs. Butler's house, and as Mrs. Motley listened to AJ explain how she wanted to be an astronaut, she girded herself for any cold shoulders she might receive from those still unhappy about what she'd done for Mrs. Crown, and by default Stew Pot.

They stopped to chat with Mrs. Powell, who couldn't say enough about how tall and pretty AJ was. Mrs. Motley asked what time Mrs. Powell planned to serve supper the next day. Mrs. Powell said three, and with a sympathetic look said that Mr. McTeer had phoned to ask if her husband could drive him to Midnight Mass. "Powell has the night off so he said he would." Mrs. Motley, hiding her disappointment, for she had driven Mr. McTeer in past years, simply replied, "Oh, I see."

When they reached the east end of the block, AJ and Mrs. Motley stood side by side, facing the neat, gray excavation with the old stone foundation.

"Well, here's where it was," Mrs. Motley said. She talked about the house, gesturing with her hands to give AJ an idea of its shape and height, and how as a little girl she could look out the west side window and see nothing but fields for blocks.

During all this, AJ occasionally glanced at the splattered wall of the two-flat. Finally she asked, "Is that were the murder man lived?" (Apparently the girl's mother or father had told her about Stew Pot.) Mrs. Motley said yes he had lived there and AJ asked: "Was it scary living close to him?" and Mrs. Motley said sometimes it had been.

AJ said she liked the garage. "It's like a little dollhouse. Can we look inside?"

Mrs. Motley said there wasn't much in there to see, but if she wanted, they could go inside. They walked down what had been the walkway on the west side of the house and across the frozen lawn to the curved brick path leading to the garage's side door.

The last time Mrs. Motley had been inside there was the day before her house had burned down. She let AJ go in first and had a shiver as she herself crossed the familiar threshold into the car exhaust smell. She pushed a switch beside the doorway engaging the motorized lift, and the alley door began to slowly rise.

AJ walked around gazing up at the empty rafters, stepped aside to avoid old oil spots on the concrete floor, and then did a twirl for no reason other than it seemed like a fun thing to do. After that she headed to the alley and looked in both directions, then came back to the front of the garage and stood at one of the windows that looked out onto the old flowerbeds. She fingered the lace curtain.

"Very nice," she said. And then something caught her eye, something to her right in the corner near where the opened door nearly touched the wall. "What's that?"

"What's what?" asked Mrs. Motley.

AJ stepped to the corner and pulled something loose from the unfinished wood-framed wall. It was a legal-sized manila envelope. Mrs. Motley had never left any such envelope in the garage. She knew immediately it must have been placed there by Stew Pot, a suspicion which was proven correct when she caught sight of the handwriting on the front: the same blocky all-caps of the longer letter.

"*Something you should know*," said AJ, reading aloud from the envelope.

Her voice displaying more anxiety than she wanted, Mrs. Motley said: "Give me that."

Surprised by her grandmother's tone and sudden look of concern, as if she—AJ—had done something wrong, the girl handed the envelope over. "Who is it from?"

Mrs. Motley, still looking at the envelope, said she'd left it inside the garage and had forgotten about it. "It's nothing important."

CHAPTER FIVE

Two Brief Encounters

Mr. McTeer must have seen AJ and Mrs. Motley from his living room, because as they were returning from the garage (the envelope folded inside Mrs. Motley's tan purse), he came out onto his front stoop and called to them. The last of the overcast moved eastward and in dramatic fashion the surroundings were suddenly all sunlight.

Mr. McTeer was as effusive in his observations about AJ as Mrs. Powell had been. He gave the girl a firm handshake which she returned, and he had fun shaking his right hand as if she had hurt him, which made AJ laugh.

Mrs. Motley asked how he was doing and he said he was fine. She then said she understood Mrs. Powell planned to serve Christmas supper at three the next day. If he wanted, she said, she could come over in the evening and give him a ride to her place. Her son would be glad to see him.

Mr. McTeer said that maybe he would come. "I have to see how tired I feel. I'll call you around six."

Mrs. Motley said that sounded fine, and not wanting to reveal any more to her granddaughter than had already been revealed, made her polite goodbye.

As she and AJ reached the sidewalk, AJ asked: "Do you like that man, Grandmother?"

"Mr. McTeer is one of my oldest friends."

"Yes, but do you *like* him?"

"He's my friend, of course I like him."

AJ wiggled her heavy eyebrows and grinned mischievously. "Like I like Otto?"

"That will be quite enough, young lady."

"I promise I won't tell my mom or dad." And then the girl broke into laughter.

As they reached the sidewalk the Hicks's middle daughter, driving a silver blue minivan, pulled up and parked in front of the Cape Cod.

Though nervous at seeing her for the first time since before Mrs. Crown's service, Mrs. Motley hoped the middle daughter would not make any sort of scene in front of her granddaughter. Mrs. Motley waved hello while at the same time not laying the cheer on too thick by smiling. The middle daughter gave a lazy wave back.

The three met on the sidewalk. The middle daughter was polite, even smiling when Mrs. Motley introduced her to AJ. Mrs. Motley then asked after Mr. Hicks. The middle daughter said he was doing about as good as could be expected under the circumstances.

"The first holiday season without Momma; it's hard on him, hard on all of us. He's at work today because lately he doesn't like being in the house, he says everywhere he looks he's reminded of her. We've decorated the place and have a tree because the kids will expect that when we're all here for dinner tomorrow; but Daddy's heart is not in it."

Mrs. Motley nodded in sympathetic agreement. The middle daughter fixed her with a gaze and said: "Could I have a private word with you?" Mrs. Motley told AJ to please excuse them a moment and the two women moved up the walkway out of easy earshot.

"Mrs. Motley, I'm baffled as to why you did what you did. I just don't understand."

"In some way I feel responsible for what happened to Mrs. Crown. If I had only realized earlier what Stew Pot had planned . . ."

"Yes, yes, I get all that, but after what he did at my mother's service, how could you give Stew Pot a service for his mother? He got to stand solemnly at her service. Whatever thoughts were running through that mind of his, he got to think those thoughts in peace; he got to see his mother sent away with dignity. He didn't have someone running in and acting the fool and making a mockery of it all. We, I mean me and my family, just feel betrayed. My mother was your *best friend*. Daddy was in tears when he found out about what you did. He kept asking me: *Why is Mrs. Motley doing us this way?* I had no answer for him."

"I felt it was the Christian thing to do for the woman—Stew Pot or no Stew Pot."

"And you'd do it again?"

"Yes, I would."

The middle daughter gazed at the ground and then back at Mrs. Motley. "I know you usually come around the day after Christmas to visit with us, but this year I don't think that would be a good idea." She peered at the ground again. "I am so angry with you right now, we all are, and I don't know how long it'll be before we're not angry."

"Will you let me know when you aren't?"

"I will, I will. But don't expect a call anytime soon."

They looked each other in the eye and said their goodbyes. As the middle daughter turned to go inside, Mrs. Motley said: "You know I love you all?"

"I know," said the middle daughter over her shoulder.

CHAPTER SIX
Carnal Knowledge

Later that afternoon, with AJ taking a nap and her son and Joyce still out, Mrs. Motley went to the other guest room and locked the door. Sitting on the closed sofa, she pulled the envelope from her purse and unfolded it. (In the garage, as soon as she had read the "something you should know," she'd realized the envelope was the "item" Gerald had referred to in the second letter.) She pulled out a black-and-white photograph, now creased across the middle. It was a picture of her husband. From the level of his baldness she estimated the picture to have been taken a year or so before his death. He was sitting with another man, a Black man who looked to be of similar age, clean shaven and deeper in hue. The man had a full head of hair, but not in the afro style so popular at that time. The two were sitting on what looked like the grass of a park, although she could not tell where because the image of the two men, taken with what must have been a telephoto lens, filled most of the frame. Her husband had his right leg raised at the knee and his hands clasped around his shin, his other leg extended on the grass in front of him, the lower part cut short by the white border of the photo. The man next to him, like her husband, wore an open-collared white shirt with the sleeves rolled up and dark dress slacks. He supported himself on an extended arm resting on the grass between himself and her husband, his left leg raised and his right leg folded partially under him, also cut off by the picture bottom. His head was tilted down and his face was not completely visible, blocked in part by the raised hand that held a lit cigarette smoked halfway to gone. The men were in the shade of what looked like some sort of bush behind them on what seemed to be a summery day. Something must have just struck the two as funny because both had laughing smiles on their faces. And though there was nothing either man was doing in the photograph that looked in any way untoward, Mrs. Motley knew immediately what it meant.

For one, her husband had not been one for sitting in the park on the grass with his sleeves rolled up. In all their years together had he ever done anything so casual while wearing dress clothes? Not that she could remember. And had she ever seen him, even in their happiest moments, looking as carefree—as if he were finally right where he wanted to be—as he appeared in the photograph? No, she couldn't say that she ever had.

The mystery of who had taken the picture was solved when she flipped it over. Written on a taped slip of paper, in Stew Pot's blocky all-caps, was the inscription: MR. MOTLEY AND FRIEND. There was also a flattened strip of negatives taped to the back. In a moment of clarity similar to what Mr. McTeer had experienced after their kiss, Mrs. Motley realized that knowing for sure why her husband had felt their marriage was in trouble was going to be a lot harder to live with than not knowing had ever been. Why, even in these first painful moments of that knowledge, she was already nostalgic for her earlier blissful ignorance.

After leaving the block she and AJ had continued their Parkland tour, going to Eden Rest, Wesley-Allen, the grade school, and finally Flipper Park where they strolled on the walkway alongside the Cal Sag. The whole time it had taken all of Mrs. Motley's steely resolve, developed so long ago, to not let the terror over what might be inside the envelope overtake her. She had kept her talk and countenance engaging and cheerful, her own dread increasing the closer they got to the ranch house. She had told herself she had to prepare for the worst, but not once had she thought the worst would be what she saw before her now, resting on her lap with a crease across the middle. The crying overwhelmed her at that point. It was not as intense as what she'd experienced over learning her marriage had been in trouble or after the death of Mrs. Hicks or the destruction of her house; however, the grief was much fiercer. It was like something physical that squeezed her lungs and caused her to gasp as she sobbed, her throat becoming sore from the labored breaths.

Eventually the crying stopped (after how long, she could not have told you, nor at what point she'd taken off her glasses), as much a case of exhaustion as anything, leaving her too tired to even wipe her glistening face. So, she told herself, she was to have not even a smidge, not even so much as a shred, of warm memory about her marriage. And she questioned whether more revealing photographs of her husband and this man were stored somewhere in the two-flat, or Lord help her in some police department evidence bag. Mrs. Motley held the negative strip to the light of the nearby window. As best she could see, the other images (the photograph was the last of the six) were equally innocent looking—no hand-holding or kissing or other lovey-dovey.

The laundry room was just to your right as you came into the kitchen from the garage. It had an old-fashioned hard metal laundry sink. Mrs. Motley burned the photograph, negatives, and envelope in there, using a long kitchen match to ignite them. As she watched the flames blossom and the smoke unfurl, she sent up a thanks that AJ had asked to see the inside of the garage, for if she hadn't, she—Mrs. Motley—would have never gone inside the place and her son, on his trip to get the rakes and the garden hose and so on, would have found the photographs and very likely come to the same conclusion she had. He had idolized his father in the way children often do, even when the father is so emotionally distant that he might as well be living in the next county. (Just as she herself had idolized her own emotionally distant father? Just as Stew Pot had idolized his abusive father?) And as the burnt paper and plastic curled and undulated and shrank in the flames, she questioned why her son should be spared. Why should he not know who his father truly was? She was going to have to deal with this, why not he? *The truth is the light*; isn't that what her mother had always said? *The truth will set you free*? But then she thought of Mrs. Hicks's middle daughter and their conversation on the walkway, the hurt that had been so evident on the younger woman's face. And Mrs. Motley thought that perhaps enough people had already been pained by her acts of good intention, her sense of right. And what was right, exactly? And what do you say to the pain of someone who felt horribly wronged by your right?

CHAPTER SEVEN
A Few Words of Advice

Mrs. Motley's son and Joyce returned in the middle of the afternoon toting stuffed shopping bags. AJ was still asleep and after Joyce retired to the master bedroom to nap, Mrs. Motley asked to speak to her son in the other guest room where she closed the door behind them. A striped pattern of sunlight and shadow, produced by the partially open blinds, laced over them and the closed sofa bed where they sat facing each other.

"I want to talk to you about last night," she said.

"Mom, Joyce and I already worked that out today—"

"Let me finish, please. Then you can speak. You should not have gone to Minton's. You should have been here when your wife and daughter woke up. You should have been here to eat supper with them. Although I have never been happy about you being in the army, I know you're a good soldier, that you care for the men and women you serve with, especially those placed under your command. *My country, my comrades, and I am third*—isn't that the quote?"

"Yes, something like that."

"Well, you have to look at your family the same way. You have to think: *What is it that they need?* You have to consider their needs just like you do the needs of those serving under you. And not just the big things like anniversaries and birthdays, but the little considerations, like putting off going to Minton's so you could be here when they woke. After a few years of being married to your father, I realized there were certain things I was never going to get from him in terms of emotional intimacy. I made my peace with that. But Joyce is not me. She will not put up with it. You keep doing stuff like last night and you'll lose her again, lose her for good."

Looking and sounding very concerned, her son asked: "What's the matter, Ma?"

"I'm fine."

"Ma, I didn't just meet you five minutes ago. I know when you're upset. What gives?"

"I just don't want you to mess this up. Today Alison-Jean and I walked through the neighborhood and over to the old block and I haven't been that happy in a long time. I want her in my life on a regular basis, or as regular a basis as I can with her in Oklahoma. I don't have my house and I don't have your father. Call me selfish, but there it is."

Her son, not convinced she was completely leveling with him, leaned over and took her in his arms, feeling her slight warm frame within his, the smell of her that he had known all his life, and he told her he would do better with Joyce and their daughter. "I swear, Momma, I promise."

And Mrs. Motley knew that her son meant what he said here in the moment. The question she had was, would he actually do it over the long haul? Would he?

CHAPTER EIGHT

On Christmas Day in the Morning

The next morning Mrs. Motley was up well before the rest of her family, who awoke around six. Unlike every other day of the year, she did not dress right off the bat; with her hair pinned loosely up, she joined the others in jammies, robes, and slippers at the Christmas tree.

Mrs. Motley was very happy with her haul, which included a large collection of CDs, nearly sixty in all, to replace the records she had lost, along with a stereo system with a five-disc player and four large speakers. It took her son awhile to set the whole thing up, but when he finally did! She had never heard *The Messiah* in such precise clarity! She had bought her son a box of deluxe cigars and a humidor to keep them in, and Joyce got jewelry and a gold necklace. When AJ opened her presents from her grandma, she could hardly believe her eyes. Mrs. Motley had called her son a few weeks before about presents for her. He'd given her the heads-up on the girl's cowboy fascination and Mrs. Motley had gotten a hold of two books, *The Negro Cowboys* and *The Black West.*

After the present-giving was done, they dressed and went to Wesley-Allen for Christmas service, Mrs. Motley sitting in the church with a full family for the first time in decades. She took her usual fourth-row aisle seat with the others to her immediate right. She was so happy that later on, back at the house, she felt no rancor when she overheard Joyce say softly to her son that Wesley-Allen looked "just a little ragged. I don't want to have our wedding next June in there."

CHAPTER NINE

To the Lord, Praises Be; Supper's Ready, Now Let's All Eat

The Motleys had supper at seven, the air of the house clogged with tasty smells and, with the CD player on shuffle mode, aloud with a cavalcade of Christmas music, from "My Dancing Day" to "Linus and Lucy."

Mrs. Motley's family surprised her by arriving at the peach dining room in dress clothes—Joyce wore a black skirt suit, AJ a collared blue blouse and slacks, and her son a gray suit and paisley tie. (She herself wore a red silk blouse and a pine-green pencil skirt.)

At the back wall of the dining room was a wide window looking out on the treeless yard. Mrs. Motley sat at the window end of the table and her son at the other, with his back to the living room passageway and the twinkling Christmas tree.

When it was time for blessing, Mrs. Motley reached one hand to Joyce and the other to Alison-Jean. Her son did the same, and when they bowed their heads Mrs. Motley said: "Dear God, thank You for allowing us to gather as family for the first time in many years. We thank You for seeing us through another year. Some we know, who were here to break bread last Christmas, are not with us and their presence is sorely missed by their families as they gather. We thank You for this home and for this food; for we know there are others, all over the world, that are not enjoying such plenty. Finally, we thank You for Jesus, who You sent so that we might have life eternal. In His name we say amen."

Alison-Jean had only eaten turkey once in her life and nothing like the behemoth Mrs. Motley had cooked; it was covered with a thick glaze of honey and seasoned from the inside with lemons and mangoes and onions and garlic. Nor had she ever had dressing like the cornbread and prosciutto concoction placed on the table in a wide deep dish, or the four-cheese macaroni-and-cheese casserole, or the black-eyed peas done with maple bacon, or the sweet potato pie that carried a touch of cinnamon.

"Oh, Momma," said AJ through a mouth of food, "you have to learn how to cook this." And Joyce said, "We have already discussed me and cooking." And AJ swallowed and said: "Then Papa, you learn how." And Joyce said dryly, "He cooks worse than I do." And Mrs. Motley's son said: "Wrecking food kept me out of the mess hall." And AJ turned to Mrs. Motley and said: "Grandmother, can I come stay with you during the summer so I can eat good food?" And Mrs. Motley said: "Sure, as long as it's all right with your parents." And her son, in a pretend tone of accusation, said: "I see what you're up to now, old woman; you just want to kidnap my child. Up here for the whole summer indeed." And Joyce, in a voice of mock admonition, said: "Wait a minute now, let's not be too hasty." Then she said to Mrs. Motley: "You'll take AJ for the *entire* summer?" And Mrs. Motley said: "The doors of the Motley Arms are always open." And Joyce said, "I'm going to hold you to that." And they all laughed, AJ rocking in her seat and sing-songing: "I'm coming up here for summer." And as Mrs. Motley looked down the length of the crowded and bountiful table, her family feasting with her at long last, she told herself that if the loss of her old house was the price she had to pay in the positive/negative scale of life, in which you never get everything you want and can only hope to get some of what you most need, then she could accept that price.

CHAPTER TEN
With Friends and Family

As the dishes were being cleared, Mrs. Powell called and said she and her husband wanted to visit along with Mr. McTeer. By nine thirty p.m. they were all in the living room conversing, save for AJ who sat on the floor, her back against the couch frame, reading one of the books Mrs. Motley had given her.

Mr. Powell asked Mrs. Motley's son when he was going to retire, and Mrs. Motley said: "Not soon enough." And her son laughed and said: "I got my twenty years this month; so, come December 2003, I'll be thirty years and out." And Mrs. Motley said: "We just have to hope the country can stay out of any more wars till then. And Joyce said: "Amen to that." And Mr. McTeer asked Mrs. Motley's son what he thought of the Don't Ask, Don't Tell directive the president had sent down that fall, and Joyce said: "To each his own." And Mr. McTeer said to Joyce: "Having once been a soldier yourself, I'm surprised to hear you say that." Before Joyce could answer, Mr. McTeer added: "The president is wrong. You can't turn a blind eye to degenerate behavior. It cuts into the heart of military discipline. And that costs lives."

Mrs. Motley, sitting on the other end of the couch, made a slashing motion with a hand and said: "I am not having my Christmas collapse into a political argument." And her son said: "We weren't arguing." And Mrs. Motley said: "Or a political discussion. Talk about something else." And that's when the bell rang.

Mrs. Motley got up from the couch and opened the door. It was Vernon Paiger.

Wearing his dark wool coat and no hat, he stepped inside and greeted everyone, getting a warm response from all except Mr. McTeer, who merely nodded.

After Mrs. Motley introduced him to Joyce and AJ, Vernon told her he had come bearing gifts. She looked at him puzzled. He went back

outside, closing the door. She glanced at the others and shrugged to
show she had no idea what he was up to, which she did primarily for
Mr. McTeer's benefit, lest he feel she had set him up for this. She could
see by the cross look on his face, however, that he was not buying it.

Vernon was gone for almost a minute when the bell rang again.
Mrs. Motley opened the door and this time he was standing there
with a little charcoal-gray schnauzer dog in the crook of one arm and
a calico cat in the other.

"What's this?" asked Mrs. Motley.

Vernon stepped inside smiling, dog and cat darting their heads
around, sizing the joint up. AJ shot from her place as if pulled by a
magnet. In front of Vernon she began hopping in place, touching the
dog's whiskery snout and the cat's jowly face.

Mrs. Motley looked surprised, but not happily so. Again she asked,
"What is this?"

"Well," Vernon said cheerfully, "I was thinking, you're in this
house by yourself, you could use some company. So I went to the shel-
ter and saw these two. I didn't know if you were a dog or cat person,
so I got both. They're spayed, housebroken, and have had all their
shots. Don't worry about a cat box and litter. I got that outside. I also
brought cat and dog chow, food and water bowls, and a dog leash. So,
which one do you want?"

Mrs. Motley was about to respond when Alison-Jean grabbed her
arm. "Oh, Grandmother, keep them both. I can play with them when
I come to visit. Pleeease."

"I really don't want a dog or a cat, honey," said Mrs. Motley. And
Joyce, from one of the club chairs, said: "Baby, if your grandmother
doesn't want them . . ." Mrs. Motley's son said: "When I was a boy,
AJ, she wouldn't let me have a dog, either." And Mrs. Motley said to
him: "That's because I knew you wouldn't take care of it." And her
son said: "You just didn't want any animals in your house." And AJ
began jumping again and saying: "Please, please," and her son said
with a smirk: "I seem to recall someone saying something about putting family first." Mrs. Motley shot him an arched-eyebrow look. He
laughed. Then she turned to AJ and said: "Okay." And AJ, all happy,
said: "Both?" And Mrs. Motley, sounding resigned, said: "Yes, both of
them."

Vernon bent over and gently set the animals on the floor where they commenced walking about in a tight area. AJ got on her knees and began playing with them and Mrs. Motley's son said: "This calls for champagne." He got up and Mrs. Motley, looking warily down as the cat circled her feet, said: "I don't want any, it goes straight to my head," and her son said: "What do you think it's for?"

After the bubbly was poured into plastic flute glasses (AJ included), and with the group of them standing around the dining room table, Mrs. Powell called for a toast. Mrs. Motley's son said: "To us and those like us—" and Joyce cut him off with a light slap on his thigh. Mr. McTeer, knowing the profane army toast, grinned, but only briefly. "Your call, Ma," said Mrs. Motley's son, and she said: "To those we can touch today." And Mr. Powell said: "Here-here." And they all tapped glasses.

CHAPTER ELEVEN
Hat in Hand

On New Year's Eve, in the early afternoon, wearing her tan beret and trench coat, Mrs. Motley walked over to Mrs. Butler's house. The other woman, answering the door in an adult muumuu, was understandably surprised at the visit and fixed Mrs. Motley with her usual hard gaze. Mrs. Motley saw heavy strain in those eyes—more wrinkles than she remembered at the outer corners and mottled skin below—which she assumed was from the anxiety all that business with Reggie had caused, and was still causing. (Word had gotten back to Mrs. Motley, via someone she knew at Parkland High, that some of the colleges which had been courting Reggie with basketball scholarships had withdrawn their offers upon learning that he'd been taken into custody on arson charges. Her source telling her: "The kid is a good basketball player and all, but he's not *that* good." This source had also said that Reggie's grades had slipped some since the fall.)

Mrs. Butler did not invite Mrs. Motley in. Speaking bluntly, Mrs. Motley asked if there was any need for volunteers at the food pantry. Surprised yet again, Mrs. Butler's expression was quickly replaced by an even harsher look. "Why are you asking?"

"I have a lot of time on my hands. I thought I could help."

"Help with what?"

"With whatever needs doing."

Giving a contemptuous smirk, Mrs. Butler said: "Oh, I get it. You're feeling guilty over your failures and mistakes of the last ten months and now you want to assuage that guilt by slumming for a while at the pantry. No thanks. I'm not interested in your pathetic attempts to atone."

"With all due respect, this is not about you. It's about the people the pantry serves."

"Don't you stand at my door and lecture me."

"I'm offering to help. Do you want it or not?"

Mrs. Butler used her smirk again. "What do you think is going to happen? You think it'll be like some after-school movie where two adversaries become friends by serving a common cause?"

To this Mrs. Motley snorted lightly and said: "I have no interest in being your friend. I don't like you."

"Then why volunteer at the panty?"

"It's close. Again, do you want my help or not?"

Mrs. Butler stared at her hard, as if she expected Mrs. Motley to falter and break eye contact. Mrs. Motley didn't. The smirk returned for a third run.

"All right then, we serve hot breakfasts the first and third Saturdays of the month. The next first Saturday is in two days."

"I know when it is."

"Prep starts at six a.m. You be there on time or don't bother coming. And show up ready to work. I don't tolerate slackers in my panty. I don't truck guff either. My word goes."

"I'll be there."

Mrs. Motley turned and walked away, leaving Mrs. Butler standing in the doorway. When Mrs. Motley was halfway down the walkway, Mrs. Butler called out: "Six a.m. sharp, Motley!"

Without turning or stopping, Mrs. Motley raised a hand and gave it a single wave, as much to show her irritation as to acknowledge she had heard Mrs. Butler, who responded by closing the door with something just less than a slam.

"Battle axe," Mrs. Motley muttered, turning onto the sidewalk.

Later, back at the ranch house with a cup of tea at the dining room table (the others off on another trip to another mall), Mrs. Motley conceded that Mrs. Butler had to some degree been correct in regards to the motivations that had brought Mrs. Motley to her door. Since seeing the photograph Stew Pot had taken of her husband, she had been doing a lot of thinking, and one of the conclusions she had come to was that her life of gentlewoman widowhood had to stop. Her present home situation had had something to do with the decision too. While comfortable, the new place had none of the charm of her old house and the idea of spending her days sitting around there did not appeal to her. She had to get out, do something. But she didn't want to do just anything to fill the time. Not join a book club or garden group. She felt compelled to do something of value, something beyond herself. She had decided to volunteer at the pantry for the very reason she had given Mrs. Butler: it was close and was the first thing that had come to her mind. As for working for Mrs. Butler, after all she'd been through since Stew Pot's return, the thought of the woman's bluster did not scare; besides, she imagined doing a good job would irritate Mrs. Butler far more than Mrs. Butler's gruff would ever irritate her.

Sipping her tea, Mrs. Motley told herself the food pantry was just a start. Chicago had to have plenty of places needing the free service of a retired teacher, places where she could do some real good. With that matter settled, at least in terms of strategy, her thoughts shifted to a personal issue that had also been very much on her mind lately. And she was about to mull it over again when she was cut short by the sound of her family returning.

CHAPTER TWELVE

To Be or Not to Be—That Is a Question?

The next morning, Vernon Paiger called Mrs. Motley a little past six and after wishing her a happy New Year, he asked what she was doing.

"I'm about to walk this dog," she said. "I was going to wait and let AJ do it, but it's pacing around like it needs to do its business real bad and I don't want that happening in my house."

Vernon said as long as she was going out, he'd join her. She told him he needn't bother. But when he said, "There's something I have to tell you," she said, "Okay."

Moments later she was in her coat, wool hat, and gloves, the dog straining the leash as it led her down the walkway. (It amazed her how much strength there was in so small an animal.) Vernon was waiting on the sidewalk, a black faux-fur hat on his head and gloved hands stuffed in the pockets of his dark coat. Mrs. Motley tugged the dog to the left and they stepped from the shadow cast by her house and into the sunny intersection.

"So what is it you have to tell me?" she asked, hoping it wasn't more proposal stuff.

Keeping his steps in pace with hers, Vernon said: "You know I have sources here and there. Well, some are at the Cook County jail. I got a call early this morning that Stew Pot killed himself overnight."

Mrs. Motley stopped in her tracks, pulling the leash to keep the dog from moving forward. "How?"

Vernon raised a black-leathered hand above his head and made an upward yanking motion while tilting his head sideways. He repocketed the hand and said: "Shirt tail tied to the upper section of a bed frame."

Mrs. Motley's face went gloomy, but she shook the look off with a slight movement of her head. "Why do I feel so sad?"

"Because he was a human being?" said Vernon.

"And why am I not surprised at what happened?"

"Because it's not all that surprising, what with that multiple-personality stuff rattling around in his head."

On the other side of the intersection they passed back into the block-long stretch of shadow cast by the row of houses on their left; here and there a noisemaker or a piece of crepe dropped by some drunken celebrant the night before.

"It turns out," Vernon continued, "that Stew Pot's lawyer did order a psyche exam. He'd had several sessions. Sometimes those things get you the opposite of what you're after. The shrink goes at the questions too strong in a particular direction, let's say, and the humane part of the patient, the part that's been buried for years but is still in there ticking, gets a true sight of the horrors that he's committed, and he can't bear it."

"Do you think that's what happened?"

"Could be. Or it could be something else entirely. That shrink stuff is not exact science."

After two more blocks they reached the north side of Flipper Park. The stand of trees cast long lines of shadow across the grass that was frosty and crunchy underfoot. When the dog picked a spot by one of the trees to squat and dump, Mrs. Motley made a disgusted face.

"You'll get used to that," said Vernon, smiling.

"That's easy for you to say. I've managed to live my whole life just fine without animal companionship. That was really unfair of you to show up carrying pets while my granddaughter was here. Just the sort of ploy you'd expect from a politician."

Vernon shrugged. "What can I say? It's my nature. But I'm betting that in a month you three will be fast friends."

"The pooch seems to have already developed an affinity for me. Every night he parks himself under my sofa bed to sleep." She glanced down at the fresh poop. "Oh shoot, I didn't bring anything to clean it up with."

Still smiling, Vernon said that as alderman, he'd grant her a reprieve this time and not call a police officer and have her ticketed.

There were only a few other people in sight. A hundred-plus yards away to their left was a man in a purple ski coat so puffy it seemed inflated, who was walking a boxer dog, and even further away in that direction, a lone runner was moving at modest speed.

They sat on a bench facing the walkway running parallel to the Cal Sag where she and AJ had strolled on their Parkland tour, the channel flowing slowly just beyond the bare bush branches of the rocky bank. From off a ways to the west, on their right, traffic could be heard from the high Western Avenue overpass, along with the shushing of water at the filtration station; meanwhile at their feet, the whiskery dog paced about, its attention taken first by a squad of sparrows hopping across the rocks, then by two squirrels temptingly running around some thirty feet to the right.

"So what did you decide to name the little varmint?"

"He's not a varmint," Mrs. Motley answered without thinking. Then, pronouncing the W as a V, she said that since the dog was a schnauzer, she had named it Wilhelm.

"Like the kaiser?" he asked. And she said she hadn't even thought of that connection.

They were quiet for a bit, then she said: "I can't help but feel that somehow we—by that I mean me and the people from my old block—were partially responsible for what happened with Stew Pot. Maybe if we'd just left him alone, not provoked him with that Erma stunt and those signs, not killed his dog, maybe he'd have gone on that pilgrimage with Brother Crown and been happy. And he, Crown, and his mother would be alive."

"Or," Vernon countered, "he might have gone on the pilgrimage and flipped out at some later date and killed Crown in his sleep and come back and done in his ma, or set off a bomb at a revival meeting, or machine-gunned a busload of nuns. Who knows what he might have eventually done? I sure don't, and neither do you. So give yourself a break."

"I'm sorry, but I can't help it. There were actions I've taken the past ten months because I thought they were the right things to do, and not only did those things not work, they often caused suffering and death. If I'd given those letters to Stew Pot's lawyer, maybe the lawyer would have picked up on that 5-32 and 32 quicker, because he or she would have had more experience dealing with people like that, and then Mrs. Crown could have been warned before she cooked up that food laced with her first husband's old poison, and she and Brother Crown would be alive.

"If I'd given the letters to Stew Pot's lawyer, he or she would have given them to the psychiatrist who did those exams, and maybe that would have been a major influence in how the psychiatrist approached things and maybe the exams would have gone better, and maybe Stew Pot wouldn't have killed himself. I got rid of those letters because I was angry that Stew Pot had once again pulled me into his messy world. I wanted the letters out of my hair as quick as possible."

"Again, don't be too hard on yourself. You're a very wise woman."

"I haven't been feeling too wise lately."

"You know what they say the key to wisdom is?"

"What?"

He grinned. "The key to wisdom is knowing that you don't know."

"Well, if that's true then I'm a genius." After yet another bit of quiet, she said: "Do you believe in God?"

"Yeah, but mine is a more holistic sense of God. Not God as a guy with a beard keeping a list on everybody and checking it twice. For me, God is everything: the stars, the heavens, the earth, the water, the plants, the animals—us. Everything's God."

Mrs. Motley looked at him sideways with a *Say what?* expression.

Vernon made a palms-up gesture. "You asked."

"But if that's true, then Satan is part of us."

"Exactly," Vernon said. "Folks like to think Satan is a villain outside themselves twirling a mustache, when in fact, he or she or it is as much a part of us as our foot or elbow. That's why evil is so hard to fight. To deny evil, we have to deny part of ourselves."

"And if we embrace goodness?"

"Then we embrace the God in us, which is always there for us to tap into if we allow it."

"So how'd you come up with this approach?"

"It was the only one I could think of that made any sense to me."

"So I suppose you think of me and my beliefs as provincial?"

"Not in the least. My grandma had a saying: *Each one to his own liking said the woman who kissed the cow.*"

Mrs. Motley laughed. "My mother used to say that too."

Vernon nodded once. "It's a good saying. If more people operated on that principle, I suspect the world would be a much better place."

"I wonder if your political enemies would consider you so understanding."

"Just because you believe in live-and-let-live doesn't mean you have to let folks run all over you. And for the record, the only people I've flattened were people who were dead set on trying to flatten me."

"Of course, you'd say that even if it weren't true."

"More than likely."

"I wonder if Stew Pot's religion, as confused as it sometimes was, was a desperate attempt to keep the evilest part of him at bay."

"That's possible, I suppose. But we'll never know the answer to that either."

After a stretch of silence, she said: "I need to be alone now."

"Okay. You want me to take the dog back to your house?"

"No, that's all right."

Vernon stood, and while pulling his gloves tighter, he said, "This latest Stew Pot business will be all over the local morning news shows. You might want to screen your calls and keep on the lookout for reporters today."

She said she would do that.

He placed a hand gently on her shoulder and brought his mouth close to her ear. Although there were no other beings nearby except Wilhelm and the few sparrows hopping about the rocky banks, he spoke softly: "If there's anything you need . . ."

She said she understood, and thanked him, and then he said: "I don't dislike Mr. McTeer, I just don't think he deserves you."

"Well, that's for me to decide, isn't it?"

"That it is." He lightly patted her shoulder a couple times and told her to have a good day, or as good a day as she could manage under the circumstances.

She waited until the sound of his footsteps crunching on the grass could no longer be heard, then waited a little more. When she turned to look in the direction he'd gone, she saw him standing in front of the stand of trees with a wide smile on his owlish face.

He pointed a gloved forefinger at her and called out: "Gotcha! That's one point for me." Then he turned around and moved into the lanes of tree shadow and light.

She turned back to the olive-drab currents of the Cal Sag. The sparrows took off, leaving Wilhelm with nothing to yearn for. The dog sat down.

"Vernon, Vernon, Vernon," muttered Mrs. Motley. She would not exactly call him the grand prize, but then again he wasn't a booby prize, either. Yet he was an alderman, and so many of them seemed to be just a step away from being indicted. Of course, Vernon had never been indicted; investigated plenty of times yes, but never indicted. Which meant Vernon was either very lucky or very skilled at his skullduggery, *or* not as dishonest as a lot of people thought.

"Now you're rationalizing," she said aloud. She thought of Mr. McTeer on Christmas night and his comment about Don't Ask, Don't Tell. That had very much rubbed her the wrong way, something about the absolute certainty of his unforgiving tone; a reaction that had surprised her. Later on, she attributed it in part to what she had found out about her husband on Christmas Eve. As painful as it was every time she thought of the photograph—and oh my, was it ever painful, her eyes wincing right now in reaction to the image—and as wrong as she thought his betrayal had been, she did not feel her husband was a degenerate. Over the last few nights on the sofa bed, with Wilhelm sleeping below, she had asked herself if she would have felt better if the other person in the photograph had been a woman. After much thought, she'd come to the conclusion that the major difference for her would have been that her husband's love for another woman was something that she could, in theory at least, understand, whereas his love for a man, like Erma's love for women, was a complete mystery to her. But then, wasn't everyone a mystery? When you thought about it, what did you really know about the secret code of conduct another person decided to build him or herself around? Only when some magician was working a trick—with a novel or a movie or a play—did you ever know the true motives of people, and those magical creations, despite all appearances to the contrary, were not real. What real people presented to you as their genuine selves could not even be called the tip of the iceberg. She now saw it as more like the snow dust of the iceberg that blows around in all sorts of unexpected ways. What did she know of the true inner workings of her parents, or grandparents, or of her own son? You moved through life surrounded by mysteries you would never solve. And even on those rare occasions when you did know a bit more than just the snow dust of another person's true self, if you knew maybe the first layer of snow's-worth of a person, as she did with Mr. McTeer, such knowledge didn't necessarily guarantee or get you anything. She was sure that great philosophical minds of long ago had already hashed this issue out, and that the great philosophical minds of today might consider her somewhat sappy, but she had never seen these things so clearly in her own mind before, so it was intriguing and fresh for her.

A jogger approached quickly on her right, a short, thin, dark man with a double chin and dark face stubble, dressed in a tight-fitting, shiny black body suit with ear muffs over his otherwise bare head, huffing and puffing little clouds with shoes slip-slapping on the walkway. He glanced at her as he passed. She nodded and he nodded back. Wilhelm stood, emitted a single bark, and sat back down.

She wondered what the young man thought of her: *Old lady with a pet dog; sitting in the park because she has no place else to be or anyone to be with.* She would have liked to have said to the jogger, who was already a good ways off, that she had people. She had her son's family. They were back. Her old house was gone, but they were back. Her old house, that grand cocoon with all that furniture, and chandeliers, and balustrades, and family heirlooms and such, was gone, which had left her naked and exposed to herself, forcing her to realize, over these past two months, that she was lonely, that she was a lonely old woman getting older, and that she had been lonely for a long time—from even before her husband had died. And no matter how much the dog and cat might grow on her, she was going to stay lonely unless she took steps to address the situation. Seeing her son and Joyce together made her lonely, the kiss from Mr. McTeer had made her very lonely, had reminded her not of what she had, but what she'd never had, and which now, in the throes of her loneliness, she realized she very much wanted, which was to love someone without reservation who loved her without reservation—to not settle for less than what she needed. Mrs. Powell had it. Mrs. Hicks had had it. So she knew it was possible. It would be nice, she thought, to know what that was like before she died, to see if it felt as good to experience as it looked from the outside when she saw others experiencing it; although she realized it might all well be too late, for she was old and getting older. Vernon had said: "Each one to his own liking." She wondered if he had meant what he said. He'd sounded like he had, but as she had learned through her newfound knowledge of her husband (the thought of that photograph again; another wince), one could never be too sure. But then, hadn't she just decided that there was no surety in that game? To love and be loved without reservation before she died. She had already outlived her parents by nearly thirty years, which was either a sign of her good health or a sign she had already pushed the genetic envelope of longevity pretty far and was way closer to the end than she'd like to admit, which meant there might not be much time for reflection and contemplation about where she might go for her love without reservation. Maybe she'd meet someone at one of her places of future volunteerism. Maybe she'd meet a single, volunteering man who was not too old or too young who was also looking for love without reservation *and*, and this was important, not interested in having a woman to wait on him hand and foot for every single solitary thing. (She wasn't going down *that* road again.) The sort of man she wanted was definitely not Mr. McTeer, for he had all sorts of reservations about all sorts of things, which made her loving him without reservation impossible. Because she was old and getting older she'd have to act before she died and her shell was planted with her grandparents and parents and husband a ways down the Cal Sag at Eden Rest. The reality of their graves was not painful to her, though her memories of them were bittersweet, because she believed in Heaven. Not the cartoon paradise peopled by white-robed angels with tiny white wings and golden harps who walked across puffy white clouds, but a state of being where one was the purest essence of oneself without the clumsy encumbrances of the physical body. But before she experienced the thrill of that she wanted to know what love without reservation was like, she wanted to feel that, like she was feeling the sunlight right now, the sun that had warmed the earth for billions of years and had never asked for anything in return—was that a kind of love without reservation? She supposed cynical types would call such an endeavor by a woman her age folly. Well, let them scoff if they wanted. The way she saw it now, she had to do something while she waited to become the purest essence of herself—assuming she was granted that—she had to do something while she did her penance of guilt for the rights she'd done that had hurt others. (That was how she would always see it.) Before she got to be her purest essence she wanted to know the joy of a loving husband's hug. (She wanted the naughty lovey-dovey stuff too, which for her was made all the more tantalizing by its being naughty.) She wanted the simple joys of the body that came out of a love without reservation. An old woman getting older could dedicate herself to worse things, she supposed. Love without reservation was a simple pleasure, really, like the sunlight on her face right now, like sitting on a bench in the winter's cold—but healthy and alive!—with a little dog at your feet and looking out at the olive-drab Cal Sag Channel. When she was a young girl it had been narrow enough to toss a stone easily across, and now, in its widened form, it looked as if it had been there forever, carved by the whims of nature.

Mrs. Motley looked to her left, to the east, over the intersecting patterns of the distant treetops, the branches like arms reaching for the sun which looked, on that clear morning, as if it were poised just above them. The sun still there burning in the here and now, thank God.

THE END

Author's Note

Back in 1971, when I was nineteen and I told my parents I wanted to be a writer, I'm sure they must have worriedly wondered: *But how will he earn a living? How will he eat?* However, they didn't say no. Iris and Charles May, whose formative years were the Great Depression and World War II, and who were nothing if not prudent parents, did not say to me, their oldest child, "Sorry, Eric, you're going to have to do something practical." I've had to fight a lot of battles in my time, but one battle I never had to fight was justifying to my parents what I wanted to do with my life. They allowed me to attend a college where the arts and communication disciplines were (and still are) at the center of things, and where I got the best training an aspiring artist could have asked for.

At Columbia College Chicago my classes included film, radio broadcasting, journalism, drawing, and, most importantly, writing workshops using the Story Workshop method (originated by John Schultz) where my classmates and I, instead of spending an entire semester on nothing but critiquing each others' work to Hell and gone, were immersed in a classroom dynamic that emphasized the important connection between oral storytelling and the written word in an atmosphere of genuine subject and voice permission, which allowed each of us to find our individual paths to our strongest stories and storytelling voices. I've taught workshops myself for thirty years using that method (John gave me my first teaching job in 1976) and Story Workshop is as exciting for my students now as it was for me when I first encountered it.

In regards to teaching, thanks as well to Lee Hope who gave me the opportunity to work as a faculty member at the Stonecoast and Solstice writers' conferences where I met so many wonderful people. I must also make mention of all the editors, reporters, and copy editors I worked with at *The Washington Post*, especially then–Metro Editor Milton Coleman who gave a novice writer a shot at reporting, and the guys I worked with on the paper's Obituary Desk: Bart Barnes, Richard Pearson, and J.Y. Smith. On the obit desk I learned to write fast and how it's possible to be elegant and concise in the narrative voice at one and the same time.

As a writer, I've been a very lucky man. Words cannot adequately convey the gratitude I feel for those who have shown so much confidence in me (in some cases with little if any hard evidence to go on) and who've given me the opportunity to live the charmed existence that has been my writing and teaching life.